Edited by
Shannon Ravenel

NEW STORIES
FROM THE SOUTH

The Year's Best, 1993

Algonquin Books of Chapel Hill

Published by
Algonquin Books of Chapel Hill
Post Office Box 2225, Chapel Hill, North Carolina 27515-2225
a division of Workman Publishing Company, Inc.
708 Broadway, New York, New York 10003

ISSN 0897-9073
ISBN 1-56512-053-1

CONTENTS

PREFACE
Is the South Still Southern?

"With a handful of exceptions, the 17 stories here are neither from nor of the South. They give us neither an old South nor a new one, but wander off in directions that have more to do with the writing-school sensibility, with its implacable focus on self, than with the land of Faulkner and O'Connor, Welty and Percy, Foote and Crews, Warren and Taylor."

> —Jonathan Yardley
> From a review of *New Stories of the South:*
> *The Year's Best, 1992, The Washington Post,*
> October 28, 1992

"What [young Southern writers] seem not to understand is that the South has changed. For a writer interested in the South, the most interesting question is now: Is the South still Southern? . . . But take a tour of much recent Southern writing, as it was my misfortune to do not long ago, and what you're likely to find is a lot of quaint, warmed over Southernisms that bear no more connection to contemporary Southern reality than does the patois of Greenwich Village."

> —Jonathan Yardley
> *The Washington Post,* January 25, 1993

Whatever Mr. Yardley is looking for in Southern fiction, it's clearly not what I'm looking for. If I understand him, he's against fiction of and about the "self," a subject he evidently believes to have been over-rated and over-promoted in the university writing programs. He is further perplexed by whether or not the South is still Southern.

That much I understand. But is Mr. Yardley saying that Faulkner, O'Connor, Warren, Percy and the rest of the Southern writers he misses eschewed self for region? Does he mean they were less interested in character than in local color? That they ignored psychological insight in their rush to sociological judgment? Does Mr. Yardley believe that Faulkner's, O'Connor's, Warren's, and Percy's "selves" played no part in their fiction?

I don't know the answers to these questions. But I do know what distinguishes my expectations of fiction from his. He wants fiction to concern itself with abstract concepts. I want it to create characters so convincing that I can, for the time of the story, live their lives. I want fictional characters who compel me to join them in their dilemmas, their decisions, their discoveries. If they can do that, I don't care if those characters are the "selves" of their authors or the man in the moon.

More often than not, the successful fictional character is created in a specific environment. If that setting is "Southern," it seems reasonable to call the fiction "Southern." So long as the setting does its job helping to develop the character, how the environment measures up on some hypothetical historical yardstick that calculates New or Old South is irrelevant. Good literary fiction is not written to inform regional sociology. Its purpose is to expand human intimacy.

I've not often been taken to task for selecting stories that are *too* Southern. On the contrary, I have frequently been accused (and not only by Mr. Yardley) of having stretched my own definition of the South to include stories that don't have an obvious regional identity.

I'm willing to accept some blame for that. I go along with Flannery O'Connor's theory that "The woods are full of regional writers, and it is the great horror of every serious Southern writer that he will become one of them." Since great characters are what count in this series, if I have to stretch conventional boundaries to include them, I will. I've probably done it again this year. Several stories in this collection are by writers from the South whose settings can be identified no more specifically than as contemporary American suburbia. These stories are wonderful by virtue of characterizations that don't depend on the details of place as much as they do on the mood of the times. David Huddle's "Trouble at the Home Office" deliciously illuminates a certain kind of male chauvinism getting its comeuppance in a reverse date-rape. Jill McCorkle flips that coin in her irreverent "Man Watcher" whose narrator might very well have instigated the trouble in Huddle's home office. Barbara Hudson's exquisite "Selling Whiskers" takes a child inside the timeless, floating world created by a mother who is mad. And the sun that sets on the aging hero of Richard Bausch's "Evening" is a universal one.

Nonetheless, a good many of this year's stories are set in specific Southern environments that weigh heavily in the creation of the characters. Small town Texas is where the retired couple in Annette Sanford's "Helens and Roses" have parked their new mobile home. Texas is where they have lived. Texas is where they will die . . . two old Texans still in love. Coastal Louisiana is where Robert Olen Butler sets his remarkable story, "Preparation," about one Vietnamese woman's good-bye to another. (Thousands of Vietnamese refugees have settled there so aren't they, by contemporary logic, part of the "New South"?) Paula Gover's "White Boys and River Girls" could not take place anywhere else than in its small southern Georgia community. Nor could Dan Leone's "Spinach" take place anywhere but in the Spinach Capital of the World, Alma, Arkansas. And if Pinckney Benedict had set his story about small town officials dumbfounded by a pickup truck full of dead dogs anywhere but in the South, I'm not sure we could have suspended our disbelief!

As for Old vs. New South, a few stories here do present the kind of South that we might agree no longer exists. "A Jonquil for Mary Penn," Wendell Berry's beautiful story of marriage, depends for its characterization on the author's memory of farm life as he knew it long ago. Elizabeth Hunnewell's fictional family works out its "Family Planning" in the Richmond of the late 1940s when children weren't being sexually educated by TV. And in "Prisoners," Wayne Karlin uses a Civil War setting to illuminate two sets of characters—one historic, the other contemporary—as a black Vietnam vet searches for his illegitimate daughter and a sense of his own ancestry.

It's evolving moral codes that confound characters in the stories set in a contemporary South: in Tony Earley's "Charlotte," a Yuppie fern bar is the scene of an all too modern romance; for the contracting business partners in Dennis Loy Johnson's "Rescuing Ed," Little Rock's new liberalism is both promise and threat; the prosperity that connects sections of Atlanta with Hilton Head Island creates the background in Kevin Calder's funny "Name Me This River"; and even Peter Taylor takes on an up-to-the-minute ethical dilemma in a Memphis hospital in "The Waiting Room."

As I see it, the great virtue of fiction is that it allows a reader to live as many lives in as many settings as there are good stories. The first and last stories in this year's collection are vivid examples of that virtue. If you're not an elderly black woman living in a dangerous section of our nation's capital and dependent on the changing rules of the Social Security Administration, read Edward Jones's "Marie." If you have never been the parent of a disfigured child, read Lee Merrill Byrd's "Major Six Pockets." These stories answer the questions real fiction writers ask.

Shannon Ravenel
Chapel Hill, North Carolina
1993

PUBLISHER'S NOTE

The stories reprinted in *New Stories from the South, The Year's Best, 1993* were selected from American short stories published in magazines issued between January and December 1992. Shannon Ravenel annually consults a list of 85 nationally distributed American periodicals and makes her choices for this anthology based on criteria that include original publication first-serially in magazine form and publication as short stories. Direct submissions are not considered.

NEW STORIES
FROM THE SOUTH

The Year's Best, 1993

MARIE

(from *The Paris Review*)

Every now and again, as if on a whim, the federal government people would write to Marie Delaveaux Wilson in
one of those white, stampless envelopes and tell her to come in
to their place so they could take another look at her. They, the
Social Security people, wrote to her in a foreign language that
she had learned to translate over the years, and for all of the years
she had been receiving the letters the same man had been signing
them. Once, because she had something important to tell him,
Marie called the number the man always put at the top of the
letters, but a woman answered Mr. Smith's telephone and told
Marie he was in an all-day meeting. Another time she called and
a man said Mr. Smith was on vacation. And finally one day a
woman answered and told Marie that Mr. Smith was deceased.
The woman told her to wait and she would get someone new to
talk to her about her case, but Marie thought it bad luck to have
telephoned a dead man and she hung up.

Now, years after the woman had told her Mr. Smith was no
more, the letters were still being signed by John Smith. Come
into our office at Twenty-first and M streets, Northwest, the letters said in that foreign language. Come in so we can see if you
are still blind in one eye. Come in so we can see if you are still
old and getting older. Come in so we can see if you still deserve
to get Supplemental Security Income payments.

She always obeyed the letters, even if the order now came from a dead man, for she knew people who had been temporarily cut off from SSI for not showing up or even for being late. And once cut off, you had to move heaven and earth to get back on.

So on a not unpleasant day in March, she rose in the dark in the morning, even before the day had any sort of character, to give herself plenty of time to bathe, eat, lay out money for the bus, dress, listen to the spirituals on the radio. She was eighty-six years old and had learned that life was all chaos and painful uncertainty and that the only way to get through it was to expect chaos even in the most innocent of moments. Offer a crust of bread to a sick bird and you often draw back a bloody finger.

John Smith's letter had told her to come in at eleven o'clock, his favorite time, and by nine that morning she had had her bath and had eaten. Dressed by nine-thirty. The walk from Claridge Towers at Twelfth and M down to the bus stop at Fourteenth and K took her about ten minutes, more or less. There was a bus at about ten-thirty, her schedule told her, but she preferred the one that came a half hour earlier, lest there be trouble with the ten-thirty bus. After she dressed, she sat at her dining room table and went over yet again what papers and all else she needed to take. Given the nature of life—particularly the questions asked by the Social Security people—she always took more than they might ask for: her birth certificate, her husband's death certificate, doctors' letters.

One of the last things she put in her pocketbook was a knife that she had, about seven inches long, which she had serrated on both edges with the use of a small saw borrowed from a neighbor. The knife, she was convinced now, had saved her life about two weeks before. Before then she had often been careless about when she took the knife out with her, and she had never taken it out in daylight, but now she never left her apartment without it, even when going down the hall to the trash drop.

She had gone out to buy a simple box of oatmeal, no more, no less. It was about seven in the evening, the streets with enough commuters driving up Thirteenth Street to make her feel safe. Several yards before she reached the store, the young man came from behind her and tried to rip off her coat pocket where he thought she kept her money, for she carried no purse or pocketbook after five o'clock. The money was in the other pocket with the knife, and his hand was caught in the empty pocket long enough for her to reach around with the knife and cut his hand as it came out of her pocket.

He screamed and called her an old bitch. He took a few steps up Thirteenth Street and stood in front of Emerson's Market, examining the hand and shaking off blood. Except for the cars passing up and down Thirteenth Street, they were alone, and she began to pray.

"You cut me," he said, as if he had only been minding his own business when she cut him. "Just look what you done to my hand," he said and looked around as if for some witness to her crime. There was not a great amount of blood, but there was enough for her to see it dripping to the pavement. He seemed to be about twenty, no more than twenty-five, dressed the way they were all dressed nowadays, as if a blind man had matched up all their colors. It occurred to her to say that she had seven grandchildren about his age, that telling him this would make him leave her alone. But the more filth he spoke, the more she wanted him only to come toward her again.

"You done crippled me, you old bitch."

"I sure did," she said, without malice, without triumph, but simply the way she would have told him the time of day had he asked and had she known. She gripped the knife tighter, and as she did, she turned her body ever so slightly so that her good eye lined up with him. Her heart was making an awful racket, wanting to be away from him, wanting to be safe at home. I will not be moved, some organ in the neighborhood of the heart told the heart. "And I got plenty more where that come from."

The last words seemed to bring him down some and, still shaking the blood from his hand, he took a step or two back, which disappointed her. I will not be moved, that other organ kept telling the heart. "You just crazy, thas all," he said. "Just a crazy old hag." Then he turned and lumbered up toward Logan Circle, and several times he looked back over his shoulder as if afraid she might be following. A man came out of Emerson's, then a woman with two little boys. She wanted to grab each of them by the arm and tell them she had come close to losing her life. "I saved myself with this here thing," she would have said. She forgot about the oatmeal and took her raging heart back to the apartment. She told herself that she should, but she never washed the fellow's blood off the knife, and over the next few days it dried and then it began to flake off.

Toward ten o'clock that morning Wilamena Mason knocked and let herself in with a key Marie had given her.

"I see you all ready," Wilamena said.

"With the help of the Lord," Marie said. "Want a spot a coffee?"

"No thanks," Wilamena said, and dropped into a chair at the table. "Been drinkin' so much coffee lately, I'm gonna turn into coffee. Was up all night with Calhoun."

"How he doin'?"

Wilamena told her Calhoun was better that morning, his first good morning in over a week. Calhoun Lambeth was Wilamena's boyfriend, a seventy-five-year-old man she had taken up with six or so months before, not long after he moved in. He was the best-dressed old man Marie had ever known, but he had always appeared to be sickly, even while strutting about with his gold-tipped cane. And seeing that she could count his days on the fingers of her hands, Marie had avoided getting to know him. She could not understand why Wilamena, who could have had any man in Claridge Towers or any other senior citizen building for that matter, would take such a man into her bed. "True love," Wilamena had explained. "Avoid heartache," Marie had said, trying to be kind.

They left the apartment. Marie sought help from no one, lest she come to depend on a person too much. But since the encounter with the young man, Wilamena had insisted on escorting her. Marie, to avoid arguments, allowed Wilamena to walk with her from time to time to the bus stop, but no farther.

Nothing fit Marie's theory about life like the weather in Washington. Two days before, the temperature had been in the forties, and yesterday it had dropped to the low twenties, then warmed up a bit with the afternoon, bringing on snow flurries. Today the weather people on the radio had said it would warm enough to wear just a sweater, but Marie was wearing her coat. And tomorrow, the weather people said, it would be in the thirties, with maybe an inch or so of snow.

Appointments near twelve o'clock were always risky, because the Social Security people often took off for lunch long before noon and returned sometime after one. And except for a few employees who seemed to work through their lunch hours, the place shut down. Marie had never been interviewed by someone willing to work through the lunch hour. Today, though the appointment was for eleven, she waited until one-thirty before the woman at the front of the waiting room told her she would have to come back another day, because the woman who handled her case was not in.

"You put my name down when I came in like everything was all right," Marie said after she had been called up to the woman's desk.

"I know," the woman said, "but I thought that Mrs. Brown was in. They told me she was in. I'm sorry." The woman began writing in a logbook that rested between her telephone and a triptych of photographs. She handed Marie a slip and told her again she was sorry.

"Why you have me wait so long if she whatn't here?" She did

not want to say too much, appear too upset, for the Social Security people could be unforgiving. And though she was used to waiting three and four hours, she found it especially unfair to wait when there was no one for her at all behind those panels the Social Security people used for offices. "I been here since before eleven."

"I know," the woman behind the desk said. "I know. I saw you there, ma'am, but I really didn't know Mrs. Brown wasn't here." There was a nameplate at the front of the woman's desk and it said Vernelle Wise. The name was surrounded by little hearts, the kind a child might have drawn.

Marie said nothing more and left.

The next appointment was two weeks later, eight-thirty, a good hour, and the day before a letter signed by John Smith arrived to remind her. She expected to be out at least by twelve. Three times before eleven o'clock Marie asked Vernelle Wise if the man, Mr. Green, who was handling her case, was in that day, and each time the woman assured her that he was. At twelve, Marie ate one of the two oranges and three of the five slices of cheese she had brought. At one, she asked again if Mr. Green was indeed in that day and politely reminded Vernelle Wise that she had been waiting since about eight that morning. Vernelle was just as polite and told her the wait would soon be over.

At one-fifteen, Marie began to watch the clock hands creep around the dial. She had not paid much attention to the people about her, but more and more it seemed that others were being waited on who had arrived long after she had gotten there. After asking about Mr. Green at one, she had taken a seat near the front and, as more time went by, she found herself forced to listen to the conversation that Vernelle was having with the other receptionist next to her.

"I told him . . . I told him . . . I said just get your things and leave," said the other receptionist, who didn't have a nameplate.

"Did he leave?" Vernelle wanted to know.

"Oh, no," the other woman said. "Not at first. But I picked up some of his stuff, that Christian Dior jacket he worships. I picked up my cigarette lighter and that jacket, just like I was gonna do something bad to it, and he started movin' then."

Vernelle began laughing. "I wish I was there to see that." She was filing her fingernails. Now and again she would look at her fingernails to inspect her work, and if it was satisfactory, she would blow on the nails and on the file. "He back?" Vernelle asked.

The other receptionist eyed her. "What you think?" and they both laughed.

Along about two o'clock Marie became hungry again, but she did not want to eat the rest of her food because she did not know how much longer she would be there. There was a soda machine in the corner, but all sodas gave her gas.

"You-know-who gonna call you again?" the other receptionist was asking Vernelle.

"I hope so," Vernelle said. "He pretty fly. Seemed decent too. It kinda put me off when he said he was a car mechanic. I kinda like kept tryin' to take a peek at his fingernails and everything the whole evenin'. See if they was dirty or what."

"Well, that mechanic stuff might be good when you get your car back. My cousin's boyfriend used to do that kinda work and he made good money, girl. I mean real good money."

"Hmmmm," Vernelle said. "Anyway, the kids like him, and you know how peculiar they can be."

"Tell me 'bout it. They do the job your mother and father used to do, huh? Only on another level."

"You can say that again," Vernelle said.

Marie went to her and told her how long she had been waiting.

"Listen," Vernelle said, pointing her fingernail file at Marie. "I told you you'll be waited on as soon as possible. This is a busy day. So I think you should just go back to your seat until we call your name." The other receptionist began to giggle.

Marie reached across the desk and slapped Vernelle Wise with all her might. Vernelle dropped the file, which made a cheap, tinny sound when it hit the plastic board her chair was on. But no one heard the file because she had begun to cry right away. She looked at Marie as if, in the moment of her greatest need, Marie had denied her. "Oh, oh," Vernelle Wise said through the tears. "Oh, my dear God . . ."

The other receptionist, in her chair on casters, rolled over to Vernelle and put her arm around her. "Security!" the other receptionist hollered. "We need Security here!"

The guard at the front door came quickly around the corner, one hand on his holstered gun and the other pointing accusingly at the people seated in the waiting area. Marie had sat down and was looking at the two women almost sympathetically, as if a stranger had come in, hit Vernelle Wise, and fled.

"She slapped Vernelle!" said the other receptionist.

"Who did it?" the guard said, reaching for the man sitting beside Marie. But when the other receptionist said it was the old lady in the blue coat, the guard held back for the longest time, as if to grab her would be like arresting his own grandmother. He stood blinking and he would have gone on blinking had Marie not stood up.

She was too flustered to wait for the bus and so took a cab home. With both chains, she locked herself in the apartment, refusing to answer the door or the telephone the rest of the day and most of the next. But she knew that if her family or friends received no answer at the door or on the telephone, they would think something had happened to her. So the next afternoon, she began answering the phone and spoke with the chain on, telling Wilamena and others that she had a toothache.

For days and days after the incident she ate very little and asked God to forgive her. She was haunted by the way Vernelle's cheek had felt, by what it was like to invade and actually touch the flesh of another person. And when she thought too hard, she imagined that she was slicing through the woman's cheek, the way she had sliced through the young man's hand. But as time went on she began to remember the man's curses and the purplish color of Vernelle's fingernails, and all remorse would momentarily take flight. Finally, one morning nearly two weeks after she slapped the woman, she woke with a phrase she had not used or heard since her children were small: You whatn't raised that way.

It was the next morning that the thin young man in the suit knocked and asked through the door chains if he could speak with her. She thought that he was a Social Security man come to tear up her card and papers and tell her that they would send her no more checks. Even when he pulled out an identification card showing that he was a Howard University student, she did not believe.

In the end, she told him she didn't want to buy anything, not magazines, not candy, not anything.

"No, no," he said. "I just want to talk to you for a bit. About your life and everything. It's for a project for my folklore course. I'm talking to everyone in the building who'll let me. Please . . . I won't be a bother. Just a little bit of your time."

"I don't have anything worth talkin' about," she said. "And I don't keep well these days."

"Oh, ma'am, I'm sorry. But we all got something to say. I promise I won't be a bother."

After fifteen minutes of his pleas, she opened the door to him because of his suit and his tie and his tie clip with a bird in flight, and because his long, dark brown fingers reminded her of delicate twigs. But had he turned out to be death with a gun or a knife or fingers to crush her neck, she would not have been surprised. "My name's George. George Carter. Like the president." He had the kind of voice that old people in her young days would have called womanish. "But I was born right here in D.C. Born, bred, and buttered, my mother used to say."

He stayed the rest of the day and she fixed him dinner. It scared her to be able to talk so freely with him, and at first she thought that at long last, as she had always feared, senility had taken hold of her. A few hours after he left, she looked his name up in the telephone book, and when a man who sounded like him answered, she hung up immediately. And the next day she did the same thing. He came back at least twice a week for many weeks and would set his cassette recorder on her coffee table. "He's takin' down my whole life," she told Wilamena, almost the way a woman might speak in awe of a new boyfriend.

One day he played back for the first time some of what she told the recorder:

> . . . My father would be sittin' there readin' the paper. He'd say whenever they put in a new president, "Look like he got the chair for four years." And it got so that's what I saw— this poor man sittin' in that chair for four long years while the rest of the world went on about its business. I don't know if I thought he ever did anything, the president. I just knew that he had to sit in that chair for four years. Maybe I thought that by his sittin' in that chair and doin' nothin' else for four years he made the country what it was and that without him sittin' there the country wouldn't be what it was. Maybe thas what I got from listenin' to Father readin' and to my mother askin' him questions 'bout what he was readin'. They was like that, you see . . .

George stopped the tape and was about to put the other side in when she touched his hand.

"No more, George," she said. "I can't listen to no more. Please . . . please, no more." She had never in her whole life heard her own voice. Nothing had been so stunning in a long, long while, and for a few moments before she found herself, her world turned upside down. There, rising from a machine no bigger than her Bible, was a voice frighteningly familiar yet unfamiliar, talking about a man whom she knew as well as her husbands and her sons, a man dead and buried sixty years. She reached across to George and he handed her the tape. She turned it over and over, as if the mystery of everything could be discerned if she turned it enough times. She began to cry, and with her other hand she lightly touched the buttons of the machine.

Between the time Marie slapped the woman in the Social Security office and the day she heard her voice for the first time, Calhoun Lambeth, Wilamena's boyfriend, had been in and out of the hospital three times. Most evenings when Calhoun's son stayed the night with him, Wilamena would come up to Marie's and spend most of the evening sitting on the couch that was catty-corner to the easy chair facing the big window. She said very little, which was unlike her, a woman with more friends than hairs on her head and who, at sixty-eight, loved a good party. The most attractive woman Marie knew would only curl her legs up under herself and sip whatever Marie put in her hand. She looked out at the city until she took herself to her apartment or went back down to Calhoun's place. In the beginning, after he returned from the hospital the first time, there was the desire in Marie to remind her friend that she wasn't married to Calhoun, that she should just get up and walk away, something Marie had seen her do with other men she had grown tired of.

Late one night, Wilamena called and asked her to come down to the man's apartment, for the man's son had had to work that night and she was there alone with him and she did not want to be alone with him. "Sit with me a spell," Wilamena said. Marie did not protest, even though she had not said more than ten words to the man in all the time she knew him. She threw on her bathrobe, picked up her keys and serrated knife, and went down to the second floor.

He was propped up on the bed, surprisingly alert, and spoke to Marie with an unforced friendliness. She had seen this in other dying people—a kindness and gentleness came over them that was often embarrassing for those around them. Wilamena sat on the side of the bed. Calhoun asked Marie to sit in a chair beside the bed and then he took her hand and held it for the rest of the night. He talked on throughout the night, not always understandable. Wilamena, exhausted, eventually lay across the foot of the bed. Almost everything the man had to say was about a time when he was young and was married for a year or so to a woman in Nicodemus, Kansas, a town where there were only black people. Whether the woman had died or whether he had left her, Marie could not make out. She only knew that the woman and Nicodemus seemed to have marked him for life.

"You should go to Nicodemus," he said at one point, as if the town were only around the corner. "I stumbled into the place by accident. But you should go on purpose. There ain't much to see, but you should go there and spend some time there."

Toward four o'clock that morning, he stopped talking and moments later he went home to his God. Marie continued holding the dead man's hand and she said the Lord's Prayer over and over until it no longer made sense to her. She did not wake Wilamena. Eventually the sun came through the man's venetian blinds, and she heard the croaking of the pigeons congregating on the window ledge. When she finally placed his hand on his chest, the dead man expelled a burst of air that sounded to Marie like a sigh. It occurred to her that she, a complete stranger, was the last thing he had known in the world and that now he was no longer in the world. All she knew of him was that Nicodemus place and a lovesick woman asleep at the foot of his bed. She thought that she was hungry and thirsty, but the more she looked at the dead man and the sleeping woman, the more she realized that what she felt was a sense of loss.

Two days later, the Social Security people sent her a letter, again signed by John Smith, telling her to come to them one week hence. There was nothing in the letter about the slap, no threat to cut off her SSI payments because of what she had done. Indeed, it was the same sort of letter John Smith usually sent. She called the number at the top of the letter, and the woman who handled her case told her that Mr. White would be expecting her on the day and time stated in the letter. Still, she suspected the

Social Security people were planning something for her, something at the very least that would be humiliating. And, right up until the day before the appointment, she continued calling to confirm that it was okay to come in. Often, the person she spoke to after the switchboard woman and before the woman handling her case was Vernelle. "Social Security Administration. This is Vernelle Wise. May I help you?" And each time Marie heard the receptionist identify herself she wanted to apologize. "I whatn't raised that way," she wanted to tell the woman.

George Carter came the day she got the letter to present her with a cassette machine and copies of the tapes they had made about her life. It took quite some time for him to teach her how to use the machine, and after he was gone, she was certain it took so long because she really did not want to know how to use it. That evening, after her dinner, she steeled herself and put a tape marked Parents/Early Childhood in the machine.

. . . My mother had this idea that everything could be done in Washington, that a human bein' could take all they troubles to Washington and things would be set right. I think that was all wrapped up with her notion of the gov'ment, the Supreme Court and the president and the like. "Up there," she would say, "things can be made right." "Up there" was her only words for Washington. All them other cities had names, but Washington didn't need a name. It was just called "up there." I was real small and didn't know any better, so somehow I got to thinkin' since things were on the perfect side in Washington, that maybe God lived there. God and his people . . . When I went back home to visit that first time and told my mother all about my livin' in Washington, she fell into such a cry, like maybe I had managed to make it to heaven without dyin'. Thas how people was back in those days . . .

The next morning she looked for Vernelle Wise's name in the telephone book. And for several evenings she would call the number and hang up before the phone had rung three times. Finally, on a Sunday, two days before the appointment, she let it ring and what may have been a little boy answered. She could tell he was very young because he said hello in a too loud voice, as if he was not used to talking on the telephone.

"Hello," he said. "Hello, who this? Granddaddy, that you? Hello. Hello. I can see you."

Marie heard Vernelle tell him to put down the telephone, then another child, perhaps a girl somewhat older than the boy, came on the line. "Hello. Hello. Who is this?" she said with authority. The boy began to cry, apparently because he did not want the girl to talk if he couldn't. "Don't touch it," the girl said. "Leave it alone." The boy cried louder and only stopped when Vernelle came to the telephone.

"Yes?" Vernelle said. "Yes." Then she went off the line to calm the boy, who had begun to cry again. "Loretta," she said, "go get his bottle . . . Well, look for it. What you got eyes for?"

There seemed to be a second boy, because Vernelle told him to help Loretta look for the bottle. "He always losin' things," Marie heard the second boy say. "You should tie everything to his arms." "Don't tell me what to do," Vernelle said. "Just look for that damn bottle."

"I don't lose noffin'. I don't," the first boy said. "You got snot in your nose."

"Don't say that," Vernelle said before she came back on the line. "I'm sorry," she said to Marie. "Who is this? . . . Don't you dare touch it if you know what's good for you!" she said. "I wanna talk to Granddaddy," the first boy said. "Loretta, get me that bottle!"

Marie hung up. She washed her dinner dishes. She called Wilamena because she had not seen her all day, and Wilamena told her that she would be up later. The cassette tapes were on the coffee table beside the machine, and she began picking them up, one by one. She read the labels: Husband No. 1, Working, Husband No. 2, Children, Race Relations, Early D.C. Experiences, Husband No. 3. She had not played another tape since the one about her mother's idea of what Washington was like, but she could still hear the voice, her voice. Without reading its label, she put a tape in the machine.

. . . I never planned to live in Washington, had no idea I would ever even step one foot in this city. This white family my mother worked for, they had a son married and gone to live in Baltimore. He wanted a maid, somebody to take care of his children. So he wrote to his mother and she asked my mother and my mother asked me about goin' to live in Baltimore. Well, I was young. I guess I wanted to see the world, and Baltimore was as good a place to start as anywhere. This man sent me a train ticket and I went off to Baltimore. Hadn't ever been kissed, hadn't ever been anything, but here I was goin' farther from home than my mother and father put together . . . Well, sir, the train stopped in Washington, and I thought I heard the conductor say we would be stoppin' a bit there, so I got off. I knew I probably wouldn't see no more than that Union Station, but I wanted to be able to say I'd done that, that I step foot in the capital of the United States. I walked down to the end of the platform and looked around, then I peeked into the station. Then I went in. And when I got back, the train and my suitcase was gone. Everything I had in the world on the way to Baltimore . . .

I couldn't calm myself down enough to listen to when the redcap said another train would be leavin' for Baltimore, I was just that upset. I had a buncha addresses of people we knew all the way from home up to Boston, and I used one precious nickel to call a woman I hadn't seen in years, cause I didn't have the white people in Baltimore number. This woman come and got me, took me to her place. I 'member like it was yesterday that we got on this streetcar marked 13TH AND D NE. The more I rode, the more brighter things got. You ain't lived till you been on a streetcar. The further we went on that streetcar—dead down in the middle of the street—the more I knowed I could never go live in Baltimore. I knowed I could never live in a place that didn't have that streetcar and them clackety-clack tracks . . .

She wrapped the tapes in two plastic bags and put them in the dresser drawer that contained all that was valuable to her: birth and death certificates, silver dollars, life insurance policies, pictures of her husbands and the children they had given each other and the grandchildren those children had given her and the great-grands whose names she had trouble remembering. She set the tapes in a back corner of the drawer, away from the things she needed to get her hands on regularly. She knew that however long she lived, she would not ever again listen to them, for in the end, despite all that was on the tapes, she could not stand the sound of her own voice.

Edward Jones was born and raised in Washington, D.C. In addition to *The Paris Review*, his stories have appeared in *Essence*, *Callaloo*, and *Ploughshares*. His book of stories, *Lost in the City*, won the 1993 PEN/Hemingway Award and was a finalist for the National Book Award in 1992.

PHOTO CREDIT: JERRY BAUER

There is not much more that can be said about "Marie." Its Southernness comes from the mindset of the main character; at heart, despite decades in the city, she remains a country person because the country, that peasant world, was where she was molded.

Tony Earley

CHARLOTTE

(from *Harper's Magazine*)

The professional wrestlers are gone. The professional wrestlers do not live here anymore. Frannie Belk sold the Southeastern Wrestling Alliance to Ted Turner for more money than you would think, and the professional wrestlers sold their big houses on Lake Norman and drove in their BMWs down I-85 to bigger houses in Atlanta.

Gone are the Thundercats, Bill and Steve, and the Hidden Pagans with their shiny red masks and secret signs; gone is Paolo the Peruvian who didn't speak English very well but could momentarily hold off as many as five angry men with his flying bare feet; gone are Comrade Yerkov the Russian Assassin and his bald nephew Boris, and the Sheik of the East and his Harem of Three, and Hank Wilson Senior the Country Star with his beloved guitar Leigh Ann; gone is Naoki Fujita who spit the mysterious Green Fire of the Orient into the eyes of his opponents whenever the referee turned his back; gone are the Superstud, the MegaDestroyer, the Revenger, the Preacher, Ron Rowdy, Tom Tequila, the Gentle Giant, the Littlest Cowboy, Genghis Gandhi, and Bob the Sailor. Gone is Big Bill Boscoe, the ringside announcer, whose question "Tell me, Paolo, what happened in there?" brought forth the answer that all Charlotteans still know by heart—"Well, Beel, Hidden Pagan step on toe and hit head with chair and I no can fight no more"; gone are Rockin' Robbie Frazier, the Dreamer, the Viking, Captain Boogie Woogie, Harry the Hairdresser, and Yee-Hah O'Reilly the Cherokee Indian Chief. And gone is Lord Poetry and all that he stood for, his archrival Bob Noxious, and Darling Donnis—the Sweetheart of the SWA, the Prize Greater Than Any Belt—the girl who had to choose between the two of them, once and for all, during THE FINAL BATTLE FOR LOVE.

Gone. Now Charlotte has the NBA, and we tell ourselves we are a big deal. We dress in teal and purple and sit in traffic jams on the Billy Graham Parkway so that we can yell in the new coliseum for the Hornets, who are bad, bad, bad. They are hard to watch, and my seats are good. Whenever any of the Hornets come into the bar, and they do not come often, we stare up at them like they were exotic animals come to drink at our watering hole. They are too tall to talk to for very long, not enough like us, and they make me miss the old days. In the old days in Charlotte we did not take ourselves so seriously. Our heroes had platinum blond hair and twenty-seven-inch biceps, but you knew who was good and who was evil, who was changing over to the other side, and who was changing back. You knew that sooner or later the referee would look away just long enough for Bob Noxious to hit Lord Poetry with a folding chair. You knew that Lord Poetry would stare up from the canvas in stricken wonder, as if he had never once in his life seen a folding chair. (In the bar we screamed at the television, Turn around, ref, turn around! Look out, Lord Poetry, look out!) In the old days in Charlotte we did not have to decide if the Hornets should trade Rex Chapman (they should not) or if J. R. Reid was big enough to play center in the NBA (he is, but only sometimes). In the old days our heroes were as superficial as we were—but we knew that—and their struggles were exaggerated versions of our own. Now we have the Hornets. They wear uniforms designed by Alexander Julian, and play hard and lose, and make us look into our souls. Now when we march disappointed out of the new coliseum to sit unmoving on the parkway, in the cars we can't afford, we have to think about the things that are true: Everyone in Charlotte is from somewhere else. Everyone in Charlotte tries to be something they are not. We spend more money than we make, but it doesn't help. We know that the Hornets will never make the play-offs, and that somehow it is our fault. Our lives are small and empty, and we thought they wouldn't be, once we moved to the city.

My girlfriend's name is Starla. She is beautiful, and we wrestle about love. She does not like to say she loves me, even though we have been together four and a half years. She will not look at me when I say I love her, and if I wanted to, I could ball up those three words and use them like a fist. Starla says she has strong lust for me, which should be enough; she says we have good chemistry, which is all anyone can hope for. Late in the night, after we have grappled until the last drop of love is gone from our bodies, I say, "Starla, I can tell that you love me. You wouldn't be able to do it like that if you didn't love me." She sits up in bed, her head tilted forward so that her red hair almost covers her face, and picks the black hair that came from my chest off of her breasts and stomach. The skin across her chest is flushed red, patterned like a satellite photograph; it looks like a place I should know. She says, "I'm a grown woman and my body works. It has nothign to do with love." Like a lot of people in Charlotte, Starla has given up on love. In the old days Lord Poetry said to never give up, to always fight for love, but now he is gone to Atlanta with a big contract and a broken heart, and I have to do the best that I can. I hold on, even though Starla says she will not marry me. I have heard that Darling Donnis lives with Bob Noxious in a big condo in Buckhead. Starla wants to know why I can't be happy with what we have. We have good chemistry and apartments in Fourth Ward and German cars. She says it is enough to live with and more than anyone had where we came from. We can eat out whenever we want.

Yet Starla breaks my heart. She will say that she loves me only

at the end of a great struggle, after she is too tired to fight anymore, and then she spits out the words, like vomit, and calls me
bastard or fucker or worse, and asks if the thing I have just done
has made me happy. It does not make me happy, but it is what
we do. It is the fight we fight. The next day we have dark circles
under our eyes like the makeup truly evil wrestlers wear, and we
circle each other like animals in a cage that is too small, and what
we feel then is nothing at all like love.

I manage a fern bar on Independence Boulevard near downtown called P. J. O'Mulligan's Goodtimes Emporium. The regulars call the place PJ's. When you have just moved to Charlotte
from McAdenville or Cherryville or Lawndale, it makes you feel
good to call somebody up and say, Hey, let's meet after work at
PJ's. It sounds like real life when you say it, and that is a sad thing.
PJ's has fake Tiffany lampshades above the tables, with purple and
teal hornets belligerent in the glass. It has fake antique Coca-Cola
and Miller High Life and Pierce-Arrow Automobile and Win-
chester Repeating Rifle signs screwed on the walls, and imitation
brass tiles glued to the ceiling. (The glue occasionally lets go and
the tiles swoop down toward the tables, like bats.) The ferns are
plastic because smoke and people dumping their drinks into the
planters kill the real ones. The beer and mixed drinks are expensive, but the chairs and stools are cloth upholstered and plush,
and the ceiling lights in their smooth, round globes are low and
pleasant enough, and the television set is huge and close to the
bar and perpetually tuned to ESPN. Except when the Hornets
are on Channel 18 or wrestling is on TBS.

In the old days in Charlotte a lot of the professional wrestlers
hung out at PJ's. Sometimes Lord Poetry stopped by early in
the afternoon, after he was through working out, and tried out a
new poem he had found in one of his thick books. The last time
he came in, days before THE FINAL BATTLE, I asked him to tell
me a poem I could say to Starla. In the old days in Charlotte you
would not think twice about hearing a giant man with long red
hair recite a poem in a bar, even in the middle of the afternoon. I

turned the TV down, and the two waitresses and the handful of hard cores who had sneaked away from their offices for a drink saw what was happening and eased up close enough to hear. Lord Poetry crossed his arms and stared straight up, as if the poem he was searching for was written on the ceiling or somewhere on the other side, in a place we couldn't see. His voice was higher and softer than you would expect the voice of a man that size to be, and when he nodded and finally began to speak, it was almost in a whisper, and we all leaned in even closer. He said,

> We sat grown quiet at the name of love;
> We saw the last embers of daylight die,
> And in the trembling blue-green of the sky
> A moon, worn as if it had been a shell
> Washed by time's waters as they rose and fell
> About the stars and broke in days and years.
> I had a thought for no one's but your ears:
> That you were beautiful, and that I strove
> To love you in the old high way of love;
> That it had all seemed happy, and yet we'd grown
> As weary-hearted as that hollow moon.

P. J. O'Mulligan's was as quiet then as you will ever hear it. All of Charlotte seemed suddenly still and listening around us. Nobody moved until Lord Poetry finally looked down and reached again for his beer and said, "That's Yeats." Then we all moved back, suddenly conscious of his great size and our closeness to it, and nodded and agreed that it was a real good poem, one of the best we had ever heard him say. Later, I had him repeat it for me, line for line, and I wrote it down on a cocktail napkin. Sometimes, late at night, after Starla and I have fought, and I have made her say "I love you" like "Uncle," even as I can see in her eyes how much she hates me for it, I think about reading the poem to her, but some things are just too true to ever say out loud.

In PJ's we watch wrestling still, even though we can no longer claim it as our own. We sit around the big screen without cheering and stare at the wrestlers like favorite relatives we haven't seen in years. We say things like Boy, the Viking has really put on weight since he moved down there, or When did Rockin' Robbie Frazier cut his hair like that? We put on brave faces when we talk about Rockin' Robbie, who was probably Charlotte's most popular wrestler, and try not to dwell on the fact that he has gone away from us for good. In the old days he dragged his stunned and half-senseless opponents to the center of the ring and climbed onto the top rope, and after the crowd counted down from five (Four! Three! Two! One!) he would launch himself into the air, his arms and legs spread like wings, his blond hair streaming out behind him like a banner, and fly ten, fifteen feet, easy, and from an unimaginable height drop with a crash like an explosion directly onto his opponent's head. He called it the Rockin' Robbie B-52. ("I'll tell you one thing, Big Bill. Come next Saturday night in the Charlotte Coliseum I'm gonna B-52 the Sheik of the East like he ain't never been B-52ed before.") And after Rockin' Robbie's B-52 had landed, while his opponent flopped around on the canvas like a big fish, waiting only to be mounted and pinned, Rockin' Robbie leaped up and stood over him, his body slick with righteous sweat, his face a picture of joy. He held his hands high in the air, his fingers spread wide, his pelvis thrusting uncontrollably back and forth in the electric joy of the moment. Then he tossed his head back and howled like a dog, his lips a gleeful red O turned toward the sky. Those were glorious days. Whenever Rockin' Robbie walked into PJ's, everybody in the place raised their glasses and pointed their noses at the fake bronze of the ceiling and bayed at the stars we knew spun, only for us, in the high, moony night above Charlotte. Nothing like that happens here anymore. Frannie Belk gathered up all the good and evil in our city and sold it four hours south. These days the illusions we have left are the small ones of our own making, and in the vacuum the wrestlers left behind, those illusions have become too easy to see through; we now have to live with ourselves.

About once a week some guy who's just moved to Charlotte from Kings Mountain or Chester or Gaffney comes up to me where I sit at the bar, on my stool by the waitress station, and says, Hey man, are you P. J. O'Mulligan? They are never kidding, and whenever it happens I don't know what to say. I wish I could tell them whatever it is they need in their hearts to hear, but P. J. O'Mulligan is fourteen lawyers from Richmond with investment capital. What do you say? New people come to Charlotte from the small towns every day, searching for lives that are bigger than the ones they have known, but what they must settle for, once they get here, are much smaller hopes: that maybe this year the Hornets might really have a shot at the Celtics, if Rex Chapman has a good game; that maybe there really is somebody named P. J. O'Mulligan, and that maybe that guy at the bar is him. Now that the wrestlers are gone, I wonder about these things. How do you tell somebody how to find what they're looking for when ten years ago you came from the same place and have yet to find it yourself? How do you tell somebody from Polkville or Aliceville or Cliffside, who just saw downtown after sunset for the first time, not to let the beauty of the skyline fool them? Charlotte is a place where a crooked TV preacher can steal money and grow like a sore until he collapses from the weight of his own evil by simply promising hope. So don't stare at the NCNB Tower against the dark blue of the sky; keep your eyes on the road. Don't think that Independence Boulevard is anything more than a street. Most of my waitresses are college girls from UNCC and CPCC, and I can see the hope shining in their faces even as they fill out applications. They look good in their official P. J. O'Mulligan's khaki shorts and white sneakers and green aprons and starched, preppy blouses, but they are still mill-town girls through and through, come to the city to find the answers to their prayers. How do you tell them Charlotte isn't a good place to look? It is a place where a crooked TV preacher can pray that his flock will send him money so that he can build a giant water slide—and they will.

But PJ's still draws a wrestling crowd. They are mostly good-looking and wear lots of jewelry. The girls do aerobics like religion and have big, curly hair, stiff with mousse. They wear short, tight dresses—usually black—and dangling earrings and spiked heels and lipstick with little sparkles in it, like stars, that you're not even sure you can see. (You catch yourself staring at their mouths when they talk, waiting for their lips to catch the light.) The guys dye their hair blond and wear it spiked on top, long and permed in back, and shaved over the ears. They lift weights and take steroids. When they have enough money they get coked up. They wear stonewashed jeans and open shirts and gold chains thick as ropes and cowboy boots made from python skin, which is how professional wrestlers dress when they relax. Sometimes you will see a group of guys in a circle, with their jeans pulled up over their calves, arguing about whose boots were made from the biggest snake. The girls have long red fingernails and work mostly in the tall offices downtown. Most of the guys work outdoors—construction usually; there still is a lot of that, even now—or in the bodybuilding gyms, or the industrial parks along I-85. Both sexes are darkly and artificially tanned, even in the winter, and get drunk on shooters and look vainly in PJ's for love.

Around midnight on Friday and Saturday, before everyone clears out to go dancing at The Connection or Plum Crazy's, where the night's hopes become final choices, PJ's gets packed. The waitresses have to move sideways through the crowd with their trays held over their heads. Everybody shouts to be heard over one another and over the music—P. J. O'Mulligan's official contemporary jazz, piped in from Richmond—and if you close your eyes and listen carefully you can hear in the voices the one story they are trying not to tell: how everyone in Charlotte grew up in a white house in a row of white houses on the side of a hill in Lowell or Kannapolis or Spindale, and how they had to be quiet at home because their daddies worked third shift, how a black oil heater squatted like a gargoyle in the middle of their living room floor, and how the whole time they were growing up the one thing they always wanted to do was leave. I get lonesome sometimes, in the buzzing middle of the weekend, when I listen to the voices and think about the shortness of the distance all of us managed to travel as we tried to get away, and how when we got to Charlotte the only people we found waiting for us were the ones we had left. Our parents go to tractor pulls and watch "Hee Haw." My father eats squirrel brains. We tell ourselves that we are different now, because we live in Charlotte, but know that we are only making do.

The last great professional wrestling card Frannie Belk put together—before she signed Ted Turner's big check and with a diamond-studded wave of her hand sent the wrestlers away from Charlotte for good—was ARMAGEDDON V—THE LAST EXPLO-SION, which took place in the new coliseum three nights after the Hornets played and lost their first NBA game. ("Ohhhhhh," Big Bill Boscoe said in the promotional TV ad, his big voice qua-vering with emotion, "Ladies and Gentlemen and Wrestling Fans of All Ages: See an unprecedented galaxy of SWA wrestling stars collide and explode in the Charlotte Coliseum . . .") And for a while that night—even though we knew the wrestlers were mov-ing to Atlanta—the world still seemed young and full of hope, and we were young in it, and life in Charlotte seemed close to the way we had always imagined it should be: Paolo the Peruvian jerked his bare foot out from under the big, black boot of Com-rade Yerkov and then kicked the shit out of him in a flying frenzy of South American feet; Rockin' Robbie Frazier squirted a water pistol into Naoki Fujita's mouth before Fujita could ignite the mysterious Green Fire of the Orient, and then launched a B-52 from such a great height that even the most jaded wrestling fans gasped with wonder (and if that wasn't enough, he later ran from the locker room in his street clothes, his hair still wet from his shower, his shirttail out and flapping, and in a blond fury B-52ed not one but *both* of the Hidden Pagans, who had used a folding chair to gain an unfair advantage over the Thundercats, Bill and Steve). And we saw the Littlest Cowboy and Chief Yee-Hah O'Reilly, their wrists bound together with an eight-foot leather thong, battle nobly in an Apache Death Match, until neither man was able to stand and the referee called it a draw and cut them loose with a long and crooked dagger belonging to the Sheik of the East; Hank Wilson Senior the Country Star whacked Captain Boogie Woogie over the head with his beloved guitar Leigh Ann, and earned a thoroughly satisfying disqualification and a long and heartfelt standing O; one of the Harem of Three slipped the Sheik of the East a handful of Arabian sand, which he threw into the eyes of Bob the Sailor to save himself from the Sailor's Killer Clam Hold—from which no bad guy ever escaped, once it was locked—but the referee saw the Sheik do it (the rarest of wrestling miracles) and awarded the match to the Sailor; and in the prelude to the main event, like the thunder before a storm, the Brothers Clean (the Superstud, the Viking, and the Gentle Giant) outlasted the Three Evils (Genghis Gandhi, Ron Rowdy, and Tom Tequila) in a six-man Texas Chain-Link Massacre Match in which a ten-foot wire fence was lowered around the ring, and bald Boris Yerkov and Harry the Hairdresser patrolled outside, eyeing each other suspiciously, armed with bullwhips and folding chairs, to make sure that no one climbed out and no one climbed in.

Now, looking back, it seems prophetic somehow that Starla and I lined up on opposite sides during THE FINAL BATTLE FOR LOVE. ("Sex is the biggest deal people have," Starla says. "You think about what you really want from me, what really matters, the next time you ask for a piece.") In THE FINAL BATTLE, Starla wanted Bob Noxious, with his dark chemistry, to win Darling Donnis away from Lord Poetry once and for all. He had twice come close. I wanted Lord Poetry to strike a lasting blow for love. Starla said it would never happen, and she was right. Late in the night, after it is over, after Starla has pinned my shoulders flat against the bed and held them there, after we are able to talk, I say, "Starla, you have to admit that you were making love to me. I could tell." She runs to the bathroom, her legs stiff and close together, to get rid of part of me. "Cave men made up love," she calls out from behind the door. "After they invented laws they had to stop killing each other, so they told their women they loved them to keep them from screwing other men. That's what love is."

Bob Noxious was Charlotte's most feared and evil wrestler, and on the night of THE FINAL BATTLE, we knew that he did not want Darling Donnis because he loved her. Bob Noxious was scary: He had a cobalt blue spiked Mohawk, and if on his way to the ring a fan spat on him, he always spat back. He had a neck like a bull, and a fifty-six-inch chest, and he could twitch his pectoral muscles so fast that his nipples jerked up and down like pistons. Lord Poetry was almost as big as Bob Noxious, and scary in different ways. His curly red hair was longer than Starla's, and he wrestled in paisley tights—pink and magenta and lavender—specially made in England. He read a poem to Darling Donnis before and after every match while the crowd yelled for him to stop. (Charlotte did not know which it hated more: Bob Noxious with his huge and savage evil or the prancing Lord Poetry with his paisley tights and fat book of poems.) Darling Donnis was the picture of innocence (and danger, if you are a man) and hung on every word Lord Poetry said. She was blond, and wore a low-cut, lacy white dress (but never a slip), and covered her mouth with her hands whenever Lord Poetry was in trouble, her moist green eyes wide with concern.

Darling Donnis's dilemma was this: she was in love with Lord Poetry, but she was mesmerized by Bob Noxious's animal power. The last two times Bob Noxious and Lord Poetry fought, before THE FINAL BATTLE, Bob Noxious had beaten Lord Poetry with a folding chair until Lord Poetry couldn't stand, and then he turned to Darling Donnis and put his hands on his hips and threw his shoulders back, revealing enough muscles to make several lesser men. Darling Donnis's legs visibly wobbled, and she steadied herself against the ring apron, but she did not look away. While the crowd screamed for Bob Noxious to Shake 'em! Shake 'em! Let 'em go! he began to twitch his pectorals up and down, first just one at a time, just once or twice—teasing Darling Donnis—then the other, then in rhythm, faster and faster. It was something you had to look at, even if you didn't want to, a force of nature, and at both matches Darling Donnis was transfixed. She couldn't look away from Bob Noxious's chest and would have gone to him (even though she held her hands over her mouth and shook her head no, the pull was too strong) had it not been for Rockin' Robbie Frazier. At both matches before THE FINAL BATTLE, Rockin' Robbie ran out of the locker room in his street clothes and tossed the prostrate Lord Poetry the book of poetry that Darling Donnis had carelessly dropped on the apron of the ring. Then he climbed through the ropes and held off the enraged and bellowing Bob Noxious long enough for Lord Poetry to crawl out of danger and read Darling Donnis one of her favorite sonnets, which calmed her. But the night of THE FINAL BATTLE, all of Charlotte knew that something had to give. We did not think that even Rockin' Robbie could save Darling Donnis from Bob Noxious three times. Bob's pull was too strong. This time Lord Poetry had to do it himself.

They cleared away the cage from the Texas Chain-Link Massacre, and the houselights went down slowly until only the ring was lit. The white canvas was so bright that it hurt your eyes to look at it. Blue spotlights blinked open in the high darkness beneath the roof of the coliseum, and quick circles of light skimmed across the surface of the crowd, showing in an instant a hundred, two hundred, expectant faces. The crowd could feel the big thing coming up on them, like animals before an earthquake. Rednecks in the high, cheap seats stomped their feet and hooted like owls. Starla twisted in her seat and stuck two fingers into her mouth and cut loose with a shrill whistle. "Ohhhhh, Ladies and Gentlemen and Wrestling Fans," Big Bill Boscoe said from everywhere in the darkness, like the very voice of God, "I hope you are ready to hold on to your seats"—and in their excitement 23,000 people screamed *Yeah!*—"Because the earth is going to shake and the ground is going to split open"—*YEAH!*, louder now—"and hellfire will shoot out of the primordial darkness in a holocaust of pure wrestling fury"—they punched at the air with their fists and roared, like beasts, the blackness they hid in their hearts, *YEAHHHHHH!* "Ohhhhhhh," Big Bill Boscoe said when they quieted down, his voice trailing off into a whisper filled with fear (he was afraid to unleash the thing that waited in the dark for the sound of his words, and they screamed in rage at his weakness, *YEAHHHHHHH!*). "Ohhhhhh, Charlotte, ohhhhhhh, Wrestling Fans and Ladies and Gentlemen, I hope, I pray, that you have made ready"—*YEAHHHHHHH!*—"for . . . the FINAL . . . BATTLE . . . FOR . . . LOOOOOOOOOVE!"

At the end of regulation time (nothing really important ever happens in professional wrestling until the borrowed time after the final bell has rung) Bob Noxious and Lord Poetry stood in the center of the ring, their hands locked around each other's thick throats. Because chokeholds are illegal in SWA professional wrestling, the referee had ordered them to let go and, when they refused, began to count them out for a double disqualification. Bob Noxious and Lord Poetry let go only long enough to grab the referee, each by an arm, and throw him out of the ring, where he lay prostrate on the floor. Lord Poetry and Bob Noxious again locked on to each other's throats. There was no one there to stop them, and we felt our stomachs falling away into darkness, into the chaos. Veins bulged like ropes beneath the skin of their arms. Their faces were contorted with hatred, and turned from pink to red to scarlet. Starla jumped up and down beside me and shouted, "*KILL* Lord Poetry! *KILL* Lord Poetry!"

Darling Donnis ran around and around the ring, begging for someone, anyone, to make them stop. At the announcer's table,

Big Bill Boscoe raised his hands in helplessness. Sure he wanted to help, but he was only Big Bill Boscoe, a voice. What could he do? Darling Donnis rushed away. She circled the ring twice more until she found Rockin' Robbie Frazier keeping his vigil in the shadows near the entrance to the locker room. She dragged him into the light near the ring. She pointed wildly at Lord Poetry and Bob Noxious. Both men had started to shake, as if cold. Bob Noxious's eyes rolled back in his head, but he didn't let go. Lord Poetry stumbled, but reached back with a leg and regained his balance. Darling Donnis shouted at Rockin' Robbie. She pointed again. She pulled her hair. She doubled her hands under her chin, pleading. "*CHOKE* him!" Starla screamed. "*CHOKE* him!" She looked sideways at me. "HURRY!" Darling Donnis got down on her knees in front of Rockin' Robbie and wrapped her arms around his waist. Rockin' Robbie stroked her hair but stared into the distance and shook his head no. Not this time. This was what it had come to. This was a fair fight between men and none of his business. He walked back into the darkness.

Darling Donnis was on her own now. She ran to the ring and stood at the apron and screamed for Bob Noxious and Lord Poetry to stop it. The sound of her words was lost in the roar that came from up out of our hearts, but we could feel them. She pounded on the canvas, but they didn't listen. They kept choking each other, their fingers a deathly white. Darling Donnis crawled beneath the bottom rope and into the ring. "NO!" Starla yelled, striking the air with her fists. "Let him DIE! Let him DIE!" Darling Donnis took a step toward the two men and reached out with her hands, but stopped, unsure of what to do. She wrapped her arms around herself and rocked back and forth. She grabbed her hair and started to scream. She screamed as if the earth really had opened up and hellfire had shot up all around her—and that it had been her fault. She screamed until her eyelids fluttered closed, and she dropped into a blond and white heap on the mat, and lay there without moving.

When Darling Donnis stopped screaming, it was as if the spell that had held Bob Noxious and Lord Poetry at each other's throats was suddenly broken. They let go at the same time. Lord Poetry dropped heavily to his elbows and knees, facing away from Darling Donnis. Bob Noxious staggered backward into the corner, where he leaned against the turnbuckles. He held on to the top rope with one hand and with the other rubbed his throat. "Go GET her!" Starla screamed at Bob Noxious. "Go GET her!" For a long time nobody in the ring moved, and in the vast, enclosed darkness surrounding the ring, starting up high and then spreading throughout the building, 23,000 people began to stomp their feet. Tiny points of fire, hundreds of them, sparked in the darkness. But still Bob Noxious and Lord Poetry and Darling Donnis did not move. The crowd stomped louder and louder (*BOOM! BOOM! BOOM! BOOM!*) until finally Darling Donnis weakly raised her head and pushed her hair back from her eyes. We caught our breath and looked to see where she looked. It was at Bob Noxious. Bob Noxious glanced up, his dark power returning. He took his hand off of his throat and put it on the top rope and pushed himself up higher. Darling Donnis raised herself onto her hands and knees and peeked quickly at Lord Poetry, who still hadn't moved, and then looked back to Bob Noxious. "DO it, Darling Donnis!" Starla screamed. "Just DO it!" Bob Noxious pushed off against the ropes and took an unsteady step forward. He inhaled deeply and stood up straight. Darling Donnis's eyes never left him. Bob Noxious put his hands on his hips and with a monumental effort threw his great shoulders all the way back. *No,* we saw Darling Donnis whisper. *No.* High up in the seats beside me, Starla screamed, "*YES!*"

Bob Noxious's left nipple twitched once. Twitch. Then again. Then the right. The beginning of the end. Darling Donnis slid a hand almost imperceptibly toward him across the canvas. But then, just when it all seemed lost, Rockin' Robbie Frazier ran from out of the shadows to the edge of the ring. He carried a thick book in one hand and a cordless microphone in the other. He leaned under the bottom rope and began to shout at Lord

Poetry, their faces almost touching. (*Lord Poetry! Lord Poetry!*)
Lord Poetry finally looked up at Rockin' Robbie and then slowly
turned to look at Bob Noxious, whose pectoral muscles had
begun to twitch regularly, left-right, faster and faster, like heart-
beats. Darling Donnis raised a knee from the canvas and began to
crawl toward Bob Noxious. Rockin' Robbie reached in through
the ropes and helped Lord Poetry to his knees. He gave the
book and the microphone to Lord Poetry. Lord Poetry turned
around, still kneeling, until he faced Darling Donnis. She didn't
even look at him. Five feet to Lord Poetry's right, Bob Noxious's huge chest was alive, pumping, a train picking up speed.
Lord Poetry opened the book and turned to a page and shook
his head. No, that one's not right. He turned farther back into
the book and shook his head again. What is the one thing you
can say to save the world you live in? How do you find the words?
Darling Donnis licked her red lips. Rockin' Robbie began flashing his fingers in numbers at Lord Poetry. Ten-eight. Ten-eight.
Lord Poetry looked over his shoulder at Rockin' Robbie, and his
eyebrows moved up in a question: Eighteen? "YES!" screamed
Rockin' Robbie. "EIGHTEEN." "Ladies and Gentlemen," Big
Bill Boscoe's huge voice suddenly said, filled now with hope, "I
think it's going to be Shakespeare's Sonnet Number Eighteen!"
and a great shout of *NOOOOO!* rose up in the darkness like
a wind.

Lord Poetry flipped through the book, and studied a page,
and reached out and touched it, as if it were in Braille. He
looked quickly at Darling Donnis, flat on her belly now, slither-
ing toward Bob Noxious. Lord Poetry said into the microphone,
"Shall I compare thee to a summer's day?" Starla kicked the seat
in front of her and screamed, "NO! Don't do it! Don't do it!
He's after your soul! He's after your soul!" Lord Poetry glanced
up again and said, "Thou art more lovely and more temperate,"
and then faster, more urgently, "Rough winds do shake the darling buds of May," but Darling Donnis crawled on, underneath
the force of his words, to within a foot of Bob Noxious. Bob

Noxious's eyes were closed in concentration and pain, but still his pectorals pumped faster. Lord Poetry opened his mouth to speak again, but then buried his face in the book and slumped to the mat. Rockin' Robbie pulled on the ropes like the bars of a cage and yelled in rage, his face pointed upward, but he did not climb into the ring. He could not stop what was happening. *Please,* we saw Darling Donnis say to Bob Noxious. *Please.* The panicked voice of Big Bill Boscoe boomed out like a thunder: "Darling Donnis! Darling Donnis! And summer's lease hath all too short a date: sometime too hot the eye of heaven shines, and often is his gold complexion dimm'd!" But it was too late: Bob Noxious reached down and lifted Darling Donnis up by the shoulders. She looked him straight in the eye and reached out with both hands and touched his broad, electric chest. Her eyes rolled back in her head. Starla dropped heavily down into her seat and breathed deeply, twice. She looked up at me and smiled. "There," she said, as if it was late in the night, as if it was over. "There."

Tony Earley is a native of Rutherfordton, North Carolina. He attended Warren Wilson College and the University of Alabama, where he recently received his MFA in Creative Writing. His work has appeared in *Harper's* and *Tri-Quarterly,* and will soon be anthologized in *Best American Short Stories*. Little, Brown and Company will publish his short story collection, *Here We Are in Paradise,* in January 1994.

PHOTO CREDIT: JANE ALEXANDER

I wrote this story very quickly, after listening for two years as the narrator, through two awful short stories and three chapters of an equally bad novel, whined about his life. His girlfriend wouldn't say that

*she loved him. Poly/cotton shirts made his back itch. Only his sworn prom-
ise that he personally knew* professional wrestlers *kept me listening to
him at all. At the time it seemed profound to me that Charlotte's professional wrestlers—this part of the story is true—were replaced by an
actual NBA franchise. When I think about it now, it still does. I'm surprised that every writer in North Carolina didn't write a story about it
before I did. As I write this, the Charlotte Hornets are 33–29 and apparently on the way to their first playoff appearance. I hope that the narrator
of "Charlotte"—whose name I still don't know—finds that event meta-
phorically significant because, quite frankly, I could use the work.*

Barbara Hudson

SELLING WHISKERS

(from *Story*)

One day Edna Sarah's mother sent her out to sell the dog. He was not an ordinary dog, and certainly it was not ordinary in her neighborhood to try and sell a dog by going from house to house, but Edna Sarah, who was ten, did not have much choice; or so she felt.

When her mother told her what she was thinking, it was during supper, a rather measly supper, but that was her mother's excuse for selling the dog, which Edna Sarah knew was completely false. The house was stuffed with food. The cabinets in the kitchen were overflowing. The refrigerator was threatening to burst. If Edna Sarah opened the door to the pantry, a can from the highest shelf always fell out, so she had given up trying. Besides, her mother had a nose that could sniff out the smallest crack in a bag of raisins, a food Edna Sarah had not thought of as particularly aromatic, crouched last week in the linen closet, the door suddenly flung open, her mother there, her hand quick, no food between meals, she snapped, the bag of raisins gone, the door slammed shut.

In fact, Edna Sarah had begun to think of the food in the house as not food at all but artifacts. She knew that her mother kept boxes of Girl Scout cookies stacked in her closet, and the big chocolate candy bars that kids sold to make money for organizations stuffed in her drawers, six-packs of small green Coca-Cola bottles under her bed, and lots and lots of bags of oyster crackers strewn around the room as though they were decorator pillows. Everything was well packaged and well sealed and had a long shelf life.

"I think we should sell Whiskers," her mother said. They were seated at the table in the kitchen, which was bare except for their plates and utensils. Edna Sarah was picking at a Vienna sausage. She had two on her plate. Of course, Whiskers had few whiskers, but her mother had wanted a cat to keep the mice population down. They had no mice and they had no cat, but they did have a purebred West Highland terrier with one eye; and they did have food but it was inaccessible, a word that hit Edna Sarah in her gut and her soul the first time her teacher defined it.

"I don't want to sell Whiskers," she said.

"I know you don't want to," answered her mother. She ran her noticeably thin fingers through her sheer blond bangs. "Who ever wants to sell their pet? Their trusty and beloved pet."

"Somebody, maybe," said Edna Sarah, looking down, "but not I."

"Why can't you say 'me'?" Her mother pierced the remaining Vienna sausage on her plate with a fork. "It's not normal."

"Not me," she answered, twisting the end of her long blond braid. "I'm not going to sell him."

"But, dear," her mother leaned forward, the Vienna sausage clinging to her fork, "can't you see how we've been brought to this?"

"I guess so," said Edna Sarah. She tapped her roll. It made a hollow sound. She could actually remember a Sunday morning last fall when her mother had made pancakes, the warm, buttery smell rising into Edna Sarah's bedroom and her father calling out for her to come. The night before, they had stayed up late, all three of them, lying on a quilt in the grass to watch for falling stars. But even then there were signs: three pancakes each, no more, the rest of the batter scraped into a clean mayonnaise jar to grow mold in the back of the refrigerator. "I haven't lost my commission yet," her father laughed. Her mother tightened the lid on the jar and looked at Edna Sarah. There are never any guarantees, baby. Her father rose from the table, the crossword puzzle in his hand. After the holidays he was gone, a lieutenant commander in the navy, away on his ship for another six months.

But they were fine, her mother said when the ombudsman called; and yes, she would be at the meeting, to the commander's wife; and of course Edna Sarah could go to the movie with Adrienne (even as the food disappeared from their plates, a little here and a little there). These days Edna Sarah ate every bite of her lunch at school, paid for with her allowance, and put the nonperishables in her backpack for the weekends. To anyone who asked, she said she was having a growth spurt, but it set her apart, the care she took, even from her friends. She guessed she understood how she and her mother had come to this.

"I guess so?" Her mother's voice rose. "I guess so? The evidence is everywhere." And she swept her arm around the room, across the overstuffed pantry, the burgeoning refrigerator, and the cabinets that would not close. "Whiskers," she called, "come here," and he dutifully came, his ears up, his tail wagging, his nose poised, the one good eye wide and open, the other gone, its eyelid sunken and shriveled. He was a good dog. "Whiskers," she said, "you are eating us out of house and home," and she gave him the Vienna sausage off her fork. He smacked and chewed and licked his lips, and then he came over to Edna Sarah's chair. She looked at her mother's plate and the empty fork. Yes, her mother had given Whiskers a Vienna sausage, although it broke all the rules. So Edna Sarah took one of hers and gave it to Whiskers and stroked him on the head.

"Good God!" her mother yelled. "You have given the dog the last bite of food in the house!"

It was useless for Edna Sarah to point out the remaining sausage on her plate, let alone the roll. They no longer existed. She stood up from the table and pushed back her chair. "How much do you want me to sell him for?"

"Two hundred dollars," her mother answered. "It's the least

we can ask for such a fine animal." Then she rose from the table and took her plate to the sink and carefully scraped what was not there into the disposal. "And, dear," she turned back, "please don't come home until you've sold him. It's a terrible thing to ask, I know, but we are simply that desperate." Edna Sarah looked at her mother and saw that she believed every word she was saying.

So Edna Sarah went to the closet and got the new retractable leash her mother had bought only recently and put it on Whiskers —he wagged his tail and grinned—then together they walked several blocks to a part of the neighborhood where nobody knew her. The evening was warm. The light was soft. The daylilies were blooming. She started to whistle "She'll Be Coming Round the Mountain When She Comes," Whiskers sniffing here and there and lifting his leg to pee a little.

The first house she decided to try was on Maplewood, a white house with a red tile roof and a big yard edged with flowers. There was a sliding board and a sandbox and a long swing hanging from a tall tree. She imagined the lift she could get out of that swing, especially with a decent push. In fact, she remembered having once seen a man on his knees at the front flower bed. She rang the doorbell. The man came to the door.

"Yes?" he said, and smiled. He was tall and slender and was wearing a white T-shirt and khaki shorts and looked to Edna Sarah like someone who might like to wrestle with his children on the floor. She had seen some fathers do this. She smiled at the man and picked up Whiskers and held him in her arms.

"Would you like to buy my dog?" she asked. "There's nothing wrong with him, except one of his eyes is missing." Whiskers was quiet in her arms.

The man came out onto the porch. "My mother has a Westie named Duffy," he said and reached out and stroked the dog's head. "What's his name?"

"Whiskers," she answered.

"Hello, Whiskers," he said. Whiskers's shriveled eyelid twitched and he wagged his tail against her arm. She heard the voice of a child inside and what must have been the voice of the mother. She strained her ears. "Why are you selling him?" the man asked.

"Oh, you know," she said, stroking Whiskers's back, "sometimes people get tired of their dogs." Just then a little girl pushed open the storm door and ran up beside the man. She was fair and slender and had a headful of thick dark hair and was wearing a dress.

"Doggie!" she said. "Beautiful doggie!" The man reached down and picked her up and showed her how to touch the dog. Edna Sarah was ecstatic. They would buy Whiskers and she would come back to visit him and they would all wrestle on the carpet and push one another on the swing and she would stay to help the mother fix dinner and eat it.

"Look," laughed the little girl. "He's kissing my hand."

"I know," said Edna Sarah. "He likes you." And she stroked Whiskers's back and smiled.

"How much are you selling him for?" the man wanted to know.

"Two hundred dollars," she told him. "It's the least we can ask for such a fine dog."

"He is a fine dog." Then the man put the little girl down and told her to run inside and ask her mother to help her put on her pajamas; she stared at Edna Sarah.

"I have a boo-boo," she said, "a very bad boo-boo." She pointed to a Band-Aid on the side of her knee, just below the hem of her dress.

"My goodness," said Edna Sarah.

"Do you want to see it?" she asked, and reached for the Band-Aid, just as the mother came out onto the porch, tall and slender with short dark hair. She smiled at Edna Sarah, scooped up the little girl, and they disappeared into the house. Edna Sarah heard the child say, "I was talking to that girl."

"I know," the mother answered. "You're very precocious."

Edna Sarah smiled at the man. "So," she said, "would you like to buy my dog?"

He smiled back but his eyes were tired. "I guess not. The yard

isn't fenced in. The house is small. My daughter is unpredictable."
He touched Whiskers's nose.

Edna Sarah put Whiskers on the porch and straightened his
leash. "I have to be going," she said, then, "Come on, buddy,"
and down the steps they went.

"Good luck," the man called.

"Thank you," she answered, but did not turn around. She
walked straight across the street to the house on the other side, a
tall yellow house with dark green shutters and an overgrown sort
of yard. Someone had left a wagon with a high, straight handle
on the front walk. Edna Sarah rang the doorbell. A black woman
opened the door. She was tall and robust and said, "Hi," just as a
little boy about the size of the little girl across the street pushed
himself around the woman's legs and stood poised on the thresh-
old. Edna Sarah could see that he was not her son, his hair blond
and wavy, but he was sturdy, a very sturdy little boy.

"Das a dog," he said.

"Would you like to buy him?" Edna Sarah asked. She picked
up Whiskers and looked at the woman. "He's a purebred West
Highland terrier with a missing eye, but you would never know it
from the way he acts, and he loves children." Whiskers's shriveled
eyelid twitched.

"I want to touch dat dog," the little boy said.

"Why are you selling him?" the woman asked, and she picked
up the little boy, who stretched his hand toward Whiskers. Edna
Sarah moved forward so that he could touch the dog.

"Gently," she said, then looked back at the woman. "My mother
wants me to sell him." Somehow it was easier to tell the truth the
second time.

"Lord, what a horrible thing to do to a child. How old are
you?"

"Ten." Edna Sarah stroked Whiskers's head and he wagged his
tail against her arm, flap, flap, flap.

"Ten years old and out selling your dog on the street." The
woman shook her head. "What in the hell is wrong with your
mother?"

"Hell," said the little boy.

"Shush." The woman looked at Edna Sarah.

"It's complicated," she answered.

The woman laughed and said, "Haven't I heard it before?" The little boy clapped his hands. Edna Sarah smiled. Maybe the woman would buy Whiskers for the little boy and they would all become friends. They looked like people who enjoyed food, not spare and fragile and wispy like Edna Sarah's mother, like Edna Sarah herself, although that was certainly not by choice. She would be fat, if she could.

"Why don't you come in?" said the woman. "But leave the dog out here. You can tie him to that bush," and she pointed across the yard to a huge camellia. "I just can't buy a dog—this isn't my house—but maybe you'd like to have something to eat and drink with us."

"Sure," said Edna Sarah. "Come on, Whiskers."

"Whiskers?" The woman rolled her eyes and went inside. Edna Sarah took him to the bush, where she fastened the leash to a thick branch and knelt and told him how much he would like this neighborhood. Then she walked back to the house and went inside.

The smell was immediate, warm and spicy and edible. The woman came out of the kitchen and Edna Sarah followed her back in. "How about some milk and cookies?" she asked. The little boy was already seated at the table, his head tilted back, his hands around a blue cup with a lid, guzzling whatever it was inside.

Edna Sarah stood in the middle of the kitchen. "What is that smell?" she asked. The little boy brought the cup down hard.

"Mo juice," he said.

The woman chuckled, the skin at the corner of her eyes wrinkling. "Spaghetti sauce," she answered. "It's been cooking all afternoon." Then she moved a little closer. "Have you had your supper?"

"Mo juice," said the little boy. Edna Sarah looked at him. The woman looked at her. Edna Sarah hesitated. It was a tricky question. Whose version of supper were they talking about?

"I did have some," she finally said, "but it was very important to my mother that I get to work on selling the dog."

"MO JUICE!" yelled the little boy, and he banged his cup on the table.

The woman drew closer. "Financial problems?" Her voice was low. "Everybody has them."

"Well, yes," said Edna Sarah. BANG, BANG, BANG went the cup. "Now that I think about it." It was the simplest explanation.

"How much does your mother want for the dog?" The woman moved to the refrigerator and opened it. Edna Sarah scanned the shelves. Where was that spaghetti sauce?

"Two hundred dollars," she answered, "but I'm willing to negotiate." The woman took out a bottle of apple juice and poured some of it into the little boy's cup as he banged his hands on the table.

"There you go." She handed him the cup and patted his head, then moved to one of the cabinets to open it. "It's a crime. Sending a child out to sell a dog for that much."

"Cookie, cookie!" yelled the little boy.

The woman turned. "Now you wait a minute," she told him, her face bending close to his, her voice firm, "we have a guest," and she extended the package to Edna Sarah, who looked her straight in the eye and asked if there was any more spaghetti sauce.

"Child," she said, "I'll fix you a whole plate."

"Gib me a cookie!" yelled the little boy. "Pease!" BANG, BANG, BANG. The woman gave Edna Sarah a push toward the table. "Now sit down and give this boy a cookie or two."

An hour later, when Edna Sarah stood up from the table and walked to the door, she knew that she had seen and smelled and tasted kindness; even her stomach protruded to a point she had never thought possible. Once outside she looked back twice, to wave, before the woman and the little boy turned to go in, then she knelt beside Whiskers to unhook his leash and saw his shriveled, sunken eyelid and knew that if she touched it, in that moment, it would begin to rise and fill and Whiskers would be whole. She felt that good.

But what if his new eye made him trip, the way people with new glasses sometimes did? Then she saw that the light was beginning to fade from the sky and the trees were growing dark and if the next house did not buy Whiskers, she would have to hide him in the garage and tell her mother this: that the people who had bought him were very respectable and had not wanted her to carry the two hundred dollars home alone at night and would bring the money by the house in the morning. She was welcome to call them. Then Edna Sarah would have to think of something fast.

She straightened Whiskers's leash and they walked across the yard to the next house and were still some distance from the front steps when the storm door burst open and out ran two children, the door slamming behind them. Whiskers began to bark and wag his tail and lunge forward. "Sit!" Edna Sarah yelled and his bottom dropped to the ground. "Good dog," she murmured, kneeling beside him, "good dog," and then the children were upon them, a boy younger than Edna Sarah, and a girl younger than he, or him, as her mother would say.

"Can I pet your dog?" the little girl asked, her eyes bright and focused, her light red hair standing out in every direction.

"No, Amy," countered the boy and he turned to Edna Sarah. "I don't think our mother wants us to." He had a shock of brown hair and lots of freckles and one of the cutest noses Edna Sarah had ever seen. "My name is Monty," he said, "and I'm in the first grade at Edgewater Elementary." Then he knelt beside Whiskers. "What's the dog's name?"

"Don't you touch that dog," said Amy, her hands fisted.

"It's okay," said Edna Sarah, stroking Whiskers. "He's a very nice dog and I don't think your mother would mind. He doesn't have any diseases or anything." The dog's tail beat against the ground.

"See," Amy said and pushed Monty a step backward.

"Cut it out," he snapped and was about to push her in return when they both saw Whiskers's shriveled eyelid. "Oh dear," Amy lowered her voice and looked at Edna Sarah, "he hurt his eye."

"Not exactly," she told them and scratched Whiskers's ears. "It's just missing."

"Gross," said Monty.

"Well, you could say gross," she conceded, "but I like to think it makes him a one-of-a-kind dog. How many dogs do you know that have only one eye?" Monty shook his head; Amy followed. "How many people do you know?" Suddenly he began to jump up and down.

"I do, I do," he yelled. "My dad has a friend," his jumping slowed, "who wears a," he stopped, his mouth twisted in concentration, "uh," suddenly he grinned, "patch," and he brought his right hand up to cover his eye.

"Yeah," said Amy and she brought her hand up too.

"Well, you know what?" said Edna Sarah. "If you buy this dog, you could make a patch to put over his missing eye, just like a pirate." She could hardly believe she had thought it up on the spot, it was so perfect. "How would you like to own a pirate dog?"

"Cool," said Monty.

"Cool," said Amy.

"Then why don't you go get your parents?" said Edna Sarah.

Monty looked at Amy. "You go."

"No, you go," she answered.

"I'll go," said Edna Sarah.

"No," said Amy, "it's my turn," and off she ran.

The mother and father came out together, Amy in the lead. Edna Sarah stood up to greet them. Whiskers was sniffing something Monty had pulled from his pocket.

"So they corralled you into the yard," the dad said. He was tall, with dark hair and blue eyes and a mouth that, well, Edna Sarah could see that he liked to tell jokes.

"No," she said, "not at all," and looked at the mother, whose hair was short like the mother's across the street. "They like my dog." Then she smiled and called Whiskers to come and told him to sit. She stroked his head. "He's very obedient." The mother knelt and stroked him, too.

"I've had dogs all my life," she murmured. The father rolled his eyes.

"So have I," said Edna Sarah. "Okay, Whiskers. You may get up." And she pushed the button on the retractable leash so that he could run. "He's a purebred West Highland terrier."

"Whiskers," said the father. "I won't even ask you that story."

Edna Sarah smiled. "It's a very funny joke." The father turned.

"Monty! Amy! Watch it!" he yelled. Edna Sarah spun around. Amy was trying to take Whiskers's leash off at the collar while Monty stroked the dog's head.

"Not now, Amy," she called, "maybe in a minute."

"So you already know their names." The mother stood up. She had a tired smile, like the man across the street.

"Oh, they're very friendly," said Edna Sarah. Then she noticed how dark it was getting and that the crickets were beginning to chirp. "In fact, they're so very friendly, I'd like to sell them my dog."

The father laughed but he caught himself. If Edna Sarah had not so recently eaten a plateful of spaghetti, she would have cried. Somehow the fullness of her stomach fortified her. As it was, she bit her lip.

"Come on, Monty and Amy," the father called, "say good night. It's time to go in." Whiskers was running back and forth between the two of them, still on the leash. They ignored their father.

"How much are you asking?" said the mother.

Edna Sarah hesitated. She did not really want to sell Whiskers, and she knew that asking for two hundred dollars almost guaranteed that she would not. On the other hand, she did not really want to take him home tonight and hide him in the garage. It was damp and moldy and she could not keep her mother out of there forever.

"Five dollars," she said.

"Five dollars," the mother called to the father.

"Five dollars!" yelled Monty, raising both his hands. "I have five dollars! My own pirate dog for five dollars!"

"Please, Daddy," said Amy, "please," and she ran over and grabbed his leg.

The father turned to Edna Sarah. "Is there anything else we should know about this dog?"

She thought. "He's had all his shots. He's never going to have any children." She paused. "He's completely housebroken. And he knows how to sit." She looked at Whiskers, his tail wagging, his mouth open. "And he has only one eye but it doesn't slow him down."

"I can see that," said the father.

"How should we, uh, treat the other one?" asked the mother.

Edna Sarah looked at the shriveled, sunken eyelid. "No special way," she said. "It's all sealed up." Then she glanced at the father. "I've told your children they could make him a patch." He smiled.

"What about his papers?" asked the mother.

"Oh, everything's in order," Edna Sarah answered. "I can bring them by."

"Well." The father looked at the mother.

She grinned. "You've been wanting a reason to fence in the backyard."

"A dog! We have a dog!" yelled Monty, and he ran over and hugged Edna Sarah, and Amy grabbed her from behind. Suddenly, she did not want to give Whiskers to them at all, because why should they have more of what they already had? It was clear that nobody would need playing with, not even Whiskers.

She handed the leash to Monty and showed him how to clip and unclip it and how to work the retractable button and told him to take good care of his new dog and maybe she would see him at school sometime.

His eyes lit up. "Sure," he said. Then she took the five dollars from the father, thanked him, folded the bill, and put it into her pocket.

"It was nice meeting you," she told them. Monty and Amy were already running toward the porch, Whiskers ahead of them. The father shook her hand and the mother touched her shoulder, then together they turned toward the house. "I'll have to get some dog food," the mother said. The father looked back.

"Would you like a ride home?" he asked. "It's getting dark."

"No, thank you," she answered, "it's just around the corner," and she waved.

She walked home slowly, her hands in her pockets, aware of the hazy blue lights of the television sets that were on and thinking about the five-dollar bill. It could buy her something to eat when the time became critical, and critical it was becoming. Soon there might be a whole weekend when her mother offered Edna Sarah nothing more than a couple of Vienna sausages, and in a matter of weeks, she was not counting, school would be out altogether. Tonight she would simply tell her mother that Whiskers had seen a cat, a tabby with a white face and dark paws, and had pulled the leash from Edna Sarah's hands, run after the cat, and was gone forever. She knew other dogs that did it all the time. Of course, they usually found their way home, or the owners retrieved them, but there was always the exception, and Edna Sarah sensed, accurately enough, that this was the nature of the world in which she was living.

As she approached her house, the second-story dormers dark, she saw the wavering blue light of the television in the den. She climbed the two steps to the front porch, unconsciously pausing to wait for Whiskers, and was about to open the storm door, when the front light came on and there stood her mother. She was dressed in a green silk kimono, her long blond hair loose about her shoulders, the points of her elbows hidden by the breadth of her sleeves. She opened the door and gathered Edna Sarah into her arms.

"Baby, baby," she whispered, "I was so worried," and kissed Edna Sarah all over her face, her mother's mouth dry and smelling like chocolate. Then her mother straightened and looked out across the porch, into the night. "Where's our Whiskers," she asked, "our precious Whiskers?"

"I sold him," Edna Sarah answered, "for five dollars," and she brought out the money. She was too tired to think of anything else. Her mother stared at the bill. Edna Sarah shook it. "Here," she said, "it should help you buy something for supper tomorrow night."

Her mother took the money and fingered it gingerly. "I'll see what I can do." She smiled at Edna Sarah. "It's the least we deserve, giving up our dog like that," and she folded the five-dollar bill and slipped it into the pocket of her kimono and patted it. Then she took a deep breath (as though she were inhaling the stars from the sky), and slowly began to turn her head from side to side until her pale fine hair swung out all around her. Edna Sarah waited. Her mother's head became still; she lifted a hand to push her hair behind her ear.

"Tomorrow," she said, as she held the storm door open for Edna Sarah and they stepped into the darkness of the hall. "Tomorrow," she said again, her nose, mouth, and chin in silhouette, all of them sharp, with edges that could cut Edna Sarah, "I will buy a cat. I will buy a cat who will sit in my lap and purr."

Edna Sarah felt the lump rise in her throat and the tears start in her eyes. She bit her lower lip. Her mother did not see or hear. The room was dark. Clearly, there were other things on her mind. She left Edna Sarah standing in the hall.

After a while, she rummaged through her pockets and found an old crumpled tissue and took it out and blew her nose. Then she climbed the stairs to the second floor and walked down the smooth carpeted hall to her bedroom. She turned on the light and went to the bottom drawer of her great-grandmother's bureau, where she found her favorite nightgown. It was long and made of blue ticking flannel, with eyelet lace at the cuffs and the collar and around the yoke, much too hot for that time of year, but what did she care? She put it on and buttoned the three buttons at the back of the neck and shook it out and turned until the hem made a perfect circle.

She had a hard time falling asleep that night, but as she did, she thought about Whiskers. She was taking him for a run on her skateboard, as she sometimes did. He was such a smart dog. He simply ran alongside her as she pushed her leg against the asphalt and brought it up again. They were sailing down Maplewood. The skinny family with the flowers and the yard toys was there. The black woman and the little boy. He was sitting on her shoulders. And Monty and Amy, jumping up and down on the curb, egging her on, their mother and father waving from the porch. Whiskers was so happy. She had never seen him happier, his ears back, his legs extended, his mouth open to catch the breeze. And where were they sailing, where? Somewhere over the rainbow, she guessed. Or maybe coming round the mountain. They would know when they got there. And what a surprise it would be.

Her eyes flew open. The room was dark. The television was on. The upstairs was quiet. Cautiously, Edna Sarah rose from the bed and tiptoed down the hall to her mother's room, where she eased the door open. Her mother was not there, so she eased the door shut, turned on the overhead light, and went to the closet. She stood on the stepladder and pulled down a box of peanut butter cookies. From there she went to the bureau, where she found a chocolate candy bar with almonds, and then to the bed, where she pulled out a six-pack of Coca-Colas. On her way out, she picked up a bag of oyster crackers. There was no sound from downstairs.

Once she was back in her own room, she closed the door and pushed a chair up underneath the knob, then sat on the bed and put the food around her, clockwise, in the order of its nutritional value: the oyster crackers first, the Coca-Colas last. At least the candy bar had nuts. When that was done, she crawled to the open window at the head of the bed and lifted the screen. She managed to get all the food into a pair of her black tights, except the Coca-Colas; she took only one bottle, dropped to the toe of a leg, the candy bar slid beside it, the cookies next and the oyster crackers last, stuffed across the seat. She tied the other leg around her waist and took the whole thing with her as she made her way out the window and onto the roof.

There she sat, perched on the dormer, her nightgown twisted around her knees, her sleeves pushed to her elbows, her feet pressed into the pebbly asphalt roofing, eating something of everything and drinking the whole Coke. The first bites hung in her mouth like forbidden fruit, but after that, she would have gladly given them up for a hot baked potato and some fresh green beans and a lick on her hand from Whiskers. She wrapped what was left into a tight ball and threw it as far as she could into the side bushes, where she knew she could retrieve it before school, if the raccoons did not get it.

Yes, a day was coming when she would have to tell someone. But not tomorrow. Tomorrow her mother was going to get a cat, and, well, that was something she had always wanted.

Barbara Hudson was born in El Paso, Texas, and currently lives in Cullowhee, North Carolina, where she teaches part-time at Western Carolina University. She received her MFA from the University of Pittsburgh and her stories have been published in *Apalachee Quarterly, Quarterly West, Story,* and anthologized in *New Stories from the South, The Year's Best, 1991.*

PHOTO CREDIT: NINA ANDERSON

I wrote "Selling Whiskers" when I was living in Norfolk, Virginia, on the edge of what I have always thought of as a very Southern neighborhood, people sharing recipes and children, picking up each other's mail,

bringing over vegetables in the summer, having drinks together and cook-
outs. Into the middle of all this, one evening a little girl came to our house
(it is true) trying to sell her one-eyed dog, or so my husband told me. No
one could say who she was or where she lived, nothing except her mother
had made her do it. A few weeks later I began to write this story.

Dan Leone

SPINACH

(from *The Paris Review*)

T he name is Stamps. Not mine, his. Steven Stamps to be exact is the name, but folks around here, which is Tucson, A-Z, prefer calling him as Bluto on account of what he keeps in his shoe, on account of the story goes along with it. His story, not mine. My story is quite a bit different.

What's in the shoe, and has been there coming on thirty years, so you have some idea what it likely smells like by now, is a black and white picture. In his shoe. And this picture, in case you ain't seen it yet, which case you must've just got in town two-three minutes ago, while he was asleep there with his head on the wall out there and didn't see you, dreaming about your-guess-is-as-good-as-mine; well, anyways, this here picture is a old photograph, circa 1961, of Bluto's ex-wife, the late and extremely wonderful, beautiful, honorable, good singer, and generally good-natured Mary Ann Stamps. The only photograph of its kind, I might add, meaning the only one Bluto or me or anyone we know about has got with her in it, her being the late and so on Mary Ann Stamps.

The place of the picture is Alma, Arkansas, which is known as the Spinach Capital of the World. Alma, Arkansas. The people of the picture is Mary Ann, young Mary Ann, standing in front of the Alma Spinach Cannery with her arm around Popeye, meaning the life-size plaster and paint likeness thereof, which, far as I know, is still standing out front of the cannery, still being fresh painted every April or so by Corky Parm, still welcoming people off Highway 71 to the Spinach Capital of the World.

Yes, sir . . . Popeye the Sailor Man . . . that Popeye look on his face, the pipe, the pants, the forearms, holding up a can—you guessed it—a can of spinach. Mary Ann has got her arm around all this, and she is smiling and happy. Who wouldn't be? Two days before, she got married up in Buffalo, where she and him come from, and was subsequently on her way with him to Mexico for a honeymoon. And behind the brand-new wedding-present camera was a dashing young man, equally attractive as her back then, believe it or not: Steven Stamps. Bluto.

What our Bluto says now, and what he's been telling to people for coming on three decades now, upon showing to them this here picture, is that Popeye stole his girl, see, and here is the proof—the picture—which is how he come to be known as Bluto in the first place, instead of his real name, which is Steven. Truth is, if Mary Ann got herself left behind in Alma, Arkansas, thirty years ago and on the same exact day as this picture, it wasn't Popeye the Sailor Man's fault no more than it was mine or yours. If she got left there all alone with I-mean-nothing but the clothes off her back—which she did—then that's because Bluto himself done her dirty. Of course, he'll tell you she had it coming to her, on account of a big fight they had over some fried chicken, and there was a fight, but that ain't why he left her no more than Popeye is. He lost his head and bailed out is what. The boy flat out chickened out on being married, way I seen it, which is something I could almost understand in a guy, on account of I did almost the same exact thing a year or so later.

Why am I telling you this? Because it's the only love story I know—that's why. It's the only real-life love story I know of. And I happen to be in it. I was born and brought up in the Spinach Capital of the World, you realize, and in 1961 I was pulling levers at the Alma cannery, like everyone else I knew. And it was Monday, which was—along with Tuesday, Wednesday, Thursday, Friday, and Saturday—my day for eating fried chicken dinners at The Shack, Alma's noted eating establishment, right off Highway 71, right off Interstate 40, directly across from the cannery.

It was Monday. Steven and Mary Ann were sitting at a table by the window when I come in after work. They'd already ordered, but didn't have food yet. I sat down and ordered the same thing as what they had ordered: fried chicken. Biscuits and corn.

"You want some spinach?"

Hell no. Nobody eats spinach in the Spinach Capital of the World. But *they* ordered spinach—that's how I come to know them as being from Buffalo, or at least not Alma, Arkansas.

That and the camera, which was setting on the table in between them, like a game of chess. They were both looking at it . . . staring at it and not saying nothing, like they already come to realize that only one of them was going to wind up leaving this little Arkansas town. It had to be building up. You know— right? It had to come out of somewhere.

Shortly after the chicken come is when they commence to fight, but first let me tell you what they looked like before things got ugly, which was like this: they were young and they were beautiful. He had that greased-back black hair like guys from the city had it in them days. Clean white shirt. Black leather jacket. She had black hair, too, black like you ain't seen black except if you been in the desert like I have at night. No moon. And movie-star eyes. They were made for each other, these two, and they knew it. Hell, I knew it, too. All you had to do was look at them, and you knew it. I reckon all they had to do was just look at each other.

So they been high school sweethearts up in Buffalo and just got married two days prior, never even been outside of New York and maybe P-A until now. I found all this out later. They were taking the scenic route, 71, through the Ozark Mountains that day, and Mary Ann a hundred percent loving every minute of it. Thought she'd died and gone to heaven, she told me. Told me she was actually pinching herself, and that she almost passed out . . . stuff like that.

Steven was meantime just driving and not saying anything or in any way sharing in Mary Ann's pinching herself on account of the sight-seeing and almost passing out and so on, which she at the time attributed to his concentrating on the road, the road being curvaceous and mountainous in that region.

And then they commence to get hungry, the next town being Alma, and one thing leading to another like I already described it until finally their fried chicken was served, which is when the fighting got under way and transpired as follows:

Mary Ann said the chicken was the best fried chicken in the history of the world. (Which is true, by the way.)

Steven said really? He didn't think it was all that great.

Mary Ann said what are you talking about?

Steven said his mother's fried chicken was the best fried chicken in the history of the world.

Mary Ann said really? She didn't like his mother's fried chicken at all it was too greasy she just ate it to be polite.

Steven said you bitch you are out of your mind.

Mary Ann said what the hell has got into you?

Steven said me? What the hell has got into you? You haven't been yourself last couple days.

Mary Ann said me? *You* haven't been yourself last couple days you're crazy what the hell has got into me?!

Steven said don't make a scene.

Mary Ann said *you* don't make a scene.

Then they both commence to start throwing fried chicken at each other.

The waitress, the cook, nobody in the place, myself included, knew what . . . we were all just looking, like we were watching a movie or something. Then when he finally realizes everyone is looking at them, Steven stands up, says, "Let's go."

"I'm not going anywhere until you apologize to me," Mary Ann says. She was crying now . . . there was a piece of chicken in her hair. "You're my husband, goddamn it," she says. "I'm your wife. We're married."

Steven, he puts some money down on the table . . . puts some money down on the table, and he says real quiet and friendly-like: "Let's go, Mary Ann."

And she don't answer. Got her face in her hands and she's flat-out wailing at this point.

Steven waited a few seconds, and I mean *seconds,* and then he turned around and left. We all heard it and seen it: the car door slamming, the engine starting up, the tires kicking up some gravel. And all of a sudden he's gone. Only two days after saying they do. Just drove away and left her there, just like that . . . crying her eyeballs out like a baby.

"Jesus Christ," the waitress said, not being able like the rest of us to believe what she just seen. "That son of a bitch." And she gone over to their table and took the chicken out of Mary Ann's hair.

Everyone was saying he'll be back. Don't worry.

I didn't know whether or not he'd be back or not . . . but I did know a couple of things, which were one, I was going to be there for the whole episode, one way or the other, and two, I felt sorry for the girl and kind of liked her, too, which is easy enough to admit now, thirty years later and four big states away, on account of all else that has transpired since; but at the time I was allowing that I just felt sorry for her. I said he would be back just like everyone else was saying, and I don't pretend to know what they were all thinking, but I was thinking: Please don't come back. Please don't come back. Please don't come back.

He didn't come back.

I'd finished up on my chicken, ate dessert maybe three-four times, and drank about enough coffee to keep the entire night shift awake down the cannery. And then it was eleven o'clock. Closing time.

I was already sitting with her by then.

"If he don't come back," I'd said, pulling up a chair, being systematically careful not to sit in his, "I am hereby officially offering to drive you home. Where you live?" I was thinking, Kansas City, St. Louis . . .

She said Buffalo.

I stammered this way and that for a minute and finally said something to the effect of Alma, Arkansas, not being all that half bad a place to live in once you got used to it.

She smiled, and I said, "I will take you to Buffalo."

"Thank you," she said.

"But he'll be back," I said. "Don't worry. But if he don't come back," I said, "on the outside chance that he don't come back, I will drive you to Buffalo."

You realize I didn't have a driver's license or exactly a car while I was saying all this, although I could've probably come up with something.

"And if you need a place to stay tonight, I'm offering to put you up," I says to her. "I got a sofa bed. It ain't too far from here."

"Thank you," she said. She said thank you. Like it was me doing her the favor . . . which it was, technically speaking.

"We can put a note on the door here," I says, "case he come back during the night."

"Okay. Thank you."

"Name's Chuck," I said.

"I'm Mary Ann."

"He seems like a really nice fellow," I says, "like a fine young gentleman—I mean that. I mean, I know you were having some troublesome times there, but I reckon he'll be back shortly. What's his name?"

"Steven," she said.

I wrote "Dear Steven" on a napkin. "Case you come back," I wrote, "Mary Ann is staying at . . ." and I commence to describe to him where she was staying at, which is where I live, at the time.

"I like the Ozark Mountains," Mary Ann said.

"That's the spirit," I said.

We put the note up on the door of The Shack, but Steven never come back. The most anyone in Alma ever heard from him again was that the restaurant begun to get photographs in the mail addressed to Mary Ann Stamps c/o The Shack, Alma, Arkansas, no zip. No explanation. Nothing. The photographs being pictures of each state's welcome-to sign along the highway. In other words: WELCOME TO OKLAHOMA. WELCOME TO TEXAS. WELCOME TO NEW MEXICO. WELCOME TO ARIZONA. And then the last one she received was TUCSON CITY LIMITS and then nothing after that, so we just reckoned that was where he wound up and still was: Tucson. Which turned out to be right, as you can see for yourself.

Well, time eventually passed, with her still staying on my couch, and Mary Ann did not ask to go back to Buffalo. Her folks shipped down some of her stuff and belongings, like clothes and books and general stuff like that, and she got herself a job teaching music at Alma's grammar school. Turns out she could play the piano and sing, which was more than anyone else in Alma could say for themselves. And she used to every now and again take me down the school with her at night and play the piano and sing for me . . . not "fifteen miles on the Erie Canal" either or "for beautiful, for spacious skies, for amber waves of grain" or anything like that, like I reckon she sung with the children, but different songs. Songs you might be likely to hear in a dance hall or on the radio. Love songs. After a while I commence to start getting some ideas in my head, which was already there to begin with, in between you and me. I loved her. Maybe *she* was getting the ideas, I don't know, but I loved her more than anything I ever loved up to then, including the fried chicken at The Shack, which we'd been knocking off together regular—but not as regular as I been knocking it off before all this happened, Mary Ann being also good at cooking and more than happy to do so on account of staying at my apartment and all.

What I'm trying to get at is that middle of the night one night, while I'm dreaming about spinach, that being what you dream about in Alma, if you're working, Mary Ann commence to come up off the couch and into bed with me.

"Chuck?" she said. "Oh, Chuck," she said, with her hand on

my chest, as I recall. "Wake up, Chuck. We're in love." She loved me, see.

Understand this: we weren't made for each other, me and her. I was nothing like Steven and I was nothing like Mary Ann. First off, I was a country boy. Like I said, I was born and brought up in Alma. When my folks moved to Little Rock, I stayed in Alma on account of one, I already had a job at the cannery, and two, I was in love—dead serious—with the fried chicken at The Shack. Which reminds me of a joke of mine, goes like this: Every now and again somebody come in here from the university or something talking about this book and that one. Always reading a book—you know the type. Then they say, "You like poetry, Chuck?" I say, "Yes." Then they say, "Well, what kind of poetry you like?" And I say, "Chicken. Deep-fried. That's the only kind of poultry I know." That's the joke.

Another thing is that I was not good-looking, not even in 1961. Mary Ann and Steven could've stepped right out of the movies, like I maybe mentioned already, but I couldn't've stepped out of anything. Big and freckled. Sandy, wavy hair.

So what did I have going for me? I don't know, except that I was there, for one thing, and I'm a nice enough guy, which you like to think accounts for something. Well, I reckon it did, on account of there was Mary Ann in bed with me, saying we was in love. And me thinking: we sure as hell are . . .

Now, Mary Ann had been in contact with Mrs. Stamps, Steven's mother, his father being already long dead on account of brain tumors; and, anyways . . . she, the mother, had even less of a idea than we did as to Steven's situation and/or whereabouts. Mrs. Stamps, being generally a good-natured and generous woman, far as I could make out, was embarrassed sick over her son's irresponsible and unexplained disappearance, and always offering to help out . . . even send down some money if she needed it, but Mary Ann said no.

Then, after we been in love together a couple, two-three

months, Mary Ann starts coming up with some fancy and fine-sounding ideas about me and her building us a log cabin up in the mountains, which sounded like a fine idea to me, long as we had a car to get to The Shack with. The only other thing being, of course, that she was a married woman, technically speaking.

Then Mary Ann commence to start talking to friends of hers in New York, friends who had friends who were lawyers and such, and they had us seeing it this way: that after a certain allowance of time—one year, to be exact—without her hearing from Steven and also not even knowing his whereabouts, Mary Ann would be considered by law as "abandoned" and could then commence to divorce him plus or minus him having any input on the subject. Then we, meaning me and her, could get married, which we were planning on doing but hadn't allowed exactly one year yet, before which some sad news come down from Buffalo.

Mrs. Stamps had been killed in a all-of-a-sudden and awful way, meaning a car crash.

Now Mr. Stamps being already dead, and what with Steven missing in action, so to speak, and Mary Ann all the while still officially married to him, after all, there was being sent to her, Mrs. Steven Stamps, a check for the settlement of the estate, which was not a earthshaking amount of money, but it was a amount of money, which is always a nice thing to have sent you, you figure.

Mary Ann was crushed. "I can't believe I said that about her fried chicken," she said. We were sitting at the table and the letter stating all this news was setting on the table in between us. Mary Ann was crying her eyeballs out.

"Poor woman," I said.

"I can't believe I said that about her fried chicken," she says again.

"There, there," I says.

"She was a good cook," says Mary Ann. "She was a really good cook."

"I'm sure she was, honey," I said, and so on, until I was up and over by her, hugging her hard as I could while she cried her eyeballs out into my stomach. "I love you, Mary Ann," I says.

"I love you, too," she says, "Chuck." And then I commence to start crying in my own right, crying right along with her.

Here was the thing: Mary Ann, being all them things I said she was earlier, and add to that philosophical, she didn't want nothing to do with this amount of money being sent her. Far as she was concerned, this here amount of money belonged rightfully and especially to Steven, and as long as his whereabouts were findable, she reckoned, he ought to be found and given it, the philosophy behind which being that if she was already intending to be not married to him in order to marry me, which she was, then it wouldn't sit right to be on the other hand receiving this here money on account of still being married to him. "Can't have it both ways," she said.

Personally, I had a different philosophy on the subject, but I also believed it to be Mary Ann's own business. Also, I could kind of part ways follow her line of reasoning on it. You can't have it both ways. Well, she could've had it both ways, technically, only she didn't want to, and I had to respect that, even if I didn't understand it. Truth is, I loved this woman by now more than I could ever even explain it to you, as you already know, and nothing meant more to me than that, including said amount of money.

Well, she chewed on it for some time before she come up with a plan, and this is what she come up with: she would cash the check, and I would take the money to Tucson, dipping into it as needed for travel expenses and such, the idea being to make every attempt at locating Steven's whereabouts and then to subsequently and simultaneously inform him of his mother's passing and hand over the amount of money, rightfully his. After which I would return to Alma, Arkansas, the Spinach Capital of the World, and marry Mary Ann, not to mention living happy-ever-after with her in a log cabin in the mountains. With a car.

If I couldn't locate him in Tucson, I was to systematically follow up on any and all information I was able to find out about where else he might be, which included going there in person and looking for him until I reached the end of the line, the line being the last knowable information regarding his whereabouts, at which point I was to take the amount of money, whatever was left of it, and symbolically deposit it in his name at the nearest bank . . . whatever city I happen to be in when his trail stops. After which I would head back home to Mary Ann and happy-ever-after and so on.

Way I seen it, I couldn't lose. I had to give up my lever-pulling job at the cannery, but that was first off highly re-gettable, and secondly, after however many years of canning spinach five days a week, I reckoned I was overdue for some adventure . . . The other thing being that I was more than happy to be the one doing the delivering, in spite of it was her idea, on account of reasons I already spelled out for you. Like I said, these two were made for each other in a way that we flat-out were not. They belonged together like pigs and mud, and I knew it; whereas we were more like pigs and, I don't know, iced tea or poetry. So if it was her making the delivery, well, supposing she actually found him? What then? Them being made for each other, like I said.

That's why I was happy not to worry about it, because it was me on that bus, watching them same exact signs pass by which he had sent back pictures of: WELCOME TO OKLAHOMA. WELCOME TO TEXAS. WELCOME TO NEW MEXICO. WELCOME TO ARIZONA. TUCSON CITY LIMITS.

Populationally speaking, Tucson is a big enough city, especially in comparison/contrast with a place like Alma. There's maybe four-five hundred thousand people these days, which is a lot of people, especially if you think about it. On the other hand, there's a awful lot of space out here for them to live in, so it can seem pretty small, more so than it is. The streets are long and wide. You can walk around downtown on a Sunday afternoon, for example, and only see four people and probably know maybe three of them. That's how it is now. In the early sixties it was even smaller seeming, which made my job that much more reasonable.

I called up Mary Ann soon as I come into town, commencing to tell her where I was staying at, which was the Hotel Congress, directly across from the bus terminal. I then explained to her how I had had a good trip and was itching to get started on the looking-for, come tomorrow, and so on.

"I love you," I said.

"I love you, too," she said.

And we hung up.

Want to hear something sad? That was the very last time ever we spoke them words to each other, much as I loved speaking them, and much as I loved hearing them spoken by her in reference to me. And true as they were.

What happened next is that I went to sleep in my paid-for hotel room and woke up the very next morning early, at which point I commence to start looking for Steven and/or his whereabouts. Turns out not only had he been there, as reckoned by me and Mary Ann, and not only did most everybody I come across recognize who it was I was talking about, but also they known him to still be there, as well as where to find his whereabouts: in the desert.

Word was he'd messed up his car a ways outside of town, at which time he commence to come into Tucson by foot, acquire himself a room at the selfsame Hotel Congress, and generally run out of money by way of drinking himself nutty in the hotel's tap-room, as well as several other local establishments, until he was not only flat-out broke but, by all accounts, one hundred percent insane and haywire. If I wanted to find out his location, they all said, I was to drive out about fifteen miles west on Interstate 10, on into the desert. And a fellow going by the name of "Biker," a former drinking buddy and personal friend to "Bluto," as he called him, even offered to drive me there. "I go out there once a week or so," this guy Biker says, "see if he needs anything, or if maybe he come around."

"What's he eat?" I says to Biker. We were in Biker's car, traveling west on 10.

"He don't eat much," this Biker says. "People stop and give him something," he says. "Take his picture, try and talk to him. He's well known along this stretch of highway here, your friend," he says, and he then commence to refer to Steven as "Cactus Man."

"Cactus Man?"

"You'll see," this Biker says. "The man is pretty far gone," he says. "It's about time someone come to claim him."

"I didn't come to claim him, exactly," I explained to this Biker fellow, commencing to get more and more nervous concerning the mental and philosophical condition of Steven Stamps, alias Bluto, alias Cactus Man. I then commence to confide how I was delivering a unhappy message to Steven having to do with the passing of his mother by way of a sudden and unexpected car accident. I also mentioned in passing phase two of my mission, wherein I hand over to Steven a certain amount of inheritance money, and just around that time exactly, don't this here Biker fellow swerve off the highway and into the breakdown lane, screeching the car to a complete and total stop and causing me to all of a sudden regret ever mentioning said amount of money to a guy I just hardly know named Biker, not to mention in *his* car and in the middle of the desert.

Then I seen him: Steven. Bluto. Cactus Man. He was standing all alone out there a couple hundred feet from the highway, just standing there under the sun and simultaneously holding up in the air both of his arms, then being bent at the elbows, and the whole picture being a fairly accurate imitation of the saguaro-style cactus you find in the desert this part of the country.

"Here's our man," says Biker, getting out of the car.

"Biker," I says, myself getting out of my side of the car and all the while keeping both eyes on yonder Steven–Bluto–Cactus Man. "Biker," I says, "how you reckon this here news of mine is bound to go over with him?"

"He can't get too much worse off than what he already is," Biker says as we commence to begin walking toward him.

I'd never been to the desert before this, leastwise not this kind of western-style desert, and I'd always reckoned it to be mostly sand on account of misinformation I must've received in school; but what I was unexpectedly walking upon for the first time turns out was actually hard and stony ground, which I liked the sound of . . . crunching under my feet. I was on solid ground. I was on ground that wouldn't give, and looking down at my feet, thinking the thoughts I was thinking, that whatever else might happen, at least I knew I wasn't going to sink; well, it distracted me from the general unease and nervousness I already said was building up inside of me: thinking maybe I should've called Mary Ann before I come out here, knowing his condition, in case she so chose to do anything differentwise, like bring him back with me or else put him in a institution. On account of her being all them things I mentioned earlier, in addition to philosophical, I didn't reckon just leaving him out there off his rocker in the desert would sit any better with her than keeping the money would've sat. These were the things been tugging at me all along, and from what the solid ground and its crunchy nature were now distracting me, like I said.

"Hey, Bluto," Biker said. We were there.

I looked up and seen him. "Hi, Bike," Bluto says, looking exactly like a crazy man in the desert would be reckoned to look. His formerly slick black hair was become long, dirty, and drier than peanuts, and his clothes was hanging on him like they probably hung on hangers, meaning limp, lifeless. His face, meantime, was dirty as dirt and one hundred percent minus a expression. Not happy or sad or nothing. I knew him to be twenty years old, but he looked about forty. "Who's the cowboy, Bike?" he says, meaning me.

"This here's Chuck," says Biker.

"Hi, Chuck," says Bluto.

"Hi, Steven."

"How you doing, Chuck?" Bluto said.

"Pretty good," said me. "I have to talk to you though. I have something to tell you."

"Biker," Bluto says, "did Chuck ever see the picture?"

"Why don't you go ahead and show it to him," says Biker.

Bluto commence to laugh. "I'm a cactus," he says, right there in front of us. "A cactus can't show it to him."

"Come on, man," says Biker.

"It's in my shoe," Bluto says. He lifts up his left foot up off the ground a little bit, which was the first time he moved anything aside for his mouth.

I looked Biker's way and he just shrugs, so I go on over to Bluto and unlace the shoe, took the shoe off his foot, and took out the picture. And there she was.

"Popeye stole my girl," he says. "My wife. Name's Mary Ann."

"I know," I said, and I reckon I was looking too long and hard for his taste at that picture, but I couldn't help it on account of there she was, smiling right next to Popeye the Sailor Man, and on account of it was *my* hometown, *my* girl, who I loved like I said beyond explanation and all, missing her already and wanting to get this business over with and get back to her and so on, and what was this picture doing in *his* shoe when everything in it, way I seen it, was mine? "She sent me," I says.

Bluto lifts his foot up that little bit again and says, "Put the picture back, okay?"

I put the picture back in his shoe, as instructed, and I put the shoe back on his foot and so on until it was done, and he commence to say, out of nowhere, "Did my mother die?"

I looked at Biker, and he just shrugged.

"Matter of fact," I says, "she did."

Bluto laughed. "I'm on a roll," he says. "Are you planning to marry my wife?"

I didn't say nothing to that, on account of I was speechless.

"Two for two," he says.

"That ain't why I'm here," I said, and I simultaneously dropped in the vicinity of his feet the envelope containing what was left of the amount of money, which was most all of it, being his rightful inheritance. "Your money," I said.

Well, whoever said money ain't important as everything else in the world ain't never been without it enough to know, I reckon. I could already see Bluto softening up some on account of having it again, and he took himself a minute to swallow and say, real polite and kind of quiet-like: "Thank you, Chuck," and, "Will you fellows do me a little favor?"

"What is it?" I said.

"Take some money out of that there envelope," he says, "and go get me about ten cheeseburgers and a large Coke."

"Hell, yeah," says Biker, although I was personally inclined to start commencing my way back east soon as possible, what with Mary Ann waiting on me; whereas Biker, thinking otherwise, says, "Hell, yeah, we'll do that for you."

"Get something for yourselves, too," Bluto then says.

Which is what we done exactly. We come back with twenty cheeseburgers and three large Cokes and a couple of fifths of bourbon, and it was by this time commencing to get dark, but Bluto had us a fire going already, and was already doing what you do with a fire out in the desert—just sitting there, staring on into it.

"What happened to the cactus?" Biker said, passing around the first round of burgers.

"It's a day job," says Bluto. "And no one can see you at night, anyways. And it's too cold. And I've got money now . . ." and there then continued forth from his mouth a long list of reasons to stop being a cactus—not only at night but in general—the list lasting clear through the third round of burgers, with some of the reasons being barely audible on account of his chewing, but all of them being for the most part valid. The last reason he gave, and likewise the most reasonable, was he said, "And it's crazy." Then he said, "Yes, boys, I believe my cactus days to be over."

"That's the spirit," Biker said.

And then I was thankful we stayed on, having witnessed first-handedly the transformation of our boy Bluto from a all-the-way haywire psycho saguaro-imitating nutcase to a generally healthy and philosophically normal member of society, meaning I no longer had to worry over his condition not sitting right with Mary Ann and possibly further complicating the getting-on-with of our mutual and simultaneous plans, them being one, getting married and two, so on.

Another thing was I come to realize how much in fact I actually like this here western-style desert. I loved the ground and I loved the night sky . . . and I loved watching the saguaros dancing around in the light from the fire, all happy-like, like little children, only bigger. I reckon the desert hit me same way as the Ozark Mountains must've hit Mary Ann. It was love at first sight. I wanted to live there.

We'd already done knocked off all the burgers and Cokes and roughly half of two fifths of bourbon, just talking about this and about that, what normal people talk about, you know: life. And then Biker, having a job somewhere working the night shift, had to get going and subsequently got going while meantime I had passed out, and Bluto tended the fire.

You realize I had seriously and all out intended to get back to Arkansas and Mary Ann and so on soon as possible, seeing as my mission was already above and beyond accomplished, way I seen it, what with Bluto not only having his news and money but being cured from his mental and philosophical craziness as well. But one thing led to another, however, commencing with the coming back of Biker after work next morning with two more fifths of bourbon, a cooler filled with beer, and three cowboy hats.

Two years later I was still in the desert, Biker and his car having long since moved to Phoenix together, leaving Bluto and myself—the best of friends, inseparable comrades, kindred spirits, and so on and so forth—to take turns hitchhiking into town for supplies and the like, meaning mostly liquor, water, and food, except we also went ahead and splurged on a couple of luxurious items: sleeping bags, a change of clothes, a harmonica, a guitar, and a frying pan. We had us as well a five-gallon bucket Biker left behind, which we'd fill it up with water each trip into town. Then

we'd let it set out all day in the sun, and later that evening one or
the other of us would have us a shower, the other one standing
atop the cooler, slowly and gradually emptying this bucket over
his head. In this way, and in others like it, we were having what
you would have to call the time of our life, just staring into the
fire, drinking, philosophizing, eating beans and other styles of
food we reckoned real cowboys to have eaten, and yodeling all
night until we'd gone ahead and either lost our voice or else first
just flat-out got spooked by the sound of it.

One time early on we talked about Mary Ann and how much
we both loved and missed her and what her qualities were, and
then I asked Bluto his opinion on something I already told you
was puzzling me: why did he reckon a lady with her qualities and
being the type of woman she was, which wasn't mine, would up
and fall in love with me in the first place, my lack of good looks
notwithstanding?

"Why do you think?" Bluto said.

"My theory," I said, "is that I am a nice guy and a generally
good person and that that accounts for something after all."

"You want to know what I think?" he says. "I'll tell you what I
think, if you promise not to take it personal."

"Okay," I says.

"She loves you," he says, "because you're the opposite of me
and because she hates me for doing her dirty. It doesn't have
anything to do with what you are, but what you aren't."

I commence to start taking it personal, but then I did some
pondering on what I was and wasn't, the outcome of which was
me not being able to tell the difference in between the two, when
it come right down to it. I was ugly, for example, and I wasn't
good-looking. Same thing. I was friendly, and I was not un-
friendly. And so on, until I couldn't've took what Bluto said personal even if I wanted to, on account of it not meaning anything
at all, way I seen it.

That same night Bluto went ahead and asked me the big and
obvious question, like this: "Will you be going back to her soon?"

This was early on, like I said—maybe two-three weeks into our desert days is all . . . shortly after Biker left us, in other words, and back when there was still a reasonable possibility for me going home. I was lying on my back by the fire at the time, and there was a half-empty bottle balancing upon my stomach, with the desert sky all spread out in front of me. I was all focused in on a star, which I liked to engage in this time of night, being just before dawn. What I'd do, I'd pick me a star and try and stare it down, the object being to stay awake just long enough to watch this here star disappear into blue sky, until it was all the way and completely gone. Sometimes I would win, and sometimes the star would win.

"Bluto," I says, "in between me and you, I want to go back to her. I want to be getting back there so bad I am all out and one hundred percent *afraid* of how bad I want to be getting back to her."

"Don't worry," Bluto says, across the fire from me and poking at it with a stick. "I won't tell nobody."

"Well," I says, "it's like this . . ." And I then sat up and commence to confide to him my whole entire life story, starting out with how I was born and then grew up and never having no brothers or sisters, and how I never had no girlfriends, on account of this and that . . . not knowing what all this had, if anything, to do with the issue at hand, but reckoning maybe if I just kept talking on it for long enough, it would eventually come down to something. Truth is, I didn't know why I was poking around in this here fire cowboy-style with Bluto every night when I could've been back home getting married and eating fried chicken.

It occurred to me later on, not while I was laying it all on Bluto that night, which I'll get back to in a minute, that before I ever begun all-the-time dreaming about Mary Ann, much as she was on my awake-time mind, I first commence to dream about the other thing: the chicken. Every time I went to sleep, that was all I dreamed about was fried chicken at The Shack. Then, after the first whole year or so gone by without me ever up and going back, and once it was by my reckoning too late to do so without suffering from certain consequences, that's when I commence to start all-the-time dreaming her: Mary Ann. Mary Ann. Mary Ann.

Sometimes she'd be crying her eyeballs out in these dreams, and sometimes she'd be other-handedly happy and cheerful, with either way amounting to me feeling deeply and all around regretful, not to mention sorry and sad—but this was only while I was dreaming and inside of the dreams that I was feeling suchwise. While I was awake, I was one hundred percent fine and okay and still having the general time of my life, except that I begun looking closer at the cars going by on the highway, now and again and halfway thinking on the possibility that maybe there was a chance she'd come after me and my whereabouts, just like I come after him and his, and likewise find me and either take me away with her or maybe even stay on and be with us, but of course none of them kinds of things was going to happen.

Anyways, seeing how this here reckoning and transpiring took many years to come by and transpire, respectively, it was not included in my original discussion on the issue that I was trying to explain to Bluto, as well as myself, early on in our desert days. Instead, I that night come out with my whole entire life story, simultaneously hitting the bottle and poking the stick around in the fire until finally I conclusioned and summarized by saying, "I don't know why I'm still here. How about you?"

But Bluto already fell asleep while I was still talking, what with his chin down on his chest and his stick no longer poking but just setting there in the fire, on fire and fuse-like, commencing to burn his hand except for and on account of me having the presence of mind to let him go of it for him.

We didn't talk much more about Mary Ann and going back after that and instead went back to philosophizing about altogether different kinds of things. That and eating beans and so on. This went on, like I said, for roughly two years. And then one day the money run out, which is exactly when and why we finally gathered up what little earthwise possessions we had and caught us a ride back into the city. Tucson, A-Z. Which, on account of the fine weather, is not a bad place to be homeless in, if you got to be homeless somewhere.

I reckon I preferred the desert, if it come down to it, and I reckon I'd've been every bit as well off if I was back in Alma . . . But, anyways . . .

Bluto, on the other hand, being a city boy at heart, fit in natural and easy to the city lifestyle. He was everybody's best buddy back then, starting out with the showing them of the picture in his shoe—how Popeye stole his girl. Then when it come around to names and he'd say: "Call me Bluto" . . . well, you had to love him.

He'll still show you that picture, too, thirty years more-or-less later, but people just ain't interested in them kind of pictures anymore. Only thing'll perk up most folks these days is if Mary Ann were naked in it, or Popeye, depending on the looker. There's no audience anymore for a honest-to-God picture of a decent woman and a decent sailor in a decent small town in Arkansas. Except for me.

I could have gone back to Arkansas. I could have any time gone back there, you realize, easy as rubber-heeling it on out as far as the highway and holding up my thumb. But on top of everything else, which is why I wasn't already there in the first place, I was afraid of some new things, like, on account of the passage of time, Mary Ann would beat the shit out of me, for example, or worse yet, she wouldn't. Or maybe she got tired waiting around and married some other spinach-canning freckle-face fried-chicken-loving and fine upstanding resident of Alma, Arkansas.

But even though I never tried calling her up or otherwise getting in touch with her for communicational purposes, she was all-the-time on my mind, believe it or not. She was on Bluto's mind, too, except in a entirely different kind of way, like she was in that picture of his: more of a novelty than a genuine, real-life dilemma. There was never any question about him going back.

Well, about ten-fifteen years ago, back when we were both of us still on the street together, it all become irrelevant anyways. What happened is I finally run into a old Arkansas buddy of mine from the cannery, and he filled me in on some back-home news I did not want to hear, on account of what it was: Mary Ann was dead. She had in fact gave up on me, turns out, after a unsuccessful telephone-style attempt to locate my personal whereabouts and all the while no longer hearing from me, either, whereupon she rightfully commence to reckon I too had done her dirty. And she had in fact, upon reckoning suchwise, up and married somebody else and even built for themselves a cabin up in the Ozark Mountains, which was the one thing I was glad about to hear. Except that then she died, just exactly while giving birth to their second baby, which is something I don't mind saying has absolutely no business happening this day and age, with all our scientific know-how, and especially to a person as all-around good-natured and all them other things as Mary Ann was.

"Bluto," I says to Bluto, "Bluto, buddy," I says, "Bluto, I just run into a old pal of mine from Alma and heard me some awful news," I says.

And the bastard did it again. He up and outs with it: "Mary Ann is dead."

I didn't say nothing, but just shook my head on account of one, it was true, and two, I didn't know how in the hell he already knew it.

"Shit," he says, putting it mildly, and then other than that he basically took it like he took it when his mother died, which was as if it weren't nothing to get all worked up in reference to.

For me, things changed. I didn't want to be living on the street no more, for one thing, so I took me a job, which I still have, cleaning up rooms at the Hotel Congress. I work for room and board and a small amount of spending money, and I help out my friend Bluto when he needs it, like sneaking him into my room on rainy or cold nights, which are few and in between, and I try much as possible to keep him some food in his stomach. I would give him the clothes right off of my back if he would take them, which every now and again he does.

It's like this: I reckon I owe it to him on account of him taking care of me, financially speaking, in the beginning. I also owe it to Mary Ann on account of I let her down, and what with Bluto being the closest as I can come to her now, what with him being more like her than anyone else . . . coming from the same place and remembering some of the same memories and all . . . And he even looks like her a little bit, I reckon, although I don't know how much of that reckoning is only in my head. For another thing, I love him.

And for one more thing, he's got that picture of her, that beautiful goddamn Popeye picture I been trying to tell you about, which will some day be mine if and when Bluto ever dies, which everybody does, I'm told. And I don't care how old or how yellow this here picture is or even what it smells like by then, being kept as it is in his shoe and so on. That picture means more to me than Bluto will ever know, on account of I am in it. You see that building yonder behind Popeye, that long gray Arkansas-style sad and sorry-looking building, in contrast against which Mary Ann's last-of-the-good-times smile dances even to this day like saguaros in the light from a fire? Well, that there is Alma's spinach cannery, and I am inside of it, as you know, only much younger then, like Mary Ann, and smiling a entirely different kind of smile—more like the beginning of good times. Look closer, and you can see me through the gray. That's me. I'm pulling a lever, see, and pulling and pulling and pulling and then pulling again with one hand, smiling, and with the other hand waving at the camera, hello to the next thirty years or so—while meantime behind from me and on account of my pulling, portions of spinach are methodically falling into tin cans, which are methodically closed, labeled, packaged, and shipped into homes all around the country, where young boys will methodically be told to eat it and shut up if they ever want to be strong.

Dan Leone lives in San Francisco. His stories have appeared in *The Paris Review, The Quarterly, Black Warrior Review, The Crescent Review,* and others. This is his second time in *New Stories from the South.* "Spinach" won *The Paris Review*'s 1992 John Train Humor Award.

PHOTO CREDIT: REBECCA JANE GLEASON

For some reason (perhaps because I am weak and stinky?) I have never been able to write about places where I lived. I have never lived in the South. However, I did accidentally stop at Alma, Arkansas, a couple years ago. I was there for about an hour and didn't eat any fried chicken. A couple days later I spent another hour in Tucson, then drove home through the desert and wrote this story. About a year after it was done, I wound up camping outside of Tucson, went back to Alma, ate some great fried chicken at a great little restaurant, and took some pictures with Popeye—wish you were here.

Richard Bausch

EVENING

(from *The Southern Review*)

He was up high, reaching, retouching the eaves of the house, thinking about how it would be to let go, simply fall, a man losing his life in an accident—no humiliation in that. He has paused, considering this, feeling the rickety lightness of the aluminum ladder—and then he heard the car pull in. His daughter Susan's little red Yugo. Susan got out, pushed the hair back from her brow, and looked at him, then waved peremptorily and set about getting Elaine out of the carseat. It took a few moments. Elaine was four, very precocious, feisty, and lately quite a lot of trouble.

"I want my doll."

"You left it home."

"Well, I want it."

"Elaine, *please.*"

Their contending voices came to him, sounds from the world; they brought him back. "Hello," he called.

"Tell Granddaddy hello."

"Don't want to."

Elaine followed her mother along the sidewalk, pouting, her thumb in her mouth. Even the sight of Granddaddy on a ladder in the sky failed to break the dark mood. Her mother knelt down and ran a handkerchief over the tears and smudges of her face.

"I'll be right down," he said.

"Stay," said his daughter in a tired voice. From where he was on the ladder, he could see that she looked disheveled and over-worked—someone not terribly careful about her appearance: a young woman with a child, going through the confusion and trouble after a divorce. He had read somewhere that if you put all the world's troubles in a great pile and gave everyone a choice, each would probably walk away with his own.

"Mom inside?" his daughter said.

"She went into town. I don't think she'll be gone long."

"What're you doing up there?"

"Little touch-up," he said.

"When did she leave?"

He dipped the brush into the can of paint. "Maybe ten minutes ago. She just went to get something for us to eat."

"Is the door open?"

"Go on in," he said. "I'll be down in a minute."

"It's okay," she said. "Finish what you're doing. You only have a little light left."

"Susan, I wouldn't get it all if I had a whole day."

"Well, really. Stay there," she told him, and went on inside with Elaine, who, a moment later, came back out and stood gazing up at him, her hands clasped behind her back.

"You're up high," she said.

"Think so?"

"Granddaddy?"

"Just a minute, honey."

He waited, listening. Susan was on the phone. He could not distinguish words, but he heard anger in the tone, and of course he was in the usual awkward position of not knowing what was to be expected, how he should proceed.

"I can come up there if I want to, right?" Elaine said.

"But I'm not staying up here," he told her, starting down.

"Are you going to bring me up there?" she said.

"No, you don't want to come up here," he said. "It's scary up here. The wind's blowing and it's so high an eagle tried to build a nest in my hair."

"An eagle?"

"Don't you know what an eagle is?"

"Is it like a bird?"

When he had got to the ground, he laid the paint can with the paintbrush across the lidless top on the bottom step of the porch, then turned and lifted her into his arms. Everything, now, even this, required effort: the travail of an inner battle that he was always on the point of losing.

"Well," he said. "You're getting so big."

She was a solid, dark-eyed little girl, four years old, with sweet-smelling breath and beautiful creases in her cheeks when she was excited or happy.

"Is an eagle like a bird or not?"

"An eagle," he said, turning with her, "is exactly like a bird. And you know why?" A part of him was watching himself: a man stuffed with death, charming his granddaughter.

She stared at him, smiling.

"Because it *is* a bird," he said, and held her up.

"Don't," she said, but she was still smiling.

He brought her back down. "I just wanted a kiss. You don't have a kiss for me?"

"No," she said in the tone she used when she meant to be shy with him.

"Are you in a bad mood?"

She shook her head, but the smile was gone.

"You don't even have a kiss for me?"

She sighed. "Well, Granddaddy, I can't because I'm just exhausted."

"You poor old thing," he said, resisting the temptation to suppose she had half-consciously divined something from merely looking into his eyes.

"Put me down, now," she said. "Okay?"

He did so, kissed the top of her head, the shining hair. She went off into the yard, stopping to examine some of the little white blooms of clover dotting that part of the lawn. It was her way. She enjoyed being watched, and this was a little ritual the two of them had often played out together. He would stand and observe her, trying to seem puzzled and curious, and occasionally she would glance his way, obviously wanting to make certain of his undivided attention. Sometimes they would play a game in which they both narrowly missed each other's gaze; they would repeat the pattern until she began to laugh, and then all the motions would become exaggerated.

Now she held her dress out from her sides, facing him. "Granddaddy, what do you think of me?"

Pierced to his heart, he said, "I think you're just beautiful."

She sighed. "I know."

Behind him, in the house, he could hear Susan's voice.

"Mommy's mad at Daddy again," Elaine said.

She stood there thinking, and then she did something that he recognized as a characteristic gesture, a jittery motion she wasn't quite aware of: her dark hair was long; it hung down on either side of her little face, and now and then she reached up with her left hand and tucked the strands of it behind the ear on that side of her head. The one ear showed.

In the house, now, Susan was shouting into the phone. "I don't care about that. I don't care."

"Daddy was cussing," Elaine said, standing there in the yard. "It made Mommy cry."

He waited. But she said nothing; she was again interested in the clover. And Susan's voice came from inside the house. "I don't give a goddamn what anybody has or hasn't got."

"Granddaddy," Elaine said from the yard. "You're not watching me."

"Okay, baby," he said, "I'm watching you."

"See my dress?"

"Beautiful," he said.

"Granddaddy, are you coming with me?" Again, she tucked the

strands of hair behind the one ear. He walked over to her and, when she reached for it, gave her his hand.

"Where are we going?" he asked.

"Oh, just around."

She took him in a wide circle, around the perimeter of the front yard.

"Isn't this nice," she said. A little girl the bulk of whose life would be led in the next century. The thought made him pause.

"Granddaddy, come on," she said impatiently. "Men are so slow."

"I'm sorry," he told her. "I'll try to do better."

Again, they heard her mother's voice. "You can do without a goddamn radio in your car."

"Mommy wants to see Grandmom," Elaine said.

"What about me?" he said, meaning to try teasing with her.

"Grandmom," Elaine said, with an air of insistence.

There had been times during the months of his daughter's recent troubles when he had sensed a kind of antipathy in her attitude toward him, which was almost abstract, as though in addition to other complications she had come to view him only in light of his gender. He had even spoken to his wife about this. "I suppose since I'm a representative of the same sex to which her ex-husband belongs, I'm guilty by association."

"Stop that," his wife said. "She's upset, and she wants to talk to her mother. There's nothing wrong with that. Besides, don't you think it's time you stopped interpreting everything to be about you?"

"Oh, no," he said. "I'm clearly not in this at all. I'm the ineffectual, insensitive daddy kept in the dark."

"Oh, for God's sake, William."

His wife's name was Elizabeth. For almost forty years now he had been calling her Cat, for the first three letters of her middle name, which was Catherine. Others of their friends did so as well, and she signed her cards and letters with a cartoon cat, long-whiskered and smiling, a decidedly wicked look in its eye. She had even had the name printed on the face of the checkbook: it read William and Cat Wallingham. They were the only married people in Stuart Circle Court these days. "The only traditional couple," William would say, "in this cul-de-sac." And in what his wife and daughter would indicate was his way of joking at the wrong time and with the wrong words, he would go on to point out that this was literally true. The college nearby—where he had spent the bulk of his working life as an administrator—had begun to expand in recent years, and the neighborhood seemed always to be shifting; houses were going up for sale, or being rented. The tenants came and went without much communication. There were no older couples nearby anymore, and the living arrangements were often confused or uncertain. The only other married people in the cul-de-sac were a stormy young couple who had already been through two trial separations, but who were quite helplessly in love with each other. The young woman had confided in Cat. Sometimes William saw this woman working in her small fenced yard—an attractive, slender girl wearing tight jeans and a smock, looking not much out of high school. He almost never saw the husband, whose job required some travel. But it was often the case that they were in the middle of some turbulence or other, and sometimes Cat talked about them as if they were part of the family, important in her sphere of concerns. Last year, William would come home from work (it was the last one hundred days before his retirement; he had been counting them down on a calendar fixed to the wall in the den), and he would find the young neighbor sitting in the living room with Cat, teary-eyed, embarrassed to have him there, already getting up to excuse herself and go back to her difficult life.

When his daughter's marriage began to break, William found himself thinking of this couple across the way, their tumultuous separations and reconciliations, their fractious union that was apparently so . . . well, glib, and also, in some peculiar emotional way, serviceable—or at least it seemed so from the distance of the other side of the street. He had felt a kind of amusement about them, waffling back and forth, ready to walk away from each other with the first imagined slight or defection, no matter their talk of love, their supposed passion; and for a crucial little while in the very beginning of Susan's divorce, he'd found it difficult to believe her marriage could really be ending, thinking of the impetuous couple across the street. It had felt so much the same, coming in to find Susan sitting there with the moist eyes and the handkerchief squeezed into her fist—Susan showing the same anxiousness to get out from under his gaze. Perhaps Susan still held all this against him; and he knew he had seemed badly insensitive to her trouble. In fact he had bungled everything, had taken a stance that became almost impossible to abandon, since he rather liked Susan's husband, and honestly believed that the two of them were better together than apart. He had made these feelings known, and now that she was in the process of getting the divorce, she had distanced herself from him.

"Granddaddy," Elaine said, pulling him a little, and then letting go. "I don't want to go for a walk anymore." She ran across the yard to the largest of two willow trees, under which there was an inner tube hung on a rope. Parting the drooping branches, she entered the shade there, and in a moment she'd put her head and chest through the inner tube. Then she lifted her small feet and was suspended there a moment, swinging slightly, obviously having forgotten him. He waited a little and, when he was certain she was occupied, he went into the house. It was cool in the dim hallway. Susan made a shadow at the other end, still talking on the phone. She did not look up as he approached.

"I know that," she said. "I know."

He waited.

"Well, I don't care what he says. It's been late every month, and this is not amicable anymore."

He went back out onto the porch. Elaine had lost interest in the swing, was just standing with her hands on it, staring out at the road, singing something to herself. He walked along the front of the house to where the porch ended in flagstone stairs. His wife had planted rosebushes here, and they were climbing the trellis he'd erected; they formed a thorny arch under which he stood.

Part of the daily portion of his trouble was that he had been having difficulty sleeping: the nights were long, fitful, and pervaded with a nameless dread; and when he finally drifted off, it was with the knowledge that he would be awake with the dawn, feeling nothing of his old appetite for the freshest hours of the day, finding himself sapped of energy, vaguely fearful, sick at heart, and more gloomy than the day before.

"Get busy doing something," his wife had told him. "You were never the type to sit around and let things get the best of you."

No. Yet he couldn't bring himself to say the word aloud.

"I'm going to make an appointment for you."

"I'm not going to any damn head doctors. There's nothing wrong with me that I can't take care of myself."

He could not put his finger on exactly where or how this present misery had begun to take hold; but it had moved in him with the insidious incremental growth of a malignancy. The first inkling of it had come to him almost a year ago, on the occasion of his seventy-fourth birthday when the thought occurred to him, almost casually, as though it concerned someone else, that he had now gone beyond the age at which his father's life ended. He had the thought, marked it with little more than mild interest—he may even have mentioned it to Cat—and then he experienced a sudden, fierce gust of desolation, a taste of this awful, this abyssal gloom. The recognition had come, and what followed it had felt like some leveling force inside him. But that feeling had passed, and there had been good days—wonderful days and good weeks—between then and now. He would not have believed that the thing could seep back, that it could blossom slow under his heart, changing always only for the worse. But it had; it had crept into his soul and ruined his ability to concentrate or to feel much of anything.

Tonight, it was almost insupportable.

One of the tenets of the religion he had practiced most of his adult life was that if one kept up the habits of faith, faith would be granted; he had hoped the same was true of just going through the days.

Now Susan came out and slammed the door shut behind her.

"Everything all right?" he managed.

She stirred, seemed to notice him, then looked out at the street. "I hate this time of day."

He thought she would go on to say more, and when she didn't, he searched for some response. But she had already left him, was striding over to Elaine. Perhaps she might be about to leave, and how badly he wanted not to be alone, now! When she lifted Elaine and put her in the swing, he hurried over to them, eager to be hospitable. Elaine sat in the swing with her chubby legs straight out and demanded that she be pushed higher, faster. Susan was obliging her. "Just for a little while," she said.

"Mom should be here any minute," William said.

"Where'd she go, anyway?"

"She was going to get some Chinese. Neither of us felt like doing anything in the kitchen. I had this—touching up to do."

"I don't want to get in the way of dinner," she said.

"Don't be absurd."

"Mommy, push me higher."

"I'm doing the best I can, Elaine."

"You didn't like the swings when you were Elaine's age," he said. "Do you remember?"

"I was a-f-r-a-i-d," Susan said. "I don't want her to be that way."

"Stop spelling," Elaine said.

"You just be quiet and swing."

William said, "Do you remember when I used to push you in this swing?"

She touched his arm. "Do you know how often you ask me that kind of question?"

"You don't recall it, though."

"Do you recall asking me this same question last week?"

"Well," he said. "I guess I don't. No."

Now she frowned. "I'm just teasing you."

"Well?" he said. "*Do* you remember?"

"I don't remember," she told him. "You dwell on things too much."

He said, "You sound like your mother."

"It's true. You've always been that way."

Now he was irritated. "All right."

"Men are such babies," she said. "Can't you take a little teasing?"

"If I'm going to be asked to represent a whole sex every time I do any damn thing at all, I guess not."

"Oh, and I suppose you never talk about women that way."

"I always thought such talk was disrespectful."

"Okay, I won't tease then—all right?"

They said nothing for a few moments.

"Was that Sam you were talking to on the phone?"

"At first."

"Higher," Elaine said.

"Hold on," said Susan.

He walked back to the porch and sat down on the bottom step, watching the two of them in the softening shade of the tree. The sun was nearing the line of dark horizon to the west, and through the haze it looked as though its flames were dying out. It was enormous, bigger than it ever seemed in midday. His daughter, still standing under the filamentous shade of the willow tree, turned to look at him, apparently having just noticed that he had walked away from her. He put both hands on his knees, trying to appear satisfied and comfortable. But his heart was sinking.

She walked over to stand before him. "Did you and Mom have a fight or something?" she asked.

"Not that I know of."

"Ha."

"We never fight anymore."

"Maybe you should."

"I can't think why." He smiled at her.

"You bicker all the time instead of fighting."

He said, "What's the difference, I wonder?"

A moment later, he said, "Are the two of you talking about me?"

"I never said that."

"What's there to talk about?" he said.

"Dad."

"We've been married almost forty years," he said. "What's there to talk about?"

"Are you saying you're bored?"

"Jesus," he said. "Are *we* going to have a fight?"

"I'm just asking."

"Is your mother bored?" he said.

"Oh, for God's sake. You don't think she'd tell me a thing like that, do you?"

"I was just asking."

"To tell you the truth, she doesn't talk about you at all."

"Well," he said, "I wouldn't. You know, there's not much to say."

"Do you still love each other?" his daughter asked suddenly. "Sam and I lasted five years and I can't imagine why. It's kind of hard to believe in married love, you know."

"Can't judge the rest of the world by what happens to you," he said. "Married love just takes a little more work, maybe."

"Why do I feel like you're talking about me and not Sam?"

"I'm not," he said. "I didn't have anybody specific in mind."

As they watched, the young woman from across the street drove up. She got out of the car and made her way over to them, having obviously come from her job at the college: she wore a bright flower-print dress and high heels. She was carrying a package.

"Cat's not here?" she said, pausing. She had addressed Susan.

"She'll be back soon," William said.

The young woman hesitated, then came forward. "Could you give her this for me? It's a scarf and earrings."

"Why don't you give it to her?"

"No, I've really—I've got to go."

Susan took the package from her.

"There's a—I put a card with it."

"Very nice," Susan said. "It'll make her very happy."

"We're moving," the young woman said. "He got a job back home. I get to go home."

"I'm sure she'll want to see you before you go."

"Oh, of course. We won't be leaving until December."

"Well, she'll be very happy."

"Thank you," William said, as the young woman went back along the walk. They watched her cross to her house and go in, and then Susan said, "You know the trouble with us?"

"What," he said.

"We'd never inspire that kind of gratitude in anyone."

"I'm too old to start trying," he said.

She shrugged. "Anyway, you haven't answered my question."

"Which question is that?"

"Whether or not you and Mom are still in love."

He looked at her. "It's an aggressive, impolite, prying question, and the answer to it is none of your business."

"Well, I guess you've answered it."

"Goodness gracious," he said with what he hoped was a sardonic half smile. "I don't think so."

Somewhere beyond the roof of the porch, birds were calling and answering one another, and over the hill someone's lawn mower sent up its incessant drone of combustion. The air smelled of grass, and of the paint he'd been using. A jet rumbled across the rim of the sky, and for a time everything else was mute. As the roar passed, his granddaughter's voice came faintly to him from the yard, talking in admonitory tones to the air.

"Imaginary friends," Susan said with a rueful little smirk.

They were quiet. William noticed that the bottom edge of the sun had dipped below the burnished haze at the horizon.

"I thought you said she'd be here any minute."

"She just went to get some carry-out," William said. "But you know how she can be."

"We really don't talk about you, Dad."

"Okay," he said.

"We talk about my divorce and about men who don't pay their child support and we talk about being sort of sick of living alone all the damn time—you know?" Now she seemed about to cry. It came to him that he was in no state of mind for listening to these troubles, and he was ashamed of himself for the thought.

He said, "Well, she'll be home soon."

His daughter turned from him slightly. "You know the thing about Mom?"

"What," he said, aware that he had faltered.

"She knows how to blot out negative thoughts."

"Yes," he said.

"She thinks about other people more than she thinks about herself."

He did not believe this required a response.

"You and I," his daughter said. "We're selfish types."

He nodded, keeping his eyes averted.

"We're greedy."

In the yard, Elaine sang brightly about dreams—a song she had learned from one of her cartoon movies, as she called them.

"I wouldn't be surprised if Mom ran off and left us," Susan said. "I mean I wouldn't blame her."

"Well," William said.

They waited a while longer, and now Elaine wandered over to sit on her mother's lap. "Mommy, I'm thirsty."

It was getting toward dusk.

"What if she did leave us?" Susan said.

He turned to her.

"I wonder what we'd do."

"I guess we'd deserve it," he said.

"No, really," she said. "Think about it. Think about the way we depend on her."

"I've never said I could take a step without her," said William.

"Well, there you are."

"She doesn't mind your confiding in her, Susan. She doesn't mind anyone's confidence. Christ, that girl across the street—" He halted.

"Well," she said, holding up the package. "She gets the pretty scarf and earrings for her efforts."

"That's true," he said. For an instant, he thought he could feel the weight of what he and this young woman, his only child, had separately revealed to Cat; it was almost palpable in the air between them.

The light was fading fast.

"Granddad." Elaine had reached up and taken hold of his chin.

"What?"

"I said I want to go inside."

Susan said, "We heard you, Elaine."

"Well, God," said Elaine. "Why didn't he answer me."

"Be quiet."

"We can go in, honey," William said.

"I'm getting worried," said Susan.

He stood. "Let's go inside. She'll pull in any minute with fifty dollars' worth of food." But he was beginning to be a little concerned, too.

Inside, Susan turned on a lamp in the living room, and the windows, which had shown the gray light of dusk, were abruptly dark, as if she had called the night into being with an emphatic gesture. They sat on the couch and watched Elaine play with one of the many dolls Cat kept for her here.

"You don't suppose she had car trouble," Susan said.

"Wouldn't she call?"

"Maybe she can't get to a phone."

"She was just going to China Garden."

"Did she say anything else? Is there anything else she needed?"

He considered a moment. "I can't recall anything."

In fact, her departure had been a result of his hauling out the ladder and paint cans. He had thought to follow her advice and get himself busy, moving in the fog of his strange apathy, and when he had climbed up the ladder, she came out on the porch.

"Good God, Bill."

"I'm all right," he said.

"What in the world."

"I'm just putting myself to work."

"I don't feel like cooking," she said, almost angrily.

"No," he said. "Right."

She stared at him.

"It's a few cracks. This won't take long."

"I'm getting very tired, William."

"This won't take long."

"Don't fall."

He said, "No."

"If I go out to get us something to eat, will you eat?"

"I'll eat something."

"Is this going to be to enjoy or merely to survive?"

"Cat."

"I'll go to China Garden. Is that all right?"

"You sure you feel like Chinese?"

"Just do me a favor and don't fall," she said.

And he had watched, from his shaky height, as she drove away.

Now, he turned to his daughter, who sat leaning forward on the sofa, as though she were about to rise. "Is that the car?" They moved to the front door and looked out. The driveway was dark.

"Maybe we should call the police and see if there's been any accidents," Susan said.

"It's just a little over an hour," said William. "Maybe it's taking longer to prepare the food."

She stopped. "Let's go there."

"Susan."

"No, really. It's only ten minutes away. Let's go there and we'll see her there and we can relax."

"Let's just wait a few more minutes."

Clearly reluctant, she moved past him and into the living room, where Elaine sat staring at her own reflection in the dark television screen.

"It's time to put the dolls away," Susan said to her.

"I'm still playing with them."

"Is there anything," William began. "Do you want to talk?"

"I just came to visit. There wasn't anything."

"Well," William said. "You had all that difficulty on the phone."

"Oh, please," she said.

He was quiet.

"Why don't you put the ladder away," she said. "And the paint? If she pulls up and sees it all still there it might scare her."

"Why would it scare her?"

"Oh, come on, Daddy. You haven't been much like yourself the last few weeks, right?"

He went out onto the porch. It was full dark now, and the crickets and nightbugs had started their racket. Perhaps Cat had found it necessary to confide in her daughter about him; if that was so his place in the house was lonely indeed. He was ashamed; his mind hurt.

The moon was half-shrouded in a fold of cumulus, and beyond the open place in the cloud a single star sparkled. He took the ladder down, set it along the base of the house, then closed the paint can and put the brush in its jar of turpentine. Twice he saw Susan standing at the door, looking out for her mother. And when Cat drove in, Susan rushed out to her, letting the screen door slam. The car lights beamed onto the corners of the house, and he felt the burst of energy from Susan's relief, the flurry and confusion of his wife's return. Cat stood out of the car and held up two packages. He stood there watching her from the dim end of the yard. She came up the walk.

"What're you doing?" she said.

How he admired her! "Putting things away," he said. He had meant it to sound cheerful.

"I hope you're hungry."

He was not hungry. He watched them go up the steps of the porch and into the house, Susan leading the way, talking about the absurd county caseworkers and their failures, their casual attitude about broken laws, court orders left unheeded. Then he made his way around to the garage and put the paint can and the glass jar on the shelf there. The night was cool and fragrant. From inside he heard Elaine shout a word, and his wife's high-pitched laughter.

Now they were calling him from the porch. They were all three standing in the light there.

"I'm here," he said. "I was just putting the paint in the garage."

"You'd better be hungry, old man," Cat said, from the top step, in the old way of commanding him, and out of the long habit of her affection. "I've got a lot of good food here."

"A feast," Susan said.

"Tell me you're hungry," said Cat.

"I'm famished," he said, taking the step toward them. Trying again, gathering himself.

Richard Bausch lives in rural Virginia with his wife, Karen, and their five children. His most recent books include *The Fireman's Wife and Other Stories,* and the novels *Violence* and *Rebel Powers.* A new collection, *Rare and Endangered Species,* will appear in spring 1994. His stories have appeared in *The Atlantic Monthly , Esquire, Harper's, The New Yorker, Redbook, The Southern Review,* and other magazines, and he has been  widely anthologized, including *The Granta Book of the American Short Story, Best American Short Stories, New Stories from the South,* and

O. Henry Prize Stories. He is currently on a Lila Wallace–Reader's Digest Writer's Award grant, which has allowed him to devote full time to his writing.

PHOTO CREDIT: KAREN MILLER BAUSCH

"E*vening" came about, at least partially, because I wanted to deliver in print a little unconscious gesture my second youngest daughter Maggie makes with her lovely long hair. It's a way she has of tucking it behind her left ear, and when I see it, I who am old enough to know how it is to be stuffed with death, feel something crack way down. It is in fact what is always meant by Joy. And if I may be forgiven for the pompous sound of all this, I'll go on to say that it is the true subject of most good stories. In any case, this story began with Maggie's little motion, and the big fissures it opens inside me when she does it, the feeling that I could very easily laugh and cry at the same time. If I were to write a poem about it, if I were good enough to write a poem about it, I probably would have stopped there. But I had to make a story, and so I took the gesture and the sense of joyous heartbreak it gives and exaggerated the circumstances. I made the pool into which that little gesture would drop much darker, and much less stable. And I remember that, last winter, several months after I'd written the story, I had occasion to read it back to myself, and was appalled at the despair in it—maybe even a little frightened for myself, seeing the huge darkness at the heart of the thing. What in the world could I have been riding over during the weeks I was writing it? It made me think of Lowell's great line in "Skunk Hour"—"I myself am hell." I like to think that all my stories, long or short, tend toward the light, toward reconciliation and even, sometimes, redemption. I don't know about this one. This one glares at me from the dark, and, as Lowell so powerfully said in the same poem, "will not scare."*

Jill McCorkle

MAN WATCHER

(from *The Crescent Review*)

What's my sign? *Slippery when wet.* Do I want to see your etchings? *No.* Have you seen me somewhere before? *Maybe, since I've been somewhere before.* What's my line? Well, I've got quite a few, all depends on what I'm trying (or not trying) to catch. It's not so hard to pick up a man; matter of fact it's one of the easiest things I've ever done. A good man? Well, that's something entirely different. Believe you me, I know.

My stepsister Lorraine is always saying *Like, I don't know where you're coming from.* If I say I've got a migraine headache, she says, "*Like, I don't know where you're coming from.* I have the kind of migraine that *blinds* you. The doctor says I might have the very worst kind of migraine known to man. My migraines are so horrendous I've been invited to go to Duke University for them to study me." You get the picture. *Like, I don't know.*

Lorraine knows a lot about everything and she has experienced the world in a way nobody can come close to touching. Still, when it comes to sizing up men, I've got her beat. I sit back and size them up while she jumps in and winds up making a mess of her life. When she opens her mouth in that long horsey way of hers, I just say, *Like, I don't know where You're coming from.*

I've thought of publishing a book about it all, all the different types of the species. You know it would sort of be like Audubon's bird book. I'd call it *Male* Homo Sapiens: *What You Need to Know to Identify Different Breeds*. Natural habitats, diet, mating rituals. I'd show everything from chic condos to jail cells; from raw bloody beef to couscous and sprouts; from a missionary position (showers following) to an oily tarp spread out behind a Dempsey dumpster. I'd break it all down so even the inexperienced could gain something. Of course there are a few questions that I haven't quite worked out, yet, like why is it considered *tough* for a man (usually a big city macho type) to grab himself and utter nasty things (such as an invitation to be fellated) to another man? Is there something hidden there like in those seek-and-find pictures? And why don't men have partitions between urinals? Is there a history of liking to watch or something? Does it all go back to the Greeks and Romans where a little homosexual activity was perfectly in order, like a good solid burp at the end of a meal? I'm still working on a lot of topics, as you can see, but quite a bit of my research is already mapped out.

You know, you got your real *fun* guys that you love to date but you wouldn't want to marry—they'd be addicted to something and out of work about the time you hatch the first kid. Then you got the kind who might do all right in a job and lead a relatively clean life, but they bore you to tears. (I'm talking the kind that gets into little closet organizers and everything zipped up in plastic.) And you've got the kind you ought to leave alone—period. (I'm talking worthless pigs and middle-aged crazed sleezos. That's where Lorraine screwed up, on both accounts, and I've told her so on many occasions. Her husband, Tim, likes to drink beer and scrunch the cans on the side of his head. He likes to chew tobacco while drinking beer and talk about what him and the boys *done and seen* while *hunting up some good fat quail and some Bambi*. He wears army fatigues and drinks some more beer and talks about needing to get some sex (actually, he uses all the slang terms for a woman's anatomy). He drinks still more beer and talks about needing to take a leak.

"Well just be sure you put it back," I said not long ago, and Lorraine and her mother (my evil stepmother) gave me a long dirty look. My name is Lucinda, after my real mother's mother

(I go by Luci), but every now and then I refer to myself as Cinda and bare my size six-and-a-half foot just so they have to take a good look at themselves: mean ugly stepmother and self-centered stepsister, both with big snowshoe-type feet.

"Take a leak. Put it back. That's a good one now," Tim said and shuffled through his magazines until he found one of his choosing for a little bathroom time, *Soldiers of Fortune* or *American Killer,* something like that. Lorraine and Mama-Too—as she *used* to beg me to call her when Daddy was still alive—were still staring. They have accused me of turning my back on my family and our natural ways because I lived in Washington, D.C., for a year, where I worked as a secretary in some very dull and very official office where there were a lot of very dull and very official men. I was there when there were rumors that this senator who wanted to be president (there are *loads* of men who fit into this particular *Homo sapiens* profile) had a mistress. This fellow always wins the election with the help of people like my stepbrother-in-law who believe that there should be a gun in every home and school cafeterias eternally stocked with that delicious vegetable, the Catsup. What I still don't understand is who in the hell would go with that type? I'm an expert on these things and oftentimes am led by curiosity, but I have my standards. I mean if you were the *wife* at least you'd live in a nice house in Georgetown or Alexandria, the fella wouldn't utter a peep if you dropped a few thou. But just to *go* with him—good God. Lorraine's friend, Ruth Sawyer, has dated a man for fifteen years with nothing to show for it. Stupid, I say. I left D.C. (which was fine with me) when Daddy got so sick. I was allergic to those cherry trees the whole country raves about in the spring. Still though, if I ever even refer to the Smithsonian, Lorraine and Mama-Too roll their eyes and smirk at each other.

"You'd be lucky to get a man like Tim," my stepmother had said.

"Like I don't know," I told her. "There are very few men in his category."

"That's right." Lorraine nodded her head as she flipped through her husband's pile of arsenal magazines to find one of her beauty ones. Tim's breed happen to travel in camouflage clothes, but they like their women to sport loud and gaudy feathers and makeup. But of course she had enough sense to know that I was not being serious, so she turned quickly, eyes narrowing. "What do you mean, his category?"

"Not many men who read about the defense of the great white race while taking a leak," I said.

"Har de har har," Lorraine said. She has not changed a bit since they came into our lives not long after my mother died of liver disease. Mama-Too worked in the office of the funeral parlor, which was convenient. I called her a "widower watcher" then, and I still do. My daddy was not such a great man, but even he was too good for Mama-Too.

Before Lorraine met Tim, she dated the man who I file in the middle-aged crazed sleezo slot. You know the type, someone who is into *hair* (especially chest) any way he can get it: rugs, minoxidil, transplants. That poor grotesquerie would've had some grafted on his chest if he could've afforded the procedure. He'd have loved enough hair on his head to perm and chest hair long enough to preen. You know the type of man I mean, the type that hangs out in the Holiday Inn lounge like a vulture sucking on some old alcoholic drink, his old wrinkled eyes getting red and slitty as he watches young meat file through the doorway. He likes chains and medallions and doesn't believe in shirt buttons.

"You're some kind of bad off, aren't you, Lorraine?" I asked one night after her *man* left, his body clad in enough polyester to start a fire that would rival that of a rubber-tire company. "I bet he couldn't get it up with a crane." My daddy was dying of lung cancer even as I was speaking, though we hadn't gotten him diagnosed yet, and he let out with a laugh that set off a series of coughs that could have brought the house down.

"Don't you have any respect?" Mama-Too asked and I turned

on her. I said, "Look, I am over thirty years old and my stepsister there is pushing forty. It isn't like he can send me to my room and keep me from going to the prom. Besides," I added and pointed to him, "he wasn't respecting me when he and Mama were out cutting up all over town, pickling their livers and getting emphysema while I was babysitting every night of the week to pay for my own week at Girl Scout camp, which I ended up hating with a passion anyway because it was run just like a military unit."

What I didn't tell her, though, (what I've never told anyone) is that going to Girl Scout camp gave me my first taste of self-sufficiency. It had *nothing* to do with the actual camp, but was in my getting ready for it. I found stability in my little toiletries case: my own little personal bottles of shampoo and lotion. *My* toothbrush and *my* toothpaste. These smallest personal items represent independence, a sensation you need forever. Otherwise, you're sunk. I liked having everything in miniature, rationed and hidden in my bag. For that week (the only way I made it through their bells and schedules) I was able to pull myself inward, to turn and flip until I was as compact as one of those little plastic rain bonnets. It was the key to survival, and it had nothing to do with the woods (though I'll admit the birds were nice) or building a fire (I had a lighter). It had nothing to do with what leaves you could eat (I had enough Slim Jims along to eat three a day). It was my spirit that I had found. Of course I lost it the very next week once I was back home and doing as I pleased when I pleased, but I couldn't forget the freedom, the power my little sack of *essentials* had brought me.

"You could have benefited from the military," Mama-Too said after I'd run down my career in the Girl Scouts. She was ready to spout on her late great husband Hoover Mills and his shining military career. I told her his name sounded like an underwear or vacuum cleaner company.

"I have said it before," I told her, "and I'll say it again. I would never have a man of the church, and I would never have a man of the military. I don't want anybody telling me what to do or inspecting me." I emphasized this and looked at Mama-Too.

"Who's to say they'd have *you?*" Lorraine said.

"I could have that old piece of crap who just left here if I wanted him," I told her and my daddy erupted in another phlegm fair, coughing and spewing and laughing.

"We are in love," Lorraine informed me, and to this day I remind her of saying that. I remind her when Tim is standing close by so I can watch her writhe in anger. I remind her whenever we ride by the Holiday Inn. I'll say, "Here to my left is the Holiday Inn, natural habitat of Lorraine's former lover, the middle-aged crazed sleezo of the Cootie phylum, complete with synthetic nest and transplanted feathers." Now whenever I say anything about Tim, the Soldier of *Un*fortune, she responds that same way: "I love him." I miss not having my daddy there to choke out some good belly laughs. Those attacks always bought me enough time for my comeback.

"It's easy to fall in love," I always say, "easy as rolling off a log, or if I were Mama-Too's boyfriend (a new one, just that fast!), easy as rolling off a hog."

"I know your soul is in the devil's hand," Lorraine says. "You wouldn't know love if it bit you."

"Oh, yes I would and oh, yes it has," I say. "It's easy to fall in love. What's hard is *living* with it. And if you can't live with it, you're better off without it." I wanted to add that Mama-Too had done a fine job killing off love but I let it ride.

I've never gotten into all that love/hate rigamarole like some women do. If I want lots of drama, I'll turn on my TV set. Any time of day you can turn on the tube and hear women talking about things they need to keep to themselves. I hear it when I go to the spa. There we'll be, bitching about cellulite and sweating it out in a sauna, and somebody will start. She'll talk about how her eye has been wandering of late, how her husband bores her, how he just doesn't turn her on, nothing, zippo. "What do you do for a wandering eye?"

"See the ophthalmologist?" I ask. "Go down to the livery stable and get yourself some blinders?"

"Oh, be serious, Luci," they say. "You *do* like men, don't you?"

It's amazing how whenever a woman is asked this question, other women get real uncomfortable while waiting for the answer. They check to make sure that no private parts are exposed for the wandering eye of a lesbian, which I am not. Still, I let them sweat it.

"I like men the same way I like people," I say. "Some I do and some I don't."

"You know what we mean," they say, and they all lean forward, more skin than swimsuits showing in this hot cedar box.

It's like a giggle fest in that sauna anytime you go. Something about the heat makes everybody start talking sex and fantasy. I tell them that they need some hobbies—get a needlepoint kit, bake a loaf of bread. The truth of it all is that I'm ahead of my time. I have already figured out what I need to live a happy healthy life and I'm no longer out there on the prowl. If my life takes a swing and I meet Mr. Right and settle into a life of prosperity then so be it and if I don't then so be it. I'm in lover's purgatory. I've seen hell and I'm content to sit here in all my glorious neutrality.

One woman who was all spread out in a tight chartreuse suit said that she had a stranger fantasy. She said (in front of seven of us) that she thought about meeting a man in a dark alley and just going at it, not a word spoken. Well, after she told that, not a word was spoken for several minutes, and then I got to feeling kind of mad about it all and I said that I just didn't think she ought to go touching a penis without knowing where it had been. "For health reasons," I added but by then there were six near naked women mopping up the floor with laughter and that seventh woman (Ms. Stranger-in-Chartreuse) shaking her head back and forth like *I* was stupid.

I was desperately seeking once upon a time. I was unhappily married to a man who wanted me to be somebody I wasn't and was forever making suggestions, like that I get my ears pinned, that I gain some weight, that I frost my hair, learn to speak Spanish, get a job that paid better, pluck off all my eyebrows, let the hair on my legs grow, and take up the piano so that I could play in the background while he read the paper. Now where was my little sack of security then? I was buying the jumbo sizes of Suave shampoo so I could afford the frostings and the Spanish tapes and the row machine. My essentials were too big to hide from the world. I once knew a girl who went to lunch from her secretarial job and never came back. I knew another girl who woke up on her wedding day with bad vibes and just hopped a jet and left her parents with a big church-wedding mess. I admired them both tremendously. I once told Lorraine she should take lessons from such a woman, and she and Mama-Too did their usual eye rolling. It wouldn't surprise me if one day their eyeballs just rolled on out like I've heard those of a Pekingese will do if you slap it hard on the back of the head.

Before I was married, I was a rock singer. I named my band The Psychedelic Psyches, you know, after the chick Cupid liked. I saw us as soulful musicians, acting out some of our better songs with interpretive dance numbers. My parents called us The Psychedelic Psychos, which I did not appreciate. There were four of us in the band: I sang and played the drums; Lynn West, a tall thin brooding-poet type, played the uke; Grace Williams, who was known for her peppy personality, could rip an accordion to shreds; my friend Margaret played the xylophone and had a collection of cow bells she could do wonderful things with. We were just getting hot on a local level when some jealous nothing type of a girl (someone like Lorraine) started calling us The Psychedelic Sapphos and spreading rumors about what we did in my GM Pacer, which we called "the band wagon."

"Oh ignore it," I told them but Lynn and Grace quit. They said they just couldn't have a connection like that, not when Lynn was preengaged to a boy at Vanderbilt and Grace was supposed to inherit her family's pickle business in Mt. Olive, North Carolina. "Good Lord," I said and flipped my hair. It was as long as Cher's and I was just as skinny if not more so. "It's a new generation." But their response told me that men and pickles came first. Drugs came first for Margaret and we tried singing a few times just the two of us, but she'd get really strung out and just go wild with a cowbell. Margaret referred to our singing engagements as *gigs*. All she talked about was gigs, gigs, gigs. She'd call me on the phone in the middle of the night to ask about a gig. Nobody wanted us and I knew that. The only real *gig* we'd ever had anyway was doing little spontaneous standups in a coffee shop downtown. Nobody wanted to hear "Blowing in the Wind" sung to a cowbell from India. Margaret liked to pass her time by doing LSD, and I passed mine by searching for the perfect male, dissecting specimen after specimen, only to find his weaknesses and toss him aside. I thought of myself as the female version of Dion's "The Wanderer." Or maybe I was "The Traveling Woman." It was wanderlust and lustwander; it got even worse after my mother died and my dad took up with Mama-Too.

I was taking pictures of being naked in a bed long before John and Yoko, *imagine,* ha ha. I met my husband at a Hallowe'en party and married him the next week. He looked much better when his face was painted up like a Martian, and I guess I kept convincing myself that there would come a night when he would look that way again. My husband believed in unemployment and a working wife and all those other things I've mentioned. Lorraine said that I should've made my marriage work, should have gone into therapy instead of running off to D.C. I've told Lorraine that I could've kept that husband, could've made a go of that lifestyle. All I had to do was become a drug addict and hallucinate that everything was hunky-dory. I probably would've wound up like my friend Margaret, getting so high you'd have to scrape her off the ceiling. Finally she got scraped off a sidewalk. I was there when it happened. She said she was so high the only way down was to jump and I was too busy talking to this matty-haired man to notice she meant business. He was wearing some of those suede German sandals that make people's feet look so wide; you know the kind, they're real expensive but they make you look like you don't have a pot to pee in and couldn't care less about your appearance. I had just asked him what made him buy those shoes, what image was he trying to fit (even then I was researching), when all of a sudden there were screams and people running to the window, the fire escape. There were sirens, a woman thinking she can fly like Peter Pan. You've heard it before. That man with the matted hair expected me to go home with him afterward. Not long after that happened I met my future husband and decided to get married. I was convinced that I had snapped to, but my snapping to was like a dream inside of a dream, a hallway of doors where with every slam I woke up all over again. I had barely begun to snap to.

That night while staring down to where Margaret was under a sheet with a little cowbell clutched in her hand, the matty-haired fellow breathing down my neck, I knew there was something powerful I needed to commit to memory but all I was coming up with was things like *lay off the stuff, don't play on fire escapes, don't let yourself become so lonely.* But like a lot of people (like Lorraine) I translated that last one as needing somebody, which leads me back to what I've already told, a marriage made in hell and me now in lover's limbo. What I know now when I think of Margaret there, is that if you can't make it in life all by yourself (and by that I mean without benefit of people and substances and gigs of whatever sort you might crave), then you simply can't make it. That's the whole ball of wax. If it happens that you meet a person who walks right in and doesn't change a hair on your head, then your pie is *à la mode.* I've found in my research that this type of male is most often the kind you can't squeeze into a category. His lines are blurred and intertwined. He's a little bit of a lot of things, and a lot of what counts. His feathers are like none you've ever seen.

I'll hold out till I drop dead if I have to and all the while I'm holding out I'll pursue my projects, my crafts, my academic studies on why some women go the route they do. Why does someone like Lorraine, who could educate herself and do better,

settle, and why can't Mama-Too, who has already killed off two
men (that I know of), give it up and take up cross-stitch? To
think that a man can fill up whatever space you have is just stupid
if you ask me. He can't do it any better than a box of Twinkies or
a gallon of liquor, and to ask it of him is unfair.

So what's my line? What's my response? These days I'm not
really playing. These days I'm constructing a little diorama of my
apartment kitchen and in it I have a little clay figure who looks just
like me and is working on a diorama of her apartment kitchen. I
have always loved the concept of infinity; it makes me feel good.
There is something about the large and small of the world, the
connections and movement between the two that keeps me in
balance. And if ever I need to feel even better about my life, I take
The Sound of Music test, which assures me that my emotions are
in working order. I have never once heard the mother superior
sing "Climb Every Mountain" or watched the Von Trapps flee-
ing through the mountains at the end without getting a lump in
my throat. It is a testament to life, to survival. I could watch that
movie again and again. When we all rented it not too long ago,
Lorraine said that the nuns depressed her. I assured her that the
feeling would be mutual if the nuns ever met her.

And speaking of religious orders, right now I'm having a nice
big argument with Mama-Too over what the rules for priesthood
ought to be. I say (just to see what *she* will say) that celibacy
means *no* sexual interaction at all, which includes people of the
same sex as well as with yourself and by yourself. "Well, how do
you propose that?" she asked. "You gonna wire them up so if
they touch themselves it'll set off bells?"

"No," I tell her. "A solemn vow to God is good enough for me."

"What do you know of God?" she asks and I'm about to tell
her when her date walks in with a fifth of bourbon and a big slab
of raw red beef.

"Why, Marty," I say to this old saggy cowboy. "I never noticed how hairy you are." He grins great big and hunkers down at the kitchen table. It's sad how easily some birds are bagged. He has molted down to a patchy skinned bone. Mama-Too will have him henpecked in no time.

I guess in a way I'm waiting for the rarest breed of all, my sights set so high I have to squint to keep the sky in focus. I concentrate on migration habits. I keep in mind that owls fly silently at night. Some people (like Lorraine) might say I'm on a snipe hunt. But, call me an optimist. I'm sitting here in a pile of ashes, waiting for the phoenix to take shape and rise.

———

Jill McCorkle, a native of Lumberton, North Carolina, is the author of four novels and most recently *Crash Diet,* a short-story collection. Her fiction has appeared in *The Atlantic Monthly, The Southern Review, Cosmopolitan, The Gettysburg Review,* and elsewhere. She has taught creative writing at the University of North Carolina at Chapel Hill, Tufts University, and is currently teaching at Harvard University.

PHOTO CREDIT: DAVID N. SHAPIRO

"*M*an Watcher" *is one of those rare stories that materialized without any plan or warning. I was driving home from work one day and while at a stoplight the story began: What's my sign? Slippery when wet. I had no idea where the piece would go, only that I had stumbled upon a voice I wanted to follow. This is a woman who is tired of looking for a relationship, and is frustrated by the women she knows who feel they have to have somebody. She is totally independent and most importantly, satisfied with herself; she is opinionated and liberated and left me feeling exhilarated. I had trouble driving. I wrote all the way home,* *nearly illegible scribbles on a pad in the passenger seat. I pulled over into the parking lot of Food Lion so that I could write faster. By the time I got to the computer, she had said everything she needed to say and worked herself full circle to a natural ending. It's not my standard story writing method, but when it happens, I don't ask questions.*

David Huddle

TROUBLE AT THE
HOME OFFICE

(from *The Southern Review*)

Let me be straightforward. I was seeing somebody, and
Susan found out. With the afternoon sunlight streaming
through our living room windows, she and I had a quiet but
definitely unpleasant chat.

Peter, she said with her lips tightening. I know these things
happen. But I'm not just going to stand by. You make your
choice. Either you're in or you're out.

We've got two kids. We agreed that I would cease seeing somebody. As of immediately. The hard line, though not unreasonable.
I chose in.

But somebody had some things to say—or to shout about in
my office. Why wasn't she asked what she wanted and who the
hell ordained my wife as the one to say when she and I were finished? Look at *her,* was she dirt, was she compost for the garden
of my marriage? Look her in the eyes, damn it, wasn't I man
enough at least to do that?

This was Julie Munroe, from Sports Spot, where I worked. I
was public relations and advertising. Julie was our senior fitness
instructor. Compact, with long dark hair and delicate features,
Julie had a physique that made our members—male and female—
blink the first time they saw her in her leotard. Julie disconcerted

people; she was small and had this girlish face, but she was the fittest person I ever met. And she took no shit.

My situation was impossible. I had a talk with the boss.

Ben Fulton and I went way back to when I came off the tour and he was looking for a tennis instructor who could attract new members to Sports Spot. In 1975 I beat Nastase in the quarter-finals at Bretton Woods—doodly-squat on the tour, but for a few years around here that credential helped make me the pro every tennis-playing housewife wanted lessons from. They signed their kids up, too.

Teaching was easy for me, easier than playing had been, and they used to say I had a natural gift and a perfect body for the game. So in those early days I had helped make Sports Spot successful, and in the last few years Sports Spot had made Ben Fulton a wealthy man.

Do you want me to fire her? he asked.

I told him no, she'd have us in court and in the papers, not to mention beating the crap out of both of us.

She could do it. He shrugged and grinned. Then he said, Tell me about her, Peter.

I can't do that, Ben, I said. But I did go ahead and share a thought or two with him about Julie, because over the years Ben has been generous with me. He gave me my own office, he looked the other way when my clients needed individual conferences, and when I burned out on teaching tennis, he let me move up to management.

She's even better than she looks like she would be, Ben, I said. She has the power, I whispered.

He nodded and gazed out his window. We were quiet for a while.

So what Ben and I worked out was that with a fax machine and a computer, there was no reason why most of the time I couldn't work at home. No reason to come into Sports Spot if my being there was going to cause a disruption.

What we said officially was that I was being given a leave of absence. This had the appearance of punishment. It calmed Julie and the other female fitness instructors who sympathized with her. A certain calming effect, Ben said on the phone and chuckled. Not too much action around here without you, Peter.

That's how we like it, isn't it, Ben? I said. I wasn't kidding. There comes a time when you want to give up all the bullshit that goes with fooling around, but I kept that to myself. Quiet around here, too, I told him, and my work is good, don't you think, Ben?

It's great, Peter, Ben said. At the edge of his voice I could hear what he wasn't saying. He had little respect for my ideas; he revised all my press releases before they went out. He was polite about it, but basically I was just the guy who produced his first drafts.

Nevertheless, there I was, set up at home on the third floor. A few years ago Susan and I had had half of the attic finished, thinking we might want to rent a room to a college student. Then Susan's grandfather died, leaving her enough money to keep us from really needing rental income. When I told her I was going to start working at home, Susan was delighted that we'd finally be able to put that room to use.

It had shelves and a skylight. Instead of a new floor, we had just put down some old carpet from our bedroom. I had to buy a desk and some chairs, but Ben insisted on Sports Spot paying for my computer and fax machine.

Maybe I wasn't an advertising genius, but brilliance wasn't what Sports Spot needed, just somebody to keep the public informed. I understood how to do that, maybe even better than Ben did.

I've never had what coaches call "a good work ethic," but I put in my hours; I put forth some effort. If I didn't give the job my all, at least I gave it my most.

And things around home were better than they had been for a while. With Julie off my mind, I was able to focus my attention on Susan. As her anger subsided, I began remembering what an attractive person I married. She's blond, tall, very thin and willowy. Suddenly I noticed what subtle taste in clothes she had, what a pleasure she was to look at. You might say that I revitalized my interest in Susan.

Susan got a promotion down at the bank, so I started taking up the slack at home. I picked up the kids at school, I washed the breakfast dishes, and most evenings I was the one who fixed dinner. I ran more errands than I used to, but that was all right because my hours were flexible.

Things are lots better, aren't they? I asked Susan one evening when we were lingering at the table after one of my better dinners. The kids were in the basement watching TV.

They're not so bad, she said, grinning off toward the dining room window in a way that I knew meant she was thinking about it. Then she got up and walked around the table, walked around behind me and ran her fingers along my shoulders. Not really so bad, she said.

I didn't mention it, but a big part of what I liked about those changes was having so many hours to myself during the day. I'd never had that experience. Hour after hour, the quiet just stretched out.

Up there in the office, I noticed how the square of sunlight from my skylight moved gradually over the floor toward me. Sometimes I just sat there, doing nothing, thinking about nothing, for I don't know how long.

Then when I did start pecking at the keyboard again, the writing went smoothly and quickly. I seemed to have composed my phrases without really having thought about them. I didn't have to force my work out the way I used to.

I began to appreciate my house. That sounds funny, I know, but you know the way you get to like a particular racquet or a pair of shoes or even a court that you play well on a number of times. It was like that, except more personal. The house was like my personal friend, good company for me, helpful.

I'd stand up from the desk, walk around, come downstairs and look out this window and that, go to the refrigerator and have some juice, pick up a magazine, listen to a record.

It felt good to spend those hours home alone. It had also begun to feel safe. Until now I hadn't been able to rid myself of an old fear of being alone in the house. Of course as an adult, I'm a big enough guy, and I've kept myself in shape. But when your job has you seeing people all the time, you never really know what's going to come at you. At Sports Spot most of the time everything had been pleasant, but there were exceptions.

Like Julie shouting at me in my office. At home, when I remembered that morning, I had to shake my head and wonder how I got through it.

I was glad to be in my own house, with the computer humming quietly and a block of sunlight just approaching my foot. That morning I was caught up on all my deadlines, the phone wasn't ringing, there was nothing I really had to do until three when the kids got out of school. I was getting an early jump on our fall membership campaign.

I thought this must be how a Tibetan monk felt when he climbed up onto some little shelf on the side of a mountain to spend the rest of his life in the lotus position, gazing down over the valley and contemplating the universe.

A noise downstairs reminded me of the one negative aspect about this working arrangement. From up on the third floor, I couldn't really hear the front or the back doorbell. If anybody came to see me on urgent business, I'd miss out on it because I wouldn't know they were down there.

But sometimes there were little noises that would catch my ear, and I'd go down to see about them. They'd be nothing but some creaking or shifting of the house. Sometimes I found that the UPS man had left a package on the back porch. But almost always it was nothing. So I tried to keep myself from being distracted and running downstairs every time I heard something.

It was like that that morning. I was in this positive state of mind and spirit. Conditions were definitely ideal. I felt that an idea was approaching, maybe a slogan for our fall membership campaign, though I knew that whatever I came up with Ben would change and then take credit for it.

But I could have sworn there was somebody else in the house. It wasn't even noise exactly but something like the floors registering weight moving across them. We've got wall to wall carpet in every room of the main floor and the second floor, and so you really don't hear footsteps in this house. You just sense people moving through the rooms. That sensation was making me uncomfortable since there wasn't supposed to be anybody down there.

So I went downstairs to check it out, and when I reached the second floor and turned the corner, I got a jolt of adrenaline.

This figure in black was moving toward me.

Hey, Peter, it spoke, and then I knew it was Julie—her features seemed to pop into focus.

Funny, the figure had seemed huge until I recognized Julie; now she was her compact self again. She had on a black blazer, a black tank top, black tights, and black sharp-toed boots. Her hair was done up in a high ponytail, her face was pale—Julie always made a point of staying out of the sun—and her mouth was a slash of crimson lipstick.

Julie, I said, I didn't hear you come in. You scared me. I kept my voice down; I didn't want to get her started yelling at me again.

She walked right up to me, keeping her hands jammed down in the pockets of her blazer. Rang the doorbell several times, she said, staring me straight in the eye, as was her way. The door was cracked a bit. So I thought I'd better just check. Didn't want to miss you, Peter, she said, after going to all the trouble of coming over here.

What am I supposed to say to that? I said. All of a sudden it made me mad to have her walking right into my house.

Whatever, she said, smiling sort of to herself and leaning to one side to peek around behind me. Nice house you've got here, Peter. Not like I imagined it at all. You should have brought me over here. I'd have had a better opinion of you.

I kept quiet, mostly because I couldn't figure out what Julie had in mind. There's this odd thing about her, or about me and her. I'm six-two and weigh right around one-eighty; she's five-three and doesn't weigh more than a pound or two over a hundred. So let's say I'm almost twice as big as she is. She was never intimidated.

I don't mean that I ever wanted her to be scared of me. But one thing I figured out from being on the tour. Size has everything to do with relationships. The advantage always starts out with the bigger person, but of course that can be changed. Little guys on the tour are always putting big guys in their place. There weren't that many players on the tour who were bigger than me.

I'm used to automatically acknowledging physical differences with women in the ways we stand next to each other and look and speak—the tones of voice we use. But Julie Munroe apparently never learned this basic principle.

At first it had annoyed me that she'd stand or sit a little closer to me than anybody else would in a similar situation—as if she were the larger person, and I ought to be the one to make room. Damn nervy woman. Then all of a sudden that nerve of hers got to be attractive. At work I'd seek her out because there was this energy that came from her, or that was generated by the two of us crowding each other's space. The charge I got from being around her was what started the whole thing.

But right then, in the upstairs hallway of my house, I was back to being annoyed. Anybody else Julie's size would have been apologizing for the intrusion. They'd be moving for the steps to head downstairs and giving me all available slack.

Julie actually nudged me over a bit with the back of her hand on my arm and walked past me toward the steps up to the attic. What's up here, Peter? she asked, not turning to look back at me.

There was that certain quietness in her tone that in the old days I'd learned to recognize as a signal. You want to come over to my place for lunch, Peter? she'd say in that tone.

But I could also feel how brittle her mood was. If I didn't humor her, I'd have a hundred pounds of trouble in my house.

I have a little study up there, I said. You want to see?

Without replying, she started up the narrow staircase to the third floor. Following her, I was forced to take note of her purposeful steps, her trim back, the slight swaying of her ponytail.

Around this time of day the skylight makes my office one of the brightest rooms I've ever been in. The space is actually a small one, but when you come up into it out of that claustrophobic staircase, your immediate sensation is one of having entered a large airy room.

Julie took off her blazer and casually dropped it to the floor. Maybe she thought I'd pick it up for her. I didn't.

Warm up here, she said, still keeping her back to me, walking toward the shelves as if she were taking a tour of the place. In all that light and in her black tank top and tights, her arms and shoulders looked pale as a statue's.

Have a seat, Julie, I told her. I sat down in my desk chair. Because I was so caught up with all my work, I didn't mind indulging her, but I definitely wanted to put the situation back into a proper balance.

No, I'm fine, she said, continuing slowly to pace around the periphery of the room, picking up one thing and another from the tops of my shelves. I've been thinking some about us, Peter. I thought it would be good if we talked.

Julie, I began, there's just no—

I'm not talking about starting up again! Julie spun around to face me. Rosy streaks appeared in her cheeks, on her neck, around her collarbone. I'm talking about . . . She turned away then, and raised her hands as if to pluck the words from the air around her head.

I waited, but she couldn't find what she wanted to say. Her hands dropped to her sides. She turned her back again and slightly bowed her head.

What, Julie? I said softly. Something about her ponytail catching the light was about to make me feel sorry for her.

She spun again and stepped quickly and directly toward me. Turn around, she said.

What?

Just turn your chair around.

I did.

I wouldn't have obeyed anybody else in that situation, but Julie was so obviously volatile right then that I didn't want to cross her unless it became absolutely necessary.

She set her hands on my shoulders and began a hard massage that was just too familiar.

Don't do this, Julie, I said. This was how we always began at her apartment. In her quiet tone she would ask me if I needed my back rubbed, and I would say yes, yes, that was what I needed. We would walk silently toward her waterbed. Then it would start. Just this way. Now her touch felt profoundly wrong, as if in busy traffic I'd suddenly been instructed to start driving through red lights.

Julie didn't stop. Her hands and fingers are amazingly strong, and she is a ruthless, deep-muscle massager. Her back rubs are like no others I have ever experienced—pleasurable, yes, but almost too painful to bear. Even when they were the prelude to our lovemaking.

Lean forward, Julie said. Automatically I did so. Previously we'd joked about these back rubs being her power move. Now I understood exactly how powerful they were. To make her stop what she was doing, I would have had to steel myself against her, mentally and physically.

Raise your arms, Julie said and lightly slapped my back. When I did as she said, she jerked my shirt up and peeled it over my head and arms. She let it fall.

Julie, I said.

She went on.

There was this pause. Her tank top fell to the floor beside my polo shirt.

Topless now, she walked around to face me. Julie's breasts are small and muscular. Now her nipples were sharply erect, and I was shaken by the look of her torso. Her body was as intimidating as a wrestler's.

Put your knees together, she said.

When I did, she straddled them and sat down, facing me. She continued rubbing my shoulders, except that now she also worked on the muscles of my arms, neck, and chest. Looking up at her serious face, the hard red slash of her lips, I had the crazy notion that she was extracting strength from my body. Her face came nearer and nearer.

When she did kiss me, it was with a tenderness that I wouldn't have expected from Julie. For that reason I didn't resist as perhaps I might have, had she tried to force me that way, too. Her thumbs brushing across my nipples, too, were gentler than any touch she'd used on me so far.

I never liked you, Julie said, but in that quiet tone that was like humming. Your body was all I ever liked. Skinny, long-muscled tennis player's body that isn't worth a damn for anything but playing tennis and sex. That's all you're good for, Peter.

While she chanted that way to me, she pulled herself closer and raised herself so that her breasts brushed my cheeks, my chin, my mouth. I confess I wanted to let my mouth respond as it ordinarily would have to Julie's doing that. I willed myself not to.

But her hand plunged down to my crotch. There wasn't anything I could do about that part of my body's response to her.

Julie, I said.

But she was smiling at me now, a clearly triumphant smile.

And undoing my belt and my trousers.

Julie, don't, I said, and I started to stand up.

Don't you, she said, and she actually thumped me in the ribs with the soft side of her fist. It wasn't a hard punch—maybe it surprised me more than anything else and just slightly knocked the wind out of me. It definitely stopped me from standing up.

She went on with what she was doing. Her advantage was that she knew my body, knew what to do. I won't say that I was helpless, but I will say that Julie was in complete control of what was going on between us.

Now stand up, she said. When I didn't do it immediately, she put her hands at my neck just beneath my ears and took hold and pulled upward in such a way that I felt half afraid that she'd snap my neck if I didn't follow her wishes. I stood up enough for her to push my pants and underwear down.

Julie, I don't want this, I said, but my idiotic bobbing erection mocked my words even as I spoke them.

Stay put, she said and stood and pulled off her boots and pushed down her tights and underwear and stepped out of them. She was fast at this—there was this quick look I had of her turning in the skylight's block of light.

Then she was back at me again, straddling me, pushed up close against me and using one hand to press my head against her chest and the other to engineer what she was apparently determined to achieve.

I thought of fighting her, and I chose not to. I wish now that I had, even though I know it would have been bloody.

When she found the fit, her coming down onto me was such a shock I couldn't help calling out. I wondered if anyone would have heard my voice.

Once she had me inside her, it was as if I had become the small person and she the large. Her hands took hold of each side of my head and she pressed her breast into my face.

Your mouth, son of a bitch, she said. Use your mouth.

I wanted it over with, which was what Julie seemed to want, too, except that she was really into it. She used both me and her hand, and she came with a yelp. She pitched upward twice more before locking herself tightly against me with her body shaking. Then she pulled away and stood up, breathing hard while she stared down at me. I hated how she looked down at me, but I couldn't do anything about it.

Dumb fuck, she said.

Then she started dressing. She took her time, as if this were her place instead of mine. After a while, it was just too humiliating to sit there with my pants around my knees. I stood and pulled them up, then bent for my shirt and put it on.

I wished she had beaten me with her fists, so that I could have hated her the way I wanted to. There was nothing I could say to her, though it seemed I had to watch her every gesture.

She used a compact and lipstick from her blazer pocket. She put them back, then used both hands to pull her ponytail tight. All the while her face and eyes ignored me. At the same time the way she moved her body told me over and over again, I had you, sucker, I had you.

Patting her pockets, looking around as if to check for anything she might be forgetting, Julie finally walked over to the staircase and gave me a final glance.

Now it's finished, Peter, she said. Her bootsteps going down the staircase were slow and loud.

In a moment I heard—or rather felt in the shaking of the attic floor—the front door slam. When I knew I was absolutely alone, I actually tried to force water to come down out of my eyes. I felt this need to let go of what I'd just been through. Crying was the only thing I could think of that might do it.

My attempts to sob sounded ridiculous. And I didn't want to do anything else I could think of. Call Susan? Call the police? Call Ben Fulton?

When I finally came down to the second floor that day, I touched the walls of the hallways and looked into my kids' bedrooms as I walked slowly past them. I ran my hand along the banister as I came down to the first floor. I was trying to think what the house must have looked like to Julie when she came into the empty foyer, figured out that I was upstairs somewhere, and decided to go up there and find me.

I set my hand on the newel post and thought hard. When I had first gone over to Julie's place, I'd followed her in, right into that immaculate living room of hers with small, framed pictures on each white wall and one bright-covered magazine in the center of a glass coffee table. I looked at all that polished wooden floor and thought to myself, So this is how she lives. She kept quiet—I did, too—while she walked me through her dining area, her kitchen, her workout space, and her bedroom. We'd said it was lunch we were there for. I stood staring down at her jungle-printed bedspread while she paced toward the window. When she turned, faced me, and asked me what I thought, I knew from her voice that the question was important, but all I could do was shrug and say, So this is where you live, Julie? While she waited for me to go on, there was a little smile on Julie's face, almost a bashful expression, but that faded. She shrugged. Yeah, this is it, she said. There had definitely been a topic there for us to discuss, but in a minute or two we'd forgotten all about it.

David Huddle was born and raised in Ivanhoe, Virginia. Since 1971 he has lived in Burlington, Vermont, where he has taught literature and creative writing at the University of Vermont. His books of poetry, short stories, and essays include *Only the Little Bone*, *The High Spirits*, *The Nature of Yearning*, *Stopping by Home*, and *The Writing Habit*. *Intimates*, which includes "Trouble at the Home Office," was published this year by David Godine. *A David Huddle Reader* is forthcoming from University Press of New England.

PHOTO CREDIT: MARION ETTLINGER

"Trouble at the Home Office" is one of the least autobiographical stories I've ever written, but it's set in my house here in Burlington, Vermont. My extreme intimacy with this house is probably what gave me the nerve to risk entering the imagined territory of what happens in the story: I could step into the dark unknown if I tightly clutched the teddy bear of what I knew so well. So what's Southern about this story? Well, the way these characters "relate" to each other is what's Southern here: there's a flirtatious decorum that breaks down—which produces *the trouble. Since I'm a Southerner who makes his home in the North, I've had to make some hard choices about what kind of a writer I am. I've written a good deal about the first twenty years of my life, but I'm fifty now, and I've had to admit that it's time to move on. Just about the time I was reconciled to being a complete exile—a Northern writer with a Southwest Virginia accent—Shannon Ravenel comes along and picks one of my pieces for* New Stories from the South. *She's right, of course; you just can't pronounce yourself a Northern writer any more than you can divorce yourself from your Southern way of seeing the world and understanding the manners men and women use in their relationships.*

FAMILY PLANNING

(from *Story*)

Mother and Minetree were dodging rice on the front steps of Saint James Episcopal Church in the middle of a snowstorm when my friends, Susannah and Mary Tyler, started talking about babies.

Mary Tyler counted on her fingers and said, "October first, 1948." She brushed a fat snowflake from her nose. "Today is January first. That means they'll have a baby on October first. Legally, you're allowed to have a baby nine months after you're married."

"Imagine a baby Gary Cooper," said Susannah. She thought Minetree looked just like Gary Cooper, especially when his hair was wet and slicked back.

Minetree helped Mother into the car and walked around to the other side, leaving handprints on the hood as he braced himself through the slush. I waved my empty rice bag at Mother's blurred face behind the JUST MARRIED sign soaped on the window. The car moved away, and I watched it until it was a black dot at the end of Franklin Street.

The last thing I wanted to talk about was babies. I was picturing Mother and Minetree in the car, Minetree blowing on his hands to get them warm, Mother fiddling with the heater button to get it going, the car smelling of icy air and her gardenia corsage, already turning brown. "Well, hello, Mrs. Fairfax," Minetree'd say. I wondered if she'd slipped over the seat to be touching him. He couldn't put his arm around her because there was a little stick to the right of the steering wheel that he pushed to make the car go. Minetree had a special car that the government had given him because he had had his leg shot off in the war. He never got the pressure quite right, so the car zoomed up and then slowed down, zoom, slow, zoom, slow, like that. They'd probably just jerked onto Broad Street and were lurching out to the west toward Charlottesville.

What did people talk about after they'd promised to love and cherish each other till death did them part? At the ceremony, Mother's voice had quivered, like the candle flame on the altar, but Minetree didn't even need Dr. Gibson to feed him his lines. He'd turned his voice up to top volume and looked at Mother as if they were in the church all by themselves, like Dr. Gibson wasn't standing between them with his prayer book open to the vows page, like I wasn't sitting in the front row in the brand-new red velvet dress Mother had given me for Christmas.

Now that Mother and Minetree were alone together, they were probably talking about romantic things, the kind of things Susannah was always quoting from her love comics. "Oh my darling, you are my life, my soul, my heart. My precious sweet, my life is meaningless without you." Riding along in the car, warm, happy, alone, they weren't thinking about me. At a moment like that, Mother wouldn't think of saying, "I wonder what Amelia is doing now." Neither of them would ever guess that I was standing in the snow with my friends talking about the baby they were going to have.

"What's the big deal about a baby?" I asked. We were sloshing over to Mary Tyler's house where I was going to stay while Mother and Minetree were at Hot Springs, and my black suede pumps were ruined. Before we left for the church, Mother had begged me to wear my boots. I didn't usually say no to my mother, except when she used to suggest that I go to camp, away from her for six weeks. I said no to that. But on her wedding day, on possibly the most thrilling day of her life, except the day she married my father and the day I was born (she always said, "Amelia, the first time I saw your little funny face was the most thrilling moment of my life"), I had said, "No!" and yelled it. Suppose Mother and Minetree got buried in a snowbank somewhere in the Shenandoah Valley and the last thought she had as the air was sucked from the car and she went whirling down the long tunnel with the light at the end was me stamping my foot and saying no about a stupid pair of boots.

"The big deal about a baby?" said Mary Tyler. "Well, for one thing, you can boss it around."

"Every story I read," said Susannah, "says only children are lonely. You're an only child. You won't be lonely with a baby."

But I'd never been lonely. I had my mother. Every summer, she took me to the Avamere Hotel at Virginia Beach for two weeks. She liked riding the waves on rubber rafts. She liked riding the whirlaway at the amusement park. If I was sick with the flu and had to stay home from school, she brought the radio upstairs to my bedroom and turned on WRNL so we could listen to "Our Gal Sunday" together. She even went to Roy Rogers movies with me. Mary Tyler said that my mother wouldn't be interested in going to Roy Rogers movies once she got home from her honeymoon. She'd have other things on her mind. Even though Mary Tyler thought Minetree was a perfect man, she said everything was going to change with him around the house. Men don't like to eat macaroni and cheese three times a week, and they make you turn off the light every time you leave your room, and you can't take the comic section out of the newspaper if it interferes with the sports section. As long as you had a man, Mary Tyler said, you might as well have a baby.

Even if Minetree took up Mother's time, I still wouldn't be lonely because Susannah, Mary Tyler, and I lived within three blocks of each other, and we'd be together the way we always had been. Susannah had a sister a year and a half older whom she fought with all the time. Susannah would scream, "I hate you," and her sister would shriek, "You make me throw up."

When we went to her house, we stuffed the keyhole to cut off the view of her sister's evil eye. Mary Tyler was the oldest of five and her whole house hummed like our school lunchroom. We couldn't have a decent conversation without someone barging in. My house was the only place we could get some peace and quiet.

My third-floor room had a slanted ceiling and three big windows facing the street. From March to October, my room was like a tree house sitting in the top of the maples, and in the winter, the wind made the branches scratch the windowpanes and we felt like we were in a cozy cottage in the forest. We put pillows on the floor in a circle with pretzels in the middle and gossiped with no interruptions from the outside world.

"What do you girls talk about all the time?" Mother asked, but she said it like she didn't expect an answer.

We were usually talking about her and Minetree.

When Minetree came home from the war and started courting my mother, Susannah and Mary Tyler were usually at my house when the doorbell rang. We'd rush to be the first to open it, to see Minetree standing in his dark blue suit with the tip of a white handkerchief sticking out of the pocket. "Hello, Min-a-tree," we'd say in chorus. By that time, Mother would have gotten to the curve in the stairs, trying to keep her grin under control.

After Minetree had squeezed my shoulder, and said, "Hi, Amelia," he'd call out, "Hail, Susannah Banana." Then, he'd make a little bow and shake hands with Mary Tyler. "Good evening, Counselor." He was a lawyer and Mary Tyler had already made up her mind to be one too. She loved what she called his "law language." On one of those nights they were going out, Mother asked him please to fasten the door properly, that she always found it flapping on its hinges when he was in charge of closing it. We heard him shut the door, rattle the handle, and say, "Witness, Julia!" Mary Tyler thought the word "witness" was just fabulous. She also liked the way he said "penitentiary" instead of "prison," that someone had committed a penitentiary offense.

"It's like legal poetry," she said.

We'd watch their two gray heads going down the front steps to the sidewalk. Susannah thought it was romantic that their hair matched. She was sure that Mother's hair turned gray gradually after she lost her first husband so young, but that Minetree's had turned in a flash while he lay on that beach at Iwo Jima staring at where his leg used to be. Minetree took one step at a time because of his artificial leg. At the bottom, he'd slip his arm around Mother's waist, and Susannah would swoon. Susannah said that none of her *True Confessions* stories matched this one— a war hero madly in love with the widow of another war hero who happened to be his oldest friend. The second war hero, who Susannah always referred to as the other man, was my father. He joined the RAF before the United States went to war and flew planes that had been shot down and patched up back to England. One of them came unpatched and dropped him in the English Channel when I was three.

All day the afternoon Mother and Minetree were supposed to get home from their honeymoon, rain filled up the gutters and flooded the streets, and as I walked home, the wind got under my umbrella and whipped it up so it sat on top of the handle like a vase. I couldn't see how they could make it back from Hot Springs in one piece. But there they were. Mother was stirring cheese sauce on the stove, wearing her same old apron that said VISIT VIRGINIA BEACH on the front, her hair beginning to frizz from the steam of the macaroni pot. Like always, the radio was on low, for company, not to listen to. The only thing different was Minetree. He came into the kitchen and hung back, waiting for Mother to stop hugging me. I didn't know whether to kiss him or not, and he looked like he didn't know what to do either. Then he did the best thing. He just stood there looking glad and said, "How's my girl?"

"Are you two going to have a baby?"

Mother sprayed the cheese sauce she'd been tasting all over the stove. Minetree felt behind him for the arms of the kitchen chair and sat down.

I rummaged around in my book bag and handed him my list of Fors and Againsts.

"Against: crying, smelling bad, throwing up, breaking things, pulling hair," he read. "For: cute."

Before they could ask why my For list was so short, I told them that Susannah wanted a boy named Gary, and that Mary Tyler wanted to be godmother so that she would have a spiritual if not legal connection to our family.

Mother said that what she wanted was to hear about what her own baby had been doing every moment she'd been away.

Every day at recess, Mary Tyler wanted to have a baby talk. She said I should watch my mother carefully in the morning. "It's a good sign if she eats her eggs and turns green."

"What about Minetree?"

"He'll be extra solicitous."

"Solicitous?"

"Yes, you know, he'll be extra attentive."

"More lovey-dovey," said Susannah.

After eating grapefruit, eggs, sausage, toast, and coffee, Mother's cheeks were still pink. But Minetree was definitely solicitous. Sometimes, he held her hand on the breakfast table. If she had wanted to rush to the bathroom, she'd have had to drag him along with her.

We spent three weeks on the reproductive system in science class. The day we talked about sperm, Mary Tyler asked Miss Hughes to trace the egg's route down the fallopian tubes and wanted to know the statistical odds for the sperm being in the right place at the right time. After class, Mary Tyler just shook her head. She said she didn't think Mother and Minetree had any idea what a tricky business the meeting of the sperm and egg was, that an egg didn't just stand around waiting.

That summer the days were long and boring and soggy with heat. The pool at the club was closed because of polio, and so

Susannah and Mary Tyler and I set up shop under the leaves of the weeping beech in our backyard with love comics, our summer reading books, and plenty of Cokes. Mother poked her head into our dim cool arbor from time to time to tell me I was going to ruin my eyes reading, and I'd say, "Uh-huh," and return to the story about Anne Boleyn whose husband, the king, got tired of waiting for her to have an heir and cut her head off. Susannah flicked ladybugs off her knees as she read her love comics, and every few pages, she practiced kissing on the back of her hand. Mary Tyler tried to ruin my concentration by making mournful sounds blowing into an empty Coke bottle.

It really bothered her that Minetree's baby would have a different last name than mine. She thought I should ask him to adopt me.

"Just imagine," she said. "The four of you enter a room of strangers. You're introduced. 'Mr. and Mrs. Fairfax, Baby Fairfax, and Amelia Harrison.' People will think you're the babysitter."

October first passed, Thanksgiving, Mother and Minetree's first anniversary, Valentine's Day, and Easter. Minetree would come up behind Mother when she wasn't looking and squeeze her so tight she told him to quit it. Then she'd turn and put her arms around his neck, and they'd go into a clinch and Susannah would say, "Hubba, hubba."

Minetree planted azaleas in front of our house. He dug up the soil and flung it over his shoulder like Luther who worked next door in the Hobsons' garden. When Minetree carried water in pails from the tap in the backyard, he swung the bottom of his wooden leg out. The knee hinges squeaked, and the heel made divots as it struck the earth. Dark red veins popped out on his neck as he lugged one pail in each hand and the water splashed out and watered his shoes. Every day when he came home from the office, he stood on the front steps and watched the azalea buds uncurl into sprays of pink and orange.

One night, I woke up and heard Mother crying. "Oh no," she wailed. I jumped out of bed and yanked my door open. I saw

Minetree hop on one foot into the bathroom where Mother was, bent over, holding her stomach. Her voice was so broken when she said, "Please, go, Amelia," it shot through my mind that it was her heart that she had lost, that lay red and splattered on the tiles. Minetree shut the door and locked it.

"Open the door," I yelled. I rattled the knob. "Let me in. I want to see my mother." I beat on the door and kicked it, and then I screamed, "You're a cripple and I hate you."

I sank down on the floor and rocked back and forth, crying into my knees. It seemed like forever before I heard whispering, running water, flushing, my mother talking to me through the door saying not to worry, she was all right, just a few more minutes and I could come in. I tried to stop crying by gulping and that made me hiccup, and then I started thinking that Minetree could never love me after what I'd said about being crippled, he'd never be able to love me like he'd love his own baby, and tears started hurrying down my cheeks again.

The lock turned and Minetree opened the door. Mother pulled me down next to her on the edge of the tub. Sometimes, she said, after a baby begins to grow, for some reason it gets sick, and it's better that the mother loses it.

"Shouldn't we call a doctor?" I asked.

"A very good idea, Amelia." Minetree was balancing himself on the washbasin, his pajama bottom all wilted where his leg should have been. "You help your mother back into bed and I'll do that."

Minetree said something to the doctor about six weeks and stomach cramps and nausea and when he got off the phone he said Dr. Beazley would see her first thing in the morning. Mother was curled around her pillow, and Minetree pulled the quilt up and we tucked it around her. He asked me if I didn't want to sleep on the chaise lounge in their room, that it would make Mother and him feel better if I was there. I lay awake for a long time listening to the shades flap against the open window, to Minetree's voice, soft as a lullaby, soothing Mother into sleep. Just before her breathing got heavy, I heard the bedsprings ping as he moved to hold her tighter. She already had one perfect child he whispered, and there was no reason to think she couldn't have another.

In early June, we were having dinner in the dining room where a portrait of my real father hung above the sideboard. Mother said that Minetree had laid down the law when he moved into our house that he didn't want a single picture of his old friend moved. So there we were, eight eyes around the dining room table, and just three people eating roast pork with crispy skin, fried apples, and mashed potatoes. I made a little circle in the middle of my mashed potatoes and asked Minetree to adopt me.

Minetree put down his knife and fork, picked up his napkin, and started matching one corner to the other.

"What's this business about adoption?" he asked.

I tried to list the reasons Mary Tyler had thought up. If they had a baby, they'd all be Fairfaxes and I'd be a Harrison; the baby would be Minetree's legally and I wouldn't; if I was in a horrible automobile accident without them, maimed beyond recognition, the hospital would look up all the Harrisons in the telephone book, and I wouldn't belong to any of them. I could die with no one I loved holding my hand.

Minetree pondered the portrait for a second, and then he cupped his hand around his mouth.

"Hear ye. Hear ye," he said. "Whereas Amelia Harrison has done me the honor of requesting that I adopt her; whereas an adoption under the statutes of the Commonwealth of Virginia requires a name change in the case of adoption; whereas her father's mother, her grandmother Harrison, would be distressed if I took her son's name away from said Amelia Harrison." He put his hand over his heart. "I swear before the company assembled that I love Amelia Harrison as if she were my own daughter, and therefore no adoption is necessary."

Mother clapped her hands and said, "Hear, Hear."

"But, Amelia," said Minetree, "if for some reason we don't have a baby, it won't shake the world. We have a nice little family right here. Plus, if we need to, we can annex Susannah and Mary Tyler."

The next week, Mother took me downtown to buy a bathing suit and we stopped for lunch at Miller and Rhoads Tea Room. Mother ordered crabmeat salad and I asked for a turkey club.

"Could we have a personal discussion?" I asked. I bit down on the end of my sandwich and a tomato slid out. "I really want you to have a baby."

She started patting the top of her crabmeat with her fork. "I went to the doctor last week."

"Well finally," I said. "When's it coming?"

She continued to neaten up her salad.

"There's something the matter with me."

"Is it your ovaries or your fallopian tubes?" I asked.

"Amelia!" She looked around at the other tables and whispered, "He can't say exactly."

"But you've already had one baby."

"I don't know if I'll have another one." She gave up trying to eat and folded her napkin by her plate. "And another thing. Please don't have a personal discussion with Minetree. Promise me."

I promised, and when the waitress brought the check, she stared at all that beautiful crabmeat lying on my mother's plate.

Every Wednesday, Minetree took me to the tennis courts at the club. He stood in one place, made a little circle in the clay next to him with his racquet, and told me to hit the ball there. He said if I did it over and over, I would learn to place the ball exactly where I wanted it. One afternoon, soon after the talk I had with Mother, we came off the court with our wet shirts plastered to our backs, and he sent me for two limeades with fizzy water. When I got back, we drank them on a green bench under a weeping willow tree. Minetree told me if I crunched the ice I would ruin the enamel on my teeth and then he said he wanted to have a talk. He gulped his limeade and wiped his forehead with the back of his hand.

"About this business of a baby. We all want one, but I don't know if we're going to have one."

"Susannah and Mary Tyler want one too."

"Yes, I know, but look, it's not always a simple business to have a baby."

"Mother says it's her fault."

"It is not her fault. It's nobody's fault. You mustn't discuss this with your mother, and there's no reason to go into any detail about it with Susannah and Mary Tyler."

I asked him if he wanted another limeade. His forehead was dripping faster than he could mop it up, even though a breeze rustled the branches of the willow tree.

It wasn't more than two days later, in the middle of a game of canasta, that Susannah sorted her hand and said that any combination of Mother's and Minetree's genes would produce a beautiful baby. I tried to joke that a baby might not be in the cards for them. My eyes started to sting and I tried blinking but that didn't work. Pretty soon I couldn't tell a spade from a club, I was bawling so hard. Mary Tyler, who was preparing to meld, dropped her cards and put her arms around me and Susannah stroked my hair and murmured, "Hush now," like a little mother. Mary Tyler said she'd had to mind her three little brothers that morning and people who have lots of children should have their brains checked.

One July evening, when the sky was still light but the air had cooled off, Mother invited my friends over for a picnic supper. Minetree roasted hot dogs and made his own mayonnaise for the potato salad. We slurped our Popsicles, lime, cherry, and grape, and stuck out our tongues, comparing colors. While we batted a shuttlecock around, Mother took home movies, "For posterity," she said. The moon came up and Mary Tyler identified it as a waxing crescent. I wondered what it would be like if there were also a playpen in the yard with a baby in it. The baby would hurl its yellow duck over the side and then put its little hands and chin on the rim to see where it landed. We'd all lapse into goo-goos, except for Minetree, who'd say something like, "That's an open-and-shut case of a perfect aim."

When Mother slapped the first mosquito, she said she guessed it was time to go in and would Mary Tyler please bring in the plates and cups. Minetree made Susannah wipe the table off and fold up the chairs. Mother told me to take away the trash. When those chores were done, we went into the living room and sat there in the softest part of the twilight, just before it slides into nighttime, talking about this and that.

Elizabeth Hunnewell was born and raised in Richmond, Virginia. She now lives in Wellesley, Massachusetts, with her husband and three children and is working on a novel. Her stories have appeared in *The Virginia Quarterly Review* and *Story* and *New Stories from the South: The Year's Best, 1991.*

PHOTO CREDIT: DAVID ZADIG

During the time I was thinking about "Family Planning," I told a friend that I could only remember being really mad at my parents once as a child. Roy Rogers was coming to town in a traveling rodeo. For some reason they were late getting me to the fairgrounds and I missed the whole thing. My friend then asked how I could have had a happy childhood and be a writer, a question that dried up my muse for months. I searched my memory for the smallest cruelty, careless put-down, an undeserved reproof, even unfair curfews, anything that I could use to evoke the dark side of life. I came up with nothing and so I began to write, hoping to prove that gentle, loving relationships could be just as potent and as interesting to read about as tortured ones.

Annette Sanford

HELENS AND ROSES

(from *American Short Fiction*)

The minute the job was done and the man drove away, leaving the trailer windows covered with toast-colored blinds drawn tight as Dick's hatband, Pep started complaining. "You can't hardly tell if it's daylight or dark since you put up these curtains."

"Blinds," Lula said, already feeling the difference they made. The cost, of course, had knocked her flat. But she'd long ago learned what you want in this world you have to pay for, and she wanted those blinds, more than new chairs or an air conditioner.

"What for?" Pep said when she brought up the subject the first time around.

"We need them," she said. She couldn't explain the pure-d fright of night coming on since they moved into town, of the dark reaching out from the houses and streets. From she didn't know where. "We need the protection," was what she told Pep.

"What I need is air," Pep said now. "Let's raise the things up."

"We just put 'em down." Lula walked back and forth, admiring the blinds. The toast color was right. It lifted the gloom of the mud-colored walls and made the rooms airy. "Stretch out on the couch if your head is hurting."

"What hurts is to think what that bozo charged."

"No more than they're worth. They dress up the place."

"Your teacups do that—and they don't stop the breeze."

The first time the man came, he came on a Thursday, one of Pep's bad days. He brought his dog. Then he started right in with how hot it was, how he'd have to step out and see about Sheri out in the van.

"Scheherazade," Lula said to Pep, back in the bedroom where he'd gone to lie down. "That's the name of the dog."

"There's a dog in the house?" His blue eyes opened. Pep missed Prince Rudy, the best hound of his life that he'd had to sell off on account of the rule Lula had made, *No dogs in town,* when they moved from the Sandies. *They can't run loose, and they sure as the dickens aren't coming inside.*

"She's out in the van," Lula said. "Sheri, he calls her."

"Who? His wife? Why don't she come in?" Pep got off the track when his head acted up. Sometimes just a minute. Or maybe all day, the way it was lately.

As a general rule, though, they did pretty well. They lived clean lives, Pep liked to say, and except for his mixups, his mind stayed clear. Clearer than hers, Lula claimed. He could tell you dates way back to the Flood, even days of the week when certain things happened, especially his dog deals, like trading the setter in '38 to Pinky McClure for a broad-nosed sow and a couple of shoats. (On a Tuesday that happened—a May afternoon right after a shower.)

"Lie there and rest," Lula said that Thursday. "When he comes back here, you can move to the front."

Lula herself had varicose veins. And hemorrhoids at night. Let her turn on her back and they started in throbbing. She had learned a trick, though—to bear down for a minute, not too hard—and the pain went away. That's all there was to it, a few minutes of pressure. Gravity, she guessed it was. Out of the blue, she knew how to do it.

"What's he coming back here for?"

"To measure the windows."

"Why?" Pep said.

"For the blinds. I told you."

The next time the man came he brought the blinds with him. He left the dog in the yard, tied to a tree. She ran all around it, yipping and yapping.

"She's a nervous animal," Lula said.

"Yes ma'am," said the man. "Spoiled rotten." He looked spoiled himself, Lula thought. He had a loose kind of look around his mouth and watery eyes set close to his nose. "She belongs with my wife, but my wife's with our daughter. In Panama City."

"Where the dictator is?"

"In Florida, ma'am. How is your husband?"

"He's all right today. He'll be out in a minute."

The man stood on a footstool. "It's the heat, I suppose, that gives him those headaches."

"Pep's ninety, you know."

"He sure doesn't look it."

"I'm eighty-two."

"You don't look it either."

Pep said again, "Let's put up the shades."

"It's nighttime, Dad."

Dad was only a name. They never had children. Never wanted them much, Pep had told his brother, which wasn't the truth. They hoped for two. Pep wanted twins. They had to fill up their lives in place of those children. Pep took up dogs. Lula settled on teacups and various things.

They were younger, of course, up on the Sandies, a little dry creek that could rise when it wanted but mostly ran quiet, bedded in sand with a few brown pools that a fish or two slept in.

They were there fifty years. Then they moved into town.

Their trailer just fit on a sliver of land next to the Quik-Stop, down a little, with a hedge in between, but the lights from the cars swept in at all hours, giving Lula the jitters.

"Like spotlights," she said. "Like they're hunting us down." She mentioned the blinds.

Pep voted for shades. "They come a lot cheaper."

"With blinds," Lula said, "you can tilt in the light and still have your privacy."

The day the man hung them he gave her some tips about which way to turn them.

"Most people get it backward. They turn the slats down." He was sweating by then. "But let's say, for example, there's a peeper outside."

It gave Lula a chill to think that there might be.

"With the slats tilted down they look like they're closed, but out where he's at, he gets the whole picture."

He sent Lula outside to prove he was right.

She told this to Pep, helping him dress. "He sure knows his business."

Pep wound his watch. "Has he brought in the dog?"

"He brought her up the steps and gave her some water. She's roped to the tree, a little fluffy orange pooch." Lula hunted her glasses, first on the dresser and then in the bathroom.

"You're wearing the things," Pep pointed out.

"For goodness sakes." Lula pushed up the nosepiece. "She's an apricot poodle."

"I know what she is. I can't think what he calls her."

"Scheherazade."

"Spell it," said Pep. He was hell on spelling. He once won a meet and was given a ribbon. CHAMPEEN it said. Lula laughed when he showed her. A spelling prize and they spelled it wrong.

"It starts with an *s,* that's all I know." But then she went on. "It's the name of that woman who kept telling stories to stay alive. In *Arabian Nights.*"

"A picture show?"

"A book when I read it. I had it in school."

School for Lula was out on the prairie. White Hall it was called. The teacher there was Miss Mabel Barnes, on her way up as an educator. She made it, in fact, to county superintendent, and on from there right into Houston. At White Hall her mission was to introduce culture.

"There are children out here that don't know a fairy tale from Adam's off ox." She was a little pale woman, born to a doctor that lived in Fort Worth when there weren't many such—female doctors.

Lula took to culture, the myths most especially, how things got like they were, why spiders make webs, that kind of thing.

Education stays with you, is what Lula said.

Viewing the blinds, she said to Pep, "I feel a lot safer."

"Safer from what?" Up on the Sandies she was scareder of june bugs than she was of the wolves. Moths gave her a tizzy, the big hairy kind that flew in the window.

Pep, however, liked all things in nature. He liked to lie in bed with the wind on his face and listen to owls. He had talked to a fellow over at the Quik-Stop that didn't even know owls made a whooping sound. "Like a cowboy yelling *yippy-ti-yo*."

"Owls hoot," the man said.

"Well, sure they do." Pep followed him out and poked his head in the car. "But they have a cry, too."

The man drove away. "Damn city fool," Pep said to Lula.

"Safe from criminals," Lula said.

Pep snorted at that. "Do you think you'll get murdered in this sleepy burg?" He had visited great cities. He once went to sea.

"It happens all over." In Lula's nightmares, crooks knocked down the door.

It wasn't much of a door, they both agreed. When they first came to town to size up the trailer—a sleek cream and beige with a bowed-out front where Pep stretched the flag—he put into words what was holding him back. "It's too smooth inside."

It was, Lula saw. A toy kind of outfit. When you knocked on a wall it didn't sound solid. It sounded, Pep said, like a cereal box.

They bought it anyway, with most of their capital. They were too old for loans is what it boiled down to. And too old for the country. What if one of them died?

When Lula met Pep she was barely fourteen. She had her hair in a net, no shoes on her feet, and was cleaning a skillet from fish she had fried that had stuck like glue. She was out by the barn and he came riding up on a no-count horse.

He was looking for cows. This was up on the Sandies where later they settled. There was brush all around with cow paths through it and lots of wild roses in hedges so thick you could bleed to death if you hung up in one and tried in a hurry to get yourself loose.

He came out of the yaupon, all dressed up on that pitiful pony, his legs hanging down almost to the ground.

"Nice morning," he said and tipped his hat.

She knew who he was from the dent in his chin and his sky-colored eyes. Her sister had told her. "You're Pepper McLeod."

He inclined his gaze to her feet in the dust. "You're the Bennett girl with the beautiful toes."

She covered them up under chicken-scratched earth. "What are you doing way off over here?"

"They told me in town to hurry on out before you got married."

"Aw, git on." But she half-believed he meant what he said.

He got off his horse. "Let me have that skillet." He went to the trough and dipped it in. "Now give me the rag."

He hung around for a while. He asked her age. She told him sixteen and changed the subject. "Do you always go riding in Sunday clothes?"

"When I'm out meeting girls."

She guessed that was true. He had girls all over, her sister said.

Then the cows came along, mooing and lowing, and gathered around him. "Here the girls are now."

She couldn't help laughing. He got back on his horse, laughing too. "Do you ever go dancing?"

"Of course," she lied. "When I want to, I do."

"How often is that?"

"When you see me you'll know."

He lifted his hat and gave her the look her sister had told her made girls pitch over and faint in the road. "Good-bye, Lula Bennett."

She loved him already. "Good-bye, Pep McLeod."

He didn't come back. He forgot her, she guessed.

In the time he was gone she got a lot older. She broke her wrist cranking a car. She bobbed her hair, got thin in the waist, bought a pair of kid gloves, and spent money on dresses that should have gone to the church.

She was working by then on a telephone switchboard and going out with men who bragged on her looks and asked her to marry them. One owned a saloon and a domino parlor and drove a Ford car the top went down on. Emmit Steele he was named, for his father the barber. He bought her a ring, but she wouldn't wear it. She said maybe she might if the sign got right.

Her sister got married. Her father died. Her mother moved off from the place on the Sandies.

Lula went there one day and found a black snake asleep in a chair. In the room that was hers, birds lay on their backs with their feet in the air.

Emmit Steele was along. "Let's get out of here."

"Wait," Lula said. She went to the window and looked at the horse trough where Pepper McLeod had scrubbed her skillet. She made up her mind. If he didn't come back she would never get married. She would stay an old maid and have put on her tombstone BORN AND DIED and not a thing else.

While the man hung the blinds Lula went to the store. Not to the Quik-Stop. She went in the car. First she took off the bedspread she covered it with to keep off the cats. Then she backed it slowly into the street.

Pep said to the man, "You could bring in your dog and let her cool off."

"She's fine outside." His name was Winkle.

"These delicate dogs keel over and die."

Winkle peered toward the yard.

"Go on with your work. I'll go out and fetch her."

Lula browsed in the store. When Pep was along she had to shop fast. He bought the wrong things. He bought everything big, the biggest bananas, big boxes of crackers that always went stale.

He was married before. Briefly, to women named Helen and Rose. One was a teacher who died right away, and the other one, Rose, fell out of love.

Lula didn't know this when Pep came back. He took her out a few times and then he said, "The day Helen died—"

"Helen who?" she asked.

About Rose he said, "We married for fun."

She took it slow after that. She went out again with Emmit Steele, and a new butcher in town who sang in the choir.

Pep seemed not to mind. He met her one day by the bank on the corner. "Whenever you're ready, say the word."

She was wearing new shoes with buckles that glittered. "Ready for what?"

"To be my wife."

"Wife number three?"

"We'll do all right. We'll make a good pair."

"Hah," she said, "you don't respect women."

"I do." He was hurt. "I have sisters," he said.

Pep sat on the couch and drew Winkle out. "What else have you done besides hanging blinds?" He fed Sheri a cookie, a gingersnap.

"I've raced horses," said Winkle, pleased to be asked.

"My business is dogs. What'll you take for Scheherazade?"

"Oh," Winkle said, "she's not for sale. She belongs to my wife."

Pep pulled on his chin. "She's got a bum leg. You'd have to whittle your price."

"There's no way I'd sell her."

"Because of your wife." Pep studied a minute on Winkle's wife. He pictured her tall, with a downy mustache. She wore suits, he thought, and had a long neck and ears that lay back, like a panther's ears.

"Winkle," said Pep, "I'm a breeder, too. We could make us some money, depending, of course, on what ails the leg."

When Lula came home she knew right away the dog had come in. She took Pep aside.

"Sheri's been in the house."

"What makes you think so?"

"Crumbs on the rug. And I smell her perfume."

"Perfume on a dog?"

"There are people that silly."

"I'm glad I was shaving."

"You should have watched out."

When they moved into town Lula put up her teacups. Not out for display, but in boxes she stored in the two bedroom closets.

They had always sat out and Pep found he missed them, the main one especially, from Miss Mabel Barnes. A plain green cup with President Wilson in black on the side.

"The trailer's too wobbly," Lula said. "They'd fall down and break."

"What good are they doing shut up in the dark?"

"I don't want to dust them."

Pep made her sit down. "I don't think that's it."

Lula twitched in her chair. "What's the matter with you?"

He gave her the look girls had swooned in the dust for. "You gave up your cups because I can't have my dogs."

"You're the beatingest man."

"I'm right, aren't I, Lu?"

He built shelves all around and helped her unpack them. "We're fixed up now."

"All but Prince Rudy."

"Rudy," said Pep, "wouldn't like it in town."

Lula held out her arms. "Would you care to dance?"

Up on the Sandies they always went dancing. Forty miles to a dance hall was nothing at all. Except once for six weeks when Pep had pleurisy. It hurt even to walk. "It sears my chest."

He was something to scare you, a big strong man and he couldn't get up. Lula hovered around. "You ought to get out. You ought to breathe in some Vicks."

"That'd sure enough kill me." He expected to die and made plans for Lula. "You could get you a job in a cafe or something."

"I'd work on a switchboard," she said, insulted.

"They've gone out of style."

"Who says so?" said Lula.

"They've gone to the dial."

She sat down and cried for all she had lost, for marrying Pep who was sick all the time, and a barren womb, and the holes in her stockings.

"Come here, little girl."

She wouldn't go near him. "Get up from the bed! And don't talk of dying."

He talked about girls. There were more than she knew of, scattered around. Even some overseas. Alice in England. And Fleurette and Marie. He forgot where they came from. "Two really nice girls."

Lula threw the green cup and gave President Wilson a crack in his glasses. Patching him up with flour-paste glue, Pep commented mildly, "It's you that I married."

"The third on the list." She was sobbing still.

"You would have been first if you'd been a day older."

Pep went to sea on the *Tarkington Trader*. A saber ship is what it was called, for the way it cut water.

It happened right funny how he got on.

He was wasting his life, his father said—a serious man who owned two ranches and had other sons that tended to business. This one he saw as a ne'er-do-well.

"What'll it take to straighten you out?"

Pep knew right away. "Five hundred dollars." He wanted a car to drive people around, land men he'd met who came in on trains from northern cities and couldn't get out to look at the prairies.

His father thought girls was what he was after. "You won't get it from me. Get out and earn it."

"Two-fifty?" tried Pep. He'd saved ninety himself. For two-forty more he could buy a Tin Lizzie.

"Not twenty-five cents," his father told him.

"Then I'm leaving the country," Pepper said.

He tried Mexico first and liked it fine, except for warm goat's milk and breakfast menudo—and the way they slit throats over practically nothing. He got out fast one night in September and went up to Corpus and hid on a ship.

"The damned thing sailed." He laughed, telling Lula.

She remembered those days when she waited, forgotten. "You were gone a long time."

"Four years on the sea."

"And two wives later."

Helen died in a dentist's chair, having a tooth pulled. About Rose, Pep said: "Rose? She was pretty."

"Let's have some air," he insisted again.

"I'll fan you," said Lula, and took up the *Post.*

The women Pep married she dwelt on in bed. At other times, too. She had in her mind delicate Helen and beautiful Rose while she stood canning pears that came off the trees that bloomed on the Sandies like lace-adorned brides.

She was married herself in a preacher's front room, wearing navy blue and a hat on her head. Then they got in Pep's truck with a hound in the back and went up on the creek and settled in.

"I know about pain, Pep. I know how to stop it."

"It's not pain exactly."

"What is it then?"

He never could tell her. "Like a fog," he explained. "Like a bag on my head. Like I don't know my name."

"You bear down," Lula said. "In a minute, it's gone."

"Bear down on my head?"

"There's another way, too." She hated to tell him because it was hard, even for her (and she was all for it). "You pinpoint the pain. You search it out with a finger of thought."

"A finger of what?"

"You concentrate, Pep. You bear down with your mind on finding the pain at the place where it starts. *Is it here?* you ask. *Is this where it is?* Wherever your mind goes, the pain disappears."

"Lu," he said, "will you bring me the aspirins?"

For a living, he farmed, a handful of acres he cleared with a mule. When he had extra cash he bet on the cockfights. He made money with dogs, but they never had water that ran from a pipe, or electric power, till they moved into town.

Pep told Lula once that Emmit Steele had got rich, driving land men all over creation. "But he hasn't had fun. He hasn't had you."

"Sit up," Lula said, "and swallow these tablets." Pep gurgled them down. She thought of the day she stood at the window and vowed not to marry any man except this one. "Are you all right now?"

"Tell me a story. One of those myths."

"Scheherazade?"

"I don't care what it is."

Lula thought back to White Hall. "She married a man that was killing his wives. She had to keep telling tales till she finally saved him."

"The woman saved *him?*"

"From his murderous ways."

Pep gave a chuckle. "You tangle things up, Lu. You don't know the truth."

"Maybe I don't."

He dropped off to sleep. Then he woke up and said, "You never have known my true feelings for women."

"Hah," Lula said, "I ought to have known."

"I've been drawn to 'em somehow."

"I guess I know *that.*"

"Like a bee drawn to flowers."

"To Helens and Roses."

"Not to their bodies." He reached out and pinched her. "Except for yours. It's what makes them go, that was what pulled me."

"Eyes were what pulled you, and thick, curly hair."

"Ah, Lula, no. What I like is to watch 'em, to watch how they do. Women," he said, "are a curiosity."

Lula saw all at once that a shiver had seized him. "Are you getting too cool?" She stopped swinging the *Post*.

"No, go on."

"Go on with what?"

"Talk," he said. "It eases my head."

"Where was I?" she asked.

He couldn't quite answer. He thought he heard owls, not their cowboy cries, but the soft feathery sounds the mice probably heard and then went into trances.

"Pep?" Lula said.

He lay very still on the rim of his name and saw in the water what amounted to fish with silver-blue sides. A long time ago he had dreamed of such fish, dreamed he had caught them with only his hands.

"You're dozing," said Lula. "Pep, are you dozing?"

She watched for his breath, for the lift of his shirt or some kind of motion. "I can raise up the blind."

She pulled on the cord and the darkness rushed in with sounds from the Quik-Stop, quick feet on the pavement.

"That man let his dog in, let her up on the couch." She circled around. "That bow in her hair and her toenails painted. But I guess it's all right. She didn't have fleas." Prince Rudy had fleas. All of his ancestors leaped with fleas.

She sat down all at once and took hold of Pep's hand. "Can you see the cabin? The swing on the porch and the moon coming up with the dogs at our feet?" She started to cry then. "Remember the dancing?"

Finally she said, when the noise at the Quik-Stop had stopped altogether, "Pep, can you hear me?" She faltered a bit and then found her voice. "Up on the Sandies we never had night. We had a long spell of light." Through her eyelids she saw it: long golden light that lasted and lasted.

Annette Sanford is a former high school English teacher who supported her earlier attempts at writing short stories by authoring twenty-five category romances under five pseudonyms. For many years her stories have appeared in a variety of magazines and literary quarterlies across the country and have been anthologized in such collections as *Best American Short Stories, Common Bonds,* and *New Stories from the South.* Her own collection, *Lasting Attachments,* won the 1990 Fiction Prize from the Southwest Booksellers Association. She is the recipient of two Creative Writing Fellowships from the National Endowment for the Arts and lives with her husband in Ganado, Texas.

PHOTO CREDIT: CHARLES SCHORRE

I am always fascinated by the way pieces of real life (mine and other people's) combine with bits of chance information, memories, and gifts from the subconscious to make a story. In the making of "Helens and Roses," a visit with an elderly couple living in a trailer provided a starting point when the husband brought out a pair of old photographs of two beautiful girls he had once been married to—one of whom, he said, he had married "for fun." His wife of fifty years listened with a look of patient amusement as he spoke of her predecessors. In following days I mulled over that look, and a series of seemingly unrelated things began to congregate around it: I kept thinking of a phrase, "a long spell of light." A man with a poodle named Sherry put up blinds in our house. I remembered a black snake I saw years ago curled in a chair in a deserted house. I heard owls on my walks in the early morning. When I began to write, these things appeared in turn, as needed. Sherry became Scheherazade and gave me direction. Lula's uneasiness with night, Pep's spells, and the "long spell of light" took shape as my theme, reminding me again of the fundamental role of mystery and magic in writing fiction. You can't do without it.

Peter Taylor

THE WAITING ROOM

(from *The Southern Review*)

Anyone could tell at a glance the two men were brothers. They entered the hospital waiting room speaking to each other in whispers, each holding his hand up to his mouth in precisely the same way. The family resemblance was unmistakable— in their features, in their gestures, even in the way middle age was beginning to tug at their under-chins. Yet their dress was so different, one's was so roughly rural-looking, and the other's so very elegantly urban; their haircuts were so different, and even the trim of their fingernails, that they seemed in a sense hardly creatures of the same species. It was nine-thirty on a Saturday morning, and these two brothers were entering the seventh-floor waiting room of the Methodist Hospital. Outside the row of windows on the west side of the room was spread the city of Memphis. In the relatively near distance out there—some eight or nine blocks away—could be seen the brick and concrete towers of the Baptist Hospital and Campbell's Clinic and the U.T. Medical complex. Two miles or so beyond that were the half-dozen near-skyscrapers of downtown Memphis, stretched out along the Mississippi River. And beyond the river, as everyone in the waiting room that morning so well knew, lay Arkansas.

In the row of chairs by the windows sat a red-haired man and two women. The man, in plaid jacket and gray trousers, was seated between the women. On his left was his sister, also with red hair, not so coppery as the man's and showing more signs of gray. The diminutive brown-haired woman on his right was his wife. All three figures were twisted halfway round in their chairs and were gazing silently out the windows. Against the north wall of the room sat a solitary young man. He was dark-haired, dark-eyed, dark-suited; he even wore dark, pointed-toe shoes. But his socks were white, and he wore a white shirt, open at the collar. When the two whispering brothers entered the room, the threesome at the window turned around. The diminutive brown-haired woman straightened herself in her chair and asked formally: "How do you find Mrs. Schofield this morning? Did she rest well?"

"She's resting nicely," said the brother in khaki trousers—the brother, that is, in a home-knit-looking cardigan sweater and high, waterproof shoes.

The other brother smiled politely and shrugged. He clearly meant, by so doing, to qualify or even contradict his brother's favorable report on the patient in question. This patient, Mrs. Schofield, was the two brothers' aged mother, who at eighty-seven lay in a coma in a private room down the corridor. The old lady's heart had begun weakening two days before, and in the time since her two sons were called to her bedside her condition had continued to worsen almost hourly. Except that he knew his brother so well, it would have been difficult for the brother in the navy blue suit (and neatly knotted houndstooth tie) to understand how anyone could describe their mother as "resting nicely." Only his brother's country timidity, he reasoned, and his country way of wishing to answer all questions as briefly as possible, could account for the falsehood he uttered in reply. And when they had seated themselves on a vinyl couch against the south wall of the waiting room, the blue-suited brother, after carefully adjusting his tie and straightening his ribbed socks, returned the little, brown-haired woman's courtesy, asking, "How is your father-in-law this morning?"

Before the woman could answer, both her red-haired husband and her red-haired sister-in-law spoke for her, spoke almost in one voice and in identical words: "He is still a very sick man." Then the two of them smiled at the rather comical coincidences of their expressions, as also did the two brothers. Apparently the coincidence struck the solitary young man across the room as being somewhat more than merely comical. He gave a sudden, loud guffaw.

Everyone's attention was at once turned on him. But in the split second required for them to direct their eyes toward him, all sign of mirth vanished from his sallow face. He gazed at them solemnly for a moment with his dark eyes. Then, casting his eyes downward and lifting one rather delicately formed hand, he pretended to brush imaginary crumbs from his shirtfront. Since he was the only decidedly young person in the room, the others were able to view his indiscretion with some degree of tolerance. Perhaps they felt especially indulgent toward him since, on the preceding two days, he had always appeared there in the company of an old woman, an old, country woman whom he had permitted to describe herself to the group—without any protest on his part—as his "grandma" and whom he had suffered to pat him on the knee or hand each time she did so.

The other occupants rested their eyes on the young man for a moment, and then they looked at one another. Regardless of this interruption, the brown-haired, little woman who had first spoken now seemed determined to give her own account of her father-in-law's condition this morning. She sat on the edge of her chair and gave two little clicks to the latch of her handbag. "Dad Jones *is* still a very sick man," she said in an almost challenging tone to her red-haired husband and sister-in-law. And in a politer tone to the two brothers on her right, she added: "But he is doing as well as could be expected after surgery—and at his age. We are quite hopeful that he may improve as the day goes on." Her husband and her sister-in-law looked at her in open dismay. Her optimistic tone seemed almost to make them laugh.

And presently they both seemed to be trying to get the attention of the brother in the houndstooth tie, to try to convey to him with a look the true state of their father's health: that he most probably would not last the day. Yet they only looked; they said nothing.

All of these people had made one another's acquaintance during the previous two days. All—even the young man seated against the north wall, as well as his grandma who was this morning in the sick room with her husband—all were aware of a number of important factors in their lives that they had in common. Each of them, for instance, had originated either on a farm or in a small town in Arkansas; the family of each had been generally dispersed and were for the most part living in Memphis, if not still farther afield; and the old persons to whose bedsides all had now come were alike not only in being regarded as "terminal cases" but in having been brought to the Methodist Hospital after long sojourns in Memphis nursing homes. This body of information about the experience they shared had not been revealed or comprehended by them in any one dramatic moment or in any series of such moments, and no open acknowledgment of it had been made at all. But during the previous days the information had been gradually and quietly assimilated. A general knowledge had been repressed, most probably, because—until this morning—there had always been present some non-Arkansan, some hospital visitor whose patient was not critically ill, some visitor whose patient was not his eldest and nearest of kin—someone, that is, who could not have understood all they had in common.

Just when the two brothers and the threesome at the window had completed their exchanges—both spoken and silent—and the brothers had seated themselves across the room from the solitary young man, there appeared in the doorway an old country woman. Although she was wearing a different dress this morning and had combed her long, gray hair more carefully than yesterday, even having inserted additional combs where her hair was thickest above the temples, she was recognized by all as the young man's grandma. She was a remarkably tall old woman with narrow shoulders and wide hips, and she wore an ankle-length dress made of a bright cotton print—orange splashes mixed with greens and blues. One could not fail to notice the dress before noticing the face of the woman, its colors were so bright and cheerful and the cut of the material so generous. She glided into view there in the wide doorway like a boat with a calico sail. Instantly upon seeing her, the dark young man turned his face away to the window. It was as though he were embarrassed by the sight. But the old woman, whose eyes were as bright a blue as any of the several blues in her dress, seemed momentarily unaware of her grandson, or at least no more aware of him than of the others present. "Well, I declare," she said, still hesitating in the doorway and looking about the room. "Well, I declare. It's nobody but *us* this morning."

Her declaration was made in a rather high-pitched drawl, and her voice revealed more astonishment than joy over the company she found. Her blue eyes, in their deep sockets, darted glances about the room as though she were made uncomfortable by her discovery, or even were frightened by it. Remaining just inside the doorway, it was almost as if she had stumbled into the wrong waiting room and might yet turn back. While she stood there, her glance did not once settle upon the figure of her grandson. Finally she repeated in a more composed and cheerful tone: "Nobody but *us* this morning."

As if in response to this somehow, the brother in the sweater and khaki trousers came quickly to his feet. "Now, don't go getting up for me," the old woman protested. "There are plenty of chairs and to spare." But the red-haired man by the window stood up also. And after him the brother in the houndstooth tie—he smiling, and somewhat shamefaced. Surely their getting up this way in a public room, for a woman whose very name they barely knew, was something none of them would have done if there had been anyone besides themselves present.

And now the wife of the red-haired man was about to inquire about the old woman's husband. She had parted her lips to speak when the old woman herself interrupted. "I do declare," she said, looking at the men who were still on their feet, "I never saw so many gentlemen in one room."

At this, her grandson came also to his feet. As he did so he continued to gaze toward the window without having once looked at the old woman in the doorway. It was as if he could not bear to look at her, or perhaps did not dare to. Yet it was his rising that the old woman seemed to find altogether overwhelming. The moment he was on his feet, she rushed to his side and threw her great frame down in a chair beside him. "Now!" she said. "Now you all sit down. Standing up that way you make me feel a thousand and one years old." She sounded positively silly, almost flirtatious. "I may have one foot in the grave," she went on, "but I still don't want everybody putting themselves out for me."

When the men had sat down again, this old country woman bent forward in her chair and fixed her gaze on the view outside the window, the view from which her grandson had still not taken his eyes. "I declare it's a beautiful day out there, despite everything," she said. "And hasn't this Memphis grown into a fine city. It don't seem like the same place it used to be. Not the town I came to fifteen years ago when my own mamma was sick and I had brought her over here to Methodist. Nothing looks the same. It's a lot prettier place now, though. Tall skyscrapers over yonder, so flat and white, like fence posts coming up so straight out of the green trees. Like so many tombstones, they are—like whitewashed tombstones in some nice, well-kept cemetery."

The old woman's burst of loquacity seemed to be amazing to everybody present. Even her grandson stole a glance at her. Yesterday and the day before—at moments when self-introductions were being made—she had rather grudgingly explained to the other visitors who she was, who her grandson was, and who their patient was, but for the most part she had remained grim-faced and silent—no less so than her grandson, himself. And now they all suddenly recognized in her a different type, recognized the garrulous old country woman whom you could not afford to encourage lest she bend your ear all day.

Except for the stolen glance from her grandson, there was no response whatsoever to her lyrical outburst about Memphis. After a moment or two of silence, during which she and the young man beside her continued to gaze out the window, she spoke again. "We had a right bad time with Mr. Glover last night," she said, her eyes still on the skyline. "He took a notion he *would* leave the hospital!"

The brother in the cardigan sweater exclaimed, "You don't say!"

The tiny, brown-haired woman sat forward in her chair, and her eyes widened noticeably.

The others looked at her with obvious interest. Who "Mr. Glover" was there could be no doubt. Even if they had not known the woman's own name was Glover, her listeners could have told from her old-fashioned, wifely tone that it was her husband she referred to. "I was nodding in my chair beside his bed," she went on, "when all of a sudden the poor patient in the *other* bed commenced shouting, 'He's out of his head. You better watch him!' Or maybe he said, 'He's out of his bed.' That's what woke me. And *there* was Mr. Glover leaning against the bed, so weak he couldn't hardly stand, peeling off his nightshirt. I hauled myself up out of my chair and asked him, 'And where do you think you're going, Mr. Glover—naked as a bluejay?' 'I want my clothes,' he said, like some bad little old boy." The old woman rolled her eyes around the room almost kittenishly. She put her hand to her mouth and seemed to laugh into it.

The young man turned and faced the old woman. "And how come you didn't send after me," he asked, "if he was making trouble?"

"Oh, you've done your share of sitting with him," she answered solemnly, and then she addressed the room: "He sat with his granddaddy many an hour of the night when he was a little fellow coming along."

"Only to keep you from having to, I did," the young man growled, turning back toward the window.

"Many's the night he'd rub his granddaddy's legs and his back and hear his complaints about how he hurt. You see, he stayed home with us till he was near twenty, and then, of course, he went off to New York City where he'd always said he was going to go when he got to be grown." She had told all of this to the room only yesterday, but it had been something dragged out of her then. "You see, we raised the boy ourselves," she continued with enthusiasm. "His daddy left his mamma and cleared out before the little fellow was a year old, and his mamma—she was mine and Mr. Glover's only child—died on us, passed away not two years after her husband left. The boy stayed with us till he was near twenty, and after he left, it wasn't long till Mr. Glover became more than I could handle. He was in such pain we didn't reckon he'd last long, so we put him over here in Mrs. Hooker's nursing home, all against his will, poor fellow."

The young man crossed his legs, and recrossed them. "You mean *I* did," he growled. And then he addressed the room: "The old guy was killing her, what with her having to wait on him hand and foot around the clock. He would have done her in, in no time. Besides which, he saw his end was coming on and, clear as anything, he wanted to take her with him was what he wanted. It was *me* that put him in the nursing home."

"Why, yes, indeed," agreed the old woman. "This here boy has sent back the money for it every month that comes. And to begin with he came back to Memphis from New York City and rented a car and came over and carried Mr. Glover over here to Mrs. Hooker's nursing home."

The young man crossed his legs again, his white socks flashing. "Against his will," he said with emphasis. "He hasn't ever forgave me for it, either. Against *her* will, too. It's a nice, clean place, though, where we put him, and they know how to look after him. He's been there four years, and *she's* still alive because of it."

"Which home is that you've had him in?" asked the red-haired man. "Did you say 'Hook's'?"

"No, Hooker's," supplied the blue-suited brother, who, like the others, had been following the young man's words with interest. "It's one of the better small, private homes here in Memphis." He was a practical businessman and spoke with authority, as someone who had made his way in the Memphis world. Since they were touching on a subject he had made a study of for the benefit of his mother, he felt his information ought to be shared and perhaps made some use of. "I believe they have an excellent staff—mostly colored—and that the food is mighty good. Their rates are just above average."

"Well, that's one I don't know about," said the red-haired man. It was a subject on which he considered himself also somewhat of an expert. "We've learned a good deal about them through trial and error," he said, smiling meaningfully at his sister. "And we've come to the conclusion that they're all about the same."

"Yes," said his sister. "Give a little here, take a little there, they're all about the same. We should know." She, too, felt that here was a subject she could speak on with some authority and therefore with some pleasure. "We've had Father in five places, all told. Each one was a little more expensive than the one before, and, as for Dad, he's liked each one we've put him in a little bit less than the one before. But they're all about the same."

"Relatively speaking, yes," said the blue-suited brother. He gave a depreciative laugh. "Anyway, however good they are, the old folks don't seem to like them. It's like sending a child to his first day of school. He doesn't like it and doesn't know it's for his own good."

The old woman shifted in her chair and cleared her throat. Then she ventured: "Well, some places, they tell me, are pretty bad."

"Ah, listen to her," said the young man, his eyes still on the window.

"Oh, yes, some of them *are* bad," said the little wife by the window. "They treat the patients—the residents, that is—like animals, as Dad Jones used to say of one place, like animals in a zoo. And I heard of another place where they regularly get the patients' medicine mixed up."

Her husband came in quickly: "That's only hearsay. And, furthermore, Dad was ever one of the worst to complain. *We* knew that as children. Even Mamma used to say so. You've just known him as an old man." He looked at his sister out of the corner of his eye, and they smiled at each other rather sadly, shaking their heads. His wife was overly indulgent, they seemed to say.

But his wife, diminutive and bright-eyed, cocked her head to one side, and as she spoke, it was hard to tell if she was addressing her husband and sister-in-law or the whole room. "I don't care," she began, "but if we had kept him at home out at Marianna, he would have been happier, he wouldn't have been so bored. Why, his mind—his memory—began to slip as soon as he left our house."

Her husband looked at her sympathetically and said, "My father stayed with *us,* and she was working herself to the bone for *my* father. She was ruining her health. People ought not to do that, not even for their *own* kin."

"We could have—," his wife began again.

But the old woman interrupted. "I don't mean to say that Mrs. Hooker's home is one of these bad ones." She was clearly afraid she had offended her grandson, and wished to placate him. "Not at all. They're nice folks there, and we were lucky to have gotten Mr. Glover in, and mighty lucky, I say, to have the money to keep him there. It's only because the boy here worked so hard in New York City and sent the money back. But, still, I do hear some of the places are pretty bad."

"They're all fairly well regulated nowadays," said the blue-suited brother reassuringly. "The quality of the meals may differ, and the beds, I suppose. I made a thorough investigation of them before we decided on one for Mother."

The other brother, in his cardigan and waterproof shoes and khaki trousers, had sat with his eyes lowered during most of this talk. Even now he kept his eyes lowered to his hands, and he spoke in a gentle and rather cultivated voice that contrasted with his rough clothing. "There's only this," he said. "There's only this: there are things that cannot be foreseen about these arrangements we make." He lifted his eyes and let his gaze move from face to face around the room. All his timidity seemed gone suddenly. "We had an uncle, our mother's brother—an old bachelor like me, he was, who farmed Mother's home place near Jonesboro after our grandfather over there died. When he, our uncle, got too old to farm and to look after himself he went into a— a church-run rest home over near Pine Bluff. What they have to do in those church-run places, you know, is sign over all their property and savings to the church home, which agrees to care for them for the rest of their lives and even give them pocket money. Well, they put him in a nice private room and all that. It was fine for the first six months or so. But he came down with a chest cold. They transferred him to an infirmary, put him in an open ward. When he improved, he found he had to be put on a waiting list in order to get his private room back. He was a timid, country fellow and hated being in the ward with all the talkative retired preachers who were there. He got worse again, and he died before he could ever get his private room back."

There was a general head shaking around the room and a chorus of *ohs*. But the blue-suited brother, who was clearly distressed by being reminded of this family story, said, "They treated the old fellow badly, no doubt about that. But there are nearly always two sides to such a story. Uncle Ned never made a good trade in his life. Yet he was very independent; he didn't consult any of the family about his agreement with that place. And Lord knows it wasn't much he had to sign over to the church. They didn't make any fortune off him, that's certain."

"Your Uncle Ned's story," said the red-haired man spiritedly, as though he were in an argument and had thought of a good point, "is just the opposite of the way the story usually goes. Your uncle went into the home of his own volition and then regretted it. My father, for instance, didn't want to go, but it became a way of life with him. Much as he has complained and moved from one place to another, he has almost never talked about coming back to us or to my sister here. He's made friends in each place and he keeps up with which ones are still around and which have passed on."

"Well, as for our mother in there," said the blue-suited brother, gesturing toward a door down the corridor, "she has made some awfully good friends and had some awfully gay times since she settled at Mount Holly, which is where she had been for three years until now. When my wife and I went by to see her on her last birthday, they were having a big birthday party for her. Why, those old ladies and old gentlemen at Mount Holly had loaded her with presents, and they were all having the time of their lives. And it isn't just the social life Mother has liked at Mount Holly. There are charity patients—even there at Mount Holly. Mother likes giving them money and clothes. And there are even colored patients, and Mother has found it interesting working out relationships with them. In fact, it is a regular microcosm of life there—not at all a feeling of isolation. I don't believe Mother has had an unhappy day since she settled at Mount Holly."

"You mean, don't you," said the brother in khaki, "since *we* settled her there."

"Yes, we had a time making her decide to go," agreed his brother in blue. "They couldn't keep her on the farm. Someone would have to be forever preparing special meals for her and driving her in town to the doctor. And here in Memphis—well, my teenage children would have driven her out of her head. And my wife and I go out—"

"That night," his brother interrupted, "when we went to her on the porch and told her we had made the arrangements at

Mount Holly, she took her cane and got up and walked without help down into the yard. She wouldn't let us help her or go with her. She went by herself. And we had a hard time finding her, later. But when we did, she laughed at us and asked if we thought she was going to do harm to herself. She kept up her teasing ways with us and her good sense of humor through it all. I still think sometimes she might have got along all right there at the farm with me."

His brother threw back his head and laughed. "Without another woman on the farm? Why, you'd have had to get married, Harry, so you'd have a wife to look after her." Now his laughter was hearty. "You know you wouldn't have liked that, Harry," he said.

The little, brown-haired wife said quite earnestly, "Yes, a woman on the place might really have made it so you could."

The bachelor brother smiled and shrugged. And the married brother said, "Anyway, she gave us quite a scare that night and, believe you me, she enjoyed it. She's always been a great tease."

"But that's nothing," said the red-haired man. "That's nothing at all to what Dad put us through. You wouldn't have thought a man with his diabetic neuritis, a serious heart ailment, and nearly blind and deaf could put us through what he did. At home, he kept firing the nurses we got him, as if to prove he didn't need looking after. And he swore that the nurses beat him whenever all the rest of us were out of the house. If the nurses beat him in his own house, he meant for us to understand, what would they do to him at a nursing home? And then finally he proposed marriage to a neighbor woman who came in to see him, promising to leave her all his property but forgetting she already had one invalid husband to take care of."

There was a general tittering in the room. Then the red-haired sister-in-law asked, "But what is one to do with old people?" It was quite as though this woman and the others present didn't understand that the old woman sitting against the north wall was really an old person who might soon be facing the fate of those they were discussing. But even the old woman herself didn't seem to realize it. With the others, she nodded sympathetically to the rhetorical question. "What is one to do?" the red-haired woman repeated. "We all wish they didn't have to end their days in those places. But I live in an apartment two blocks from here, with my husband and our two children. My husband and I both work downtown, and we're not young anymore. Yes, you know, the trouble is this: the old people's young people are not really young people any longer. And in every case there are the problems of the home and children. Life has to go on even where there are old people and sick people. The problems become just too much. It's not like the old days on an Arkansas farm where there was plenty of time and plenty of room, and plenty of hands, too, for taking care of the old folks."

"Let me tell you," the dark young man joined in abruptly, turning his eyes from the window to the room. "Yes, just let me tell you. The day when I came back home in the car I had rented in Memphis, I found my grandma here looking like a skeleton. She was worked to the bone and about fit for burying, herself. I ran up the stairs to my granddaddy's room and told him to get out of that bed, told him I knew a doctor in Memphis could cure him and get rid of all that pain in his legs and back, and told him I had the money to pay for it, which part was true. I don't think I'd ever told him a lie before in my life. And no matter how many lickings he had give me, I hadn't ever hated him before either, because in his way he was good to me when I was coming along without any dad of my own—as good to me in his way as *she* was. I hadn't ever hated him until I saw what skin and bones he had wore her down to. But I knew I had to hate him, that day, and lie to him till I got him over here to Mrs. Hooker's home, where I had already paid a hundred dollars down for him. He and I left Grandma crying in the hall there at home and I lied to him all the way over to Memphis and even after he was in his room at Mrs. Hooker's. Oh, he found out in a few days that the doctor who came to see him was nothing special and that we weren't going to let him go home again. But it was too late then. He hasn't ever forgave me, either. He hasn't ever forgave me. Every time my grandmother would go to see him there at Mrs. Hooker's, he would spend half the visit railing against me. But I had to do it, and I'm not a bit sorry. You can't let them take the living with them!"

"No," said the blue-suited brother.

"No, you can't," agreed the red-haired man. And his sister shook her head in agreement.

"But it's hard," said the little wife.

"I've found it hard," said the brother in the sweater, "to think of her ever here in Memphis when she might have been at home where she wanted to be."

The old woman shifted her weight in her chair. Then she cleared her throat and spoke openly to the whole company: "The worst part of it, though, you haven't come near touching on. And like as not, you haven't known it yet. When Mr. Glover climbed out of bed last night, and I asked, 'Where do you think you're going, naked as a bluejay?' he answered me: 'Get me my clothes, woman. I'm leaving out of here. It's going home, I am.' 'All right,' I say to him, 'but not tonight. It's some fifty miles to Mark Tree. We'll have to wait till sunup.' I could see he was half out of his head and only meant to humor him. But he said, 'It ain't your home I want to go to, woman. I want to go back to Mrs. Hooker's home. That's where the only friends I have are. That's where they know how to give me some ease.' "

Suddenly the old woman, looking out across the room to the doorway, began to shed silent tears. The young man looked up as if he had never before in his life seen her cry and so didn't know what to do. And it was just then that he and the others saw the nurse who had appeared in the doorway. Silently, the plump little nurse crossed the tile floor and stood before the old woman. "He's gone," the nurse said in a voice full of gentleness.

"What do y' mean?" asked the young man, coming to his feet.

"All right, ma'am," said the old woman to the nurse. Then she said, "Sit down, son." The nurse glanced at the young man, then turned and left the room without looking at anyone else.

"Does she mean—he's dead?" asked the young man, sitting down beside the old woman.

"No, son, he died somewhile earlier," she answered gently. "The nurse means they've taken his remains out and to the undertaker's."

"How come you didn't say so? How come you sat here talking?"

Now it was only the old woman who stared out the window. She raised her two hands to her head, lifted the combs that were just above her temples, and replaced them more firmly in her thick hair. "You wouldn't have liked being in there," she explained. "Now, you know you wouldn't," she said, as if remonstrating with a child. "Not seeing him the way he was at the last. And I didn't want you to." As she rose from her chair, her eyes seemed dry again. And as she turned from the window to leave the room, all the men stirred in their chairs. She motioned to them to remain seated. But her grandson came up beside her and placed his arm about her waist and walked beside her through the doorway. The other occupants of the room glanced at one another briefly, and then everyone watched the grandmother and grandson pass down the corridor toward the elevator, the old woman seeming to lean more of her weight on the young man with every step. Just as the doors slid closed, those in the waiting room saw the young man withdraw his arm from his grandmother's waist, turn away from her in a sudden, spasmodic motion, and quickly throw both his hands up to his face. Then they saw the old woman turn her back to the young man and hide her own face in her hands.

The people left in the waiting room looked at one another in silence. When the elevator doors were closed, not a word was spoken among them, not between brother and sister, husband and wife, or brother and brother. What could their silence mean? Perhaps until a moment before the elevator doors closed they had imagined that the death of the old man would draw his old wife and his grandson closer together, would draw them into closer understanding of each other, that for all their differences they would be of comfort to each other now. As they sat gazing down the corridor toward the closed elevator doors, they could only have been reflecting on how near the end was for their own old ones. And for them was there any other prospect than that view down the corridor and the image of the pair on the elevator, turning their backs to each other, burying their faces in their hands, each giving way to his own sobs and shedding his own tears for what he had not been able to do and all he had had to do?

Peter Taylor was born at Trenton, Tennessee, in 1917. After attending Kenyon College and Vanderbilt University he was in the army for five years and wrote most of his first book of stories there. In later years he taught at such colleges and universities as Kenyon, Harvard, The University of North Carolina at Greensboro, University of Virginia, and others. In 1987 he received the Pulitzer Prize for his novel *A Summons to Memphis*. A new collection of his stories, *The Oracle at Stoneleigh Court and Other Stories,* was published in 1993. He is married to the poet Eleanor Ross Taylor. They have two children and one grandchild.

PHOTO CREDIT: J. WILLIAM BROADWAY

M*r. Taylor declined to comment on his story. He said, laughing, "I have trouble telling the truth about my stories."*

Dennis Loy Johnson

RESCUING ED

(from *New England Review*)

U sually, the ride up to my friend Ed's place is a humdinger. You've got to drive slowly on those country roads. The trees get thicker and nearer on each side of you, and the road somewhere loses the extra lane, and then even the shoulders, and it starts to weave and to wind. If you go at the end of the day, just before dusk, it's like the air has thinned out; things look clearer and sharper. Eventually, you're in the hills, curving and twisting and leaning through the switchbacks. Then you start passing through the towns. They're small, usually just a couple of rival Baptist churches (one clapboard and one brick), a gas station–convenience store, and a few houses with big porches setting right up on the road; places with names like Pocahontas, and Romance, and Morning Light. I'm not making this up.

Then you go around a bend, there's a sign that says SCENIC VIEW, and the earth on one side of the road drops off and you're looking out into a wide valley, with a farmhouse and some acres squared off and plowed. Some animals in a pasture. It's really something. Makes me feel good about where I live, which is the state of Arkansas. It strikes me as so nice that it's almost unreal. You know it doesn't look so good to the people down there that own it all, but it sure looks fine from the mountaintop. It's like something in a dream, that's the kind of feeling it gives you.

Unless, of course, you're fighting with your wife, and she happens to be in the front seat next to you.

"If you drive any slower, we'll go backward in time," Marilyn says. She says this to the window.

"Well, that might just solve everybody's problems," I say.

"No sir," she says, "we'd all just be shorter and we'd have even less money than we got now." She shakes her head. "Boy, imagine that."

I just keep driving. I don't want to aggravate this situation. Marilyn is none too happy about having to go up to Ed's in the first place. At the moment, we've got a couple of three fights going. Money, her family, the amount of time I spend working with Ed on our carpentry business. The usual for most of us, I suppose, although it has seemed a little worse than usual to me lately. Still, what I think we're really doing when we're fighting about Ed is we're fighting about something else. But I figure we aren't going to do Ed any good if we're going at it when we arrive, whatever the hell it is. See, Ed's wife left him. We're supposed to be going to comfort him.

Which is another reason I'm driving slow. This is not something I'm anxious to get at. As a matter of fact, it's something Marilyn and me have grown damned tired of having to deal with. It's all been going on for quite a while. Before they were married, Ed and Cassandra (her real name, by the way) fussed like cats and dogs for a full year, always breaking up and getting back together again. It got so we couldn't keep track of it anymore. We never knew whether it was okay to call just the one to invite them both to dinner, or if it was better to call them both individually, or whether one was even going to come if the other was there, and so on and so forth. Then, as a way to make up from one of these fights, they decided to move to the country and get married. "I give it six months," said Marilyn. She was right on the money. When Ed telephoned this morning to say why he'd missed work, it was nearly six months to the day. I swear, there's times I think I ought to bring ole Marilyn out to the racetrack.

Now, though, she's got her legs curled up under her on the seat, and her arms are crossed, and she's heaving such powerful sighs at the windshield it's like she's trying to bust it.

So for once the ride is not as nice as it usually is, and it's not late enough in the afternoon yet for that special light, and I guess I get to driving slower and slower, because eventually Marilyn says, "The G forces are pushing the skin right off of my face."

I try to ignore this, but a little farther on she says, "The high speeds are going to give me a nosebleed."

I'm near to biting my tongue off when she says, "No tickets for speeding, just flying low."

"Goddammit," I say. There are times when all I can think of is to curse. It's a bad habit left over from the old days. Then Marilyn stops talking to me altogether.

What happens is, it becomes a flat-out God-Awful Long Drive Up From North Little Rock. By the time we get to the dirt road leading to Ed's place—it's a great house, perched on a hillside, we built it ourselves, just the two of us—by that time, Marilyn and me haven't said two words since Dahlia.

I pull into the dirt road and let the clutch out. "Look, baby . . ." I think back on how pitiful and weird Big Ed sounded on the telephone. "How could I say no?"

"You move your lips like this," Marilyn says, puckering up around a silent "no." She goes at it like a fish for a little while.

There's nothing for it but to slip the clutch back in and head on up to Ed's place at the end of that long dirt road.

Marilyn gets quiet again. She's looking out the window. Then she says, "See Big Ed run his hand through his hair. See him stare off and wag his mighty head. See the poor critter look at you with a pleading stare and mutter, 'What do I do?'"

"All right," I say as we pull up. "All right."

Marilyn can't let it go, though. She says, "And it's always great to experience Cassandra's paintings, isn't it? I think it's what you'd have to call a joy. Yes, a joy." Cassandra's a painter. She says painting is what brought her to Arkansas, believe it or not.

"A boy is what brought Cassandra to Arkansas," is what Marilyn claims.

Anyway, Ed throws open the door as we get out of the mighty land shark. He's been waiting for us, it's a real appearance. Ed is a big, barrel-chested fellow, muscular, with a tight, curly black beard. He fills up the doorway. He looks feverish, like he's been up all night. Marilyn stays a step behind me as we walk up to the bottom of the front porch. I stop and hem and haw for a minute, then look up and settle on giving Ed a firm look of solidarity.

"Raymond," he says. "Marilyn." He's got his hands shoved in the pockets of his Levi's, he's nodding at us, at the horizon, at the door sill. "Damn glad y'all could come. I appreciate it." He looks at us with red-rimmed eyes, runs a hand through his hair, wags his head, then turns back into the house. I look down at the ground and nod, knowing Marilyn's looking at me. I give her this one. I can tell by the sound of her breathing, though, that she's still mad at me, as we step up into the house behind Ed, who's having marriage problems.

When we follow him down the hall to the kitchen I think even Marilyn realizes something's up this time. A bunch of Cassandra's big paintings are stacked and leaning face against the walls. It's like someone has cleaned out a storeroom or some such. I wonder if he put them like this, or if she did. It's kind of dramatic, like somebody's saying, "I'm leaving you," or somebody else is saying, "Get out." Either way, I'm glad they're facing the wall, because Marilyn's right on this account, too: they are weird, disturbing things to look at, full of big red hearts with knives stuck in them and burning crosses and naked people with wild hair and expressions of grief. In some of them, there's naked people with expressions of grief running from dogs.

Cassandra is from New York City.

Marilyn and I slow up, taking in the paintings facing the wall like it was some kind of negative art show.

When we get to the kitchen it's like there's another show. The place is full of empty beer bottles. They're displayed on the table and along the counters and even on the windowsills.

"Boy," Marilyn says. "I think I'm gonna go powder my little nose now."

She leaves and Ed starts fooling with a small gym bag on a chair pulled out from the table. He zips it up and says, "All right, I'm all set." He seems sober. Maybe the drinking was last night.

I figure this is true when I notice a couple of wine bottles sitting with the brown beer bottles on the table. That would be Cassandra. She only drinks red wine. All that's missing are the candles. Cassandra was big on candles. Whenever you visit there's usually only candles going so everybody's face is lit from below, like in a horror movie.

"All set for what, Ed?"

"To go find her. We got to go find her." He's standing there with this gym bag.

"You know where she's at?" I ask.

"No," he says. "I got some ideas."

"Maybe she went to her mother's." I say this because Marilyn's gone to her mother's a couple of times lately, just for an overnight thing.

"I hope not," says Ed. "Her mother's dead."

Marilyn walks back into the room, one hand tossing back her hair so hard I wait for it to come flying off her scalp. She stands with her hands on her hips. Marilyn's only five-six, but she looks six feet tall, the way she carries herself.

"Who's dead?" she asks.

"Cassandra's mother," I tell her.

"Still?" says Marilyn.

"Yeah," Ed says. He's serious.

"Damn," says Marilyn.

"It's okay, she's okay on that now," Ed says. "Let's go."

"Ed wants to go look for her," I tell Marilyn.

"Her mother?" Marilyn says. "Piece of cake."

I give her a dirty look. It's like she makes me forget about Ed for a moment, but then he suddenly collapses into one of the chairs at the table. "Oh man," he says. He puts his head down. "She's never done this before."

In back of Ed, I notice one of Cassandra's paintings still on the wall of the kitchen. It's of a bunch of sheep jumping over a stone wall, at night, under a starry sky, like in a dream. Only, on the other side of the stone wall is a cliff. She has gone to great trouble to detail the smashed and bloody sheep bodies at the bottom of the cliff. I am afraid Ed might turn around and see this and be reminded of her in a powerful way, and cry out. This strikes me as a painting that can make you cry out, anyway.

Marilyn and me stand there for a minute. She looks at me like I'm supposed to do something. I look at her like what'd you say that for? When nothing comes to me she purses her lips like she's going to start doing the fish again. Her lips are parted just enough for me to see her teeth. She's got pretty teeth. She goes over to Ed and rubs a hand across his shoulders.

"Ed," she says, "you've been through this before, you know it'll work out." I can hear her just barely keeping that tone of frustration out of her voice, just barely.

"Oh man," he says again. "She never left before."

"Well, maybe not physically," Marilyn says, rubbing away at him.

"Right," I say, not exactly knowing what I'm agreeing with.

Marilyn raises her eyebrows. She's looking at me, but she's talking to Ed. "Come on now," she says. "Let's go find your loved one."

Ed hoists himself up, and Marilyn stands aside so he can go first, like he's leading and she's just along for the ride.

We go down the hall, past the stacks of paintings, to the front door. I look off through the living room as I hold the door open and wait for Ed with his gym bag and Marilyn with her attitude to troop out in front of me. The sun has just set and it's like the light has gone out of the house, but the dark hasn't come yet. The white walls in the living room look fuzzy, and you can see where

the paintings are missing. There are big extra white glowing rectangles of wall all over the room. The white in those rectangles
somehow looks more in focus than the rest of the room. It's
spooky, to tell you the truth. It's like there's an echo, like there's
some kind of echo of light.

Something in Ed's little gym bag clinks, and I ask him what's
in there, but he won't say.

We take two cars because Ed wants to have room for Cassandra
if we find her. So he gets in his truck.

"Sure, you can just toss her in back," Marilyn says, slapping a
hand on the side of the truck so it echoes in the bed.

"No, I'll have her up here with me," Ed says, looking out the
window at her, puzzled. "She'll be in the cab." Ed is looking at
her hard, like he's missed something.

"Good idea," says Marilyn. "She'll like that."

We get back in the Bonneville. It's a 1972 model, longest car
ever made. You could fit a couple of bodies in the trunk, as
Marilyn likes to say.

Ed pulls out and we follow him down the hill. He's driving slow.

"You boys sure have lost some pep," Marilyn says. "Some of
that old zing."

"Listen," I say. "This is some serious business. You ever seen
him like this? This bad? I mean, man. We've got to help him."

She folds her arms. "All right. I'm sorry. But, Bubba"—she
hasn't called me Bubba in a while now, it's a good sign—"these
things have to end sometimes. These problems that go on and
on and on—sometimes you just got to make up your mind and
change things. You can't expect people to be rescuing you all
the time."

"What do you mean?" I say. "He's looking for her, isn't he?
He's trying to fix things."

"No, we're looking for her."

"Same difference."

"No," says Marilyn, "different difference."

We pass the scenic view sign, but it's getting too dark to see anything much. Summer's dying, it's getting dark quicker these days. I'm following Ed's taillights.

We switch roads and go down the hill to Birdseye. It's a little village on the river where they're trying to develop a retirement community. We pass a giant condo complex, a place that's all wood shingles and glass, with landscaping and lots of sidewalks crisscrossing this way and that. Then we go over an old trestle bridge and we're in Birdseye. Besides old-timers, the town is also trying to attract tourists and hunters and fishermen. There are bait shops and restaurants mixed in with arts and crafts shops, where they sell quilts and beat-up furniture that they've refinished and renamed antiques. We go by Myrna's Country Collectibles. Myrna used to handle some of Cassandra's artwork, but she quit because Cassandra's stuff didn't sell real well around these parts. Little old ladies looking for quilts would waddle into her shop and run out screaming, I suspect.

Ed turns the corner onto a side street and pulls up in front of the Deer Head Tavern.

"She for sure isn't in there," Marilyn says, looking out at the neon blinking deer head. A bunch of moths are whacking up into it. There are lots of little dead spots in the neon.

"Who knows?" I say. "Come on."

Inside the Deer Head it's dark. The walls are covered with cheap paneling, and dead animal heads hang all over the place, not just deer but also a boar's head, a steer, an entire stuffed coon. There are bass mounted on plaques.

"Hmm," Marilyn says. "Lovely."

When my eyes get accustomed to the dim light I see Ed is standing up on tiptoes trying to look into all the shadowy booths.

Marilyn goes over to the jukebox and I go to the bar and get a round of longnecks. I bring them back to a table sitting in the middle of the floor. It's like an old kitchen table, Formica-topped with a split in it for a leaf.

Ed comes over and stands next to the table. He stands there holding his gym bag. "She's not here," he says.

"Sit down and relax for a minute," I say. "Let's just collect our thoughts."

Hank Williams, Jr., comes out of the jukebox. "Good Friends, Good Whiskey, and Good Loving." Marilyn comes back to the table. "Is this man an idiot or what?" she says, thumbing back at the jukebox. "It was either this or Bing Crosby singing 'How Are Things in Gloccamora?' Come on, Ed." She takes the gym bag from him and sets it on the table, then lifts one of his hands and puts it on her waist and raises his other one into dance position.

Ed pulls away a bit but she yanks him back hard. "Don't make me go back and put on Der Bingle," she tells him.

So Marilyn shuffles Ed around the floor but he's all the time looking around, keeping an eye out for Cassandra.

I sip from my beer and watch them. Marilyn's a good dancer, we used to go out all the time. She taught me the two-step, which is a pretty good dance. Ed's not having any of it, though. After a minute Marilyn gives up on him and they come back to the table.

"He wants to go next door," Marilyn says.

"What's next door?" I ask.

"The Elbow Room." She says it slowly, like it's another language she's learned and she's showing it off.

"Ed," I say, "you know she for damn sure ain't in the Elbow Room." I've been in the Elbow Room. It's even worse than this place. The locals go there to get away from the out-of-towners. Probably they go there to get away from everything. It's the kind of place where the same sad sacks sit all day, melting away on their bar stools.

"No," says Ed. "She likes to go to these places sometimes. She says it gives her ideas. For her pictures."

"Well there's a surprise," says Marilyn. "Cassandra is a woman of unsuspected depth."

"I just got these beers," I say.

"Just a quick look," says Ed. "I got to find her."

"You boys run and play," says Marilyn. "I will guard these beers with my life."

So Ed and I go next door to the Elbow Room.

It's still early in the evening, but you'd think it was near to closing time in there. There's a guy curled up with his head in his arms on the bar. I notice another guy, lighting the filter end of his cigarette. While Ed stands looking around I go up and order a beer from the fat woman behind the bar. She's wearing a T-shirt that says "Bennie's Restaurant & Bait Shack: Yesterday's Bait is Tomorrow's Plate." It's pulled tight over her bosoms, which are as big as my head, and so's her belly. Beer's cheap here.

The place is small but Ed keeps looking around even though it's clear right off that Cassandra's not around. I watch the woman behind the bar go over to a table where a man who's got a truck cap on backward wants another beer. It's clear he's already had too many, he's practically drooling as he works at something stuck to the table top. It's a label he's peeled off one of the collection of empty bottles in front of him. He thinks it's a dollar and he's trying to give it to the woman. Ed comes up and stands next to me and we watch the guy for a minute.

"Poor son of a bitch," says Ed. Then he says, "Come on."

"Let me at least finish a beer," I say, but it's not going down any easier than the guy in the truck cap.

"I can't quit," Ed says.

"I know that," I say, and I stand up off the bar stool and slap a hand on his shoulder. "I know that." I leave the beer.

Ed wants to try a place at the end of the street, down by the river. There's a big club there with strings of lights stretching from the building to a corrugated aluminum awning built over the docks. There's a big open patio with white iron tables. The place is crawling with young couples holding on to each other. They're all in new-looking summer clothes. People up from Little Rock, I guess. The kind of people the regulars in the Elbow Room are trying not to think about. They're good-looking, they have sharp haircuts and big smiles. Clothes that look expensive even though they don't cover much. Bright tank tops, wild jams, and clean white sneakers that look like they'd glow in the dark. Clothes with no meaning except some idea of fun. Cassandra would stick out a mile here, I think, in her black jeans and black T-shirts.

Ed decides we've got to go in so he can survey the bar. When he doesn't find her there, he turns and sets his chin and wades out onto the dance floor. I go to the bar, squeezing into a place between two huge nests of teased blond hair, and watch him. The place is thumping with music and kids are trying to dance. They're bumping into Ed, but they don't seem to notice him. He's just some old guy taking in the sights—it's a place that makes you feel that way, old at thirty-two. I can't hear any melody, just the thumping. Ed comes to a stop and I see him sagging a little, he's standing in the middle of the dancers like he's stunned. I have to set down another beer that's mostly full and wade in and drag him away. We go back outside and end up in a shadowy spot by the water.

"We're running out of bars," I say, "and I would like to see a beer through to completion."

He nods, thinking hard.

"Let's go back to the Deer Head," I say. "If she's in town she'll end up there." He just nods and follows me like he was a little kid.

When we get there Marilyn is still at the table but two guys in polo shirts and baseball caps are sitting with her. They're drinking our beers.

"That's my beer," I say to one of them.

The guy gives me a big smile and holds up the beer to look at it.

"Your name Bud?" he asks.

"That's Bubba," Marilyn says. She's sitting back in her chair, legs crossed, smoking. She looks pretty in a way that makes me nervous. There's an empty bottle in front of her, she's sipping from a full one. They must have bought her a beer.

"Bub?" says the guy. He looks at his label again. "Must be a misprint."

The other guy snorts.

Ed and I just stand there and look at them. Then Ed says to Marilyn, "No luck."

The two guys look at each other and shrug. The one who'd been drinking my beer puts it down and sticks his hands out, palms flat like he's keeping something away. "Hey," he says. "No trouble." Both of them get up smiling and go and sit at the bar.

"I can't find her," Ed says.

I sit down and look at the backs of the two guys at the bar.

The song on the jukebox is "I'd Rather Have a Bottle in Front of Me Than a Frontal Lobotomy." Another one of Marilyn's favorites. I wonder if one of those guys put it on for her. I'm the one with the quarters.

"They were all right," Marilyn tells me. She puts a hand on my leg but she only leaves it there for a second. "Just passing time." When the two guys look back over their shoulders at us she gives them a little wave and wiggles her fingers at them so they can see her wedding ring.

"Jesus," Ed says. He puts down his gym bag and sits at the table. Then he pounds the Formica, whaps it one with his fist. "Jesus damn."

The barmaid comes hustling over and gives us a nervous look as she plops down a round of beers. "Compliments," she says. We look off at the bar, and the two guys both touch the bills of their caps. They're wearing worried smiles now. Ed gives them a killer look. He's not even seeing them, I know, but they don't know that. Marilyn's laughing and I'm thinking about asking her what the hell she thinks she's doing.

"Do that again," she tells Ed. "Whap that table one. We could become rich in beer."

"Maybe a good bar fight would take your mind off of things, Ed," I say.

Marilyn looks at me and raises her eyebrows.

"Smash some things up," I say. "Raise a little hell."

"Boy," says Marilyn, "wouldn't that be fun? Maybe do some time in jail?"

"How do you two do it?" Ed says.

Marilyn and me both look at him.

"Oh, it's easy, I guess," Marilyn says. "We just kind of go at it."

Ed takes a long thoughtful slug of his beer and empties the bottle. Then he leans into the table.

"No, I mean, y'all fight a little, I know," he says. "But that's life. People fight. You two hang in there. You two will still be married in the morning. Me and Cassandra, each fight is like the end of the world."

We get quiet then. Ed starts another beer.

Marilyn reaches over and rubs one of Ed's hands. "You want to dance some more?" she asks. Marilyn is not a woman without compassion.

"Not just now," Ed mumbles.

She takes a drag off her cigarette—she's been smoking a lot lately—and seems to think for a minute, the smoke lacing around her head. Then she says, "What's your favorite song, Ed?"

This one snuck up on him, makes him sit back in his chair.

"My favorite song?" He's got his hand going through his hair again. "I don't know. I don't guess I have one."

"Everyone has a favorite song," Marilyn says.

I say, "Mine's 'I Got Tears in My Ears from Lying in My Bed on My Back Crying My Eyes Out Over You.'"

"I know what yours is," Marilyn says. "We're working on young Edward here."

"You got to admit, that's a funny song," I say.

"It's a damn scream," says Marilyn.

"Well, what's yours?" I ask her.

"You know mine."

"I forget."

She stubs out her cigarette. "'Whiter Shade of Pale,'" she says. "The most beautiful damn song ever written."

"God," says Ed. "I heard Willie singing that one this morning. The house was so damn quiet I couldn't stand it, I put the radio on, but it was like every song was about me and Cassandra. It was goddamn weird."

"Okay, I'll tell you something weird," says Marilyn, lighting another cigarette. "Once Ray and me had a fight so bad I had to get up and go for a walk."

I don't know what's coming here, but she looks at me and smiles, so I know at least this is something that's settled. It might be the one about the time she got so mad at me she shoved the refrigerator in front of the door so I couldn't get in. Only thing was, the door opened out, so I could just step in around the Frigidaire. Even Marilyn laughs at that one. Now, anyways.

She leans forward and tucks a strand of hair behind her ear. She taps her cigarette on the ashtray. "I went all around the neighborhood trying to calm down. I was so mad at you, Bubba."

She takes a deep drag off her cigarette, then rubs it out, half-smoked. "But I couldn't shake it off, and things started coming to me, things I should have said, so I started back to the house. I was really gonna give you what for. So I'm walking down the sidewalk past all these houses that are the spitting image of ours, and I'm just as mad as I can be. But all of a sudden there's this huge bang, like a bomb. I mean, it was really something. You could feel it. It felt like it had gone off just overhead, and then there was this concussion thing in the air—the birds stopped, and everything was all still. I honest to God thought it was the big one, like that was some kind of initial explosion, and in a minute the real one was gonna vaporize us. Doors started flying open on the houses, this pack of dogs comes zooming down the street with their tails between their legs, people came running out looking up at the sky. We're all looking around, but nothing else happens, and then everyone all at once notices this little puff of smoke hanging just over the telephone wires. So we go running there, me and about ten other people, and there's this little squirrel curled up on the ground under this telephone pole, just as peaceful as could be, like he was sleeping. Only he was deader than a doorknob. We all stood there looking at him, and then this one guy points to a transformer up on the pole and says the squirrel must have chewed a wire leading into it or something. And everyone kind of laughed a little, relieved, even though this poor little squirrel is setting there steaming. But I tell you, I was shook. I thought I was so mad, I'd sent out some kind of bad vibrations. I thought I'd blown up that dang squirrel with my mind."

"You never told me this," I say.

"You don't remember me telling you I blew up a squirrel?" she says.

"No," I say. "I'd remember that."

"I didn't tell you," she admits. "I just decided that argument was over. I wasn't ever getting that mad again. You were still pouting when I got back, though, as I recollect."

"I wasn't pouting," I say, even though I don't recall this particular time.

"You was," says Marilyn. She lights up another cigarette.

I decide I'm not even gonna grace this with a reply and I just sit back in my chair without so much as a word.

Ed knocks back his beer. "That's the most beautiful thing I ever heard," he says. "I mean that."

"You wouldn't think so if you'd seen that squirrel smoking," Marilyn says.

"What's your point here, Marilyn?" I ask. I'm not sure she's talking to Ed here. It's like she wants to get at me.

"Maybe Ed has just blown up his own squirrel, is what I'm saying. Ed, I don't know what went on between you and Cassandra last night—and I don't want to know, so hush up on that account. You just play your cards close to your chest on that one. But maybe now you and Miss Cassandra know something about getting mad. Maybe now you can start from square one. And maybe that'll make it so she's free to come back."

You could see Ed's eyes light up.

"But maybe she won't," I say. Everybody looks at me. I can't believe she got me to say this.

Marilyn just sinks back in her chair and shakes her head. Her hair shimmers, then falls back into place.

* * *

Ed starts drinking whiskey. This is Marilyn's doing. Whenever he finishes one, she fetches him another squat glass of the stuff so fast you can tell he doesn't realize, after a while, that it's a new drink. It's like one long continuous whiskey. I can see that she's decided to just get him drunk as a skunk, to make him forget things for now and just get unconscious for a while and put him out of his misery that way.

He's not going down easy, though. Every time the door opens he looks up. He's jittery, looking around, heaving sighs like he was out of breath. Then he starts fiddling with his wedding ring. He's not accepting the notion that Cassandra's cut and run, that it's really over this time. He sees it, but he's not buying it.

Somebody puts Merle Haggard on the box. "Today I Started Loving You Again."

"Oh man," says Ed. He empties a new whiskey in one gulp. "Oh man." He pushes his glass onto the table and it slides away from him on the condensation. "She's got to be somewhere."

Marilyn grabs his glass before it quits sliding. She rattles the ice. "Most likely," she says, and slips out of her chair and heads to the bar with Ed's glass.

I watch her and see her exchange a few words with the two guys in ball caps. They laugh.

"Ray," Ed says, so I have to look back at him. "I know this is asking a lot. But I've got to find her. I've got to fix things. I messed up with so many girls before Cassandra. For one damn time, I want to fix a situation I've screwed up. I can't explain it but . . . I just feel like I'm gone if I don't. Don't you feel that way, sometimes? Like Marilyn has saved you?"

Marilyn is coming back to the table, so he's talking in this wet whisper. I don't know what my answer is. Right now, I'm clenching my fists about this situation with the guys at the bar. I'm getting annoyed with Ed, too, with the whole, long time of hearing about his and Cassandra's never-ending problems. The not talking, the going off and so on—as if they were special people who didn't have to get along and live with troubles like the rest of us. What did he think marriage was? Ed, I want to say, how could you not know where your wife is? How could you miss that one little detail? Measure twice, cut once, buddy!

But that's not what I say.

"And just what the hell was that all about?" I ask Marilyn as she slides back into her seat.

"What?" she says, slipping the whiskey in front of Ed.

I nod at the bar.

"Just being friendly," she says. "We ought to ask them to sit with us, they're funny."

"I don't think so," I say.

"What am I gonna do?" Ed says. "She's got to be somewhere."

Marilyn sighs, one of those windshield-busters. "You're gonna get on with things, Ed. I know you don't see it now, but time will help. It's true what they say."

Ed is shaking his head. He gulps back the whiskey. "I can't just wait," he says.

"What else can you do?" Marilyn asks him.

Ed doesn't move, he's sitting stiff in his chair. And then there's tears spilling down his cheeks. "All day long, I kept thinking I heard her somewhere else in the house. I kept getting up and going to the next room, I'd go to the door and call her name . . ."

Marilyn is out of her chair, she's standing behind Ed and rubbing his back. "Ed," she says. "Ed, now, you listen to me."

But he shakes her off and wipes a big hand across his cheeks, then reaches down to the floor for the gym bag. He practically falls out of his chair, Marilyn's got to grab his shoulders. He finds the bag but it catches on the leg of the table and Ed yanks it up so hard the bottles and glasses rattle and clink.

"I know where she's at," he says.

Marilyn comes around to face him, sits on the edge of the table, and grips him by both shoulders. "Ed," she says. "Stay with us. You're in no condition. Try and wait it out."

"No," he blurts out. Then he stands and he's weaving a little. He's gulping for air. "Goddammit, I know where she's at."

"Ed," says Marilyn, "I think you're making a royal mistake."

"She's at Juanita's," he says. Juanita's is this Mexican place Ed and me worked on once, it's back in Little Rock, in the fancy little mall across from the capitol building.

"No, Ed, she's not." Marilyn says this like she knows for sure, and Ed hears this, and it's like something's going out of him. Like he's losing all of his air.

I stand up suddenly. "I think he should give it a try."

Marilyn presses her lips together and rolls her eyes. "Oh, sweet Jesus," she says.

"We're gonna do it," I say.

We stand there for a minute, with Ed swaying between us.

"Ed, don't you have to go see a woman about a horse?" Marilyn says.

"What?" he asks.

"Go splash some water on your face," she says. "Men got bladders like dang camels," she mutters.

"Oh," he says. "Okay." It's like he's happy someone has told him a thing he can do.

He goes off and we both stare after him. He staggers up to a door and he's staring at it, scrunching up his eyes. It takes him a minute to figure out it says DOES. Then he moves off and finds the one marked BUCKS.

Marilyn turns on me. "Just what do you think you're doing?" she says.

"What?" I say. "What?"

"Leading him on a wild goose chase, is what. Don't neither one of you see it? She's gone. She's a young girl who wants some fun and she's gone. He blew it one time too many."

"Whose side are you on?" I ask her.

"There ain't no sides to it. It's just over, it's just plain over. God almighty, this has been coming for centuries. What are you, Blind Lemon Jefferson? Little Stevie Wonder? Ray Charles?"

"But if he finds her, she'll come back. How could she not? It's clear as a bell he loves her, him looking all over the land for her."

"Ronnie Milsap?" she says. "José Feliciano?"

"Him going through hell?" I say.

Marilyn takes a step back. She's waving her arms. "Men always think like that. They always think if they put on a dramatic enough show they'll get what they want. Fireworks! Music! Maybe some bullets to dodge! That's what this is for you—you've got some big idea of rescuing Ed, like you can do it all for him."

"Well, I'm not just gonna abandon him," I say.

"That would be the best thing in the whole wide world you could do for him. He's got to face this, he's got to let it go. He won't as long as you keep firing him up."

I sit back in my chair, take a sip of beer. "You gonna start talking about blowing up squirrels again?"

"Argh!" says Marilyn, and somewhere, I know, there's another squirrel that's blown up.

Ed's coming back then, so I push back up out of my chair, just as Marilyn plops back into hers.

"You ready, Big Ed?" I ask him. I got the feeling you get when you're on a job, say, framing a house, and the light's failing, and you decide to plane just one more edge, slide just one more board into place. Your movements from tool to wood become real smooth and sure and quick.

Ed gives a hopeful little smile, then switches to this serious and determined look. "Yeah," he says. "Let's roll." He goes to hook his thumbs in his belt but he misses. He looks down at himself in confusion.

"I'm not going," Marilyn says. She's lighting another cigarette. Her hands are shaking. The match flares up in front of her face with the breath of her words.

"Oh come on," I say.

"Nope. It'll take you forty-five minutes just to get there."

"Look," I say.

"Forty-five minutes to get back," she says. "Nope, I'm staying. This is the best dang beer I ever had in my life."

"What kind is it?" Ed says.

Tammy Wynette singing "Stand By Your Man" comes out of the jukebox. Marilyn slaps a hand to her head. "Oh, lordy," she says, "I'm being affronted on all sides."

"How am I supposed to get home?" I ask her.

She looks at her watch. "I'll add on ten minutes to not find her. That'll make it eleven-thirty. I'll come get you at Ed's."

Ed's looking at his watch, his eyes all scrunched up.

"All right, fine." I get his gym bag for him and shove it into his arms, and I yank him out of there. He's still trying to read his watch.

It's pitch-black five minutes outside of Birdseye. Ed's trying to sober up, he's got his window open and the night's rushing in. I'm driving his truck hard, I can see a rooster tail of dust in the rearview as I cut down some back roads to the highway. I don't ease up until we're in the lights of the city, until we cross over the bridge from North Little Rock into town. It takes us a lot less than forty-five minutes.

When I turn onto Markham I have to slow down to a crawl. There's a lot of traffic, more people out doing the nightlife than I'd expected. It's been a long time since I was down here this late. I can see the town is changing from the sleepy little place it was when I was a kid into one of those southern success stories you hear so damn much about. We pass by the governor's mansion and it's all lit up, I imagine there's some sort of ball going on in there. People in tuxedos, probably, evening gowns, butlers. The mansion is modeled after the White House. It looks just like it, only smaller.

Then we pass the capitol. It's built to look like the real thing, too. I remember when some movie was made there about terrorists taking over the country. The movie people weren't allowed to use the real Capitol in Washington, so they came to Little Rock to use ours. This was when Ed and I had the remodeling job on Juanita's. I remember watching the movie on TV, there was a scene where they blew up the dome. The next morning Ed and I sat on the second story, sipping coffee on the raw two-by-fours we'd put up to frame out a big window, looking out at it, and wondered how they'd done that.

We have to circle the block a few times to find a parking space, finally finding one between a Jaguar and a Volvo. We're out of pickup country now. I climb out and wait for Ed to come around to cross the street with me when a little Japanese car zips past, inches away, music blaring. Some young buck with slicked-back hair hangs out the window and shouts, "Woooo!" pumping his fists up in the air. Ed and me press back against the truck.

When they're past I push off into the street but Ed stays collapsed against the truck. He's got that gym bag up in his arms the way a little girl holds her schoolbooks. I can see by the watery look in his eyes that he's still hammered. His hair is standing on end from the wind on the ride down.

"Edward?" I say.

He's looking up at the light of Juanita's.

I go back to him.

"Edward, what's in the damn bag, anyway?"

He looks down at it like he's not sure what this thing clutching his chest is.

"Oh," he says. Then he looks back at me. It's like he's looking up at me from under water. "What am I gonna say to her if she's there?" he asks.

I can see he's lost all momentum, he's sagging against the truck.

I slap the little sign, our old slogan he's painted on the driver's door.

"Just like it says right here, Ed," I tell him. " 'One Board at a Time.' Now c'mon."

I pull him along behind me and we go to the door leading up into Juanita's. There's a sign on it in red letters that says " 'Don't Even THINK About Coming into This Establishment If You Are UNDERAGE.' " I yank it open and we go in.

When we get to the top of the stairs some bruiser stops us, some former Razorback just about busting out of his official Juanita's T-shirt. He looks us over. They don't know us here anymore. It's clear we're old enough, though, so he takes my money from me, then stamps the back of our hands with a little ink stamp. Ed stands there, swaying, squinting, trying to make out what's this on the back of his hand. I have to tell him it doesn't say anything before he'll move, it's just the official Juanita's symbol, the outline of some little woman flamenco dancer with her dress twirling.

The way Ed's walking I can tell he can't see three feet in front of him, so as we make our way through the crowd I'm the one who's looking for Cassandra. We pass a booth where some people are leaving so I steer Ed into it, get him settled, and look off through the crowd some more. There's so many people she could be right in front of me and I wouldn't know it. There are young guys in white shirts with the top button fastened and the sleeves rolled up, people in jeans with creases, women in short, tight cotton dresses, their hair loose. The place has a high ceiling, divided down the middle by a brick wall. One side is like a cavern lit by neon beer signs, with a bar and a rock band at the other end of it. The other side is a dining room with small tables tucked between potted trees. Couples are leaning in together over candles in little red globes. Our booth lets us see into both rooms. It's against the big window Ed and I framed out way back when.

I give up looking for Cassandra and slide into the booth opposite Ed. I have to shout, practically, to make myself heard.

"What makes you think she's here?" I ask him. I've been picturing the final scene between Ed and Cassandra, the night before, as a sad, tearful, all-night jag. I can't imagine wanting to come here after that.

Ed's fumbling with the gym bag, trying to get it open, but the zipper's stuck. He stops what he's doing and looks up at me. His head's wobbling.

"The crowds," he says. "She says the crowds make her feel safe. We used to come here all the time. I"—he cuts a look out the window at the capitol, posing like somebody in a movie—"I proposed to her here."

I'd forgotten that. He'd done that right in front of Marilyn and me, sliding out of the booth and sinking to his knees.

A waitress comes over and I order a couple of beers, but as she walks away I'm suddenly feeling pressed for time. I'm picturing that last scene between Ed and Cassandra, and it's making me remember Marilyn, the way we left her in the Deer Head. See, she's got this rule, which is to never go off mad—she makes sure to kiss me, for example, every night before bed. It's true that some nights, when I've done something that's annoyed her, her lips have come up on me like a freight train, and I would take a step backward out of fear that she was going to head-butt me. But she's never missed a night. I'm suddenly wishing we had kissed, because the truth is, her kisses rarely hurt.

"Ed," I say, "we're running out of time."

The waitress comes back and slides our beers in front of us. She doesn't bother to clear off all the empties cluttering the table.

The band kicks into a ballad, something for couples to slow-dance to. It's still pretty loud, though. There's no making out what words of love the singer's crooning, just the bass humping along slowly.

"Oh God," says Ed, and he's going back at the zipper on the gym bag. He gives it a big yank and it rips free, and I suddenly see what he's got in there: it looks like all of Cassandra's candles. He starts plopping them down on the table, shoving them out amongst the beer bottles. There are candles in little brass holders, in little ceramic holders. There are fat ones that stand by themselves.

"Edward," I say, "what the hell?"

He pulls some matches from his pocket and starts lighting candles like crazy. I'm afraid he's going to set himself on fire.

I'm trying to pull some of the candles away so they don't catch Ed's sleeves when the waitress comes back. "Hey," she says. "You can't do that."

Ed says, "Aragum doit."

"I'm gonna get the manager," she says, and she backs off quickly.

People are looking at us now, turning from the bar, heads twisting our way over the tops of the other booths. The band seems to come clearer, there's a saxophone playing. Some wait- resses stop what they're doing, they drop their trays to their sides and stand in a small circle around us. It's like something's got to happen now.

And then it does. Cassandra steps into the clearing.

She's all in black, she's wearing long brass earrings that stretch along her neck and sparkle against her dark hair. The sleeves of her T-shirt are rolled up to show off the length of her pretty arms. Her hair is loose and thick, falling free to her shoulders. She's young and beautiful.

She steps up to the table and looks down at Ed, who's still trying to light more candles. "Hello, Ed," she says.

He stops what he's doing, freezes with a lit match in midair. He lifts his head and I can see his eyes come into focus.

"I brung the candles," he says.

"I see," she says quietly.

It's like I'm not there, it's just the two of them. I can see the waitress leading the big guy who works the door through the crowd. They stop at the edge of the circle.

Then Ed drops the lit match, it falls to the table and sput- ters out in a puddle of beer. He slides out of the booth and in one movement he's on his knees before Cassandra. "Please come home, baby," he says. "Please." Then he wraps his arms around her waist and buries his head in her stomach.

She has a sad look on her face when she gathers his big head in her arms. "Oh, Ed," she says.

Then the people all around start cheering and clapping. I think I may be the only one who hears Cassandra when she says, "I told you it would never work, baby." The crowd is clapping, they just see her holding him. Then it's like the place comes back to life, and they all turn back to the business of partying.

The big fellow from the door steps up to us. "Y'all are gonna have to leave," he says.

"It's all right," Cassandra says, and she leans over and whispers something in Ed's ear. He stands up but he doesn't pull away from her, he's clutching her close.

I'm blowing out candles like crazy. I leave them on the table, reach over, and grab the gym bag. It's still got more candles in it, I see.

I bend to Cassandra and whisper in her ear, "I can take you back, honey." Her thick hair smells nice, I notice. I don't know why I call her honey.

"All right," she says, "all right," but I can't tell if she's talking to me or to Ed.

Back outside, I help Cassandra pour Ed into the truck. She hesitates for a moment before climbing in after him, looking back at me. I put a hand on her shoulder. "We looked all over for you," I tell her. "He needs you bad."

She looks at me with an expression so sad it could break your heart, such grief on such a pretty girl. Then she just nods and slips into the truck beside Ed.

All the way back, she sits looking out the window, one arm wrapped tight around Ed, him leaning on her. She looks out at the lights of Little Rock, at the imitation White House all aglow, at the water rushing under the bridge, and then, afterward, at the total dark.

It's near to midnight when we drive up the hill to their house. There's no sign of Marilyn.

I get out of the truck feeling like I've been driving forever. Ed revives a little when he steps out into the cool night air. As Cassandra starts up into the house, he looks at her back and squeezes my shoulder and gives me a lopsided smile. "I couldn't of done it without you, buddy," he says. Messed up as he is, there's something beaming from his eyes.

Cassandra stops at the top of the stairs, turns and looks down at him, catches his look. She can't help but give him a little smile. But when she says, "Let's sit in the kitchen for a few minutes," her tone is quiet, still. I can't make out how she's feeling about things.

"I just have to wait a few minutes," I say, "for Marilyn to come get me."

"I know," Cassandra says, and goes into the house.

I follow them to the kitchen and sit in the chair by the big picture window so I can look out and see when Marilyn's coming. Ed and me built the whole house around the idea of this particular window. He'd got it in his head that the view through this window was what mattered most about his first house. It was the first thing he framed out, and everything else went up around it. We were still working on the foundation in places, but the two-by-fours outlining that window were sticking up there, waiting for us to catch up.

That window is worth looking out, though, I can tell you that. In daylight, you can see the White River in the distance, and the White is a sight. When sunset comes, it turns into a copper band, cutting off through the dark green hills. The town is invisible from this angle, you can't even see a single house or condominium. It's just the hills. Even the road is folded away out of sight into the greenery, but I know the Bonneville's headlights will cut through all that. I'll be able to see it coming.

Ed and Cassandra sit across from me, across the table covered with beer bottles. Looming behind Ed is the picture of the sheep. The room is bright in the glare of the overhead light. It makes the whole night seem unreal.

We sit for a little bit in silence, blinking, then Cassandra excuses herself for a moment and leaves the room.

Ed watches her go, smiles, and draws himself up. He's not worried about her disappearing now.

"I'll be back at work in the morning," he says to me. "Everything's gonna be all right now."

"I know," I say. "I know it will be."

"Damn," he says. "I've never been so happy in my life. Everything's gonna be all right now."

He lifts himself up and stumbles to the refrigerator and comes back with some beers. He pops one open for himself, then pops open another and places it in front of Cassandra's chair. He pushes the last one toward me and slides the opener behind it.

Cassandra comes back into the room with a candle. She clears a space for it in the middle of the table and lights it. Then, before she sits back down, she switches off the overhead light.

The kitchen slowly fills with an uncertain light. It flickers, and there are little pieces of shine where there didn't used to be. The shadows move, the appliances and squares of linoleum change size and shape, and texture.

Through the shadows on her face, Cassandra looks drawn and older than she is. She takes a sip from her beer, works to swallow it. I think how this is something she's doing for Ed, she'd rather have wine.

I fiddle with the church key, spinning it around in a circle on the tabletop. It looks like a clock going crazy. It's past time for Marilyn to come and take me home.

Ed can't take his eyes off Cassandra. He starts telling her about how he's going to put a skylight in her workroom—he calls it her "studio"—so she can have more of the natural light she loves. He tells her how they're going to go out dancing more often. He tells her about the job we just got, a big house that we're going to make a lot of money on. Enough for a trip, maybe, he says. He tells her how everything's going to be different.

Then he pauses for a moment and looks at her so hard she has to look down into her lap.

"Darlin'," he says. "Can I kiss you now? I been thinking about nothing else since you left."

She gives him that sad smile again. "Of course you can, Ed," she says.

Her eyes flutter a look at me, then back to Ed. I stand up to leave but Ed's only seeing her. He goes over to her and kneels, he's tall enough to reach her that way, and he embraces her. He kisses her briefly on the lips, then on each cheek, then tenderly on each closed eye. Her face is slack, like she's bone weary, she just accepts each one. And then he kisses her long and slow on the lips, gently and needily, but somehow increasing greedily, until she sinks into it and she's kissing him back.

I take a step back and knock into my chair. They break and I notice a thin thread of saliva pull between their lips. They look at me.

"I'm going to wait for Marilyn outside," I say. "She's going to be here any minute."

Cassandra and Ed both start to say something, but I stop them. "Just kiss each other," I tell them. "Just kiss."

They both look at me, then hang their heads together as I pass. I notice a dead sheep falling over Cassandra's shoulder. At the door, I look back and see the little flame from the candle reflecting through all the brown beer bottles surrounding it, like there was a light in each one like they were in a church. I see Ed kissing Cassandra's neck as I leave.

Outside, I sit on the steps and let the cool night air wash over me. I listen to the cicadas, my mouth dry and my head buzzing. Eventually, I hear the low murmuring of their voices. I look up at the weak light flickering in the window, it's the only light out there, and I wonder what they could possibly be saying. I hear her voice, then his, rising and falling. I can't make out the words. Then I hear Ed's voice getting louder. I can't tell if they're fighting, maybe they're excited some other way. Then I hear Cassandra, a kind of a muted wail, and my heart sinks.

What I think then is to force myself to remember when they were just dating, when she was just another of Ed's girlfriends, and he told me what it was like to make love to her. "She talks," he said, "she's a screamer, too."

"Ed," I told him, "this is not something you ought to be telling me. We're not in school anymore."

It was embarrassing, but now I hope that's what I heard. That's what I hope the kissing and the words, what I hope the whole night, has led to. I leave the porch and start off down the dirt road. I figure I'll meet Marilyn halfway.

As I go down the dirt road into the darkness, the black air is cool on my skin. I'd worked up a sweat, somehow, I don't know how. I can't see much, and the earth is crunching under my feet. That's all I hear at first.

It takes a few minutes for both my eyes and my ears to get acclimated, but when they do, I can hear the cicadas again, and occasionally an owl, and I just can barely see my feet against the slight lessening of blackness that makes up the road. But the treeline is thin at that level, so as I go down the hill, it doesn't take too long before the bastard pines start to lean in and darken things up even more, and I'm in the pitch-black that only exists in the heart of the country.

Eventually, I find a steady stride, and I can follow the road by hearing that I'm on the dirt and not the grass, and by following the parting overhead between the black trees and the starry sky. It feels like an accomplishment, to make my way through such darkness.

It'll surprise Marilyn, I think, when she comes.

And then I'm running, I'm running, and I'm very certain about my footing, which is crazy, I know even as I feel it. But I've never been so focused on anything in my life as I am on moving down that hill and into the valley. I don't think about the fact that I might come around a bend and run straight off into a parting of the trees, right into a scenic view, and get down into the valley by dying. That just doesn't seem possible.

And then, after I don't know how long, I hear a truck grinding its gears way off in the distance. Then I see its lights below me, on the main road that skirts the foot of the mountain.

I skid to a stop and watch those headlights. Then I see another pair, a car's. Only the cones of light in profile, beaming out onto the highway. I hold my breath, praying for those rays of light to turn up onto the dirt road, to transform into eye beams, to come scanning down the lonely dirt road as if looking for me, as if sensing my presence. If I saw that, saw that light looking for me, how could I not move to it? How could I not run to it, and step into it, and let it wash over me?

O, Marilyn!

Dennis Loy Johnson is an itinerant writer from Cornelia, Georgia. His stories have appeared in many literary journals, including *Ploughshares, New England Review,* and *Another Chicago Magazine,* and in several anthologies such as Doubleday's *The New Generation* and August House's *Homecoming: The Southern Family in Short Fiction.* Lately, his stories have earned him an award in fiction writing from the National Endowment of the Arts and *Black Warrior Review's* annual prize for best short story.

PHOTO CREDIT: JILL LEVINE

I was living a pretty cushy life when I first sat down to write "Rescuing Ed" a few years ago. I was living in Tennessee, where I'd long wanted to be. My writing was just beginning to appear in print. What's more, I was getting paid for it.

I was working steadily for the late, great Southern Magazine, which came out of Little Rock, and this seemed like reason enough for celebration. Every so often I would loop over the border to visit with some of that town's many talented writers and editors. Once, we went up into the hills with a brace of 30.06 rifles and blew away a temperamental typewriter, a Selectric that got what it deserved. In less rowdy moods we went after trout, up in the lower Ozarks on the shiny White River (catch & release). Often, we capped these spells by returning to Little Rock in the warm night to Juanita's Café, where we drank abbreviated Margaritas (shots of tequila).

I guess "Ed" originated in smugness. But I loved Arkansas, and I wanted to document, at least for myself, the kind of people that graced their villages with names like Romance and Morning Light. At the same time, some of my friends there were visited by trouble, and I was feeling for them. Bad times in a beautiful place have a barbed edge to them. But my own luck was on a continued roll. I fell in love with a beautiful woman who loved me back. I landed a prestigious job up north as a college prof, and began making more money and experiencing more influence than I'd ever thought possible. Amidst this comfort, I couldn't quite catch that aforementioned edge: I wrote the story about Arkansas and it was, as they say, gutless.

Two years later I'd lost both the job and the girl. Southern Magazine *was bought out by a big nasty competitor and put mercilessly to sleep. A couple of my stories went down with it. I was stranded in a cold Northern clime, in a particularly mean and rainy stretch of woods known as Pennsylvania. Somewhere in a dark winter night, I took "Ed" out of the drawer and went back at it in a white heat. I sent it off immediately afterwards, pretty much afraid to look at it. It was another act of catch and release.*

Now, another year or two further on, I can look at that story, and neither the general rise of Arkansas chic—neither the advent of Bill Clinton nor of that insipid TV show which caused an editor to delete my mention of Evening Shade—can blur for me the fact that I went to both the story and to Arkansas itself for sustenance and inspiration. These may be the reasons we write and read short stories, I don't know. I do know I hope to go back to Arkansas someday.

A JONQUIL FOR
MARY PENN

(from *The Atlantic Monthly*)

Mary Penn was sick, though she said nothing about it when she heard Elton get up and light the lamp and renew the fires. He dressed and went out with the lantern to milk and feed and harness the team. It was early March, and she could hear the wind blowing, rattling things. She threw the covers off and sat up on the side of the bed, feeling as she did how easy it would be to let her head lean down again, onto her knees. But she got up, put on her dress and sweater, and went to the kitchen.

Nor did she mention her sickness when Elton came back in, bringing the milk, with the smell of the barn cold in his clothes.

"How're you this morning?" he asked her, giving her a pat as she strained the milk.

And she said, not looking at him, for she did not want him to know how she felt, "Just fine."

He ate hungrily the eggs, sausage, and biscuits that she set in front of him, twice emptying the glass that he replenished from a large pitcher of milk. She loved to watch him eat—there was something curiously delicate in the way he used his large hands—but this morning she busied herself about the kitchen, not looking at him, for she knew he was watching her. She had not even set a plate for herself.

"You're not hungry?" he asked.

"Not very. I'll eat something after a while."

He put sugar and cream in his coffee, stirred rapidly with the spoon. And now he lingered a little. He did not indulge himself often, but this was one of his moments of leisure. He gave himself to his pleasures as concentratedly as to his work. He was never partial about anything; he never felt two ways at the same time. It was, she thought, a kind of childishness in him. When he was happy, he was entirely happy, and he could be as entirely sad or angry. His glooms were the darkest she had ever seen. He worked as a hungry dog ate, and yet he could play at croquet or cards with the self-forgetful exuberance of a little boy. It was for his concentratedness, she supposed, if such a thing could be supposed about, that she loved him. That and her yen just to look at him, for it was wonderful to her the way he was himself in his slightest look or gesture. She did not understand him in everything he did, and yet she recognized him in everything he did. She had not been prepared—she was hardly prepared yet—for the assent she had given to him.

Though he might loiter a moment over his coffee, the day, she knew, had already possessed him; its momentum was on him. When he rose from bed in the morning, he stepped into the day's work, impelled into it by the tension, never apart from him, between what he wanted to do and what he could do. The little hillside place that they had rented from his mother afforded him no proper scope for his ability and desire. They always needed money, but, day by day, they were getting by. Though this was yet another spring of the Depression, they were not going to be in want. She knew his need to surround her with a margin of pleasure and ease. This was his need, not hers, but when he was not working at home, he would be working, or looking for work, for pay.

This morning, delaying his own plowing, he was going to help Walter Cotman plow his corn ground. She could feel the knowledge of what he had to do tightening in him like a spring. She thought of him and Walter plowing, starting in the early light, and the two teams leaning into the collars all day, while the men walked in the opening furrows and the steady wind shivered the dry grass and shook the dead weeds and rattled the treetops in the woods.

He stood and pushed in his chair. She came to be hugged as she knew he wanted her to.

"It's mean out," he said. "Stay in today. Take care of yourself."

"You, too," she said. "Have you got on plenty of clothes?"

"When I get 'em all on, I will." He was already wearing an extra shirt, and a pair of overalls over his corduroys. Now he put on a sweater, his work jacket, his cap and gloves. He started out the door and then turned back. "Don't worry about the chores. I'll be back in time to do everything."

"All right," she said.

He shut the door. And now the kitchen was a cell of still lamp-light under the long wind that passed without inflection over the ridgetops.

She cleared the table. She washed the few dishes he had dirtied and put them away. The kitchen contained the table and four chairs and the small dish cabinet that they had bought, and the large iron cooking stove that looked more permanent than the house. The stove, along with the bed and a few other sticks of furniture, had been there when they came.

She heard Elton go by with the team, heading out the lane. The daylight would be coming now, though the windowpanes still reflected the lamplight. She took the broom from its corner by the back door and swept and tidied up the room. They had been able to do nothing to improve the house, which had never been a good one and had seen hard use. The wallpaper, and probably the plaster behind, had cracked in places. The finish had worn off the linoleum carpets near the doorways and around the stoves. But she kept the house clean. She had made curtains. The curtains in the kitchen were of the same blue-and-white checkered gingham as the tablecloth. The nightstands were orange crates for which she had made skirts of the same cloth. Though the house was poor and hard to keep, she had made it neat and homey. It was her first house, and usually it made her happy. But not now.

She was sick. At first it was a consolation to her to have the whole day to herself to be sick in. But by the time she got the kitchen straightened up, even that small happiness had left her. She had a fever, she guessed, for every motion she made seemed to carry her uneasily beyond the vertical. She had a floaty feeling that made her unreal to herself. And finally, when she put the broom away, she let herself sag down into one of the chairs at the table. She ached. She was overpoweringly tired.

She had rarely been sick, and never since she married. And now she did something else that was unlike her: she began to feel sorry for herself. She remembered that she and Elton had quarreled the night before—about what, she could not remember; perhaps it was not rememberable; perhaps she did not know. She did remember the heavy, mostly silent force of his anger. It had been only another of those tumultuous darknesses that came over him as suddenly, and sometimes as unaccountably, as a July storm. She was miserable, she told herself. She was sick and alone. And perhaps the sorrow that she felt for herself was not altogether unjustified.

She and Elton had married a year and a half earlier, when she was seventeen and he eighteen. She had never seen anybody like him. He had a wild way of rejoicing, like a healthy child, singing songs, joking, driving his old car as if he were drunk and the road not wide enough. He could make her weak with laughing at him. And yet he was already a man as few men were. He had been making his own living since he was fourteen, when he had quit school. His father had been dead by then for five years. He hated his stepfather. When a neighbor had offered him cropland, room, and wages, he took charge of himself, and though he was still a boy, he became a man. He wanted, he said, to have to say thank you to nobody. Or to nobody but her. He would be glad, he said with a large grin, to say thank you to her. And he could *do* things. It was wonderful what he could accomplish with those enormous hands of his. She could have put her hand into his and walked right off the edge of the world. Which, in a way, is what she did.

She had grown up in a substantial house on a good upland farm. Her family was not wealthy but it was an old Kentucky family, proud of itself, always conscious of its position and of its responsibility to be itself. She had known from childhood that she would be sent to college. Almost from childhood she had understood that she was destined to marry a solid professional man, a doctor perhaps, or (and this her mother particularly favored) perhaps a minister.

And so when she married Elton, she did it without telling her family. She already knew their judgment of Elton: "He's nothing." She and Elton simply drove down to Hargrave one late October night, awakened a preacher, and got married, hoping that their marriage would be accepted as an accomplished fact. They were wrong. It was not acceptable, and it was never going to be. She no longer belonged in that house, her parents told her. She no longer belonged to that family. To them it would be as if she had never lived.

She was seventeen, she had attended a small denominational college for less than two months, and now her life as it had been was ended. The day would come when she would know herself to be a woman of faith. Now she merely loved and trusted. Nobody was living then on Elton's mother's little farm on Cotman Ridge, not far from the town of Port William, where Elton had lived for a while when he was a child. They rented the place and moved in, having just enough money to pay for the new dish cabinet and the table and four chairs. Elton, as it happened, already owned a milk cow in addition to his team and a few tools.

It was a different world, a new world to her, that she came into then—a world of poverty and community. They were in a neighborhood of six households, counting their own, all within half a mile of one another. Besides themselves there were Braymer and Josie Hardy and their children; Tom Hardy and his wife, also named Josie; Walter and Thelma Cotman and their daughter, Irene; Jonah and Daisy Hample and their children; and Uncle Isham and Aunt Frances Quail, who were Thelma Cotman and Daisy Hample's parents. The two Josies, to save confusion, were called Josie Braymer and Josie Tom. Josie Tom was Walter Cotman's sister. In the world that Mary Penn had given up, a place of far larger and richer farms, work was sometimes exchanged, but the families were conscious of themselves in a way that set them apart from one another. Here, in this new world, neighbors were always working together. "Many hands make light work," Uncle Isham Quail loved to say, though his own old hands were no longer able to work much.

Some work only the men did together, like haying and harvesting the corn. Some work only the women did together: sewing or quilting or wallpapering or housecleaning; and whenever the men worked together, the women would be together cooking. Some work the men and women did together: harvesting tobacco, or killing hogs, or any job that needed many hands. The community was an old one. The families had worked together a long time. They all knew what each was good at. When they worked together, not much needed to be explained. When they went down to the little weatherboarded church at Goforth on Sunday morning, they were glad to see one another, and had lots to say, though they had seen each other almost daily during the week.

This neighborhood opened to Mary and Elton, took them in with a warmth that answered her parents' rejection. The men, without asking or being asked, included Elton in whatever they were doing. They told him when and where they needed him. They came to him when he needed them. He was an apt and able hand, and they were glad to have his help. He learned from them all, but liked best to work with Walter Cotman, who was a fine farmer. He and Walter were, up to a point, two of a kind;

they were both impatient with disorder—"I can't stand a damned mess," Walter said, and he made none—and both loved the employment of their minds in their work. They were unlike in that Walter was satisfied within the boundaries of his little farm, and Elton could not have been. Nonetheless, Elton loved his growing understanding of Walter's character and ways. Though he was a quiet man and gave neither instruction nor advice, Walter was Elton's teacher, and Elton was consciously his student.

Once, when they had killed hogs and Elton and Mary had stayed at home to finish rendering their lard, the boiling fat had foamed up and begun to run over the sides of the kettle. Mary ran to the house and called Walter on the party line.

"Tell him to throw the fire to it," Walter said. "Tell him to dip out some lard and throw it on the fire."

Elton did so, unbelieving, but the fire flared, grew hotter, the foaming lard subsided in the kettle, and Elton's face relaxed from anxiety and self-accusation into a grin. "Well," he said, quoting one of Walter's sayings in Walter's voice, "it's all in knowing how."

Mary, who had more to learn than Elton, became a daughter to every woman in the community. She came knowing little, barely enough to begin, and they taught her much. Thelma, Daisy, and the two Josies taught her their ways of cooking, cleaning, and sewing; they taught her to can, pickle, and preserve; they taught her to do the women's jobs in the hog-killing. They took her on their expeditions to one another's houses to cook harvest meals or to houseclean or to gather corn from the fields and can it. One day they all walked down to Goforth, in the Katie's Branch Valley, to do some wallpapering for Josie Tom's mother. They had a good time papering two rooms, and Josie Tom's mother fixed them a dinner of fried chicken, creamed new potatoes and peas, hot biscuits, and cherry cobbler.

In cold weather they sat all afternoon in one another's houses, quilting or sewing or embroidering. Josie Tom was the best at needlework. Everything she made was a wonder. From spring to fall, for a Christmas present for someone, she always embroidered a long cloth that began with the earliest flowers of spring and ended with the last flowers of fall. She drew the flowers on the cloth with a pencil, and worked them in with her needle and colored threads. She included the flowers of the woods and fields, the dooryards and gardens. She loved to point to the penciled outlines and name the flowers as if calling them up in their beauty into her imagination. "Look a there," she would say. "I even put in a jimsonweed." "And a bull thistle," said Tom Hardy, who had his doubts about weeds and thistles, but was proud of her for leaving nothing out.

Josie Tom was a plump, pretty, happy woman, childless, but the mother of any child in reach. Mary Penn loved her the best, perhaps, but she loved them all. They were only in their late thirties or early forties, but to Mary they seemed to belong to the ageless, eternal generation of mothers, unimaginably older and more experienced than herself. She called them Miss Josie, Miss Daisy, and Miss Thelma. They warmed and sheltered her. Sometimes she wanted to toss herself at them like a little girl to be hugged.

They were capable, unasking, generous, humorous women, and sometimes, among themselves, they were raucous and free, unlike the other women she had known. On their way home from picking blackberries one afternoon, they had to get through a new barbed-wire fence. Josie Tom held two wires apart while the other four gathered their skirts, leaned down, and straddled through. Josie Tom handed their filled buckets over. And then Josie Braymer held the wires apart, and Josie Tom, stooping through, hung the back of her dress on the top wire.

"I *knew* it!" she said, and she began to laugh.

They all laughed, and nobody laughed more than Josie Tom, who was standing spraddled and stooped, helpless to move without tearing her dress.

"Josie Braymer," she said, "are you going to just stand there or are you going to unhook me from this shitten fence?"

And there on the ridgetop in the low sunlight they danced the dance of women laughing, bending and straightening, raising and lowering their hands, swaying and stepping with their heads back.

Daylight was full in the windows now. Mary made herself get up and extinguish the lamp on the table. The lamps all needed to be cleaned and trimmed and refilled, and she had planned to do that today. The whole house needed to be dusted and swept. And she had mending to do. She tied a scarf around her head, put on her coat, and went out.

Only day before yesterday it had been spring—warm, sunny, and still. Elton said the wildflowers were starting up in the leafless woods, and she found a yellow crocus in the yard. And then this dry and bitter wind had come, driving down from the north as if it were as long and wide as time, the sky as gray as if the sun had never shone. The wind went through her coat, pressed her fluttering skirt tight against her legs, tore at her scarf. It chilled her to the bone. She went first to the privy in a back corner of the yard, and then on to the henhouse, where she shelled corn for the hens and gave them fresh water.

On her way back to the house she stood a moment, looking off in the direction in which she knew Elton and Walter Cotman were plowing. By now they would have accepted even this day as it was; by now they might have shed their jackets. Later they would go in and wash and sit down in Thelma's warm kitchen for their dinner, hungry, glad to be at rest for a little while before going back again to work through the long afternoon. Though they were not far away, though she could see them in her mind's eye, their day and hers seemed estranged, divided by great distance and long time. She was cold, and the wind's insistence wearied her; the wind was like a living creature, rearing and pressing against her so that she might have cried out to it in exasperation, "*What* do you *want?*"

When she got back into the house, she was shivering, her teeth chattering. She unbuttoned her coat without taking it off, and sat down close to the stove. They heated only two rooms, the kitchen and the front room where they slept. The stove in the front room might be warmer, she thought, and she could sit in the rocking chair; but having sat down she did not get up. She had much that she needed to be doing, she told herself. She ought at least to get up and make the bed. And she wanted to tend to the lamps; it always pleased her to have them clean. But she did not get up. The stove's heat drove the cold out of her clothes, and gradually her shivering stopped.

They had had a hard time of it their first winter. They had no fuel, no food laid up for the winter. Elton had raised a crop, but no garden. He borrowed against the crop to buy a meat hog. He cut and hauled in firewood. He worked for wages to buy groceries, but the times were hard and he could not always find work. Sometimes their meals consisted of biscuits and a gravy made of lard and flour.

And yet they were often happy. Often the world afforded them something to laugh about. Elton stayed alert for anything that was funny, and brought the stories home. He told her how the tickle-ass grass got into Uncle Isham's pants, and how Daisy Hample clucked to her nearsighted husband and children like a hen with half-grown chicks, and how Jonah Hample, missing the steps, walked off the edge of Braymer Hardy's front porch, fell into a rosebush, and said, "Now, I didn't go to do that!" Elton was a natural mimic, and he could make the funny things happen again in the dark as they lay in bed at night; sometimes they would laugh until their eyes were wet with tears. When they got snowed in that winter, they would drive the old car down the hill until it stalled in the drifts, and drag it out with the team, and ram it into the drifts again, laughing until the horses looked at them in wonder.

When the next year came, they began at the beginning, and though the times had not improved, they improved themselves. They bought a few hens and a rooster from Josie Braymer. They bought a second cow. They put in a garden. They bought two shoats to raise for meat. Mary learned to preserve the food they would need for winter. When the cows freshened, she learned to milk. She took a small bucket of cream and a few eggs to Port William every Saturday night, and used the money she made to buy groceries and to pay on their debts.

Slowly she learned to imagine where she was. The ridge named for Walter Cotman's family was a long one, curving out toward the river between the two creek valleys of Willow Run and Katie's Branch. As it came near to the river valley it got narrower, its sides steeper and more deeply incised by hollows. When Elton and Mary Penn were making their beginning there, the uplands were divided into many farms, few of which contained as much as a hundred acres. The hollows, the steeper hillsides, the bluffs along the sides of the two creek valleys were covered with thicket or woods. From where the hawks saw it, the ridge would have seemed a long, irregular promontory reaching out into a sea of trees. And it bore on its back crisscrossings of other trees along the stone or rail or wire fences, trees in thickets and groves, trees in the house yards. And on rises of ground, or tucked into folds, were the gray, paintless buildings of the farmsteads, connected to one another by lanes and paths. Now she thought of herself as belonging there, not just because of her marriage to Elton but also because of the economy that the two of them had made around themselves and with their neighbors. She had learned to think of herself as living and working at the center of a wonderful provisioning: the kitchen and garden, hogpen and smokehouse, henhouse and cellar, of her own household; the little commerce of giving and taking that spoked out along the paths connecting her household to the others; Port William on its ridgetop in one direction, Goforth in its valley in the other; and all this at the heart of the weather and the world.

On a bright, still day in the late fall, after all the leaves were down, she had stood on the highest point and had seen the six smokes of the six houses rising straight up into the wide down-falling light. She knew which smoke came from which house. It was like watching the rising up of prayers, or some less acknowledged communication between Earth and Heaven. She could not say to herself how it made her feel.

She loved her jars of vegetables and preserves on the cellar shelves, and the potato bin beneath, the cured hams and shoulders and bacons hanging in the smokehouse, the two hens already brooding their clutches of marked eggs, the egg basket and the cream bucket slowly filling, week after week. But today these things seemed both dear and far away, as if remembered from another world or another life. Her sickness made things seem all awry and arbitrary. Nothing had to be the way it was. As easily as she could imagine the house in its completeness, she could imagine it empty, windowless, the tin roof blowing away, the chimneys crumbling, the cellar caved in, weeds in the yard. She could imagine Elton and herself gone, and the rest of them— Hardy, Hample, Cotman, and Quail—gone too.

Elton could spend an hour telling her—and himself—how Walter Cotman went about his work. Elton was a man fascinated with farming, and she could see him picking his way into it with his understanding. He wanted to know the best ways of doing things. He wanted to see how a way of doing came out of a way of thinking and a way of living. He was interested in the ways people talked and wore their clothes.

The Hamples were another of his studies. Jonah Hample and his young ones were almost useless as farmers, because, Elton maintained, they could not see all the way to the ground. They did not own a car, because they could not see well enough to drive—"They need to drive something with eyes," Elton said— and yet they were all born mechanics. They could fix anything. While Daisy Hample stood on the porch clucking about the weeds in their crops, Jonah and his boys, and sometimes his girls, too, would be busy with some machine that somebody had brought them to fix. The Hample children went about the neighborhood in a drove, pushing a fairly usable old bicycle that they loved but could not ride.

Elton watched Braymer, too. Unlike his brother and Walter Cotman, Braymer liked to know what was going on in the world. Like the rest of them, Braymer had no cash to spare, but he liked to think about what he would do with money if he had it. He liked knowing where something could be bought for a good price. He liked to hear what somebody had done to make a little money, and then to think about it and tell the others about it while they worked. "Braymer would be a trader if he had a chance," Elton told Mary. "He'd like to try a little of this and a little of that, and see how he did with it. Walter and Tom like what they've got."

"And you don't like what you've got," Mary said.

He grinned big at her, as he always did when she read his mind. "I like some of it," he said.

At the end of the summer, when she and Elton were beginning their first tobacco harvest in the neighborhood, Tom Hardy said to Elton, "Now, Josie Braymer can outcut us all, Elton. If she gets ahead of you, just don't pay it any mind."

"Tom," Elton said, "I'm going to leave here now and go to the other end of this row. If Josie Braymer gets there before I do, I'm going home."

When he got to the end of the row, Josie Braymer was not there, and neither were any of the men. It was not that he did not want to be bested by a woman; he did not want to be bested by anybody. One thing Mary would never have to do was wonder which way he was. She knew he would rather die than be beaten. It was maybe not the best way to be, she thought, but it was the way he was, and she loved him. It was both a trouble and a comfort to her to know that he would always require the most of himself. It stirred her.

She could feel ambition constantly pressing in him. He could do more than he had done—he knew he could—and he was always looking for the way. He was like an axman at work in a tangled thicket, cutting and cutting at the little brush and the vines and the low limbs, trying to make room for a full swing. For this year he had rented corn ground from Josie Tom's mother, down by Goforth, two miles away. When he went down with his team to work, he would have to take his dinner. It would mean more work for them both, but he was desperate for room to exert himself. In two years, after the death of Josie Tom's mother, Mary and Elton would go to that farm to live. In another two years they would move to the Jack Beechum place, a good, well-husbanded farm that would give them their chance. They foresaw none of that now. They were poor as the times, and they saw more obstacles than openings. And yet she believed without doubt that Elton was on his way.

It was not his ambition—his constant, tireless, often exhilarated preoccupation with work—that troubled her. She could stay with him in that. She had learned that she could do, and do well and gladly enough, whatever she would have to do. She had no fear. What troubled her were the dark and mostly silent angers that often settled on him and estranged him from everything. At those times, she knew, he doubted himself, and he suffered and raged in his doubt. He may have been born with this doubt in him, she sometimes imagined; it was as though his soul were like a little moon that would be dark at times and bright at others. But she knew also that her parents' rejection of him had cost him dearly. Even as he defied them to matter to him, they held a power over him that he could not shake off. In his inability to forgive them, he consented to their power over him, and their rejection stood by him and measured him day by day. Her parents' pride was social, belonging, even in its extremity, to their kind and time. But Elton's pride was creaturely, howbeit that of an extraordinary creature; it was a creature's naked claim on the right to respect itself, a claim that no creature's life could of itself invariably support. At times he seemed to her a man in the light in daily struggle with a man in the dark, and sometimes the man in the dark had the upper hand.

Elton never felt that any mistake was affordable; he and Mary were living within margins that were too narrow. He required perfection of himself. When he failed, he was like the sun in a cloud, alone and burning, furious in his doubt, furious at her because of her trust in him in spite of his doubt. How could she dare to love him, a man who did not love himself? And then, sometimes accountably, sometimes not, the cloud would move away, and he would light up everything around him. His own force and intelligence would be clear within him then; he would be skillful and joyful, passionate in his love of order, funny and tender.

At his best, Elton was a man in love—with her, but not just with her. He was in love, too, with the world, with their place in the world, with even that scanty farm, with his own life, with farming. At those times she lived in his love as in a spacious house.

Walter Cotman always spoke of Mary as Elton's "better half." In spite of his sulks and silences, she would not go so far as "better." That she was his half she had no doubt at all. He needed her. At times she knew with a joyous ache that she completed him, just as she knew with the same joy that she needed him and he completed her. How beautiful a thing it was, she thought, to be a half, to be completed by such another half! When had there ever been such a yearning of halves toward each other, such a longing, even in quarrels, to be whole? And sometimes they would be whole. Their wholeness came upon them like a rush of light, around them and within them, so that she felt they must be shining in the dark.

But now that wholeness was not imaginable; she felt herself a part without counterpart, a mere fragment of something unknown, dark and broken off. The fire had burned low in the stove. Though she still wore her coat, she was chilled again and shaking. For a long time, perhaps, she had been thinking of nothing, and now misery alerted her again to the room. The wind panted and sucked at the house's corners. She could hear its billows and shocks, as if somebody off in the distance were shaking a great rug. It was like something that somebody was doing. She felt not a draft but the whole atmosphere of the room moving coldly against her. She went into the other room, but the fire there also needed building up. She could not bring herself to do it. She was shaking, she ached, she could think only of lying down. Standing near the stove, she undressed, put on her nightgown again, and went to bed.

She lay chattering and shivering while the bedclothes warmed around her. She sensed that the time might come when sickness would be a great blessing, for she truly did not care if she died. She thought of Elton, who could not even look at her, out of the day's wind that had caught him up, and see that she was sick. If she had not been so miserable, she would have cried. But then her thoughts began to slip away, like dishes sliding along a table pitched as steeply as a roof. She went to sleep.

When she woke, the room was warm. A teakettle on the heating stove was muttering and steaming. Though the wind was still blowing hard, the room was full of sunlight. The lamp on the narrow mantelshelf behind the stove was filled and clean, its chimney gleaming, and so was the one on the stand by the bed. Josie Tom was sitting in the rocker by the window, sunlight flowing in on the unfinished long embroidery she had draped over her lap. She was bowed over her work, filling in with her needle and a length of yellow thread the bright corolla of a jonquil—or "Easter lily," as she would have called it. She was humming the tune of an old hymn, something she often did while she was working, apparently without awareness that she was doing it. Her voice was resonant, low, and quiet, barely audible, as if it were coming out of the air and Josie Tom also were merely listening to it. The yellow flower was nearly complete.

And so Mary knew all the story of her day. Elton, going by Josie Tom's in the half light, had stopped and called.

She could hear his voice, raised to carry through the wind:

"Mrs. Hardy, Mary's sick, and I have to go over to Walter's to plow."

So he had known. He had thought of her. He had told Josie Tom.

Feeling herself looked at, Josie Tom raised her head and smiled. "Well, are you awake? Are you all right?"

"Oh, I'm wonderful," Mary said. And she slept again.

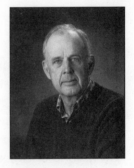

Wendell Berry is a native of Henry County, Kentucky. The main characters in this story have appeared also in other writings by him. This story is in his latest book, *Fidelity: Five Stories* (Pantheon, 1992).

PHOTO CREDIT: DAN CARRACO

I have nothing to say about the story that I haven't said in it. The story and I both are from a border state. If we are "Southern," we are only relatively so.

Pinckney Benedict

BOUNTY

(from *Story*)

It was a hot cloudless August day, and the sun heliographed off the windshield and side mirrors of Candles's truck as he drove past the county courthouse. He parked the truck at a slant against the curb, set the handbrake, unfolded himself in a leisurely way out of the cab. He was a tall man who wore walked-over workboots bound up with duct tape, wore jeans that were too short for his long legs, the denim washed nearly white.

Three kids were lounging against a boarded-up storefront across the street, and they watched as Candles rummaged in the covered bed of the truck. He pulled out the slack body of a dog, slung it across his shoulders. He held its slim forelegs in his left hand, hind legs in his right.

The least of the kids finished the cigarette he was smoking, pitched the butt down a sewer grating at his feet. The three crossed the street, hands in their pockets, took up positions behind Candles. They gestured at the man and the dog, talking in quiet voices among themselves. The least one said, "What do you figure you'll do with that'ere dog, mister?"

Candles ignored the question, kept his eyes on the sidewalk just in front of his feet. The boys conferred again, laughed. "You know it's dead, don't you?" the biggest one asked. The least one said, "Dummy," made sure his voice was loud enough to carry to

Candles. They followed him as far as the courthouse doors and then abandoned him, went back across the street to their place.

Candles pushed through the swinging doors of the courthouse. They shut behind him, and he paused a moment while his eyes adjusted to the relative dark of indoors. Then he proceeded down the hall, entered the first room he came to.

A pasty-faced character was writing on some papers there and he stopped the scratching motion of his pen when Candles entered. The character peered up at the dog settled across Candles's shoulders like a stole. "This the sheriff's office?" Candles asked.

"Three doors down, on your left," the character said, and went back to sorting through his documents.

Candles went out, walked down the hall, counting doors. When he came to the third, he opened it. "Sheriff?" he said.

A woman inside said, "This is the sheriff's office." Candles stepped in, closed the door behind him with the heel of his boot. "Can I help you with something?" the woman said. She was small, seated behind a scarred wooden desk. She wore a blue uniform blouse that had a deputy's badge pinned to the flap of the pocket. There was a rack of rifles and shotguns behind her. The weapons were secured in their case with a brass padlock.

"I guess you can," Candles said to her. He lifted the dog off his shoulders, laid it on the tile floor. It was a medium-sized brown dog that had been shot just at the base of its pointed skull. Its dark tongue lolled out of its mouth. "I believe you got a bounty on these," he said, and prodded the dog's corpse with his foot.

The deputy rose from her seat, circled the desk. She stood over the dog a moment. Then she called toward the half-open door of an inner office. "Sheriff Gallantin," she said. "Could you come here a minute?"

The sheriff came out of his office, a cup of coffee in his hand. He was a squat solid man with a belly on him, moved slowly. He wore metal taps on the heels of his shoes, and they rang against the uncarpeted floor of the office. He looked at Candles and then at the deputy, who directed his gaze to the dog. He grimaced when he saw it lying there.

"What is this?" he said. He gestured at Candles. "Did you bring that thing in here?"

"This man," the deputy said, and her voice was nicely controlled, "says that we're offering a bounty on dogs."

"Wild dogs," Candles said.

"The bounty is on coyotes, not dogs," the sheriff said. He set his coffee down on the deputy's desk. "You think we would pay people just to shoot their dog and bring it in?"

"This here's a coydog," Candles said. He knelt beside the animal, dug his hand into the ruff of hair on its neck, raised its head. The dog's loose jaw yawned open. "It's a cross between coyote and dog." He pointed the snout of the dog first toward the deputy, who stepped away, and then toward the sheriff. "Look there," he said, and gave the dog's narrow head a shake. "Don't that look like a coyote cross?"

"It looks like a dog to me," the sheriff said. He crouched with a little difficulty next to Candles, grabbed at the dog's body, tried to get his arms under it, as if he would load it back onto Candles's shoulders and that way be quit of it. When he couldn't get a good grip on the thing, he sat back. "You pick it up," he said to Candles. "Pick it up and get it out of here."

"Then you won't pay?" Candles asked. There was disbelief in his voice. "I got a whole truckload of these things parked out there," he said, and gestured behind him. "What am I suppose to do with those?" he said.

The sheriff stood, looked Candles over, appeared to consider. "It's not our office anyway," he said. He edged around Candles and the dog, stepped out into the hallway. "It's animal control you want. Let's get you down there to them and see what they have to tell you."

Candles watched him go. After a moment he grabbed the dog by its outstretched legs, hefted it back into its place. It weighed thirty or forty pounds, and he grunted as he rose from his crouch.

"Thank you for your help," he said to the deputy. She smiled at him without saying anything, returned to her desk. Candles left the office.

The sheriff was waiting for him up the hallway, at the door of the room Candles had entered earlier. Candles went to him, and the sheriff ushered him in. The pasty-faced character was still sitting there. "This is the man you want," the sheriff said, guiding Candles across the room. "This here's Leggy Gaines, your assistant dog warden."

"Animal control officer," Leggy said. He didn't stand. "What is it you want, Gallantin?"

The sheriff was grinning. "Where's Curtis?" he asked. To Candles he said, "Curtis is the real power around here. The head dogcatcher."

"Curtis is out on a call," Leggy said. "Somebody got a raccoon in their attic and it's tearing up the insulation. They're afraid it'll bite their kid or something."

"Well, I think you owe this man some money, Leggy," the sheriff said, indicating Candles. "He's gone and brought you a truckload of . . ." He paused. "What was it you brought?"

"Coydogs," Candles said. "I shot them. They been raiding my place, killing my sheep, so I set them up. They's more of them out there than what I killed. I imagine I'll get them after a while." He shifted the dog's body uncomfortably.

"Go ahead," the sheriff said. "Lay it on down. You found the place." He helped Candles to set the dog on the floor. Leggy looked at it where it lay. "This man here'll give you your bounty," the sheriff said.

"I don't know," Leggy said. He had on a pair of little round glasses, and he slid them down to the end of his nose. "I recall your office has got that bounty on coyotes, but I don't believe we've set out any kind of a policy on feral dogs or whatever."

"Our office?" the sheriff said. "We don't pay any bounty. That's you."

"Somebody pays," Candles said. "I heard."

"We do pay a small bounty on rabid animals, which would apply to dogs," Leggy said. "We have to send their heads down to the lab in the capital to get tested before we disburse that money. Maybe that's what you're thinking of."

"What kind of a bounty did you hear about?" the sheriff asked Candles. "How much?"

"Five dollars a dog. And I got a truckful out by the curb."

"In that heat," the sheriff said, and wrinkled his nose.

"Did these animals exhibit any of the symptoms of rabies?" Leggy asked. When Candles didn't answer, he said, "Stiff-legged, staggering, snap at their shadow, walk into things like they're blind. Foaming at the mouth is what most people notice."

Candles studied the image a minute. "No sir," he said. "Not that I seen, they didn't."

"There you go then," Leggy said. "It must be Gallantin's coyote bounty you're after."

"We got no bounty," the sheriff said.

"No more do we," Leggy said.

The three men stood in silence and regarded the dog in the middle of the floor. A fan that sat on a filing cabinet in the corner buzzed and rattled, sent a tepid stream of air from one side of the room to the other as it turned. Finally the sheriff said to Candles, "Well, let's see what we can do for you. You got anything in petty cash, Leggy?"

Leggy sighed, tapped a pencil against the bridge of his nose. "How many's he got?" he asked.

"How many you got?" the sheriff asked. "Six, seven?"

"Maybe fifteen," Candles said, "counting this one here."

"I don't think we can go five dollars on that many," the sheriff said. "How does two dollars a dog sound to you?"

"I don't know," Candles said. "Like I told you, I heard about a man that got five."

"Not around here he didn't," the sheriff said. "Two-fifty a head, and that's the most I ever heard of a man getting for a dead dog."

"Okay," Candles says. "If it's what you're offering, I guess I'll take you up." The sheriff looked at Leggy, who shrugged his agreement.

"You got it," Candles said. He started for the office door.

"Hold up," Leggy said. "You ain't leaving this mess here." He indicated the dog.

"Oh," Candles said, returning. "I thought you'd want it. For evidence or something."

"Well I don't," Leggy said. Candles bent and heaved the dog up. He balanced it across the back of his neck, and its legs hung down the front of his shirt. Its head trailed across his back, snout downward. The head bobbed loosely as Candles walked down the hall.

"Come on," the sheriff said to Leggy, who had not moved from where he sat.

Leggy said, "What is it you need me for?"

"To verify," the sheriff said. "We got to count the dogs he's got in his vehicle."

"You go," Leggy said. "You can count as good as I can."

"All right," the sheriff said. "We'll be back in a couple of minutes to give you the damage." He ducked out of the animal control office, followed Candles as he headed down the corridor.

Outside, Candles moved down the sidewalk with his stiff sweeping gait. Seeing what he carried, the couple of people that he met moved out of his way, rolled their eyes at the trailing sheriff as though they wondered when he was planning to haul in this demented hooligan.

One man took his eyes off Candles's figure, tugged at the sheriff's sleeve as he went by. "What you got there, Gallantin?" he asked. His breath was beery. "Coydog," the sheriff said. He pulled himself free and continued on before the drunken party could form his next question.

The three kids who had followed Candles earlier stood gathered around the bed of his old mud-colored truck. When Candles reached it, he slid the dog off his shoulders, dropped it onto the sidewalk, where it sprawled. The kids stared at him, peered into the bed of the truck, looked back at Candles again.

Candles ignored them. He reached into the truck, hauled another dog out, holding it by the loose skin at its withers and its hindquarters. It was a fawn-colored dog of no particular breed, with heavy forequarters and a narrow back end, an almost hairless whip tail. He heaved it onto the sidewalk next to the first. It lay with its head bent under its body at an unnatural angle. He reached into the truck again, extracted a third dog, a brown lanky mixed breed that had had its back broken by rifleshot, deposited it with the others.

"Whoa there," the sheriff said when he caught up to Candles. "You don't want to do that." He caught the odor that boiled from the truck, and the low buzzing of flies. "This is no place to put them dogs."

"It's a pack of them," the least kid said. "I told you it was a bunch of dogs he had in there." The three stood looking at the short line of bodies on the sidewalk.

"Just coydogs," the sheriff said to them. "Wild dogs. Nothing to worry about."

"How do you plan to count them then?" Candles asked. "We got to pull them out to count them." The bed of the truck was covered with a tarpaulin strung loosely over the high board sides. Candles leaned into the noisome space beneath the tarp, dragged another dog out, tossed it among the others.

"That'n there's a beagle," the least kid said.

Leggy came down the street in time to hear what the kid said. He was wearing a white uniform jacket that he had put on. "I don't believe I'm going to pay for any beagle," he said. He pushed his way through the little group around Candles's truck. "You told me these were coydogs, not pets," he said to the sheriff. "That was your word for it." He turned to Candles. "And I might not pay for these others here either, until their authenticity is established," he said.

Candles loomed over him, and his eyes were dark. "You told me two-fifty a dog," he said. "You didn't say that about authenticity." He flexed his big hands.

"Well, where did the beagle come from then?" Leggy wanted to know.

"How do I know where it come from," Candles said. "It was running with them others and I shot it."

"It's got trap marks," Leggy said. He bent down to the dog, which was a gray-muzzled beagle bitch. Its belly was swollen, lined with a double row of black teats. Leggy picked up its right forepaw, shook it. "I know trap sign when I see it," he said. "This leg's clear busted."

Candles's brow wrinkled. "Trap, shoot, I don't know. It was there with them others. They harry my sheep and drive them over a bluff or run them till they get a heart attack. They do it for fun," he said. He was breathing hard. "They don't even eat them."

The sheriff moved between them. "Why don't you just put them back in the truck," he said to Candles. He was hot and he spat his words. Candles stood where he was.

"They killed my cat too," Candles said.

"You pay that guy to kill dogs for you?" the least kid asked Leggy.

"Shoot, we could do that," the next biggest kid said. "How much do you get per dog?" he asked Candles, who ignored him.

"And they got in my melon patch," Candles said. "Busted open them sugar melons like they was eggs."

"He won't never answer what you ask him," the least kid said to Leggy, hooking a thumb toward Candles. "There must be something the matter with him. I believe he's simple."

"Go ahead, ask him something," the next biggest kid said.

The biggest kid had perched himself on the tailgate of the truck. He peered into the darkness of the truck bed, counted silently to himself. In a minute he declared, "They's better'n ten-eleven dogs in there, what I can see. Pretty big dogs." He hopped down from the back of the truck. "Some of 'em been there awhile too," he said.

"Anyway," Leggy said to the sheriff, "reason I come out is because Curtis called. I told him what you all were up to and he said you better stand by, on account of he wants to get a look at what was brought in. He said he wouldn't authorize no bounty without his okay."

The sheriff leaned against the fender of the truck, stood up when he recalled the carrion in the bed. He sighed. "All right," he said. "We'll wait on Curtis. He say how long he would be?"

"He was wrapping up the raccoon situation when he called. He said it might be a while."

"You got any more pets in your truck?" the sheriff asked Candles.

"I got nobody's pets," Candles said. "Just wild dogs is all."

"Wouldn't surprise me none if they were somebody's," the least kid said. "It might be he just goes around grabbing dogs. I know a lot of people that are missing their dogs around here." He looked at Candles with narrowed eyes.

"You want us to see?" the next biggest kid said. "Edgar'll go in there and check on if it's wild dogs or tame if you want." He pointed at the biggest kid.

"I'll do it for a dollar," Edgar said.

"No dollar," the sheriff said. "Don't you all have school?"

"It's summer," the least kid said.

"Okay then," the sheriff said. "You must have someplace you got to be. Why don't you take off?"

"Well sure," the least kid said. He started to cross the street, and the other two came with him. "We just thought we might could help," he said. The three of them retired to their spot in the boarded doorway.

Once there, the least one got out the makings for a cigarette, rolled himself one, stuck it in the corner of his mouth, and lit it. The kids did scissors-paper-stone together. When Edgar, the big-

gest one, lost at that, he headed out for the store on the corner
to get them all bottles of pop.

The sheriff said, "I think I'll go back to my office awhile. It's
cooler there. You fellows come get me when Curtis shows up,
won't you."

Candles looked worried. "I don't know about waiting," he said.
"It's a long way to go, back to the mountain. I got to get back to
my place."

"Stay or go. Whatever you want," the sheriff said. He started off
down the street, got half the way to the courthouse before Leggy
sang out, "Here he comes." He turned and, with the others,
watched the white animal control van as it made its way along the
street, coming toward them through the haze of pavement heat.

The brakes of the van whined as Curtis pulled to a stop beside
Candles's truck. He stuck his head out of the driver's window,
yelled, "This the place, Leg?" Leggy called back that yes, this
was it. Curtis threw the van into reverse, backed into the spot
next to the truck. When he cut the wheel at the last moment, the
van thumped the truck, and its bumper dragged a little streak of
primer from the truck's side.

"Damn," Curtis said, hopping out. He was a fat man with curly
black hair, and he walked as though his feet pained him, taking
mincing little steps. He bent down to inspect the scrape. "This
your truck, buddy?" he asked Candles, who had stepped forward.

"It's mine," Candles said.

"I'm awful sorry," Curtis said. He pressed at the scarred paint
with his fingers. "It don't look too bad though," he said, standing
up and dusting his hands against each other. "It ain't like you got
a million-dollar finish on that thing in any case, is it?" he said,
and laughed.

"No," Candles said.

"I always have trouble parking that wreck," Curtis said, jerk-
ing his thumb over his shoulder at the van. "We use to have an

old panel truck, and I could just swing it around on a dime, but this new one." He shook his head. "You ask Leggy here, he'll tell you."

Leggy nodded his head vigorously. "Curtis can't park for anything," he said.

"What's this here?" Curtis asked when he saw the dogs on the sidewalk. He sniffed at the back of the truck, said, "It don't smell any better than it might, does it?"

"These dogs," Leggy said. "We talked about these on the phone."

"I thought you said coyotes. I had to come down and check out this truck full of dead coyotes for bounty, you said."

"I never said that about coyotes. Coydogs, is what he told me," Leggy said. "I never heard of them but I figured you'd know."

Curtis turned to the sheriff. "I just snared a family of raccoons out of an attic of a house on the Tinder Road, and decided to check in before I went home. Nothing tire you out like fooling with raccoons. Just like little monkeys or something, the way they dash around."

From across the street, the least kid shouted, "That guy's been stealing dogs, Curtis. He's got Mrs. Shipley's little beagle dog right there in front of you if you look." He pinched his cigarette between his thumb and forefinger, dropped it on the sidewalk, ground it out with the toe of his tennis shoe.

"And somebody's German police dog too," the next biggest kid called out. "It's there in the truck. Edgar seen it. He told us."

Curtis snapped his head toward the kids, then back to the man. "There any truth in this?" he asked Candles, who said nothing, just backed up a couple of steps. "Sheriff?" Curtis said.

"I don't have any idea," the sheriff said. "He says he shot them running sheep on his place, and I'm as inclined to believe him as not. He's looking for a bounty price on them."

"Because we got some reports like that recently," Curtis said. "Folks missing their dogs. We thought might be it was a ring of thieves or something."

"I told him we'd give him two-fifty a dog," the sheriff said. "Your office and mine. But I guess we wouldn't have to pay him for the ones look like they were domesticated. Collars and such."

"It's more than that," Curtis said. "Statutes provide a stiff penalty if he's been killing pets. He could do time. I think you'd know about that, Sheriff Gallantin. As a peace officer and all."

Candles said, "Do time. For what?" He swept his arm over the dogs. "For this? Them's sheep killers. I lost twenty head, and just come into town because a fellow told me you'd pay." He looked a little panicked.

"I thought it was some funny business like that," Leggy said. "When he first come into the office. He give me a look up and down and it just about give me a chill."

"He said they were coydogs," the sheriff said. "I didn't know anything different."

"This beagle does look some familiar as I study it," Curtis said. He bent and prodded the dog with his forefinger. "I'll place it here after a while, if I think about it."

"You keep them," Candles said. He headed for the door of his truck, but Curtis was blocking the way. He veered aside, started to walk off down the street.

"He's getting away from you," the least kid said. Candles picked up his pace when he heard the kid's voice. The sheriff trotted after Candles, broke into a heavy run when he saw how fast the other man was moving. Still Candles pulled away from the sheriff, his long legs pumping under him. The two animal control officers stayed where they were.

"Whoa up there," the sheriff called out as Candles neared the street corner. Edgar came out of the store then, blundered without looking into Candles's path. He had three cold bottles of pop in his hands, and his eyes widened as Candles collided with him. The impact set the bottles spinning out into the street. Two of them shattered there, and the pop ran over the pavement and sizzled with carbonation. The third bottle spun on its side in the intersection.

Edgar and Candles sprawled together on the sidewalk. When Candles got up to run again, Edgar clung to him, shouting. Candles tried to shake him off, grabbed the collar of Edgar's shirt in his wide hands. He tried to thrust the kid away from him, and Edgar's shoulder blades thumped against the sidewalk.

They were tangled that way when the sheriff came up on them. He pulled them apart from each other, held on to Candles. "Don't you go anywhere," he said to Candles, who pulled away from him. He twisted the man's bony arm up behind his back, forced him to his knees. "Just cool down," he said into Candles's ear. Candles was trembling. Edgar continued to shout behind them.

"You fight with me and you'll wind up in a whole world of trouble," the sheriff said. He stood Candles up, pushed him against the brick wall of the store.

Edgar stood up, darted into the middle of the street. He kicked around among the shards of bottle glass, picked up the unbroken pop. He inspected it with a critical eye. "This's all that's left," he told the other two kids when they rushed up to him. They gathered around Candles and the sheriff, who was patting him down.

"Give him a good poke in the ribs," the least kid said.

"You ain't even got your nightstick, nor handcuffs," Edgar said. "He knocked me down and busted my pop. He like to killed me." He held out his scraped and bleeding hands as testimony.

"You ever heard of obstructing justice?" the sheriff asked them. When Candles stirred, the sheriff hissed at him, "You ever heard of resisting arrest?" Then, to the kids again, he said, "Scat."

They stood watching a moment longer. The least kid put his hands on his hips, pursed his lips like he intended to say something more. Then the three of them turned in a body and sauntered to the corner store. The storekeeper stood in his door, wiping his hands on his apron. "Everything all right, Sheriff Gallantin?" he said.

"Give them a soda, will you?" the sheriff said. The storekeeper led the kids inside.

Tucked into Candles's right boot, snug against his lean calf, the sheriff discovered a long bone-handled folding knife. He opened it, squinted along the blade, tested the edge against the hair on his arm. "Some sharp pigsticker," he said.

"Skinning knife," Candles said into the wall.

The sheriff shoved him in the middle of his back. Candles's head struck the brick wall, and his lower lip began to bleed. "I'll ask you when I want to know something," the sheriff said. He closed the knife, slipped it into his pocket. He propelled Candles along the sidewalk in front of him.

"You busted him, Gallantin," Leggy said as Candles and the sheriff approached the truck and the animal control van. "We saw it. Plenty righteous," he said. The sheriff said nothing, kept Candles moving toward the truck.

"We got the evidence right here," Curtis said. He climbed out of the back of the truck, wearing a white surgical mask over his nose and mouth. His hands were covered by a pair of thick leather gauntlets. He dumped the body of a young Alsatian onto the pavement and pulled the mask down around his neck.

"What are they doing with my dogs?" Candles asked. He spoke softly because of his injured lip. The sheriff threw open the driver's-side door of the truck. Candles craned his neck around to see what Curtis and Leggy were up to.

"Get in there," the sheriff said. Candles climbed into the truck, sat staring forlornly out the open window at the sheriff, who closed the door.

"You got your keys?" the sheriff asked.

"Sure," Candles said. He dug in one of his pockets, held the truck keys up. They were secured by a couple links of light chain to a round leather tag. Candles held the keys out as though the sheriff might want to take them from him.

"No," the sheriff said. "I don't want your keys. Just start this thing." He marched around the truck, said to Leggy and Curtis, "Get them dogs in the truck."

"Wait a second, Gallantin," Curtis said. "You got no jurisdiction here. You don't tell animal control what to do."

"No," the sheriff said. "I guess I don't." He leaned down and picked up one of the dogs. He grimaced at the hairy feel of its hide in his hands, sighed as he heaved its limber weight into the bed of the truck. It struck with a muffled thump against the other dogs.

He grabbed the forepaws of the Alsatian, but he couldn't lift the dog off the ground. After a moment's hesitation, Leggy took up the dog's back end, and they swung the heavy body over the board tailgate and into the truck. As the two of them loaded the rest of the dogs, Candles cranked the truck. The starter motor spun and spun and finally the engine caught. Dark exhaust plumed from the tailpipe. Curtis stood back and watched.

The last dog to go into the truck was the beagle. When he had pitched it in, the sheriff walked back to the cab of the truck. "There you go," he said to Candles. "You're all loaded up. Now roll." He leaned into the window, spoke softly. "And don't come back here with another mess like this."

When Candles opened his mouth to speak, the sheriff held up a forestalling hand. "I don't need to hear it," he said. "I'm not sure exactly what went on here," he said, indicating the back of the truck, "and I don't believe I care to know."

"What do I do with them now?" Candles asked.

"Hell, I don't care," the sheriff said. "You got a shovel?"

"Sure," Candles said.

"Dig a big hole," the sheriff said. "Dump them in it. Cover them with caustic lime. Fill the hole back up."

"I never figured on nothing like this when I come down," Candles said.

"You bet you didn't," the sheriff said. He stepped away. Candles forced the truck into first gear, stalled it out. The truck rocked back to where it had been. Candles grimaced, twisted the key again, but the truck refused to start.

"Flooded it out," Leggy said. Candles cranked the truck again, and this time it roared to life. Candles gave it the gas and bumped one wheel up over the curb as he pulled into the street. He narrowly missed a sedan that was passing. The sedan's driver blew his horn, waved a fist. Candles turned the truck north and headed away from the men, out of town.

After he was gone, Curtis climbed into the animal control van without a word, slammed the door behind him, pulled out of his parking space. "Curtis'll be okay here after a while," Leggy said. The van slowed for a stop sign, rolled through it, rounded a corner. "It's just he doesn't like people to order him around."

"Sure," the sheriff said. "Curtis is okay. I imagine I know how he feels." The two of them walked toward the courthouse together.

The three kids wheeled back onto the street, swigging their pop, at about the time Leggy and the sheriff reached the courthouse. As the kids were moving to take up their place at the storefront, a long-limbed redbone hound came wandering up the street and sniffed at the section of sidewalk where the bodies had lain.

"Check that out," the least kid said. "He don't even know it's a massacre of his own."

The redbone moved from one spot to another, snuffing. The least kid picked up a small stone from the street, shied it at the dog. The stone skittered off the pavement, and the redbone raised its head, pricked its ears. The other two kids pitched rocks as well. The redbone yelped, broke for cover. It holed up under an old Malibu wagon across the street and lay there, watching the kids warily from between the car's wheels.

"Hey," the sheriff called from the doorway. "You want to leave that hound alone."

"Okay," the least kid said. The three of them parleyed, dropped the few stones they had gathered. They darted glances at Leggy and the sheriff, disappeared down a dusty side alley.

Leggy spat dryly on the sidewalk and went on into the courthouse. The sheriff peered down the alley. He squinted after the kids, but the day was bright and the space between the buildings was filled with shadows. He shaded his eyes, couldn't make out their progress at all.

The redbone pulled itself out from under the Malibu, glanced around. When it saw that the kids were gone, it headed back up the street the way it had come. It zigzagged from one side of the road to the other, nose down, nails clicking against the hardtop.

The sheriff stayed where he was until the dog too was out of his sight. A big garbage bin stood next to him, just outside the courthouse doors. The sheriff patted at his pockets one after the other, at length withdrew Candles's skinning knife. He turned it in his hand, ran his thumb over its flawed bone handle. Then he tossed it into the bin, where it slipped down among the papers and crumpled pop cans and assorted trash to thump against the metal bottom. The sheriff pushed against the wide doors of the courthouse, which opened smoothly for him on their oiled hinges, and passed inside.

Pinckney Benedict grew up and continues to live on his family's dairy farm just north of Lewisburg, West Virginia. He was educated at Princeton University and the Writers' Workshop at the University of Iowa. He has published two collections of short stories, *Town Smokes* and *The Wrecking Yard*. His stories have appeared in *Ontario Review, Southern, Wigwag,* Italy's *Grazia, The Oxford Book of American Short Stories,* and a number of other magazines and anthologies. A novel, *Dogs of God,* is forthcoming from Nan A. Talese Books/Doubleday.

PHOTO CREDIT: C.C.F. GACHET

For years a sheep-farming neighbor of ours has conducted a running battle with our local pack of wild dogs; he provided the initial inspiration for the character of Candles. My family has had its share of *unfortunate run-ins with the dogs also. They eat cats and harry livestock on a regular basis. Weary of the encounters, I thought, "Okay, I'll kill a few of the bastards." In writerly fashion I sat down at my typewriter before turning to the trap or the rifle. Not long after I finished "Bounty," a feral dog chased my wife across the yard. She lost her footing on our porch and plunged headfirst through the screen door and fractured her arm. So probably I got my actions in the wrong order.*

Kevin Calder

NAME ME THIS RIVER

(from *Indiana Review*)

T he summer Camille DeLand turned eighteen she decided
to go live with her grandmother, Ms. Navada Farra De-
Land, on Hilton Head Island, because she was tired of listening
to her mother and father telling her about all the talent she had
that was going to waste. Tired of the doors that slammed and
slammed and slammed.

She called her earth-sister Winnie.

"Well, what are you going to do all summer?" Winnie asked. It
came as no surprise to Camille that Winnie would be absolutely
prostrate with anguish at the news. As if saying good-bye was
easy on Camille.

"For that matter, what am *I* going to do all summer? I thought
we were swimming on the swim team this year. I thought we
were going to get tans and play tennis."

"I'm going to write a novel, darling," Camille said into her
old black phone. Her parents had had a private line installed in
her room because they were bad about taking important phone
messages. "And I might even take voice lessons from Lady Faith
Hollis. My grandmother said she's coming to stay with us."

"What about Vanderbilt?" Winnie wondered. "Well, I guess
you'll be back in time for us to fix up our room. I'm so excited
about it, aren't you? I mean, Bonner Hall. Jane-Gower Whitley

told me that's where all the cool people live. What are you talking about 'voice lessons'? How does Navada know you can sing? I know I've never heard you sing a note."

"She was a famous opera star in New Orleans in the fifties. She knows of my talent. She was in *Tosca* and *Aïda* and *La Bohème* and *Manon Lescaut*. So was Lady Faith. They were in them together. And Winnie," here came the difficult part, "I don't think I'm going to Vanderbilt. Or anywhere else."

"What, are you high, Camille? I mean, we planned all this out. If you don't go with me, who will I go to parties with? Who will listen to me talk about all the terrible things Oliver Benning says to me?"

"You'll be fine," Camille reassured her.

"You know what's even scarier? Who am I going to live with? All I can say is you never can tell what kind of basket case you're going to end up with for a roommate so I'll just keep telling myself you'll change your mind before the summer's over. My mom told me about a girl she knew at the University of Georgia who had a lesbian roommate. What if that happens to me?"

"Lesbians don't go to colleges like Vanderbilt," she said. "They're all in Massachusetts."

Then came the tactic she knew Winnie was going to use on her. "And just what does *you-know-who* have to say about all this?"

Camille put the phone on her dressing table and began combing her long red hair, gazing at herself in the mirror. Then she thought of his eyes. Green eyes that meant business when they studied you. Hypnotic and precarious and wonderful. "Oh, you must mean Michael Finnie. I'm sure it will tear him apart," she said carelessly, spraying herself with Chanel No. 19. "No boys this time," she went on. "No boys to fuck up my fortune."

"I'm envious, Camille. Life by the sea. I'm just so sad and excited and envious I don't know what to say."

"Say you'll come visit," Camille said, so thankful Winnie let the you-know-who issue drop. "Say you'll hear me sing."

She hung up and stared at herself in the mirror a long time.

She had decorated this mirror with clippings of headlines from magazines and newspapers and pictures of her favorite stars. SCIENTIST DISCOVERS PLANET IN OUR SOLAR SYSTEM one title read. And from *Mademoiselle,* SIT ON YOUR HANDS AND DON'T CALL ANYONE, LET *HIM* CALL *YOU.* A photo of Madonna.

Then she sat down on the bed and started itemizing everything in her room. There were pink cotton half-curtains with matching pink cornice boards. Mauve carpet layered with Indian rugs in varying shades of the same. There was an old black trunk that her father had taken around the world before he married her mother and could still do as he pleased with his parents' money. On the trunk were stickers from all the cities. Most prominent was a wine-colored sticker that said CAIRO in yellow letters with a palm tree making the *I.* It lay open at the foot of the bed, stacked with magnificent hand-loomed blankets done in bright colors. There were yellow ones and red ones and ones with stripes. Stripes of purple and orange and white and turquoise.

She picked up the book she'd been reading, *Speaking of Secrets,* and read two chapters.

After she'd done every single thing she could think of to keep herself from calling Michael until she was safe away on Hilton Head, she could stand it no more and dialed the number.

Michael Finnie worked at Antinori's Vintage Clothiers in Little Five Points. His job was to receive and sort out all incoming clothes. He considered himself very lucky to have this position because of all the unusual things he'd found emptying the pockets. He'd found an original Cherokee Indian wheat penny from 1902 and a book of stamps from Paris, France, and a wad of money that turned out to be three one-hundred-dollar bills.

He had shared some of his treasures with Camille: an antique wristwatch with hands that glow in the dark, and a silver ring he found in the lining of a raincoat, which bore the inscription LET ME BE NOT TO THE MARRIAGE.

The day they met Camille had wandered into Antinori's and

bought an old house dress. It was made of sea-green cotton and had the constellations all over it. All the stars connected with black thread. Michael was in charge of ringing up sales that day because the girl who usually did that had eloped with a Korean the day before.

"I certainly hope things straighten out," she said to him unexpectedly.

"I'm afraid I don't understand," he muttered, punching the keys on the cash register.

"Whatever it is you're worrying about," she replied. "I get that way over people too."

He looked at her with an elated kind of recognition as he folded the dress. He'd been thinking just that moment that he would leave no more messages on Corinne Sykes's answering machine. He'd had his share of relentless pursuit.

His keep-everyone-at-a-safe-distance nature rose up inside him, taking control, and he said, "So what are you supposed to be, a mind reader?" He surprised himself with his sharp tone.

"More of a facial expressions reader. If we're going to put a label on it," Camille said and smiled. "I'd love to work in a place like this," she said looking at the row of old wig stands. "I like the makeup on those mannequins. They must be from the sixties."

Michael let his guard down just long enough to have a daydream about driving around with Camille in a 1968 convertible Mustang. In his vision she was smiling the smile she'd just flashed him and saying the most interesting things.

"Listen, darling," she sighed in her best captivating Audrey Hepburn voice. "Why don't we catch the French movie that's playing at the Ellis. Let's see," she said, putting a finger up to her lip and looking from side to side. "And afterward we could get a bottle of wine and walk along the Chattahoochee. That is, of course, if you don't already have plans."

A series of familiar wheels began spinning in Michael's head. A chain reaction that felt like soft breath on his neck. He felt it in his arms. Down low in his back near his buttocks. At least it would be entertaining, he thought. At least it would be something out of the ordinary. She seems like the type who would do all the talking.

They agreed to meet at the Ellis theater at seven.

The movie turned out to be so long and so boring Camille had to go to the bathroom twice. Then they went and had chardonnay at Mick's. They sat there making fun of the movie. Then they had more wine and drove out to the river and had sex three times on its grassy banks and the rest is history.

"I've been reading poetry," he said on the phone upon hearing the news.

It thrilled Camille that Michael was so into soul-searching. And that he drove a Volvo and that he was twenty-three years old and lived in an apartment by himself in Virginia Highlands.

"I can't believe you're doing this. But I must confess this is not entirely unexpected," he said.

"But the only person I told was Winnie," Camille said.

"No. What I mean to say is that I know so because of the dreams. I've been having dreams about the swallow trapped in the house. It flies around banging and banging into the windows as I try and save it. That is the dream of impending doom.

"Anyway, I have to read you this poem," he said. "Would you like me to read it to you?"

"Oh, please do," she squealed. "Please read it to me."

" 'You Who Never Arrived,' by Rainer Maria Rilke," he said and began to read.

> *You, Beloved who are all*
> *the gardens I have ever gazed at,*
> *longing. An open window in*
> *a country house—, and you almost*
> *stepped out, pensive, to meet me.*
> *Streets that I had chanced upon,*
> *you had just walked down and vanished.*
> *And sometimes, in a shop, the mirrors*
> *were still dizzy with your presence and*

startled, gave back my too-sudden image.
Who knows? Perhaps the same bird
echoed through both of us
yesterday, separate, in the evening.

"Oh, God, what a beautiful poem," she said looking out her window over the lawn. It was first dark. A dreamy twilight. A hue the color of tea and jonquils thrown over the houses, which stood tall and dark. The streetlights and fireflies just beginning their night watch.

I will go to Hilton Head and write a novel, she was thinking. I will not think about Michael Finnie and how I want him to ask me for my hand in marriage. All the air in Atlanta has been breathed up.

"You have to make me a copy of that divine poem," she said. "I have to hang up now. My dad says we're heading out at seven and I still have things to pack."

"I'll write you all the time," he said.

"Try to visit me if you get the time, although I know you'll be working."

"This is killing me," he added. "This saddens me so."

She hung up the phone and stuck it under the bed. She put on a Moschino nightshirt that had EXPENSIVE SLEEPWEAR embroidered across the chest in red, and finished getting her things in order. She packed three nightgowns and two bathing suits and a dozen books and some walking shorts and some jeans and T-shirts and a blank book with the Little Prince on the cover. She made a hanging bag with a suit and two dresses and some rayon pants. She stuffed her socks and underwear in the corners of the bag.

At twelve-thirty she was still awake.

"You still up, honey?" It was Camille's father. He was standing in the doorway with light from the hall behind him. He looked tall and sad like an old faithful tree.

"Just finished packing," Camille said.

The light was dim and gold in Camille's room.

"It's going to be a different kind of summer around here with you missing," he said walking into the room.

"Why don't you take some time to write, or take voice from Mama's friend," he began, "but come back and go to . . ."

"I'm not talking to you about it," she said, burying her face down in her book. "I'm not having this exhausted conversation again."

He sat down on the bed next to her and put his face in his hands, caressing his forehead.

"It just breaks my heart to see you make this mistake," he said. "I think if I could just understand why . . ."

Camille put her book aside and reached down into her old-fashioned crocodile traveling bag and withdrew a pack of Camels. "Because, darling," she said as she lit the cigarette. "Not all the greats went to college. Michelangelo didn't learn sculpture in a classroom. How do you think Gauguin learned to paint Tahiti?" She leaned over into her father's space and whispered, "*He went there.*"

She got up and paced around the room. "You know, Dad," she said, "when an artist studies art he must first learn so much shit about doing it the right way that what's expected of him becomes the art. His real talent is locked away inside him forever. All gone away and hidden."

He stood up and faced her, assuming the strong arm of fatherly power. "I'm sorry you can't see this from my perspective," he said sternly.

They stood eye to eye. "Same to you," Camille said and blew a big cloud of smoke that lingered blue under the light from the lamp on the nightstand. It turned like a clockwork of blue wheels.

He walked across the hall and climbed in bed with his wife, Celia, the mother of his beautiful crazy redheaded daughter who caused him so much worry.

"You've let her do as she pleases all her life," he said. The ceiling fan above the bed stirred long pieces of Celia's auburn hair.

It floated about her face like a spiderweb. "That's what's wrong with her."

"Nobody can do anything with her," Celia said, half-asleep. "Don't blame me for it. She'll be back here in two months begging us to let her go off to school.

Ms. Camille Rochelle DeLand, Private Journal:
Summer, 1988

June 15, 1988

Dear Trustworthiness,

There she stands, I was thinking when I laid eyes on my famous grandmother as she stood flailing her arms wildly at us when we drove up in the driveway. She was so tiny and skinny among all the plants on the front porch. Ms. Navada Farra DeLand, of New Orleans, Louisiana, and Atlanta, Georgia, and Hilton Head, South Carolina. All five feet and two inches of her, dressed in a white sleeveless summer dress and yellow leather sandals and a light blue scarf tied around her waist and red lipstick. She still dyed her hair blond. A divine image of loveliness.

After Dad left we could talk. I had been dying to talk to someone for hours. I refused to speak to him in the car. I just slept and read the whole way down. I finished this book I've been reading. It was called *Speaking of Secrets*. By an author from Argentina. It was about this wonderful, sad woman named Louise who was of French-Russian descent. She lived in Paris, France, and married this handsome man named Pierre who beat her every chance he got until she went to court about it and lost because people thought she was making it up. Then she left him and had two lesbian affairs with women she hardly knew at all. She saw Pierre on the street one day years later and shot him and was sent to prison. It was a coed prison in the South of France. She started fucking the prison guard (his name was Didier) and so they fell in love. He helped her escape and they went to live in the German Black Forest. The end was so wonderful. It ended with her looking out the window over the lake that was in the front yard of their house while he made a fire in the stove. It was such a moving story.

Anyway, Navada and I talked and I told her about everything that's going on. We were sitting in the solarium surrounded by stained glass windows drinking Cokes and eating Fig Newtons and I said, "Well, I'd have to say he's crazy about me. But it's not quite what you'd think, really. Perhaps the hardest part of all was when I told myself there needed to be a change."

"Love never changes," Navada said.

"I told him I was writing a novel. And about the voice lessons. We'll probably get married someday. After I've published the novel."

"It's wonderful you want to write. Did you know that when you were two years old you displayed signs of genius? I said to your father, 'That child is going to do something great,' and I'm as sure of it today as I was then.

"Lady Faith might come sometime next week. She'd be delighted to give you voice lessons. We're going to be doing a lot of practicing this summer. You know, going over some of the old operas we did in New Orleans. I'm not sure how successful it will be on my part but I'm sure she can still sing like a bird."

"I'd love to hear you sing again," I said.

"And you've found someone you really like," she said, chewing a Fig Newton. In the sunlight that beamed in through the stained glass her hair looked tall and orange and hard from hairspray. I wanted to tap on it with my fingernails.

"Yes. I look at it like this, Navada. Everyone needs someone to fuck. A significant other. An extension of the inner self. Michael understands about freeing the soul and astral flight. Most people go along with their lives and miss the boat. They don't grasp a single goddamn piece of it."

"Oh, Camille!" she said. "Please don't say those ugly words. It sounds so terrible. Christians don't give in to . . ."

I listened to all I could about Christians and went upstairs to my room and wrote Michael a letter.

Dear Michael, (I wrote)

Picture this: a three-story wooden house painted blue with burgundy trim with a deck that overlooks a garden with the most gorgeous colorful flowers and shrubs and ivies, and past that a dark ocean with whitecaps going out farther than you can see. The inside of the house is sunny and drafty. Old houses like this one keep cool in the summer without any air-conditioning. The rooms connect through doors and hallways and closets. My bedroom is on the top floor over to the left. I have a set of French doors that lead out onto my own little private sun patio. I miss you so much already. There is a maid named Delila and twelve closets (four of which are walk-ins) and there are two more flower gardens in the front yard. My bathtub is on legs off the floor like they used to make them around the turn of the century. Sometimes when I'm taking a bath I imagine you're in the tub rubbing the soap on me.

A poem has come to me in a dream. I haven't started the novel yet. Here is the poem:

> *If someone says they've seen me*
> *painting the notions of Earth*
>
> *tell them I say live and let live*
> *for Love, which is all we know*
>
> *is a monument of strength.*
>
> *I am a river of consciousness,—*
> *water seeping through rocks at the oracle.*
>
> *Name me this river.*
>
> *I have flown in my nightgown*
> *over the mountain.*

Please write and tell me what you think. The novel is going to be about war heroes and their wives and deceit and anger and love. It's going to be about seduction.

And Michael, although we may not hear the echo of the same bird, the same moon and stars will bathe us in their light.

Always,
Camille

P.S. ". . . what I do
       and what I dream must include thee, as the wine
       must taste of its own grapes."
That is part of a poem by Elizabeth Barrett Browning. My grandmother has the best library.

. . . I will send this poem to Michael. He is one of the most literate people I know. His apartment is filled up with books. Books stacked everywhere.

Navada is calling me from somewhere outside so let me wrap this up for now.

Back in Atlanta, Michael sat in the waiting room of his therapist, Dr. Josephine Philby. He went to see Josephine every Thursday. He was reading an article in *Time* about babies, how it takes forty-eight hours for the sperm to hook up with the egg and how some pregnancy tests are only accurate eighty-two percent of the time. That figure changes depending on what brand you use. He thought about the night before. He thought about his come swimming around in Annie Campbell. How while she'd slept he'd lain on his side, utterly miserable, watching the fireflies out the window. Annie was on the pill. There would be no egg.

Dr. Philby stepped out and invited Michael into her office. He saw the same couch and two Queen Anne chairs and the Persian rug and the bookshelf with the same five titles over at the end. She never read the books. The same titles were always in a row. Second shelf to the left.

"It's a pattern, I'm telling you, Josephine." He started talking before they sat down. "It's this same goddamn pattern that's making me so goddamn nervous all the time. Let's sit on the floor," he insisted. "It's too much of a cliché on the couch."

Josephine obliged silently. She sat down and propped herself up against one of the chairs.

She must be about forty, Michael thought, looking at his therapist. Blond and not at all doctor-looking.

He imagined her writing a thesis and cutting on a cadaver. Her red painted fingernails digging around in the dead person's stomach.

"What pattern are we speaking about?" she asked him. "If you're going to make me sit on this floor for an hour we'd best make ourselves as clear as we can." She laughed and tossed her hair back.

None of this was funny to Michael. He found Dr. Philby very antiseptic, but someone had to help him get away from his prison. He saw the guards. They were the ones who wrote the laws about breaking people's hearts.

"It's this dream I have all the time," he began. "Only it's more than a dream because this one part of it is always following me around. During the day."

"Do you want to tell me about it now?"

"I've been captured by everyone I've gone out with in the last year. That constitutes seven women. They have tied me to a chair underneath a giant black attic fan. What do fans mean?"

"I don't interpret the symbols. Tell me how it makes you feel."

"Awkward," Michael said. "Backed into a corner. They all have this look on their faces like *Now you're getting what you wanted and aren't you happy about it.* It's very sarcastic. They take turns approaching me with silver knives. They lay the knives on the floor at my feet in a circle that goes around the chair.

"I think it means I'm threatened. I can tell you this much. I won't let anyone get close to me. I can't. I'm afraid of the repercussions. Take Camille for instance. She is this girl who has been a companion to me this year. She is one of the most beautiful wonderful women I have ever met. I thought at first it would be like all the others—a sexual thing where we just did it and that was that? But it's different. I know she loves me. I love her. But

I hold her at a distance. She's eighteen years old but you'd never know it. We only screwed once so I can't exactly say I'm using her for that.

"We went camping last November in Tennessee. I drove because she wanted me to. For three days and nights we were together in the woods. There were waterfalls and mountains and deer. We didn't have a tent so we slept in sleeping bags under the stars. Nothing happened. I know she wanted something to happen because of the way she looked at me when we were lying there in the sleeping bags. She'd even take all her clothes off when we went under the waterfall. I would say there is no chemistry between the two of us but I don't believe it. There could be chemistry. And I really like her. Yet this terrible pattern of finding people to care about takes hold of me when I already have what I need and am not satisfied. I am just not goddamn satisfied.

"And then I go out and get a little pussy and think I'm in love and two weeks later I hate the girl I've been fucking and move on . . ."

Josephine's mind began to leave the office. She was sorry for the misgivings of life. She would write any prescriptions her patients wanted. Do you want Valium? You take some. You won't care if the goddamn house burns down. Down, down, down. My blame lies in the grave with my father, she thought. I buried it when he died because it's unhealthy. We do not allow unhealthiness at the Manor. Or uncleanliness or anyone being misguided by too many questions. At the Manor we hold hands and worship in harmony with Dr. Black Hawk. We sit by the fountain before we go to work and tell one another that we are one and God hugs each one of us through Dr. Black Hawk and we are in trouble with Him if we do not pay our rent on time.

July 5, 1988
Dear Faithful Journal,

Lady Faith Hollis arrived last week. The day she arrived Navada and I had been shopping at this fabulous mall called Shelter Cove. We'd been to Lord & Taylor where I bought a red cotton dress and two jumpsuits and some socks and a white T-shirt that says CHANEL on it. (I'm going to wear the T-shirt with my black jeans and my all-gold jewelry.) Then we went to Polo/Ralph Lauren and I got a white skirt and two antique necklaces and a pair of sandals. I'm getting off track here. I was going to tell you about Lady Faith.

Navada and I were still in the driveway getting our packages out of the trunk when this big white Cadillac pulled in. It had a license plate on the front that said PRAISE. At that point all I could see behind the windshield was a giant hat and some sunglasses. It wasn't till she got out I could see all of what must have been three hundred pounds of her. The hat she wore was made of straw and she had on a bright yellow muumuu. Yards and yards of yellow madras.

She got out and ran over to Navada and kissed her and then she grabbed me and pressed me against her and I became lost in all the cloth.

Then she spoke: "It must be you," she said and looked at Navada holding my cheeks in her hands. She smelled like a mixture of perfume and mothballs and liquor.

As soon as we were inside the house I said I had some letter writing to do and so I'm up here writing this. I got a letter from Winnie in the mail last Thursday, June 30.

Dear Camille-Darling, (it said)
Everyone is so sad you're gone but we understand why you left. Have you been writing? I haven't done much of anything except put up with Valarie Lipsy. We lay out at the pool at the club. She's the worst tennis player I've ever seen. The only reason she even tries is to impress her father and that boy she's so crazy about. Russell Hall. How could anyone like Russell Hall? She goes on and on about him, saying things like, That man knows how to lay pipe. If she knew how stupid she sounded. Goddamn rednecks.

See? I wish you would come on back now. We've got to think about what we're going to do with our room. I saw

Michael Finnie when I went in Antinori's. I was just walking around browsing when he came bounding out of the back room. He said he saw me through the curtain and wanted to know if I'd heard from you and I said, No I haven't, but I'm sure she's written to you. He told me you had and for you to expect a letter with a collage on the back of it any day now. He looks forlorn. Languid. You love him and you're going to fuck everything up if you don't hurry up. Think about it. We have to leave for Vanderbilt on September 1. When will you see him if you stay there so long? I guess you'll probably write me back and remind me it was my idea the two of you needed space. You remember what I read to you about Pursuit-Distance Relationships don't you? Well, don't overdo it, darling.

When are you going to invite me down there? How are the singing lessons? Who do you hang around with? I'm sure I'll end up calling you to get all the answers to my questions.

Ciao,
Winnie

Dear Winnie, (I wrote back)

Love is eternal. It is flying low in a private airplane with the windows open. Nobody knows the destination and nobody wants to. It's forbidden to ask where you're going. It satisfies all we need from this world. Love is champagne. If we do not drink it we will never get a buzz from it. In case you're wondering, I didn't pay any attention to you when you read me that bullshit about Pursuit-Distance. I love you, Winnie. You are the best friend I have. You are my earth-sister. I would love it if you came down here.

Sincerely,
Camille

I haven't done any singing yet. Navada and Lady Faith practice all day long every day. Just the two of them. It's like being at the Met. Women of voice. Perennial talent. Stick-to-it-iveness.

I have to tell you about last night. I have two charming friends here who live on my street. Their names are Terri-Anne and Ida. I remember Navada mentioning them before I came to Hilton Head. They tell me they think I'm the neatest person they ever met and that they could tell me anything. Terri-Anne works at a gift shop in the mall for the summer. She's from Missouri. She has an old convertible. When we go out in it she wraps her head in a Hermès scarf and we all wear sunglasses.

Last night Ida threw a dinner party. She is house-sitting for her Aunt Frieda who is gone all summer producing a play in Alabama. We had the place to ourselves. Just the three of us at first. We made spaghetti and sat in the formal dining room. We were eating and listening to classical music (Debussy's *L'Apres-midi d'un Faune*) and drinking cognac. Terri-Anne had too much cognac. I don't know whose idea it was to drink that with dinner. She started saying every other word in French. She asked us, "How would you two like some male company? I could *téléphoner à des garçons si vous voulez bien, mes chères*."

She got on the phone and in thirty minutes the house was full of *garçons*. Five boys in the living room. Theodore and Dan and Rob and Wesley and Jody. Jody was the most appealing, that's for sure. Curly black hair and a T-shirt with angels eating watermelon on it and old jeans.

When he walked into Ida's house he walked over to her and said, "Quick, Ida! Do a magic trick. Put a spell on someone."

Ida closed her eyes and raised her arms and threw her head back and waved her fingers in the air. She opened her eyes and they looked at each other and laughed. Her arms glided down around his shoulders. They hugged and kissed and both of them commented on how too much time had passed since they last got together.

The business about the magic trick was unabashed creativity. I knew he drank from the same well I did. A mysterious, rugged-looking boy. An unfixed tomcat. Wild and delirious.

I was sitting next to Terri-Anne on the couch pretending to watch a movie when the rest of them came into the living room. As soon as he finished saying his hellos with Terri-Anne, Jody looked at me and said, "What's your name?" and I said, "Camille," and he said, "Come with me," and led me by the hand into the kitchen and filled my glass with some wine they'd brought with them and pretty soon we were on the front porch getting stoned off a joint he'd been saving in his small Indian wallet.

I was feeling deliciously anesthetized.

It hit me then who he was. He was the one Ida and Terri-Anne were always telling me I needed to meet because I would think he was the biggest trip. They were always saying, There's this guy we know who is an artist and he says the kind of things you say. You'd love him. You two would have so much to talk about.

"I'm gay," he said. "Let me get that out on the table."

I had no idea what to say to that. "Come on," I said. "Let's go look at the ships." We finished smoking and got in his car and drove out to one of the fishing docks.

We were on the dock and I was studying the reflections from the water on his face. I guess when he was stoned he had an affinity for profound philosophical thought. He said, "One of the disciples of Sigmund Freud asked him point-blank, 'Master, what's it all about?' And Freud replied, 'Love and work.' For me it is painting. I hope Ida's not pissed that we left like that."

"Oh, she won't be mad." I was looking down at the black water, how it swirled underneath the dock. It looked like Jody's hair. "I'll tell her we started talking and went for a drive. It's the truth, anyway. My friend Deidrie and I learned all about telling the truth this spring."

"I don't think a little white lie hurts. You know, just to spare someone's feelings if they ask you why you haven't called and you say you just can't say, Because I don't like you or anything you have to say.

"Look at those lights way out there," he said pointing out at the ocean."

"They're lighthouses," I said. "Probably for the shrimp boats that go up and down the shore all day long."

"Or the military."

"I hate the military. They'll think up any goddamn old thing to make the men in uniform look important. I never could figure out what sailors do on ships. All day and night aboard a ship."

"I know what I'd do if it was me on the ship with all those men," he said, and looked at me. Imagine saying that. God, he cracks me up.

"This morning I went to see Matthew play the cello in the Savannah Symphony. Matthew is my lover. We studied together at Columbia. He studied musicology and the cello and I studied him and art."

I was galvanized and kept silent and took it all in.

"It touches me in an unknown way to see a group of people who've made something as intangible and wonderful as music their obsession," he said.

"I know what you mean," I said. "Giving something of themselves back to the universe. That's why I'm going to be a writer," I told him. "It's what I know."

"I've tried lessons on the cello but it doesn't work," he said. "I'm afraid I'm not exceptional when it comes to that kind of concentration. You have to come over to my apartment tomorrow and you can write and I'll paint."

I just love talking to him. We talked for hours and hours and when I got home I knew I had made a true friend. A boyfriend. Only, of course, not really. I have an open mind when it comes to things like that. It doesn't bother me he wants to stick his dick inside Matthew.

Later,
Camille

Camille put her journal on the top shelf of the closet and went out on her balcony. The sky was absolutely sapphire blue and the ocean calm and infinite. The sea air has healing powers. She remembered her mother saying that from when she was small.

From downstairs she heard Navada vocalizing. She went in the bathroom and filled up the tub. She got in and did swimming motions and then lay there with the door cracked, listening while her grandmother's voice rose from downstairs and bounced half of an aria from *Tosca* around the bathroom walls.

She thought about Jody some more. She'd been thinking about him all night long.

She got dressed and took Navada's Mercedes over to Jody's apartment.

The door was unlocked and she went in. She called and called wandering through all the plants and paintings. Propped everywhere were wonderful paintings of angels and women and shells and rivers. The sound of her shoes on the hardwood floor made her feel conspicuous.

Jody was nowhere to be seen.

She looked out the window on the back door in the kitchen and saw him in the backyard doing something with some sort of barrel. She unlocked the back door and ran down the steps to join him, so glad he was home.

"Well, hello!" he said when he noticed her. "Just taking a look at the bees. They're just like my children."

"I didn't know you had a beehive," she said. "Are they the mean kind or can you let them crawl on you?"

"You can do it but you have to wear gloves. I lost the gloves last week. Matthew lost them, actually. He was gardening or something."

Camille leaned over and looked down inside the hive. Thousands and thousands of bees. Some of them were landing on her. "There are so many of them. Do you know how many are in there?"

"Nope," he replied. "You'd think there were at least enough to make me some honey. But they never have."

He raised his voice and said, "And God descended down upon them and said, *You will have a dysfunctional beehive,* and then it was so. The curse of the infertile bees. For Jody Forest, anyway."

They went into his apartment and Jody showed her some of his work.

"I would show you what I'm doing right now but I hate for anyone to see my unfinished projects," he said walking down the hall to the bedroom. "For fear I might change my mind about a color or a layout after I've shown it to them. That would alter their first impression. You don't realize it until you start painting how important a first impression can be. It can either be something breathtaking or something horrifying. An embarrassment to the art world."

"You shouldn't say things like that," Camille said. "It makes it seem as if there is only one way of self-expression. I don't think I like art critics."

Jody opened a door to a small workshop. He was telling Camille about how his style changes. How there remains an underlying similarity between all of the paintings, but how the ideas behind them evolve, much the same way people grow close and grow distant and are forever indecisive.

They sat down on a small sofa that was covered with a floral-printed sheet. Camille reached down and picked up a photo album off the floor and began thumbing through it. In it were pictures he had taken of his work. Snapshots of things to be painted. There were also photos of some of the things he'd sold or given away.

"This is one I'm going to do next when my project is over," he said, pointing to a photo of a woman wearing a snowsuit in the middle of a city. "I saw her on the street when I was in New York and had to take her picture."

"She's beautiful."

When the grand tour was over they went out to lunch and she took him over to her house and Lady Faith sang for him. Then they met Terri-Anne and Ida at the beach and they went walking. It was pitch-black when she got home.

That night she found herself still awake at four. She got up and put on a silk robe and went downstairs to the kitchen. She opened the refrigerator door and took out a pie pan full of banana pudding. She sat down at the table and ate half of it. Then she got the inclination to begin her written masterpiece.

She grabbed a sheet of typing paper and a magazine to bear down on. She sat in a wicker chair in the den and wrote:

You shall know the truth, Michael Finnie, and the truth shall make you free: You are a spider for not writing me any letters.

Then she wrote a poem:

In this kitchen we call life
all the cooks are high.
I wanted to make an appointment
with you for Saturday.

I was told you were hiding
and could not be contacted . . .

Then she wrote:

Prologue: London, 1944.

A dignified woman named Helene sits in an antique chair, remembering the veins of her father's hands as he traced lines of Tennyson along the page, as he read to her by the saintly glow of a fire. He spoke in a wistful and methodic voice, barely his own, and she could but close her eyes to live in the pictures cast by the words on her eyelids. It is a memory of childhood. She is dreaming of this as she waits.

It saddens her in a nameless way to think of the house so empty now. She used to believe in entertaining.

Now, except for Helene, the house is silent and abandoned; clothes hanging silently in closets. Pictures in the dining room smiling over a dusty table into the darkness.

Her flame burns low tonight. Seconds turning to hours creeping past on hands and knees, she waits, she waits . . .

She was pleased with what she'd written. She ate an oatmeal cookie and went out on the porch and smoked two cigarettes and went to bed.

The next morning she got up and wandered into the kitchen and poured herself some coffee. From the window over the sink she could see Navada walking on the wooden walkway toward the ocean. She was carrying a bag of bread for the sea gulls. It was windy and overcast.

The clock said eleven-thirty. She had not planned on sleeping that late. She was going to devote the entire day to her novel.

Something was touching her feet. She looked down and saw Asia licking her toes. Asia was her grandmother's Siamese cat.

"Good morning, darling cat," Camille said. "Men can be such dicks, don't you agree? Yes they are. I'm going to write a novel about it. The ones you want know it and put you through the goddamn wringer. They wring and wring and wring until you're so nervous you don't know what you're doing. Then comes the issue of making love. You know what I'm saying, Asia. When you want them to throw you down on the bed and stick that thing inside you so far you can't see straight."

Camille was looking around through all the cabinets for something to eat. She did not want Cream of Wheat. She did not want grits or Oat-Bran and Raisin cereal or a biscuit that Delila made.

She settled for cold leftover pizza from the refrigerator and took it over to the table and began eating it out of the box.

Asia jumped on the table and meowed and Camille was feeding her pieces of pepperoni. "Let me ask you this, Asia," she continued talking to the cat. "What does a girl have to do anymore to get laid? I want more than just talking and going to movies. I know the *who* and the *how much* but it's not working. God, I've been so goddamn horny. It's not the same when you do it alone. Don't get me started on the subject of masturbation. I mean, who wants to do that all the time?"

"We manage somehow, don't we?" Asia said. "It could be worse. They could strip you of your womanhood the way they did me."

Camille put the pizza box on the floor and let Asia finish up what was left. She raised her head and saw Delila standing in the doorway to the kitchen.

Delila had heard every word of that. In her day such talk from a lady was unheard of. Black or white. It was vulgar and bitter. So common.

Camille walked in her silk robe out to the mailbox at the end of the driveway. *It was there.* The long-awaited letter from Michael. She saw the return address and the collage on the back of the envelope. The collage was a collection of famous fashion models. There was a small piece of paper that ran down the center that said OUT WITH THE IN CROWD.

She stood at the end of the driveway and read,

My dear Camille, (he wrote)

Everything in the universe reduces to energy which takes two forms: mind and matter. All day long everyone is trying to control the matter with the mind. Try as they must to change this physical assumption. Do you know what they're forgetting? They're forgetting the matter is also energy and could very well have a will of its own.

We are shoving along in our predisposed directions all the same. Shovels and hammers and screws and nails in our hands. I am ready. The graves we dug yesterday are already filled.

Where are you, baby? And when are you coming home to me?

Love and so infinite the source,
Michael

P.S. I loved the poem.

I can't wait to read what you've written of the novel.

She went inside and sat down at the table and wrote four chapters. It was five-thirty when her father called to give her the news.

"Honey, I've got the best news you could possibly hear," he said. "You won a trip! Some contest you entered. Now the man gave me the number and he said you needed to call him yourself."

"What contest? I don't remember entering a contest. It's probably one of those condominium advertisements."

"No. I don't think it was. He said he was calling from the airlines."

Camille took down the number and hung up. She went up to her room and got in bed and stayed there a long time trying to remember what contest she entered. And then it came to her.

The week before she left for Hilton Head she'd gone with Michael to an exhibit at the High Museum. It was a display of exotic flowers called "Art in Bloom."

She remembered three things about entering the contest. That there was a big poster for KLM Airlines behind the contest booth with red tulips on it, a field of red tulips, and that the card she filled out asked if she was a member of the High Museum, in which case she answered no because she is not a member, and that it was a trip for two to Paris.

The next two weeks were exciting and sad and hurried. The man who was in charge of the contest had said to her on the phone, "You can either go on the first of August or the fifteenth. It's for a week. The plane goes from Atlanta to Amsterdam and then you get the first available flight to Paris."

"It's for two isn't it? I can take a guest."

"Oh yes, yes, of course. Listen, I'll send you all the information and the tickets and a brochure about the hotel."

"Thank you. I'm so excited. Thank you so much."

The first thing that happened was her birthday/going-away party. It took place at Ida's house. Winnie had come down from Atlanta to take Camille home and was there for the party.

Everyone huddled around Camille and tried to talk to her at the same time. Jody presented her with a picture he'd painted. It had ONE COOK'S PARADISE written across the top and below that was a shady dark blue figure reaching up for food-order tickets that were flying around his head. Out to the side was a black woman in a flowered dress flying off a bed with smoke at her heels. Underneath her was written, BABYDOLL IN JEOPARDY.

Camille had never seen anything so original. She and Jody said their good-byes and got choked up.

Navada and Lady Faith were there telling her all the places she must visit in Paris.

"You have to see all the museums," Navada said. "Your grandfather and I went to Paris on a cruise ship after the war. It was our second honeymoon. You can't waste a second. Go to the Musée de l'Orangerie and the Louvre and see all the châteaux."

"And all the famous cathedrals," Lady Faith put in. "They're all over Paris. Go to the vineyards, too. Go on a wine-tasting tour."

"And I'll be thinking of you when I see them. I wish I'd had the time to study voice with you. It was nice of you to offer that to me," Camille said.

In the car on the way back to Atlanta Camille told Winnie all about Jody and Terri-Anne and Ida.

"I guess I don't have to ask who you're taking to Europe," Winnie said.

"I'm not sure who I'm taking yet. Although I feel obligated to ask Michael because we were together when we registered for the drawing."

"Well at least you're bringing all your suitcases home. That way you won't have to go all the way back down there before we head up to Vanderbilt."

"Please let's not get into that. I'm going to cross that bridge when I get to it. *Carpe diem.* We might just decide to stay in Europe permanently. I may never come back from this trip."

They drove a long while in silence while Camille worked on her novel. Then Winnie said, "I have this funny, bad feeling. I don't want to scare you or anything, Camille, but I have the feeling something's up. Something we don't know about."

"Is there something wrong with the car? Is it driving okay?

Why don't we pull over and get something to eat. With me being so quiet this whole way you probably have road-monotony."

They stopped at Donut World and split a box of forty-five donut holes and had Cokes.

As soon as they were back on the road Winnie said, "You know? I don't feel anything bad is going to happen anymore."

"Of course not, Winnie. Nothing bad will happen now. I mean, how could it?"

At eight o'clock Michael came to get Camille in the old Volvo and took her to the Dessert Place. He kept saying things like, "I'm so glad my best friend's home again," and, "I can't believe you're in this car with me."

"There's something I need to tell you, Camille," he began after the waiter brought their coffee. "I hope it's not going to make you mad or hurt your feelings." Both of his elbows were on the table. He held his mug with both hands and took a sip of coffee.

"You can tell me anything. What could you possibly say that could hurt my feelings? That's what relationships are based on isn't it? Communication and honesty. Go ahead. I want to learn."

"Well, I went out with Annie Campbell while you were at Hilton Head. But we're not really seeing each other. I don't know if I even like her. She's already started using the 'l' word and it's all moving entirely too fast if you—"

"Say no more." She set her coffee cup down silently on the table and stared at her rings.

"I don't know how you feel," he continued. "I feel like you're my best friend. I've had more of a relationship with you this year than I've had with anyone. I want you to know it's not you who has the problem, it's me."

Camille started giggling.

"What's funny?"

She raised her head and met the green eyes she'd imagined watching her hair blow around the top of the Arc de Triomphe.

"I'm relieved," she said and threw her head back in laughter. She slapped a hand down on the table.

"You are?"

"Yes. I'm so relieved. Darling, if you knew the load you just took off my shoulders." She smiled her charming, flattering smile and went on, "I was going to tell you about this guy I was dating at the beach and didn't know how to say it. His name is Jody and he's one-third Cherokee Indian. We dated all summer. This makes everything so much easier."

They sat and talked and laughed together for an hour and Camille told him all about how she was going to decorate her room at Vanderbilt. "Jody loves to paint things green. He's offered to paint my room at the dorm." She proceeded to tell him all about her novel and the new clothes she was going to buy to take with her and she gave a full description of the mountains of Tennessee as they stand cold and red and mysterious in the fall on all sides of the university.

"I think it's ridiculous we have to sit here in this airport and wait for so long. I've never heard of a two-hour advance check-in," Winnie was saying in the International Concourse at Hartsfield International Airport.

"Relax, Winnie. It's so they can find all the bombs before we get on the plane."

"Jesus Christ, Camille. Don't say things like that. You know I hate the idea of flying over the ocean. Much less the threat of terrorism."

"If you'll take notice," Camille said leaning forward in her seat in the departure lounge, "it looks like it's all Arabs in charge of cleaning the planes. See? Look out that window. There they are putting the luggage in."

"Oh, stop it, Camille! I'm serious. Tell me why you're taking me instead of you-know-who. You haven't really said much about it the last couple of days."

"Well, I'd been doing some thinking while I was at the beach this summer. I just decided that since I'm leaving soon there's just no point in investing so much of myself into a relationship. Of course he was devastated by it. I just said to him, We can always remain the best of friends. It's gotten too hard for me to have to be preoccupied with all this dating business while I'm trying to write my book and get ready to go off to college. I guess he took it a lot better than what I'd expected."

Then a voice announced the boarding for KLM flight 416 to Amsterdam.

After dinner and watching half of a Mel Gibson movie, Winnie was busy making a daily itinerary for the week in Paris and trying not to think about how high up they were in the air.

Camille stopped watching the movie and unfolded her tray table and began writing on her dinner menu.

Epilogue: Somewhere in the Greek Isles, Summer 1956
(Worry about what comes in the middle when you get home from Paris)

What is there left to be hoped for that has not been attained? Helene wondered as she stood on the shore of the vast blue ocean, letting the breeze scatter her hair and burying her feet in the sand.

From here she could see Reginald coming down from the house carrying breakfast on a silver tray. It had been their daily ritual since they'd been in Greece to have breakfast on the beach. "Helene!" he called out, settling himself down in the sand, unfolding a towel for her to sit on. "Helene!"

She waved her arms around signaling she'd seen him. It was too difficult at this moment to disentangle herself from the water. She smiled his way flashing reflections of the morning sun, still low on the horizon, from her sunglasses.

She remained in her divine exile a few moments more, dreaming. Of the tuxedo Reginald had worn the night before, of touching his cheek and holding his hand in the taxi on the way home early that morning, listening while a faint voice on the driver's small radio sang "You Don't Know How Loveable You Are."

Camille looked over at Winnie, who was still flipping through her *Let's Go Europe* book, and said, "I'm going to hang the picture Jody made for me over my bed in our room. We'll do the whole room in green."

She turned out her light and looked out the window. She could see the reflection of the moonlight on the water. It shined in little luminous pieces like scales on a fish or sequins on a black dress.

She put her head back on the seat and thought about how lucky she was to be flying over the ocean blue going to Paris, France.

And then she was sitting in the top of a tree watching Helene picking apples in the orchard. She was putting the apples in a basket she carried over her arm. "Helene! I'll see if we can stop over in England and visit you. We need to get acquainted." And Helene was overcome with joy and jumped up and down and did a little dance. Helene so serene. I will be more like Helene. She wears a long flowered dress and no shoes. She sleeps under her airplane chair like the Madonna with her arms folded. She carries no baby. She is not afraid of spiders.

Kevin Calder is a native of Atlanta, Georgia, and has lived in London and Paris. He currently lives in Fayetteville, Arkansas, where he is working toward a Master of Fine Arts in fiction and teaching French at the University of Arkansas. His fiction has appeared in *Indiana Review*. He is finishing a first novel, tentatively entitled *Looking for an Angel in the Cyprus Trees*.

PHOTO CREDIT: ALAN CALDER

Months before I sat down to write this story, I was living in an upstairs room in Paris, dreaming of my characters. I listened to their sighs as they waited for things to clarify inside my head and for me to get sensible and read them their part. I actually wrote their story down when I was on Tybee Island, Georgia, at the summer house of my best friend. I took long solitary walks on the beach and then in the middle of a poker game I announced I had to have blank paper at once. I shuffled through the drawers in her house until I found a legal pad and I began to write "Name Me This River." I wrote and wrote and wrote. I made my friends sit around the dining room table and listen to me read the story aloud. I created this story to remind myself and my readers to laugh at ourselves and at the sometimes hopeless things we do in the name of love.

Paula K. Gover

WHITE BOYS AND RIVER GIRLS

(from *The Virginia Quarterly Review*)

Yolanda was working tables at the Tenderloin Ballroom that summer we collided. While she wasn't my regular type, she was the kind I sometimes picked up with in between the tall, blond, cool-drink-for-the-eyes numbers I prefer, the kind that don't give you nothing to think about much except for the smell of their hair. Not that Yolanda wasn't a looker in her own rights—small, dark-eyed, skin so pale like she'd never seen daylight. The kind with "Slow down, Donnie-boy, watch the road now" written all across her face. She wasn't my regular type.

Take Cynthia, for instance. That's who I'm hanging out with these days. Three inches under my six foot two, small white wedges of skin at her breasts and hips when she peels off her bikini, eyes green as kiwis. She's working on a portfolio for a modeling agency out of Savannah. Hopes to make it into videos with the house band from the Tenderloin. And she might. Her brother Marvin works lights for the band, and he knows someone who knows someone who could maybe help now that the band's got a recording contract. She's from Tyler, like me, and says she remembers me from when I played on the football team, but she's just enough younger than me so it's okay I don't remember her. And she's slimmed down since back then, she says, though I don't say nothing about that. Only I know how she fusses about the pale stretch marks on her bottom and radiating out like a starburst from her nipples, but they're not visible to no one but me. Or so she says.

Last weekend Cynthia worked a car show in Macon, stretching all five foot eleven inches of her attributes across machine-waxed hoods and bumpers and quarter panels. She's got the glossies developed already and tucked into her portfolio just so. She takes great pains in arranging them in special order, holding them up under the light in the dining el, the tips of her nails at the corners, going, "What do you think, Donnie, this one or this? Which first? Which one is the real me?" Course, aren't none of them the real her, not the Cynthia I see each morning, sheet wrinkles on her cheek and sour-breathed. But then, what do I know? So I tell her this one or that, point at the photos, smile, say they're all real nice, and that's what she likes to hear.

When the guys come around after work, I kind of flip through the portfolio, looking from the television set to their faces, acting indifferent about how they look from Cynthia in the flesh at the dining room table, clipping coupons with hair tied back, to the pages again. I go, "She's got it all right," watching them react to Cynthia's body all oiled and tanned and spread out in the photos, tucked inside those bikinis, which were never meant for swimming.

Cynthia's big dream is a condo on the coast—full basement, white shutters, privacy fence, the whole shot. We drive around Sundays after church and stop at the open-house signs near the beach, going twenty miles in either direction from the city. She says commuting is stylish these days. We walk up the narrow white sidewalks to the display models, real proper, like we was married or something, me in a clean shirt for once, her all wobbly on heels in her church clothes, and only I know she's not wearing any panties.

Cynthia and I got this two-bedroom apartment in Garden City off Highway 21. It's cheap because the airport's right there back of the place, and, to be honest, our neighbors are mostly poor working people, but I kind of like that, you know. Feels like I'm where I belong. But when someone asks Cynthia where we stay, she smiles and tells them, "In the city," slow-voiced and lying so pretty they believe it, and I don't understand that, but women are like that, ask anyone.

It doesn't take much to keep Cynthia happy, just keep saying how God-awful-nice she looks and act like I can't think of nothing all day but getting home to her body all stretched out in the chaise lounge next to the pool by the rental office. She's easy to live with because most of the time she's too busy working on herself to know I'm around, sticking little foam pads between her toes and fingers, painting her nails while watching the television, flipping between "Geraldo" and soaps and music videos, studying who she wants to be, shaking bottles of polish so the little beads go clicking around. She spends two hours a day on the exercise bike in our living room, and when she's not busy puffing away there, working the handlebar levers in a crisscross, increasing the resistance on the wheel, she goes into the kitchen and runs carrots and fruit through the blender. Or she stands in the bathroom spraying some kind of tropical mess on her hair and squeezing the curls around her temples so they stay there until she washes them out in the shower.

Cynthia's only true hobby outside of "creating an image," that's how she puts it, is collecting refrigerator magnets. Now, that isn't a true hobby, not like collecting baseball cards or refinishing furniture, but she has elevated it to that status, and who's to tell her it's silly. Not me. She's got so many of them doodads they cover both doors of the refrigerator, and just recently she's taken to putting them on the front panel of the dishwasher. Our only true fight to this day was the one time I slammed the door to the icebox and half the magnets fell to the floor, smack, smack, down on the linoleum, and she threw a fit like I'd never seen, just like I'd stepped on her tail, hissing all ugly between her teeth with green facial clay wrinkling in cracks across her cheeks. Now that was a sight.

I've been promoted to crew chief for Clem Palmer's Asphalt and Paving out of Tyler and we're tarring a stretch over to Statesboro, so I pick up a magnet for her here and there to add to her collection since she threw that fit, just to show I care. Mostly I find ones of beer cans and Harley emblems, but I did find a real funny one at Red's store, a shiny naked ceramic lady with big pointed tits, holding her fingers up in a little curl, and a smile on her lips. Across her pink belly little letters say "Get a PIECE of the action," and now, I think that's real cute. Of course Cynthia says it looks just like her, and a few days after I carried it home to her, she took to referring to me as her "fiancé." Tell me how that works.

Now, Cynthia and Yolanda aren't nothing alike. Reason I got hooked up with Yolanda at all was out of sheer boredom with my regular type. That's no reason for starting something like I did, but accidents happen, what can I say? That summer, I'd just broken off with Susie Purviss, who is now married to E. Henry Broadwell, who just happens to be working for Clem Palmer in payroll, but we don't have no bad blood between us these days. Susie had broken things off once E. Henry come around, seeing as she complained she was getting too old to just keep dating like we were, and how I should ask to marry her. She's a charge nurse now there to Reidsville, pulling in a nice tidy check every week, but marriage was not in my mind two years ago, and it still isn't much in my mind today, except for those times when Cynthia goes all throaty and says, "And I'd like you to meet my fiancé." Meaning me.

So Susie and I'd broken up to her crying of, "Why can't we just get married, Donnie?" and I certainly wasn't looking for something like that again, though to be honest, that is my pattern. I'm thirty-four, and for the past ten years it's been a woman a year, give or take a couple of dry months now and then. See, you start out saying, "Now, mind you, I'm not looking to settle down just yet." And you say it right from the jump, looking those straight-teethed girls dead in the eyes, and they go, "Why, whatever gave you reason to think I'd expect that from you, Donnie, why aren't you just the most nervous man I've ever met." Then somewhere down the line it changes. They start talking about moving in together, and they go all pink-faced and smiling at babies in strollers, even the ones with spit and cereal down their chins, and they take to staring at you for long silent moments across the table at the diner next to Miss Lucille's motel. I'd just come out of a version of that and kicked around single for a couple of months, when right after the fourth of July I noticed Yolanda back of the bar, though she never so much as touched my fingers when I paid for my beer, not even handing back change. Like I been saying, she wasn't my regular type.

Most of the women I end up with are the kind that make certain you notice them first. They sit around on bar stools, smiling those glassy smiles, shaking their hair off their shoulders, lifting their drinks to their pink lips so slow it just makes you wonder. They're the type that once you finally get a couple of beers going they start making conversation from down the bar or the next table, depending on where you're sitting. They're the kind that once you're a little drunk it don't take nothing to talk to them, and they lean into you a little once you ask their names, like exchanging names was some kind of personal secret. They're the type once you've got their names straight like to go upstairs and shoot a little pool, only they don't really know how to shoot at all, asking, "Should I hit it here? There? Off the side, there? I couldn't do that, it'll never work," squealing all delighted when they sink something somewhere by accident. They're the type been noticing you all along but got it planned so when you finally park yourself next to them at the bar, when you finally look in their eyes, it's like you've just arrived on this earth and nobody else existed before you.

But not Yolanda. She'd come from school in Atlanta where she'd been studying design, though what that meant, I wasn't sure. She'd come to live with her sister Regina, an interior decorating consultant, though later I'd find out they were both from that stretch on the Walapaha back home nobody ever mentions

as a birthplace proper. The river spreads out back there so wide
it seems like a lake when you stand there near the landing. I
know the place good, even took a ride out there last spring with
Teddy, Cynthia's brother-in-law, thinking maybe I'd catch sight
of Yolanda. He's got that speed boat and we drove on down to
the landing one afternoon, down past her mama's place, back
through those trails don't even seem like a road to anywhere,
but then the pines clear away and suddenly, there it is, the old
shacks, even a couple of trailers, though how they got those back
in there is a mystery. Teddy and I took the boat on down where
the Walapaha feeds into the Altamaha, then to where that river
gets dark and winds all through the woods. My daddy used to
take me to the landing to get his liquor. They got a couple of
stills back in there, though to look, you'd never find them. The
feds come around every month or so, but the people back there
are on to that, going so dumb and simple-acting wouldn't think
they'd ever done nothing but sit home all day and read the Bible,
waiting for their welfare checks.

But that's something I found out later about Yolanda. The
summer we met I was working for Clem out of Savannah on a
contract job at Hunter Army Airfield. The Tenderloin was my
summertime watering hole. Yolanda was working there nights
and living in an efficiency apartment over her sister's office in
a three-story house two blocks from the bar. She'd had to find
a place to work within walking distance of her apartment since
she'd slammed her car into a viaduct on purpose driving home
from Atlanta. She'd just left it at the side of the road outside
Macon, can you beat that? She unscrewed the plates and took the
papers from the dash, then settled with the claims adjustor for
cash money and left the car on the shoulder. "Better than being
flat broke," she explained. And she took the job at the Tenderloin
because it let her work nights and sleep in the day, and that was
something she'd wanted.

But like I was saying, I found this out later, because at first I
just kind of kept noticing her and she wasn't putting on no show

for me, not like the cool blond eye-batting type. So I took to trying to get her to notice me, but she had this attitude about her like you didn't exist except as a body ordering beer. For instance, if I'd try to wink her down for a draft, she'd come over to my table and say, "What can I get you?"—formal, without a smile, like I hadn't been a regular there for two months and always drinking from the tap.

She wasn't my type, and I knew it. She was the kind you have to sideswipe into noticing you back, the kind you get a fix on, then let up on the gas and coast into. The boys in the crew seen it coming clear as day, saying how I ought not to mess with someone so serious-faced and unsmiling, and how didn't she look something like a witch. Trust us, they warned. But she got to me, in some deep place, how if business was slow, she'd set up a stool behind the bar and pull out a sketch pad and draw. And that's part of why business picked up for Willie B., in addition to Toujaise's band, because she drew anybody who walked in the door in two minutes flat, and she drew them perfect. She'd take out a piece of charcoal, a long black stick-looking thing didn't seem no picture could come out of, and then she'd swing it across the page, scribble back and forth with it, work her fingertips in little circles to make shadows and what have you, and that was all it took. Magic. Darryl in his Atlanta Braves jersey, Toujaise in his beret at the microphone, Sasha holding her fingers in front of her mouth in that embarrassment she has about her overbite when she's not singing, the Wonder bread man bringing in trays of kaiser rolls for the grill. She'd get the face, sketch the shoulders real quick, collar, hair, and she'd put her initials at the lower right hand corner and pin it to the wall near the register with a thumbtack.

About the third week she'd been working at the Tenderloin, I come in early on Friday. It'd rained all day, and I'd let the crew go at three. I come in the door, and Yolanda was sitting back of the bar, and I said, "All right, go on now, go ahead."

And she says, "Go ahead, what?" standing up like she's going to get me a beer or something, moving slow and cautious.

"Go ahead and draw me," I smiled, feeling a little silly, because she'd never taken to drawing me on her own, though I come in every night.

The place was real quiet, and the jukebox was turned low with Roy Orbison crying about crying out the cloth speaker, and only some gay boys in leather jackets standing around at the back drinking beer and shooting darts. She looked at me holding her face in a frown, her hands stuffed down into the pockets of those baggy black pants she always wore. Her face was all white with some kind of powder, unnatural looking in general, but nice to look at on her, just the same. She wasn't my regular type, but she was something to look at all right. She had color on her lips you can't call lipstick, dusty-like, dark as old blood, and not shiny like the stuff most girls wear, and all around her eyes was a thin black line I'd never noticed before, and lashes so thick I wanted to reach across the oak planks of the counter and touch them. Then she said, "Yeah. That's good," like she'd never really seen me before, pinching her eyes all tight and serious, studying me, not like the type what pretends to just that moment see you, but in genuine blindness to the fact I existed prior to that second. I felt like I'd just been born. Then she looked me so hard in the eyes I had to turn away for a moment. Her eyes went that deep. So, I stood there dripping rain onto Willie B.'s red carpet like some big fool in work boots, and she stood there a minute in a complete stop, and finally pulled out her sketch pad from next to the register and told me to sit there across from her.

She sat on the stool behind the bar, and I looked her over, really looked, not in the looking to pick somebody up kind of way, but seeing the narrow curve of her neck, the ridge of her spine, her head shadowing the sketch pad, seeing her scalp white like candle wax beneath her glossy black hair. She wore her hair poked up in a rubber band at the top of her head, like a little make-believe Indian feather, funny to do with hair short as a boy's, but it looked kind of nice on her. Little wisps of hair fell down on her white forehead and down the back of her neck. Then she said, "Don't look at me while I draw," even though she'd never looked up the whole time to see me looking. So I stopped looking at her, because I had been looking, she was right. So I stared into the mirror behind the bottles of liquor back of the bar, and I could see her reflection next to mine, and I looked at that, the flat pale face from the side, that little bit of nothing nose, hoops in her ears big around as a beer can, three in one lobe, two in the other. She was wearing a white T-shirt, the only thing I'd ever seen on her thin body, and she wasn't wearing nothing underneath, her small breasts barely showing except for the shadows of her nipples. She had a red leather belt through the loops at her waist, and a thong of keys hung to one side.

She held the charcoal in the tips of her fingers and used her left hand to make shadows by rubbing the flesh of the edge of her palm against the page. Her hands were pale, and the nails were short and plain, trimmed, not chewed away like some girls do, always putting their fingers in their mouths. Her face was what got to me that day, so white she seemed not to be living, and that dark stuff on her lips making me want to kiss her, and maybe she felt that, who knows.

She sat there drawing a few minutes, and I'd thought she was done when she looked up once to meet my eyes. "Hold still," she'd said, just ordering me around, though I didn't know I was moving. Then she bent back over the paper, and went to making just the tiniest strokes with the charcoal, then she looped her initials into place at the bottom of the page and said, "There." She turned the sketch pad toward me then from her lap and there I was, me, real as real. She'd got the scar at my lip just right, a shadow-like divot where I'd gone through the plate glass window at Mama's twenty years ago. She'd drawn me smiling, though I hadn't smiled the whole time she'd been working at the thing.

"Well," I said, grinning dumb-like. "Well. Looks like me, don't it now?" I grinned. I couldn't stop grinning, though I felt a fool for doing so, my mouth like a Band-Aid across my face.

Then she said real nervous-like and peculiar, "You like it, then? Tell me the truth." The reason this was peculiar was I'd never heard her ask that of anyone before, only heard her say, "See Willie B.," when a customer asked to buy a likeness, only heard her say, "That's a five spot," when her drawing went public and all. But there she was, all quiet and anxious about her drawing for the first time that I'd seen, and boy, that did something to my heart, I can't tell you.

"It's great," I said, the grin of an idiot still flowering across my face. "I like it fine," I said, feeling myself go all tender and loose inside about her concern.

She tugged at the paper and ripped it from the pad. "Take it," she said as if she was mad at me and wanted just to be rid of it or something.

"I owe you some money now," I answered, fishing my wallet by its chain from the back pocket of my jeans.

"No charge," she said, and then a smile shot to her lips, her teeth flashing all sudden in her small white face, like she just then figured something out important. "You remind me of someone," she smiled. "Take it. It's yours," she said, then a couple men in three-piece business suits come in the front door, and she walked down the bar to serve them.

To this day that whole night sticks in my head like some movie I could've watched just this morning. Yolanda worked the bar until eight, then drew pictures for the customers brave enough to come in during the storm that worked itself into a fit after the sun went down. Around eleven the electricity went out, and Willie B. set candles on all the tables and the band come up and sat near the bar, and two of them brought out acoustical guitars and made music real quiet up there at the front with Sasha singing. Willie B. didn't get no power the rest of the night, and he let Yolanda off at midnight, and she come and sat next to me at my table where two guys from the crew sat drunk and not minding their manners much. She sat there next to me, not asking if she could, knowing as well as I knew I wanted her there, small as a child, and quiet, her thigh light as a wing up against mine. She drank beer from the bottle with her lips pulling at the neck, and every once in a while would say something a little odd, like once saying, "You believe in voodoo?" which set us three drunk men into snorts. "No, really," she'd said. "You shouldn't laugh about something as serious as that," then she smiled and wrinkled her nose up in her face. Something she said set me back a little, though I was kind of laughing along with the other two guys from the crew. "My mama's a practicing witch," she said, and right after she'd said it a flash of lightning lit all the dark windows of the bar. Tony, one of the guys, went, "Oh my God," and Yolanda said, "See?"

I had a good-old-boy tired drunk going around one, and at closing said couldn't I see her home, and she nodded without a smile to her white face. So we drove my truck the two blocks to her sister's place and she took me upstairs by the hand to her room where she slept on the floor on a mattress, the moon just barely cutting through the clouds after the rain, just coming in faint through the windows.

If you'd asked me that morning where I'd end up that night, I couldn't have guessed it'd be there under the cool sheets of her bed. I'd never have guessed I'd be lying beneath her as the wind came through the open windows, her thin legs at my hips, her lips opening against mine from the first kiss. I'd never have guessed things to go like that, not with her, not lying there letting her love me with her weightless body in the rain-washed night. She'd made love to me in absolute silence, kissing from my lips to my neck to my belly, then later, riding up above me, so light I could've lifted her in my arms. Only once did she say anything at all, and then it was only, "Oh, now," announcing the squeeze of her body.

When morning come, the room was dark. She'd gotten up before dawn to draw the blinds at the windows. She slept beside me on her back with her hands at her breasts. Her breasts were small and white, and the nipples lay flat against her skin. I kissed her breasts as she slept. I kissed her nipples to points and she reached her sleepy arms around me and I moved inside her a long time before I came, and she fell back off to sleep right after.

She kept her room dark in the day and at night opened all the windows. In a bowl beside the bed, she kept three pale stones, and each morning she warmed them in her palms and chanted over them in a trance, words sounding senseless to me, but pretty how they come out of her mouth. Once I visited her with a case of heatstroke, and she boiled herbs on the hot plate and made me drink the mess from a spoon. In an hour I was well, and I'd sat naked in a chair while she trimmed my hair, collecting the pieces she cut in an envelope, sealing it closed with a press to her lips. We went on real regular that summer, her working the Tenderloin, me coming to see her at the bar after work, going home with her at closing. She never liked going out much during the day on the weekend, but I coaxed her into taking rides down the coast up toward South Carolina, and sometimes the hour inland to Tyler. She didn't like Tyler. She said it was an old sore for her. So I asked her why. And that's when she told me she'd been born on the river, though all along I'd pictured her coming from the city.

Driving into Tyler one day she said, "Okay, we always go to your mama's house. Let's go to mine this time. See what you think." We drove back into the woods and down to the landing, the sky all blue and thin with clouds. There were girls swimming at the landing in their clothes, shorts and cutoffs, wearing little stretchy tops. A couple were pregnant, their white bellies showing, and Yolanda called out to a few by name, and they come up to her and pressed her hands between theirs. One girl named Jasmine said, "Heard you're doing readings again." Yolanda nodded, then Jasmine said, "Well, what you said come true. My period come regular. I was only late." Another girl stood at the edge of the river with a small dark-haired child in sagging diapers on her wrist. Yolanda called out to them.

"Hey," she said. "Hey, over here," she said, and the child turned from the girl at the edge of the river, and walked up the beach to us. "Come on," she laughed to the child, and the child come running toward her going, "Mama, Mama," laughter all bouncing around in his chest from running on those fat white legs, and Yolanda swept him up in her arms.

She held the child against her, nosing her face at his neck and kissing his shoulders, and my skin went a little cold. She looked up at me once, dead in the eyes and staring me down. She turned away from me and walked down a soft silver path to a clapboard shed back of the tackle and bait store. I stood there on the beach and then followed behind her a minute later. She stood at the door to the shack and waited for me to catch up. "This is Joey," she said. "He's mine," she said.

"You never told me," I said as I brushed gnats from around my mouth. The gnats billowed at our heads under the thick oaks above us.

"You never asked," she said without any kind of tone to her voice. Just, "You never asked," like maybe I was supposed to guess at her life and figure it out. "So, you going to stop liking me?" she said. She didn't say "loving me," and that made me feel all messed up inside.

"Well, I'd a rather known," I said, a little bit of anger seeping into my voice, anger come out of not knowing about this baby of hers.

"I see," she said softly, just like that. "Easy come, easy go," she said, and opened the screen door to the shack. I followed her inside, the door barely closing behind us as it was hung so makeshift and poorly in its rotted frame. Inside the shack the walls were covered with feedbags, stapled to the wood in regular rows, like some kind of makeshift decorating. The shack was divided into rooms by mismatched paneling fixed to the floors and ceilings with metal angle brackets. A gas stove and sink stood at the front of the main room, and two curtains made doors to rooms in the back, though the whole thing was no bigger than a two-car garage. A thin woman sat at a gray Formica-topped table in the center of the front room. Her hair was pulled back in a braid and she wore a pink housecoat fastened with safety pins in the front. Her legs were white and thin, and small patches of broken veins roamed under the skin. A hand-rolled cigarette hung from the left corner of her mouth, lips so pale I could barely make them out. She looked up when Yolanda and I come in the door. Then she looked down at the table in front of her where a magazine lay spread out to a picture of lemon chiffon pie. She looked back up at Yolanda, fingering a cross that sank between her breasts. Then she said, "Got the money, thank you," smoke from her cigarette coming out of her lips with the words. "Bought diapers," she said, tearing the page from the center of the magazine, her long fingers working the paper free from the spine, the cross at her neck knocking against the table edge. "Don't let Nigel see you toting that boy in from town now, you hear?" I could tell the way she looked up at me quick when she said it who she meant.

Yolanda put the baby down at her feet, and he toddled over to the woman at the table and crawled up into her lap, leaning against her sagging bosom. Yolanda crossed her arms at her waist, and stared at me for a moment, then back to the woman at the table. "Mama, Nigel don't want me," she said, her voice going dark in a way I hadn't heard before. "Nigel don't want us," she said.

"Nigel don't talk like that to me," said her mother, running her finger line by line along the recipe for lemon pie. "He know you left school to work in Savannah. He know you work at some place where queers go. He know you live with your sister. He got spells going to bring you home. Ask," she stated, looking me over like I wasn't a living being. "Ask anybody here, they tell you the same."

"Nigel's got a new baby girl down the Altamaha," Yolanda said. "I don't want nothing from him, neither," she said, her voice sounding so much like her mama's I had to look to see if it was her talking at all. "Nigel ain't nobody," she said, turning to look at me real serious-like. "He's a bad kind of person. He runs people around here," she sighed. "I'm done with him. I got me a new life," she said softly, and it scared me to think she meant me.

Driving back to Savannah that night, Yolanda sat close to the door with her knees hugged up to her chin. Ten miles out of Tyler she said, "So, maybe I should have told you. So maybe I did, you'd leave me. Drop me. Stop liking me." She still wasn't talking about loving her. All she could talk of was liking.

So I go, "It's a lot to think about, I'll give you that. It's a surprise to me, what you having a baby and all. You don't look like you've had a baby. Your skin don't look stretched or nothing," I laughed, trying to cheer her up.

"I could've died with him," she said. "I was tiny and I could've died, except for Elvira's doctoring."

"You don't mean Black Bob's Elvira?" I exclaimed. "That nigger lady, that Elvira, that fat old nigger?"

She sat there in the quiet truck, looking straight ahead down the highway, but staring so hard didn't seem like she seen nothing but what was inside her head. She stared straight into the night as we passed the forestry tower going eighty, where two army jeeps stood at the mouth of the trail leading back into the wood. Two soldiers pulling fire-watch stood by the jeeps, passing in fast black shadows in field helmets, the embers of their cigarettes glowing like two red eyes in the dark. She sat there with her knees up, then she turned to me.

"You white boys got the world all figured out, don't you now?" she said, her voice tight with anger. "You get born into decent families with money to get by on, with daddies who come home at night, daddies you know by name, thinking you belong to those daddies like something God shit out of gold. You think the only decent folks are white people like yourselves, and you call good people like Miss Elvira 'niggers,' like they was something dead at the side of the road, like something without a heart or a mind. You play football and hang little cheerleaders on your wrist and sometimes they let you feel their tits, but that's it. They don't let you do what you really want to do. So, white boys like you come prowling down by the river on Friday nights, and you find girls with dark eyes and you buy their daddies' shine, and you get them to drink beside you in the woods, and you don't even remember their names the next day. White boys like you make babies and go away to school to nice places where you find some neat little someone to marry who's still got her cherry. Don't you call my family 'niggers.' Miss Elvira is blood. She raised my granddaddy at her breast when his mama died of fever, kept him as her own when nobody claimed him, a little white baby, and she saw him get in bed with her own half-white daughter, but don't nobody know that side of it. You saw my mama. She's white now, isn't she? But that don't make me true white. Black men give babies to white girls down to the river. That don't mean nothing. Everyone acts so snooty in Tyler, like us river girls aren't nothing but animals, like we don't got hearts to break and bend. But, your daddies come poking around the river, looking for something they can't get at home, and they pay for black girls in Shanty Town, just the same as black men bring their money to us girls at the river. Don't talk to me about niggers." She stopped a minute then. I was silent behind the wheel, and my fingers shook as I pulled a cigarette from my shirt pocket. She studied my silent face and my trembling fingers as I punched in the lighter on the dashboard. "My mama's French. Her family come down here from Quebec. None of us got the same daddy, except for Regina and me. You want to know who our daddy is? You want to know what white-looking Baptist come out to stick his thing in some poor white trash at the river? You want to know Miss Elvira's grandbaby's name?"

"Stop it," I whispered.

"No," she said, so fiercely it shook me inside. "You need to know the truth. You need to quit living your white boy life where the world's divided into white folks and niggers. My daddy was old man Rogers, Louise's daddy, but you wouldn't have called him a nigger, seeing as only a quarter of his blood ran true black, and he passed for white. He paid my mama to love him, then paid her to keep quiet once we come along. He come out to see her once a week all his life till he got the cancer. Louise maybe knows I'm her blood way she looks at me sometimes there in Danner's store. We don't got to say nothing. She just knows. Her daddy hurt her, you can see it in her face and how she don't need to name her own baby's daddy. But she was born there in Tyler, looking white and living white. Me, I look white. Mama's skin's so pale guess it come down to me that way. My granddaddy got killed on the river, and I seen it, I seen the knife go clean into his heart. Some woman went wild on shine and poked him with a knife till the air whistled out his lungs and blood filled his mouth. Miss Elvira come out and buried him back in the woods. Don't nobody ask questions about dead men down there. And let me tell you about girls like me. Sometimes we get free, go away, get jobs, get educated, but the river don't leave you. You seen Joey. I gotta live with that. I can't never be really free. And if you don't like me for that, I can't do nothing to stop it." She grew quiet then as the truck sailed toward the coast.

My mouth had gone dry, and the cigarette burned hot at my lips as the ember reached the filter. I tossed it out the window, into the dry brush whistling by at the side of the highway, something dangerous and awful to do. "So who is Nigel?" I said, my voice coming out high and fast. "Who's this Nigel? Some white boy?"

"He's not a white boy like you," she said softly. "I don't love him no more," she said. That was the only time I'd heard her talk about love, and she never brought it up again. "He's river family. He lives most the time in Jesup. But he's river people. And he put a spell on me early. I was only sixteen."

"A spell?" I said, and I laughed in disbelief. "A spell. That's funny."

"You white boys don't know what that means," she whispered. "You don't know what that means. He put a spell on me," she said, looking over at me as I drove toward Savannah. "He got Old Jennie to take things from my mama's house, things that belonged to me, strands of my hair, dust from the corners, and he put a spell on me. You don't know what that's like," she said, her voice thin as the air coming in the windows. "You don't know what's it's like to find yourself possessed till you faint for wanting someone, faint for what comes into your head without knowing why. That's what a spell does, sends you out in the night till you find what you're looking for, till you fall down on your knees, the fire all hot inside your middle like you were to die from it."

"So where is he now?" I asked, feeling momentarily frightened, afraid maybe something might happen to me, to us, like maybe I'd find myself driving possessed, ramming into a tree or sailing off the side of a bridge. We were alone on that dark stretch of road. Anything could happen and be made to look like an accident, seeing as I had this girl in the truck this Nigel had got under his spell enough to have a baby by him, whether I believed it or not.

"He's still around," she sighed, and then she yawned, real slow and stretching toward me across the seat like a pale night animal. Then she inched over beside me. "He can't get to me these days," she whispered, pressing her hand to my zipper.

"What about the spell?" I asked, trying to keep my voice light but feeling all heavy inside. I lifted my hips from the seat as she unfastened my jeans, keeping both hands tight on the wheel.

"It's been broken," she whispered at my ear right before she lowered her face to my lap. The moon hung in a gold plate over the low marshes and reedy banks that laced the river outside the city. The water on either side of the road lay still and black, mirroring the night on its surface. A crane lifted up from the side of the road, its wings pulling into slow strokes in the moonlight as Yolanda took me in her mouth. I trembled between her lips and put one hand to the back of her head, my fingers knitting down to her scalp, and I kept driving in toward the city, steering hard, oblivious and blind to anything but the heat of her mouth.

Later that night as we lay in her bed the wind blew in so warm we didn't need more than a sheet. I touched my hands to her face. She'd showered before coming to bed, and her skin was smooth and bare. She'd dusted her body with powder, and I ran my hands the length of her torso and then worked my fingers between her legs. "No," she'd said. "I don't want to do that."

"I want to return the favor." I smiled, thinking what she had done in the truck. But she pulled her hips back toward the wall and smoothed the sheet in a barrier between us.

"I just want to lie here beside you and think," she said. "I got too much to think about," she said, and then closed her eyes. "Sometimes I get thinking so hard my heart skips a beat. Sometimes even with my eyes closed, I can't stop thinking."

She fell off to sleep like that, with me staring at her face the whole time. She'd taken me so quick and hard in the truck that I couldn't have made real love to her if I'd wanted. I didn't have anything left. I wanted to touch her white skin, to look at every inch of her body in the light of the night, to find every inch I'd never been and kiss her in those places. But she slept beside me, and I didn't touch her. I'd never felt like that before, wanting to make love to a girl without wanting it myself. It was a sad kind of feeling, and it kept me awake until three. Then I fell asleep beside her, my arm at her shoulder until she pushed it away in a dream.

After that night, it was hard to leave her each morning. Every few weeks we went down to the landing and saw Joey, but we never took him with us anywhere, just sat with him there by the water. Some afternoons I sat with Joey under the pines by the tackle and bait store, buying him Coca-Colas and marshmallow pies while Yolanda went into her mother's shack and did palm-readings. I had her read the flat of my hand one evening at the Tenderloin, right before last call as we sat side by side at the bar. She'd held my big hand in between hers, trailing her fingers against my palms and calluses. "You'll live a nice long life," she told me, the back of my hand against her thigh. "You'll go many places, but you won't always know where you're going or why." I asked her would I ever get married, and she said, "Not soon," and I laughed, though for some reason that hurt me to hear. One late Saturday afternoon we were there at the landing and some boys from Tyler came out and swam in the river. They knew me from around, but not one of them spoke to me, just gave me sideways glances and looked at Yolanda.

The first week in September I went into the Tenderloin on Friday afternoon, looking for her. Willie B. gave me a stare when I come in the door, his face falling serious, and he got busy washing glasses as I dropped onto a stool near the register. When I asked where Yolanda was, he said, "Well, Donnie, she's gone back up to school." That was a hard thing to hear, and at first I thought he was mistaken. Seems everyone knew she was leaving but me. Seems Nigel'd come in late one night looking for her the week before, and he'd held her against the wall of the poolroom upstairs and said something right up close to her face. No one could tell what he said, he spoke so low and all. And nobody'd told me he'd been there, either, but then maybe they thought I knew, like maybe Yolanda had told me herself, but she hadn't. I stopped by to see Regina the next day, and said maybe she could tell me what to do. Maybe she could give me Yolanda's address or something. But she just shook her head.

"Just leave her be," she said in the cool of her blue carpeted office beneath Yolanda's room, her voice a river-born echo of her sister's. "She's got troubles enough, let alone some Tyler boy came hunting her down."

"I just want to talk to her," I said, standing there with my hands tight in my pockets.

Then Regina leaned back in her chair behind the desk and folded her arms at her waist. "What you have to say doesn't matter. Words can't bring her back." Then she looked past me, through the window behind me to the street. "What you going to say, Donnie, that you love her?" She lifted her head then and looked at me dead-center. "Leave her be," she sighed. "Or Nigel will see that you do."

That Sunday I hung out at the Tenderloin, shooting pool with the half of the crew that wasn't married. We drank drafts all day, and then around seven I was bent over racking the balls on the green felt table when a cool-fingered hand touched the back of my neck and I stood up straight and turned around. Nobody'd had to tell me who was standing there. Nobody'd had to tell me that tall olive-eyed boy with black hair bound back with a leather strip and a rattlesnake skin round the brim of his hat was Nigel. I seen it in his eyes sure as shit. He was wiry, thin arms hanging down into fingers strung in his belt and a knife in his boot. He was slim and tense, and I knew even beating him by forty pounds I'd never win if I fought him. The boys went quiet around me, knowing as well as I did that maybe a fight would erupt between the space of our bodies. We'd all been party to barroom punches in our days. I stood there, knowing I was whipped without even a fair match to prove it. I stared into those eyes of his, and got this peculiar hot feeling under my skin that made me feel fool for standing there. But I kept on staring into his almond-shaped eyes, the one on the left with a spot of blood in a patch near the iris. I stared for maybe two minutes when he tilted his narrow head and said, "You got something to say to me?" Course I didn't and I shook my head. I couldn't trust my voice to come out of my mouth.

"Well, I got something to say to you," he said, low in his throat, spitting the words like a sick yellow dog. He pulled a cigarette from the pocket of his plaid shirt, the sleeves cut off ragged at the shoulders, showing the tight knot of his biceps where on the left Yolanda's name lay stretched out across a heart red as new blood. They were professional tattoos, not the kind made in the middle of some drunk with a sewing needle and ink from the office supply store, real nice tattoos like the ones done in that parlor next to the front gates of the post, the one soldiers go to to have GOD-MOTHER-COUNTRY stenciled over their hearts, going into the flesh the way those words are already deep in their actual beating hearts. He took a Marlboro in his fingers, twisted the filter off, and stuck it between his pink lips, the flesh of his mouth sweet as Joey's and teeth so white didn't seem right in that poor-boy's face.

"Well, now," he said, holding a silver lighter to his face, flicking it once so the flame was not quite touching the tobacco, then he sucked in hard so the fire pulled to the tip of the cigarette and caught. The crew was behind me. I couldn't see them, but I heard them breathing close at my neck so it didn't feel so bad having to face this boy right there eye to eye, but my hands trembled in my pockets. "Well, now, I've been wondering what someone like you might look like." He smiled around the butt of the cigarette, talking smoke out his lips. "You ain't soft like I thought you might be. Suppose that comes with working asphalt," he said. Then he lifted his head real quick and all that pretend niceness dropped from his face and all his energy went to his eyes in a squeeze. "If I hear you're trying to find her I'll see you don't walk for a year. I'll see you don't walk or talk or have nothing left between your legs what works," he said in a hiss of smoke. "And I'll see she don't neither," he added, then he took the cigarette from between his fingertips and dropped it to the carpet. He stepped on the butt without lifting his eyes from my face, stepped on it exactly where it fell by my feet, never looking to see where it was. "I'll take that baby and she'll never see him again," he continued. "Lots of nice white folks'll pay cash for a baby sweet as that one." He grinned, so wide I could see the pink of his gums, then he turned, looking once over his wild-horse shoulders at me and the boys standing there dim-witted by the pool tables, not one of us breathing regular.

Love's a funny thing. Cynthia and me been together just shy a year now, and I know what's coming up next. She'll keep calling me her fiancé. She'll keep introducing me like that to her friends and the people we meet when we go into Tyler. And then someday I'll just tell her that's not what I got in mind, and she'll go to crying and buying me cards with all kinds of sweet-talk and flowers and hearts printed on the front. Then someday when I'm too hung over to be patient with her, maybe I'll slam the refrigerator door so her all-important magnets go flopping down on the floor, and she'll say something like, "See, I don't matter to you." And maybe she'll cry and maybe she'll throw something or break a glass against the wall. That's how those things happen.

I haven't heard from Yolanda and don't know what I'd do if I did. I know she is still at that school in Atlanta because she made the front page of the *Tyler Sentinel* with a show she put on at a gallery in Norcross. There was a picture of her on the front page, and she looks the same as ever, standing in front of her pictures all hung on the white wall of some building, and the show was called "White Boys and River Girls." The paper didn't actually mention her drawings, but I wouldn't expect that they would. Yolanda's not smiling into the camera, but I wouldn't expect that neither. She was a pale slip of white trash back in Tyler, somebody nobody'd ever remember from high school, not even finishing proper, just taking her General Education Degree out of night school like misfits and pregnant girls do. She was one of those girls that we wouldn't recognize proper on the street, the kind we'd search out in a drunk and forget about sober. Seeing her face on the front page of the weekly paper made me feel guilty and ignorant all over again, like I'd felt that night in the truck.

The article running alongside the photograph had a title saying "Local Girl Wins Major Award," and that seemed a sorry thing. She isn't true local and she isn't a girl, not proper, seeing the article states she's twenty-two this year. But Tyler reclaimed her in her moment of accomplishment, and if Yolanda took time out to pose for the camera and answer questions for the reporter, then she must've felt right for doing so.

I keep the article in the top drawer of our dresser in our two-bedroom apartment. Cynthia asked once why I kept it, and I told her I knew Yolanda from the Tenderloin. Seems she'd have some knowledge about things, since we both know all the same people. But Cynthia don't ask what she don't want to hear.

I think about getting married, someday, not to Cynthia, but to who I don't know. Late at night I've taken to leaving Cynthia at home where she don't even notice I'm gone for all the image-creating she does, what with *Vogue* and *Glamour* and *Elle* all open in front of her on the coffee table with the television on, nail polish bottle going clickety-click as she shakes it next to her face in one hand, punching buttons on the remote control with the other. I drive out toward the coast, across the causeways toward Tybee Island, and the lights from the truck slide over the water beneath and beside me. And those nights I get to thinking how time passes so quick you don't even know it's gone, how things happen you can't explain.

I keep a rabbit's foot on my key chain these days, and it hangs to the side of the steering wheel. I reach up to touch it every now and again, just quick. If you'd asked that summer if I loved Yolanda, I would have answered fast that I wasn't the marrying type, like love and marriage go together in answering that question. But it's funny, because when I think of her face rising up like the moon over mine, when I think of her sleeping next to me there in her dark apartment, those cool smooth stones in the bowl beside the bed, something like love comes to mind.

I get in my truck and drive places without knowing where I'm going. I put my foot to the floor and open her up, trying to outrun the inside of my head, trying to shake loose of that kind of thinking. I sit there driving, downing a cold one, going through a six-pack, stopping to piss at the side of the road, like maybe a drunk will stop me from thinking, like maybe I could forget, but I can't. I can't shake thinking about her. I don't want to tear loose of thinking about her, like it's some kind of spell. And I get to thinking maybe she's got a strand of my hair stuck away in her jewelry box, thinking maybe at night she pulls it out and warms it between her fingers, speaking over it on her knees, pulling forward in the pale curve of her narrow back. I think of those words in the breath between her lips, a slip of my hair at her fingertips, praying in river-girl tongue.

Paula K. Gover is a native of Mt. Pleasant, Michigan. Paula teaches composition at Ferris State University in Big Rapids, Michigan, where she also provides alternative methods of writing support for special needs students. While her teaching and writing career has followed a rather elongated and tangled path, she has possessed a love of both language and writing for as long as she can remember. In 1985, she earned her BA in English, then in 1987, she received her MFA in Creative Writing in Fiction from The University of Michigan. As a graduate student at U of M, she received four first-place Avery Hopwood Awards in both poetry and fiction. Her work has appeared in a number of literary magazines including *The Virginia Quarterly Review,* which selected "White Boys and River Girls" as the 1992 Balch Award for the best story to appear in *VQR* last year. Her collection of short fiction, *A Woman Like Me,* has been accepted for publication by Algonquin Books of Chapel Hill.

PHOTO CREDIT: BILL WELCH

While I'd gotten married for all the wrong reasons, in the long run, a number of good things came out of that situation, including spending three years in southeast Georgia as a soldier's wife, which is where I gave birth to my only child, Aaron, in 1979. While my ex-husband was stationed at Fort Stewart, Georgia, due to a housing shortage, we ended up living twenty-seven miles from post in the small rural village of Glennville—which was also exactly where we'd run out of gas and money after traveling from Fort Sill, Oklahoma. I've never held much store in ideas about destiny and fate, but there was something nearly magical in how the residents of Glennville responded to our plight. We'd had just enough cash for one night in a motel, but by morning, the owner of the motel had arranged for us to move into the trailer of a friend, and to pay off our rent as we could. The owner of the trailer gave us food from his garden, and the manager of the IGA let me charge $50 worth of groceries to get us started. Throughout the next three years, I found work,

*had a baby, and discovered friends at every turn. "White Boys and River
Girls" has its origins in that village, and also reflects how the different
communities allowed me to pass through their ranks without question-
ing my presence or intentions. I had friends in every corner, from bank
directors to Baptist preachers to river-folk to black residents of Shanty-
town, the reasons for which I'm still not quite certain. Part of it can be
attributed to my mother, who has always insisted that the most valuable
trait a woman can possess is the ability to listen. I haven't always agreed
with this idea as it suggests attitudes of feminine compliance, yet I also
have come to recognize how this ability has served me as a writer. I did
indeed listen as I moved through my circles of friends in that small town
in Georgia. Moreso, I remember their voices.*

Wayne Karlin

PRISONERS

(from *Prairie Schooner*)

for Lucille Clifton

Russell drove south through a warm, misty November day. The week had kept turning corners that left him facing to the past. Yesterday, interrogating a twenty-year-old white male named Jason Waxman who was suspected of dealing crack cocaine at the state college, he had inadvertently joked in Vietnamese with Trung, a California-born deputy. Trung had looked at him blankly; he affected not to speak a word. But the suspect had gone pale at the sound of the language. "You're a vet," he had said.

Russell found himself offended at the boy's fear.

"What are you, a cocker spaniel? You need to be altered?"

"You know what I mean."

He had put Waxman's thumb between his own thumb and forefinger, the boy's flesh white as bone against his skin. At the gentle squeeze he gave, Waxman began to talk. He was scared to death. Russell had learned that being offended by a stereotype didn't mean you shouldn't use it.

Now he was driving to Point Lookout to help in the search for a fourteen-year-old, half-black, half-Vietnamese girl named Kiet who had run away from a residential program for troubled adolescent girls.

He was taking his time. He doubted that Kiet would come in this direction; usually when girls went AWOL from Ruth's

House they headed north, to D.C. or Baltimore. But a figure, female, had been spotted wading out at the point, and the cold water was being dragged and searched by divers.

The girls, often inner-city kids, hated being sent to the boonies, and where he was now was the least populated area of the county: a crust of houses, white clapboard churches, and country stores along the highway, beyond them fields and forest and marsh. The farther south you went, the narrower the peninsula became until finally the Potomac and the bay pinched out the land between them. That tip of the county, of the state, was Point Lookout. The state had started from it. In 1634 the British colonists had come in two ships, *The Ark* and *The Dove,* and made the point (then called Sparkes Poynt) their first landfall after the Indies. Russell was a history buff. The progenitor of his own family—a slave named Lucius from Dahomey—had come in 1756, brought up from New Orleans by one Somerset Hallam. Russell's boss, Alex Hallam, who was white, shared ·the same family name as Russell. It wasn't unusual for blacks and whites in the county, from the old families, to have the same last name. But Alex regarded the fact with an amusement that Russell didn't know how to take.

Alex kidded him for what he called Russell's obsession with family history. But Russell didn't think he had the choice implied in Alex's teasing. He had been born, like many in his family, with twelve fingers; the extra two had been amputated when he was a baby. But he still felt the invisible ache of them on his hands, organs of an extra sense that dipped and stirred into time. Time touched him back. It wasn't a matter of searching it out. It was simply there, the weight of an internal presence. He thought the Vietnamese would understand; their ancestry and history were felt as points of reference, of lookout, in a person's soul. Though Kiet, the child he was looking for, black GI father she never knew, Vietnamese mother, only had a history of running away.

He was nearly at the beginning of the state park now. On impulse, following his line of thought, Russell stopped at the memorial to the Confederate dead, a Cleopatra needle with the names of the dead inscribed on copper plates fastened around its base. Over thirty-five thousand prisoners had been kept at the Point Lookout camp, some of them rebel sympathizers from the county. About four thousand men had died here, of disease, exposure, maltreatment. The prisoners had been packed into flimsy tents and often slept on the ground; the country was marshy and unhealthy and exposed to ill winds off the Chesapeake Bay and the river. Many must have died, Russell speculated, of broken hearts. To the west, on the Potomac side, they would have stood and stared at the shoreline of Virginia, as distant and as tantalizing as the shores of heaven. He imagined it added to their sense of hell that often their guards were ex-slaves who had joined the Union army; the prisoners', and in fact, the Union officers' diaries that Russell had read, expressed horror that black troops had been set over Confederate prisoners. Russell's family had a story about an ancestor who had been a guard and who had either abused or murdered a white Hallam, his former master. But Russell had never been able to confirm the story in any of the histories and it seemed wishful thinking to him.

In Vietnam, when he had briefly been a guard at a POW compound himself, he had tried to relate the experience to Point Lookout. But the Vietnamese prisoners, mostly starved amputees, were poor substitutes for white southerners, and the job had only caused him to lose the romantic image he had of the VC as supermen. Their filth, lethargy, and indifference had infuriated him. When he knew he'd murder someone if he had to keep looking at their faces, he'd gotten a transfer back to a line unit.

The mist draped around the monument and paled the bright green of the pines behind the iron picket fence that enclosed the area. A moldy smell clogged his nostrils and the cone of air around him turned suddenly icy, a spot he could move out of, he found, by taking a step to the right or left. He wondered if it was a trick of air currents or if his presence had stirred something. Inevitably there were ghost stories about Point Lookout. Tape recorders left overnight by park rangers had picked up voices where no people had been; whispered but distinct words without context for the listener: "Halt" "Where is it?" "A watery path." Russell had heard the tape, seen the photograph taken in the sixties of a couple sitting in a room at the Point Lookout lighthouse, a textured grayness next to them that configured, if you looked long enough, into a furiously glaring man in a Confederate uniform. All of it, voices, photographs, were ambiguous enough to disown or to own, depending on what you wanted out of the situation.

He walked to the needle, put his hand down flat, over some names. The coldness of the metal moved into his palm. He had been once, only once, to the Wall in Washington. Standing at its apex, he had felt he was winging out from his own center, the names carved inside him. He couldn't stay. But the names on this monument, even the familiar county names his fingers traced now, meant nothing to him. More than nothing; he was glad they were dead.

He looked for Hallam, as he had before, but again he couldn't find his own name on the monument.

He left the memorial and drove south. He passed the signs for the camping ground and Civil War museum, set back in the tall loblolly pines to the right of the narrow road. On the other side were several weather-beaten frame houses, their yards weedy, the knobbed silver globe of a sea-mine on a pedestal in one front yard. Then the country opened suddenly, and it was as if he were driving into water, passing from one element to the other, the road on top of a narrow stone dike, the bay vast and gray and seething with whitecaps on his left, Lake Conoy, a large pond that flowed into the Potomac on his right. He could see the river glinting through a thin tall picket of loblollies on the eastern edge of the pond. At the end of the causeway, on the bay side, was a brief wedge of grass between the road and the water. A spoked iron wheel stood half-buried near a picnic table. Russell stopped the car again, stalling, not sure why.

He got out. A boy was standing on the edge of the rocks near the grass, arm cocked, a dip net in his hand, the other delicately holding the end of a trot line. It was the wrong season and the wrong place to crab, but the boy's concentrated stillness tugged a memory out of Russell; when he was a kid he would stand like that, pulling his thoughts from the gray flowing of the water. He touched the iron of the wheel. It held a different coldness than the monument's, the coldness of the water in which it had lain. This object was from the prison camp. The land had steadily eroded since then; during the war the shoreline here extended out per-haps half a mile into the bay. On the horizon, Russell saw a ship, a freighter headed toward Baltimore, drawing a line between sky and sea. He looked at the closer water. It was cold and dark and smoothly heavy, heaving itself up, pushing against the shore.

Under the surface here would be more ruins, broken plates, chains, minié balls, the barnacle-encrusted bones of unburied white prisoners clicking against the bones of the Middle Passage that had marched here along the ocean's bottom to complete their journey, to push blindly against the mass of the continent. He tried to imagine the girl, Kiet's face, emerging suddenly, half-black, half-Vietnamese, his own past made into a construct, rising, water streaming from eye sockets and astonished mouth. A shadow passed under his gaze. He started, then grinned at him-self as he recognized the surprisingly graceful scurry and glide, a glimpsed motion that gave his mind just enough to fill in the form of a crab. He let himself glide under the surface with it, the cold water smooth over him, his stalked eyes probing the dark rocks and silt, a sediment thick with secrets and crimes. A voice, a distinct word, rose and opened in his mind, as perfectly as a bubble.

Hallam.

I am considered an educated man for one of my race, although Dr. Miles Oberle, my mentor at the New England Conservatory for Freed Africans, would undoubtedly chide me for the above phrase. You are simply an educated man, he would say. I have found, however, that while simplicity is much to be desired, it is rarely achieved and the qualification I make perhaps stems from the way I have come to regard myself. For if one thinks of education as enlightenment, of light, the pure *lux* (from the Greek *leukos,* white) that overcomes darkness, then I cannot help but think of myself as that which must be overcome.

Lux et logos. Those gilted words, engraved above the door of Dr. Oberle's study, his sanctum sanctorum, will always conjure the conservatory to me. *Lux* illuminated *logos. Lux* was the cool New England light that flowed like a blessing through the bay windows and touched a muted gleam from the polished oak furniture and floors, that awakened a warm smell, like that emanating from milk-fed, content calves nuzzling in a clean barn, from the leather-bound books lining the shelves. *Lux* glittered from the golden titles branded onto their spines. At certain times of the day, rainbow prisms of light would sparkle from the fine crystal in the red china closet, while at others globules of lemony light would move like luminous spirits over the portraits of the Fathers, Washington and Jefferson, framed on the walls, decoalesce and drip onto the blindly staring marble busts of the great thinkers: Socrates, Plato, Aristotle, Descartes. That room was to me the physical formulation of *logos* itself. Even the mahogany fireplace mantelpiece, which was decorated with a bas-relief of elephants and gilded Negro heads, their widened eyes gleeful with stupidity, their thick-lipped mouths drooped open like the mouths of idiot children, seemed contained, made ridiculous and safe by the room. Which of course was Dr. Oberle's intent in having it there. The design, he told me, was copied from the decoration over the door of the Liverpool Customs House and was emblematic of the slave trade: it was commonly said by the English themselves in those days that Liverpool's streets were marked out by chains, the bricks of its houses cemented with African blood. This too is conquered, Oberle wanted the decoration to say, conquered by the fact he dared put it there, conquered by what surrounded it: those paintings, those sculpted heads, the reasoned words standing in tight-shouldered solidarity on the bookshelves. I found it impolitic to mention the obvious paradox that the right hand, so to speak, could sculpt one set of heads while the left carved those Negro visages.

He was, after all, my mentor. I had come to the conservatory soon after I ran away from south Maryland in March of 1858, in my seventeenth year. In May of that same year, I had been asked to address an abolitionist meeting on Boston Common, a gathering attended by Dr. Oberle. My quick tongue was married to my thick ignorance, a combination that drew him to me; I suppose I seemed backward enough to benefit from his aid, yet with enough natural eloquence to promise his success. At his request, we were introduced after the rally. He asked me if I could read and write (I could. I had been taught the art at my old master's bidding, for he liked to have me read to him in the evenings). Soon after that interview, Oberle invited me to join the dozen or so other students, all runaway slaves, he had chosen to bring to the light.

For the most part, I remember my time at the conservatory with fondness; it was a flowing and tranquil passage. There are only two incidents that jar my memory. The first occurred, of all places, in Bible class. I cannot be certain why that occasion has stayed in my mind except that it marked an unusual agitation in me about a subject that had never been one I had taken with any seriousness before, my mind tending toward the rational and scientific. That day Dr. Oberle was visiting the class, which was taught by the Reverend Silas Gough; the subject was Abraham begetting a child in his old age. According to Dr. Gough, faith in the possibility of the miraculous was one message we could extract from this incident.

But what of Ishmael, I found myself asking, my voice to my surprise, to the astonishment of the others in the room (Dr. Gough stroking his beard, looking at Dr. Oberle, who stroked his own in a mirroring response), suddenly cracking with emotion. I had learned by then—I was near graduation—to affect a dispassionate coolness sharpened with just an edge of sarcasm as my persona, and the rage that seized me was, to say the least, unexpected. How could a father abandon his own child, and that child's mother, to what he surely must have thought would have been certain death in the desert, simply because Ishmael was the child of a slave? I demanded. Was he not still Abraham's son? Only, to my further consternation, I realized I had not phrased my question in these words; in my agitation I slipped back into myself. "He not be Abraham chile?" I asked. Stopping myself, looking at the startled faces around me, looking startled myself at the words that had slipped past my lips like traitors, I suddenly realized that I had risen to my feet and was shouting.

I sat down, shamefaced, my hands trembling. The extended point of the passage, Mr. Hallam, Dr. Gough said quietly, is that this miracle made Abraham the progenitor of the Hebrews, who thus could fulfill their mission of becoming the human progenitors of the Christ, the light of the world. If Abraham's blessing had gone to Ishmael, this symbolically would signify the victory of the baser forces of his nature that had resulted in the child of the lower state. Yet to leave a child in the desert, I began, but stopped when I saw the impatience clouding his face, the disappointment in the eyes of Dr. Oberle. There is always the danger, Mr. Hallam, he said, of losing one's objectivity.

That Bible class was my last before graduation and for a time I worried that my indiscretion might threaten my being chosen as valedictorian. It did not.

Commencement took place in Dr. Oberle's study. There were but twelve of us in the graduating class. I began my speech by announcing, with a beaming pride that produced a ripple of emotion from my audience, that to a man we had enlisted in the Thirty-sixth United States Colored Infantry, under Colonel A. G. Draper. We needed, I said, as we went forth to battle, to recall that we were going to be engaged in a conflict unlike any other fought in the history of mankind, a struggle engendered not from greed, not from the coveting of a neighbor's goods and chattels, nor even from a desire to break the chains of tyranny from oneself, like the struggles of the slave Spartacus or the valiant Hasmoneans. No, I maintained, here, for the first time in human history, was a battle motivated by the purest altruism, for what else could we name it when the men of one race were willing to give their lives, to fight their own brothers, in order to liberate those of another race?

As we took our position in the ranks, I admonished, when the applause had ceased, we needed to nourish our astonishment at this sacrifice in order to save ourselves from the monster of vindictive hatred that could destroy us, even in our moment of victory. We, the sons of Ham, had eaten the bitter herbs of slavery, yet—we needed to remember—without that original taste, we would not be here either; the light of *logos* would have been denied us if we'd remained in our baser, native state, exiled in the desert. White hands had rudely plucked us from that state, I said, my metaphors becoming somewhat confused in my excitement at the approval my speech was gaining; white hands had placed us in harsh servitude, yet white hands also—I nodded to the audience—had reached down and picked us up to the sun of truth and civilization. Thus, even as we fought our oppressors, we must never forget to guard against becoming like them through blind hatred and the facile satisfaction offered by retribution. In the words of Thomas Paine, I concluded (I knew my audience), tyranny like hell is not easily conquered.

As I spoke, I kept my eye on Dr. Oberle, the faculty, the trustees of the institute. Their murmurs of approval, their pale hands stroking their beards with increasing speed, as if to gauge an inner pleasure, warmed me. In a theatrical manner even the day itself joined the ceremony: a beam of light flowed through the windows, illuminating, as if to paint into my memory the details of that room. It fell on the shelves of books, it fell on the Persian carpet, on the richly gleaming oak furniture and then, inevitably, it fell on that accursed mantelpiece.

As the row of woolly-headed, mocking faces suddenly blazed before my eyes, each became a black, metastasizing cell of doubt entering my body. These fathers nodding at me, these graybeards, had brought both of us to this room and I wondered suddenly at their intent in lining us before them, as into crooked mirrors. They had brought us into their light, these white men, but they had also fashioned these heads, we were both their children and neither of us their inheritors. Was this truly such a mystery to me, who knew it in my flesh that a hand that could caress and stroke could also rend and tear? Those gaped mouths called to me, Who do you think you are, pickaninny, parrot, gibbering ape, what do you think you are doing here? I tried to force my gaze from them, but I turned my head and they melted into the faces of the faculty and trustees, faces suddenly anxious at my silence, mouths suddenly murmuring with concern instead of approval, and the metamorphosis continued so that I saw their whiteness became a row of grinning skulls that parodied the mocking African faces.

Finally, the growing mutter caused me to shake my head, shake off the vision, and I continued. But the applause when I finished my speech was more an outburst of relief than of admiration.

My graduation from the conservatory merged into a different form of education, that of the training camp, but I cheerfully endured its mindless brutality for I felt it was suffered to hone me for a nobler purpose. The earlier lessons of my slavery, which for the main part consisted of a protective retreat into expected mannerisms, came back to me at this time; they were of great value in my intercourse with my drill sergeant and white officers. At the end of our training period, we were read the news of the great scrap at Gettysburg and we became fearful the war would be over soon. I was wild with impatience, eager not to miss the tide of history.

To my disappointment, though, the Thirty-sixth did not march to be tested in the crucible of battle. Instead, we were to be sent to southern Maryland, the very place where I had endured my slavery, the cursed ground where I had buried my mother and promised myself not to return. But I was a soldier now; I had willingly sacrificed the freedom I'd taken to myself in order to extend and ennoble it. I had to, to put it simply, follow orders. The whites of the region, certainly not to my surprise, were sympathetic to the Secesh, and federal troops had had to be sent to occupy the area both in order to catch blockade runners and also to control the spies and saboteurs this poisonous pocket of rebellion spewed northward. In addition, a large prison depot had been built at Point Lookout just miles south of Scotland, where I had spent my years of servitude, and we were to help garrison it. Although the Second Regiment of New Hampshire Volunteers was already deployed at the depot, its population was growing due to the Confederacy's defeat at Gettysburg. And perhaps it was felt (although perhaps it could be the War Department was reluctant to trust us in battle) that justice would be served by assigning a regiment of colored troops as guards of their former keepers.

And so, in the beginning of May in the year 1863, behind the flags of regiment and country, I marched as official and unrelenting as a debt back to the place where I was born. There was something of the dream about it: in my uniform, armed, I moved down into a land devastated as if by the fire of my hatred. Fields had gone to weed or were growing up in pine trees; dogs and cattle were running wild. When we came to Leonardtown, the county seat, the buildings were closed, their windows boarded, and bony pigs were rooting in the main street. There were very few people who came out to see us, though I looked into every white face as if peering into a mirror, searching for the one face I knew as I knew my own to form before my eyes. But we passed only old men and women who stared at our black faces as if we had marched out of their own uneasy dreams. Only old men and women; they kept the children and the young women hidden and their able menfolk had gone to Virginia to join the rebels.

We marched south, down through the St. Inigoes district, until we passed Scotland. It was a name that, before my eyes were opened to geography, had meant only this hot, lowland place to me.

The prison camp spread itself below Scotland and onto the point, exposed to wind and water on that sandy spit. Before us were the neat dwellings of the guard regiments, the sturdily fashioned and well-maintained administrative and supply buildings, and then, beyond them, a deadline ditch, a rampart, and a city of rotting white canvas tents, acres of tents so ragged in appearance that they had the aspect of patches of diseased skin scaling off the land. They covered the country of my childhood.

What I have kept all these years since is a stink in my nostrils and pictures, daguerreotypes fastened behind my mind's eye, flash burned into my brain. Pictures. A group of emaciated prisoners arriving at the wharf, my fellow guards, ex-slaves ennobled by their suffering, tearing the rags from the backs of these wretches and throwing that clothing into the bay, so these white men stood naked in the wind, as on an auction block or an African beach. The malodorous mud alleys between the tents, puddled with urine and piled with lumps of excrement. A Negro guard shooting a squatting, bare-bottomed prisoner driven into the night by the diarrhea all of them had. A stocky, sturdy New Hampshire man shooting down with cold rage a Confederate officer who taunted him that Yankees and niggers, all guards, all in the same uniform, must be equal. Shooting him for the utterly offensive insult of that remark, this New England soldier on my side of the war. Another prisoner, a gaunt, bearded man with fiery eyes, a patriarchal figure who reminded me of lithographs I had seen of John Brown, stepping deliberately into the deadline ditch and Jim Tanner, the ex–field slave from Mississippi who had dared him to do it, just as deliberately shooting him in the head. Tanner. Tanner making prisoners driven from their tents by dysentery get on their knees and pray "fo President Lincoln and colored folks"; making them carry him on their backs as he whooped, his mud-stained, red-rimmed eyes rolling at me, fixed to mine, smiling his mockery at my look of disgust, his face one of the faces I had seen on the mantelpiece. Tanner.

He was my guide into this new country that my old country had rolled over into as if in some inexorable balancing of nature's justice. On my first day, he brought me with him into the prisoners' area. The prisoners scurried out of his way, disappearing into their tents as he walked the mud streets. Tanner was Provost Marshall Brady's favorite; he had gotten away with murder more than once, and they knew it. As we walked, he recited information about the layout of the camp, the rules involving relief of guard, the deadline, the contraband market (yes, there was commerce in hell, surely no surprise to a former slave. I have heard that Major Brady, called Beast, left the point with over a million dollars in his retirement fund). The prisoners, Tanner told me, were permitted twelve ounces of hard bread a day; if they had greenbacks they could always buy more. Or they could scavenge.

"It seems hardly enough for a man to live on, Sergeant," I said.

Tanner turned to me. The weave of tiny veins that formed a scraggly red border around his eyes seemed to glow (Old Blood-eye the prisoners, and many guards for that matter, called him, when he was not within hearing). A slow smile spread on his face. "Why you talk so white, nigger?" he asked.

"I have had schooling," I said stiffly.

He laughed. When he spoke, he seemed to exaggerate the discrepancies of his language. "Well, le'me tell you somephin, School. Lose some sixty a day, fum de scurvy. We got bowt twenty thousand take care ob. Scurvy too damn slow." He peered at me curiously. "I just gib dem dey amount. Set dey amount. You know about de amount, boy? Where you slave?"

"Here."

He laughed even louder. But the red glow stayed in his eye, smouldering like a choice he kept at hand under the choice he seemed to have made of being amused at me.

"Firs' day, field handin, I mus be six, seben year ol', dey gib me a sack," Tanner said. "Got a strap roun my neck, my mowth open, mowth a de sack open at my heart, bottom of de sack drag de ground. Also got dis basket, for when de sack full. Dey say pick, I pick. I pick, dey whip all de time fus day, cause what I doing, I settin my amount. Dat day my amount one hunert pound. Dey nevah see no six, seben year old do one hunert pound. Dat day on, at end a picking ebery day, you go down the gin house, weigh up. Undah you amount, dey whip you up. Obah you amount, dey figger you fake befo, whip you up too, next day you pick dat much. Understand, School? You wanna see mah back, times I ovah or undah mah amount?"

"I have an amount that I have carried also, Sergeant," I said (what a pompous ass I was in those days). "But I believe we must be better than they are."

The red net glowed. "Bettah. You right dere, School."

He spun around. His quickness caught a man who had been standing in the shade of a tent, eavesdropping on our conversation, in its net. I had not thought that Tanner had seen him. The prisoner was still wearing the bedraggled uniform of a Confederate captain. He stared at us strangely. He had a long, thin face and his rotted teeth, elongated by the retraction of his gums, gave it a horsy cast. He looked back and forth at our faces, then nodded and laughed to himself.

Tanner nodded also. "Come on ovah heah, Cap'n Norris," he said.

The man shrugged and pulled something from his pocket. He held it up in front of his face as he approached us, snapping it between his hands. A greenback. When his breath washed over me, I understood why he had not ducked back into his tent like the others.

"You look like a damned old whiskeyhead, Sergeant," he said, swaying. "Why don't you take this, go buy me some whiskey. From your massa, the Beast. Go fetch me some beast whiskey. Some hairy beast brew."

When he was finished, he stood, a sneer forming on his lips, then disappearing, then forming, as if he were tugged between fear and insolence. As if a part of him were remembering to be afraid.

"Dis man talkin contraband, School," Tanner said. "You head him?"

"Sergeant, a little philanthropy is all I ask." Norris gave a mock bow. "Aren't you a philanthropist, Sergeant? You look ripely philanthropic to me."

"You callin me what?" Tanner said, putting a hand behind his ear. A kind of calmness descended on his face.

"Captain Norris," I said, "why don't you take yourself out of here now."

Norris looked from Tanner to me, smiling and shaking his head as if he could not believe what was in front of his eyes.

Tanner drew his revolver from its case. I could feel that motion in my stomach.

"Sergeant," I said quickly. "Philanthropist is not an insult."

He glanced at me, then back at Norris, and smiled. "Ain't no insult? You wrong, School. Philanthropist mean nigger, doan it, Cap'n?"

He pointed the revolver at Norris. Norris stiffened, then tore open his shirt. He rubbed his filthy chest, pointing to his heart, still swaying.

"Philanthropist," he said.

Tanner cocked the revolver and fired into Norris's chest. Norris flew backward and fell into a tub that had been sunk into the mud as a latrine. I stood staring at the body, the greenback still clutched in one hand, waiting for him to get up, for the lesson to be over. The flies started gathering quickly; there were many already there. "That was cold murder," I said. But Tanner just smiled at me again, a conspiratorial smile, as if he had seen into my heart, sensed the surge of pure triumph and joy I had felt when he fired into that arrogant beast.

"Bettah," he said.

* * *

I open a tent flap, even now, in memory, in dreams, and the prisoners' faces turn to me slowly. A menagerie of the faces of my youth. Even now, in memory, in dreams, they must stay animalistic, for I can't bear to think of them as men. Sly, fox faces. Flat, snake-mean eyes that gleam with contempt, even as they opaque with fear. Bats in a cave, blinking awake. So many eyes. The tents are made to hold sixteen; we stuff in forty. Forty of them: high or low, thick or thin, though they all thinned and sharpened after a while, took on the smudged white and gray coloring of the tents as if they had become a new race. A doggish race that we kenneled, their wagging and hand-licking, their nipping at one another, their occasional snarls of defiance, their cur's stink. How they hated me. How I reveled in their hatred. How I hated them back. I raise my Sharps as Tanner had raised his revolver and I point it and I feel the freedom and the power that Tanner must have felt. If they had one head I would blow it off.

I spin around and leave that closed place, seeking air and light. I spin and spin.

Below the prison compound, surrounded by its deadline ditch and stockade, was the Hammond Hospital, a series of twenty buildings arranged like spokes in a circle. Twelve hundred patients could be held in its wards; there were over six thousand when I was at the point. At Hammond, the surgeons were another race also, a race with serrated, sharpened fingers, with strange hunger in its eyes. Among the Whydahs, I had read in a book I found once in Dr. Oberle's library, all sickness is thought to come from the curses of enemies: cure came from removing—removing first the curse and then the enemy. To those Whydah, the surgeons of Point Lookout, limbs were curses and their answer was removal also.

It was Tanner who brought me to the hospital, and Tanner of course who took me to the charnel tent, showing it to me like a choice he was putting into my mind, though I did not understand that until later. He pulled back the flap and grinned and stood to one side to let me look. The amputated legs and feet and arms were stacked neatly as cots or tent poles: legs on legs, feet fitted with feet, detached hands cupped, all their palms up. Flesh apple-fresh as stolen youth and flesh already rotted with death, moving with maggots, buzzed by obscenely fat bluebottle flies. Flesh that had blackened or browned, as if our color were contained within it, as if our color was its rot. At the sight of that horrible uniformity my mind tilted and I thought: here they build us.

I fled both the sight and Tanner's laughter and rushed behind the tent. Doubling over, I released a stream of bile, then heaved and retched, my eyes fastened to the ground. Bent over in this posture, I saw the back edge of the tent rise slightly at its bottom, as if being nudged up, and then I screamed, for from that black gap came a scuttling line of detached hands, escaping, scurrying along the ground sideways, their fingers moving like legs. I reeled up and my eyes met Tanner's mocking, red-rimmed orbs. "What sicks you, boy?" he asked, and brought his heel down hard. I heard a terrible crushing sound. We stood for a moment, our eyes locked, then I looked. Under Tanner's boot, its claws still clutching a trophy of torn flesh, was the good friend of my childhood, a Maryland blue crab, come up from the inlet that lapped near the tent to feast on the grabbers that for so long had pulled his friends and family from the water.

"Come on, School," Tanner said, "got somephin make you feel bettah."

Taking my arm, he led me away from the hospital to a section of the compound to which I had not yet been, to a tent that was identical to all the other tents. He smiled at me and opened the flap just as he had at the charnel tent.

I entered. The flap coming behind me closed me into a dream. A face I had sunken into the deepest depths of myself loosened from its weights and bobbed up, real and inescapable in front of my eyes.

"Private Hallam," Tanner said. "You find somephin you enjoy heah? Pass de time, say? Somephin bettah?"

I nodded, unable to speak.

"Yours," Tanner said simply.

There was no one else in the tent; the others must have been out on work parties. I walked toward the figure on the ground.

"Hallam," I said hoarsely, the sound of my own name in that rank, closed place startling to my ear.

"Hallam," I said again, as if to relieve myself of it, give it back to this skeleton who had given it to me.

He didn't move, only stared at me. If he recognized me, he refused to acknowledge it. As I looked at him, my eyes fastened like crab claws to his flesh, I remembered the day I had marched back into the county and saw it scorched, as if from my wishes. His body was similarly devastated. The powerful form I remembered was wasted away. His hair was mostly gone, except for a few lank, filthy strands. His face was skullish, the skin yellowed and waxy. The padded, sloped strength of his shoulders, the muscles I had seen dancing under a gleam of sweat as he punished, as he hit or drove his need forward into my mother's body, had withered to wing bone. And his hands. These were not the calloused, vein-knotted pinchers I remembered: cunning fasteners and whittlers of wood, boat-building hands, trot-lining hands, strokers, graspers, carvers, seizers, twisters, grippers of the handles of whips, of the heavy links of chains, carapaced scuttlers that moved like feeding creatures over the front of my mother's calico dress, patters of warm waves of love into the top of my head that suddenly grabbed my face, pulled it close as if to a mirror and what he saw in that mirror blossoming on his face into disgust and self-loathing. Those hands.

They had been crushed as if under Sergeant Tanner's boot, the fingers skewed and splintered, black crescent moons where the nails were torn off, the skin as black as the flesh of the hands I had seen pleading at me in the charnel tent, black as if the name he had given me like a curse had come back to him from me. He raised those terrible claws to me. His cracked lips moved and he croaked, but the words were words I might have heard if I had just come into his bedroom of a Sunday morning to help him dress for church:

"Help me, boy."

Did he recognize me? I don't know. Even after I pressed my face to his, even after I called out my name and his crime, screamed it into his face, all he might have seen was another nigger guard calling him to his account.

I pushed my rage back into my heart, a case that had hardened over the years to contain it.

"You need the hospital," I said.

At the word, a look of horror sprung onto his face. "No," he moaned. "Nooowhooo." It was the howl of a terrified dog.

"You'll die," I said.

"Help me," he whispered, looking into my eyes now as if he at last recognized me. "Feed me," he said.

The slaves in southern Maryland prepare a ham in a way, my mother told me, that they brought from Africa: it was done both for the tastiness of it and to preserve the meat in hot weather. The Negroes would take the pieces of butchered hog their owners would give them on holidays, groove the meat, and then stuff the grooves with greens and peppers and mustard seeds. My mother had often prepared this dish for Hallam. It was our old master's favorite meal.

From the guards' garden then, and from some of the traders that did business in the camp, I gathered the ingredients: kale, cabbage, cress, turnip tops, and wild onions. The ham I obtained from an old Negro man in Scotland, just north of the prison: he had lost his family when they were all hurriedly sold to Virginia before the federal troops came into the area, and he was living with the pig in a little shack outside the abandoned quarters of his master. When I asked him why he didn't move into the main house, he looked at me as if I were a lunatic. He treated that pig with affection, as if it were a child, but he needed the greenbacks and I was willing to pay.

The other guards teased me as I began to prepare the dish, but when they saw my face they stopped and formed a silent circle around me. Silent at first, but after a time they began to mutter, a steady drone of voices that seemed to hum and vibrate in the bone of my skull. "His mama . . . lak the ham . . . stuff hisself in, split fo sho . . . wah he do . . . see, see." I cut the greens and vegetables fine, and I chopped and I chopped, the salty drops of my sweat falling on them, and then I put them into a tub, and I mixed in red pepper and salt and mustard seed while all around me and in me the voices droned. I took a clean cotton shirt and I cut it up the front, the guards moaning as the knife touched and split, see, see, and I lay it open on the table. Then I tenderly laid a bed of green on the cloth and turned to the ham. I took my bayonet and cut deep crescents into the pink, giving flesh, making a crisscross pattern, the point of the knife meeting the resistance of the flesh, then my thrust breaking through, the moan around and from me increasing as if all we had passed through that was terrible beyond language had been stripped to this single, gathering sound and it was our word, our language. And I gathered up the greens in my hands, the peppers burning into the small cuts, burning the tender flesh between fingers and nails, and I stuffed that hotness into the holes I had made, pushing them in deep, deep.

I turned the ham over and repeated this process and then I lay it on the bed of green and wrapped it round and tied it shut with twine, the moaning passing lip to lip, reverberating in the tremble of my fingers, working that meat. I put the ham on the rack I'd prepared, in a deep pot of water, and I covered it. I boiled it for hours, sitting cross-legged and motionless, sweating. Then I took it from the fire and I let it cool in its own juice for the rest of that night.

In the morning I drained it and I brought it to Hallam.

The other guards followed me at a small distance, and they

stood back when I went inside. Hallam's tentmates were still there. They looked up at me with an animalistic dullness from their starved lethargy, their nostrils twitching at the smell of the meat, their mouths salivating.

"Get out," I said.

They stared at me, or rather at the bundle in my hands, transfixed, and I said the words again. As if they were a signal, my companions poured into the tent, screaming my words like echoes, kicking, beating, driving all the prisoners out. All but Hallam.

He lay as I had seen him before, befouled and stinking, his eyes unfocused. I sat down on the earth next to him.

"Hallam," I said, "do you know me?"

His yellowed eyes rolled back in his head. A brownish liquid dribbled down his chin. I seized his jaw between my thumb and forefinger, a gesture remembered by my very skin: the way he would seize me and search my face each time he would see me. His flesh felt rough and hard on its surface but rotten soft underneath, like wood undermined by termites.

"Hallam," I said.

"Hallam," he echoed hollowly.

I laughed. "Yes, Hallam. I bring you something to eat, Hallam. To give you strength. Here." With my free hand, I tore off a chunk of ham. The juice and stuffing clung stickily to my fingers. I pushed it under his nose.

"This is the flesh of your flesh," I said. "Eat of it."

He gagged, his eyes rolling. His hand came up feebly to hold my wrist, but he shrieked when we touched, his rotted fingers bursting and bleeding at the slight contact, as if something in my skin had burned him.

"Eat," I said.

I squeezed my grip until his mouth opened, the stench from the blackened stubs of his teeth and his rotted gums as strong as death. I pushed the ham and greens into that black gap, mashed it into his mouth like a grotesque second tongue. He gagged and swallowed, his eyes rolling. The pink meat mixed with the bile of his insides, his blood; it all spilled out on my hand. Behind him, the other guards watched us silently, a row of grinning heads.

"Hallam," I thought he tried to say.

"Vomit, Hallam," I said. "Vomit, Hallam. Vomit me, Hallam."

I pushed more meat into his mouth. He vomited. As if I were floating above myself, drifting up to the apex of the tent, I saw myself, Hallam before Hallam.

I rose and then I knelt and I picked him up. I cradled him in my arms as if he were my child. The bear of a man I remembered was slight, nothing. As we passed outside, the sunlight touched his panicked face and he buried it in my chest. I felt his lips flutter against my skin, as if my heart were beating outside my body.

He only raised his face when the entrance of the hospital suddenly shadowed us. When he looked up and saw where we were, a great cry issued from his lips.

"Noooo. Hallam. Noooo."

"God of Abraham, save us," I whispered into his ear, but I carried him into the darkness, to the dark gods of the Whydah.

It was two days before I could bring myself to go back to the hospital. He lay on his back on the cot, staring up at the ceiling. A bowl of gruel had been placed next to his head, apparently so he could turn his face and lap it like a dog. But either inadvertently or in order to torment him, it had not been placed quite close enough for him to "reach." The gruel was congealing, untouched. A beetle had drowned in its sticky substance.

He stared at me vacantly when I stood over him. He was shrinking into his death, the flesh melting, the skull emerging. I pulled the tattered blanket from him. His yellow flesh had sucked down to the ladder of bones in his chest. His belly was distended with bloat and bristled with a coarse black fur. Tight between his legs that purse of life, the cursed sac from which unwanted issue was released into the world, was shriveled and black, void of the appearance of flesh. But his arms, down to the stubs of his wrists, lay smooth and innocent at his sides. They weren't horrors, but seemed simply inhuman, mere sticks. Only the stumps themselves looked bad; the surgeon had cauterized clumsily and the flesh there was cracked with bleeding scabs. As I stared, he raised his two arms and brought them together in a strange fashion: the two wrists almost but not quite touching. It took me a moment before what was in his mind emerged as a picture in my own: he was grasping, as if in prayer to me, what was no longer there to grasp: his phantom hands. A prayer, I thought, for forgiveness, but then I saw that his eyes were fastened to that bowl of rancid gruel.

I looked down at him. His passivity, his cringing focus, his utter noncomprehension, suddenly enraged me. Picking up the bowl of gruel, I flung it across the tent. His cauterized wrists waved in its direction helplessly, like the broken antennae of some gigantic, foul insect. Waved at me, as I fled the ward.

I fled, but that night I came back to him. I took him up in my arms and carried him to the ward door. I waited until the sentry had passed, and I carried him outside. He was so light that when I went out into the darkness, I could imagine my arms empty, as if I were carrying smoke. Sergeant Tanner was on duty that night. I had testified in his behalf at the hearing that had been convened after the Norris shooting, a marker I'd called in, though I believe he would have let me do what I wished to do anyway. He imagined I was taking Hallam to finish him. Brother murderer he thought me, though it was murder of which I wished to be relieved. Tanner made sure that no one stopped me, questioned my burden. My burden was light as smoke in my arms and he was the very weight of my life.

I had hidden the skiff under some brush off the Potomac shore and I thought I saw his eyes widen and grow brighter when he saw the water. He was a Hallam, Chesapeake-born; his blood, like mine, run through with estuarine water, that mixture of sea and fresh, the water from the heart of the continent that flushes out its sediment and flows into and dilutes the salt tears of the ocean passage. A mix of waters that bears and nourishes its own strange, tearing bits of life, species that could not live in the unmixed, pure essence.

I rowed until the shore was a gray seam against the sky, then set the sail. A fog drew around us, and water and sky and time coalesced until I didn't know if we were floating or flying, Hallam and handless Hallam, in a gray ether in which there was only the rasping of his breath, mingling with the groan of canvas, the whistle of wind. If the wind held, it would not take me long to get to the other side, and if my luck held as well, I could avoid the Secesh patrols. I knew these waters; I'd fished them for this man's dinner, helped crab and oyster them for my mother's pot. It was a long, wild shore on the Virginia side; I'd leave him on it, one of their patrols would find him. That was my plan. That would have been my plan if I had one, but in truth there was no plan to my voyage, no *logos,* but only a pure and wordless animal need for the relief of weight.

I felt the tick of my heart beat in my palm against the tiller, like an inexorable measure of time. My hands, my skin, my ears all told me I was heading in the right direction, but for all I knew I could have been floating in a fantastical bubble toward the moon. Hallam lay against the bow of the skiff. He raised his face and looked at me through the mist, his face and form, hands gone, wrists wrapped with a breath of smoke, dissolving into that pale opalescent grayness. He smiled. He was fifteen feet from me, at the other end of the boat, but I could feel that smile print like an icy kiss on my lips. He smiled and then he cackled and rolled over the gunnel. I raced to the side and looked over, but all I could see were those two flayed stumps breaking through the mist, their phantom grip squeezing my heart. Then he was gone and I could feel him sinking, sinking, his weight growing heavier inside me as he settled deep.

It was shortly after Hallam's "escape" that I was transferred from the prison: not because of any suspicion accruing to me from Hallam's disappearance (Tanner had covered me well) but rather because my constant petitions were at last answered. So it was I finally came to the war. And while I was late to the fighting, I saw enough to relegate my memory of Hallam's last days to a small horror, only a comparative (I wanted to believe) by which to measure other horrors. I have seen paralyzed men constantly pinch and prod the flesh of their deadened limbs as if they had to endlessly demonstrate the lack of feeling to themselves. Hallam's pain and death became a vision I touched in just such a manner: only (I told myself) as a test of my numbness. I became, as all good soldiers do, a strange construct without heart or voice, designed only to advance, to aim, to shoot. A pair of feet, a pair of eyes, a pair of hands.

I returned only this far into southern Maryland: when Father Abraham was murdered by that popinjay of an actor, I was among the troops who hunted him down into Charles County, who followed him over the Potomac. I watched him burn in that Virginia barn, but I felt nothing, neither pity nor delight. All of the fires inside me had already turned to ash.

Afterward, I rode off by myself, as if to make official the desertion I had taken from my own soul, from *lux,* years before. I rode south along the river. It was still dangerous country for a black man, particularly one in a blue uniform, but the few whites I saw, furtive and emaciated, looked at me and looked away, afraid of whatever they saw in my eyes, as surely as they feared the rifle slung from my saddle.

I rode until my stomach growled with hunger, and then, as if pulled to the water, I stopped before a dock with most of its planking torn off, but with a skeleton of boards connecting the pilings that marched out into the river.

The dock was off a small meadow; as I rode down to it, I passed the bloated corpse of a cow. I stopped and dismounted. My horse calmly nibbled on the grass near it; like me, he had grown indifferent to carrion. With my bayonet, I sliced off a chunk of the maggoty meat, then cut that into small pieces. The slicing motion of my blade reminded me, for the first time in many months, of the way I prepared a meal for Hallam. I took a coil of cord from my saddlebag and I fastened the rancid hunks of meat every two feet along the line, using the trot-lining knot Hallam had taught me when I was a small boy, the string looped over itself, each loop tightened like a small noose on the meat. Then I made my way over the framework of boards to the end of the dock, and sat on the small remaining platform of cross boards between the last two pilings. Sat out over that water.

I tied the cord to a piling and threw the end into the river, then I took the slack in my hand, holding it lightly between thumb and forefinger. I had no net or bucket; inasmuch as I thought at all, I thought to pull the crabs out, one by one, and bayonet them. I sat for a long time, dangling my feet, the water flowing around me and from me in a silver stillness. The river pulled on the line, as if testing what it had on the other end. Soon I felt the smooth cord begin to tug and jerk harder against my skin, as if it had taken into itself the essence of the life feeding at it, the claws grabbing at the chunks of offal. I began pulling the line slowly in to me, gently so as not to startle the feeding crabs, feeling their slight back tug, the tug between hunger and fear on which we are all strung. Soon I could see one, then two dark shapes growing under the silvery skin of the water, their appendages moving at me like frantic fingers as they broke through the surface.

Wayne Karlin lives in St. Mary's County, Maryland, with his wife and son. He coedited and contributed to the anthology *Free Fire Zone: Short Stories by Vietnam Veterans* and has published four novels. The most recent is *Us* (Holt 1993). His short fiction has appeared in a number of literary magazines, and he has received two Individual Artist Awards in Fiction from the state of Maryland and a fellowship from the National

Endowment for the Arts. Mr. Karlin teaches at Charles County
Community College in southern Maryland and, during the summer,
at the William Joiner Center at the University of Massachusetts.

PHOTO CREDIT: JOHN KOPP

"*Prisoners*" *is one of a series of stories I've been working on, all connected by setting, by reappearing characters, and by theme. What
I can't seem to break away from in my fiction is what the world doesn't
seem able to break away from: the self-perpetuating cycle of violence
and hatred. I don't live very far from Point Lookout, the setting of
"Prisoners." As the story depicts, there was a large federal prisoner of war
facility at the Point where thousands of Confederate prisoners died of star-
vation, disease, and abuse: local people still have many ghost stories about
the site. When, in my reading, I found that a regiment of ex-slaves had
been used as guards (a deliberate choice made by the War Department
as a form of payback), I tried to imagine how I would feel if I had been
one of those slaves, suddenly given a gun and authority over the men who
had owned me. Once I had that voice in my head, the story wrote itself;
I felt it was being told to me rather than written by me, and I had to
make very few changes in it, something which doesn't happen to me very
often when I write: I'm usually a plodder, a manic reviser. I wanted the
story to connect directly to us, our time; hence the beginning set in time
present. But I also owe that, and much else in the story, to the poet Lucille
Clifton who told me of two traits that run in her family: being born with
six fingers and the ability to see ghosts. Neither seems a bad trait for a
writer to have.*

Robert Olen Butler

PREPARATION

(from *The Sewanee Review*)

Though Thuy's dead body was naked under the sheet, I had not seen it since we were girls together and our families took us to the beaches at Nha Trang. This was so even though she and I were best friends for all our lives and she became the wife of Le van Ly, the man I once loved. Thuy had a beautiful figure and breasts that were so tempting in the tight bodices of our *ao dais* that Ly could not resist her. But the last time I saw Thuy's naked body, she had no breasts yet at all, just the little brown nubs that I also had at seven years old, and we ran in the white foam of the breakers and we watched the sampans out beyond the coral reefs.

We were not common girls, the ones who worked the fields and seemed so casual about their bodies. And more than that, we were Catholics, and Mother Mary was very modest, covered from her throat to her ankles, and we made up our toes beautifully, like the statue of Mary in the church, and we were very modest about all the rest. Except Thuy could seem naked when she was clothed. We both ran in the same surf but somehow her flesh learned something there that mine did not. She could move like the sea, her body filled her clothes like the living sea, fluid and beckoning. Her mother was always worried about her because the boys grew quiet at her approach and noisy at her departure, and no one was worried about me. I was an expert pair of hands, to bring together the herbs for the lemon-grass chicken or to serve the tea with the delicacy of a wind chime or to scratch the eucalyptus oil into the back of a sick child.

And this won for me a good husband, though he was not Le van Ly, nor could ever have been. But he was a good man and a surprised man to learn that my hands could also make him very happy even if my breasts did not seem so delightful in the tight bodice of my *ao dai*. That man died in the war that came to our country, a war we were about to lose, and I took my sons to America and I settled in this place in New Orleans called Versailles that has only Vietnamese. Soon my best friend Thuy also came to this place, with her husband Le van Ly and her children. They left shortly for California, but after three years they returned, and we all lived another decade together, and we expected much longer than that, for Thuy and I would have become fifty years old within a week of each other next month.

Except that Thuy was dead now and lying before me in this place that Mr. Hoa, the mortician for our community, called the "preparation room," and she was waiting for me to put the makeup on her face and comb her hair for the last time. She died very quickly, but she knew enough to ask for the work of my hands to make her beautiful in the casket. She let on to no one— probably not even herself—when the signs of the cancer growing in her ovaries caused no pain. She was a fearful person over foolish little things, and such a one as that will sometimes ignore the big things until it is too late. But thank God that when the pain did come and the truth was known, the end came quickly afterward.

She clutched my hand in the hospital room, the curtain drawn around us, and my own grip is very strong, but on that morning she hurt me with the power of her hand. This was a great surprise to me. I looked at our locked hands, and her lovely slender fingers were white with the strength in them and yet the nails were still perfect, each one a meticulously curved echo of the others, each one carefully stroked with the red paint the color of her favorite Winesap apples. This was a very sad moment for me. It made me sadder even than the sounds of her pain, this hand with its sudden fearful strength and yet the signs of her lovely vanity still there.

But I could not see her hands as I stood beside her in the preparation room. They were somewhere under the sheet and I had work to do, so I looked at her face. Her closed eyes showed the mostly Western lids, passed down by more than one Frenchman among her ancestors. This was a very attractive thing about her, I always knew, though Ly never mentioned her eyes, even though they were something he might well have complimented in public. He could have said to people, My wife has such beautiful eyes, but he did not. And his certain regard for her breasts, of course, was kept very private. Except with his glance.

We three were young, only sixteen, and Thuy and I were at the Cirque Sportif in Saigon. This was where we met Ly for the first time. We were told that if Mother Mary had known the game of tennis, she would have allowed her spiritual children to wear the costume for the game, even if our legs did show. We loved showing our legs. I have very nice legs, really. Not as nice as Thuy's, but I was happy to have my legs bare when I met Le van Ly for the first time. He was a ball boy at the tennis court, and when Thuy and I played, he would run before us and pick up the balls and return them to us. I was a more skillful player than Thuy, and it wasn't until too late that I realized how much better it was to hit the ball into the net and have Ly dart before me on this side and then pick up my tennis ball and return it to me. Thuy, of course, knew this right away and her game was never worse than when we played with Le van Ly poised at the end of the net waiting for us to make a mistake.

And it was even on that first meeting that I saw his eyes move to Thuy's breasts. It was the slightest of glances but full of meaning. I knew this because I was very attuned to his eyes from the start. They were more like mine, with nothing of the West but everything of our ancestors back to the Kindly Dragon whose

hundred children began Vietnam. But I had let myself forget that
the Kindly Dragon married a fairy princess, not a solid home-
maker, so my hopes were still real at age sixteen. He glanced at
Thuy's breasts, but he smiled at me when I did miss a shot, and
he said, very low so only I could hear it, "You're a very good
player." It sounded to me at sixteen that this was something he
would begin to build his love on. I was a foolish girl.

But now she lay before me on a stainless steel table, her head
cranked up on a chrome support, her hair scattered behind her
and her face almost plain. The room had a faint smell, a little itch
in the nose of something strong, like the smell when my sons
killed insects for their science classes in school. But over this was
a faint aroma of flowers, though not real flowers, I knew. I did
not like this place and I tried to think about what I'd come for.
I was standing before Thuy and I had not moved since Mr. Hoa
left me. He tied the smock I was wearing at the back and he told
me how he had washed Thuy's hair already. He turned up the air
conditioner in the window, which had its glass panes painted a
chalky white, and he bowed himself out of the room and closed
the door tight.

I opened the bag I'd placed on the high metal chair and I
took out Thuy's pearl-handled brush and I bent near her. We had
combed each other's hair all our lives. She had always worn her
hair down, even as she got older. Even to the day of her death,
with her hair laid carefully out on her pillow, something she must
have done herself, very near the end, for when Ly and their oldest
son and I came into the room that evening and found her, she
was dead and her hair was beautiful.

So now I reached out to Thuy and I stroked her hair for the
first time since her death and her hair resisted the brush and
the resistance sent a chill through me. Her hair was still alive.
The body was fixed and cold and absolutely passive, but the hair
defied the brush, and though Thuy did not cry out at this first
brush stroke as she always did, the hair insisted that she was still
alive and I felt something very surprising at that. From the quick

fisting of my mind at the image of Thuy I knew I was angry. From the image of her hair worn long even after she was middle-aged instead of worn in a bun at the nape of the neck like all the Vietnamese women our age. I was angry and then I realized that I was angry because she was not completely dead, and this immediately filled me with a shame so hot that it seemed as if I would break into a sweat.

The shame did not last very long. I straightened and turned my face to the flow of cool air from the air conditioner and I looked at all the instruments hanging behind the glass doors of the cabinet in the far wall, all the glinting clamps and tubes and scissors and knives. This was not the place of the living. I looked at Thuy's face and her pale lips were tugged down into a faint frown and I lifted the brush and stroked her hair again and once again, and though it felt just the way it always had felt when I combed it, I continued to brush.

And I spoke a few words to Thuy. Perhaps her spirit was in the room and could hear me. "It's all right, Thuy. The things I never blamed you for in life I won't blame you for now." She had been a good friend. She had always appreciated me. When we brushed each other's hair she would always say how beautiful mine was and she would invite me also to leave it long, even though I am nearly fifty and I am no beauty at all. And she would tell me how wonderful my talents were. She would urge me to date some man or other in Versailles. I would make such and such a man a wonderful wife, she said. These men were successful men that she recommended, very well off. But they were always older men, in their sixties or seventies. One man was eighty-one, and this one she did not suggest to me directly but by saying casually how she had seen him last week and he was such a vigorous man, such a fine and vigorous man.

And her own husband, Le van Ly, was of course more successful than any of them. And he is still the finest-looking man in Versailles. How fine he is. The face of a warrior. I have seen the high cheeks and full lips of Le van Ly in the statues of warriors in the Saigon Museum, the men who threw the Chinese out of our country many centuries ago. And I lifted Thuy's hair and brushed it out in narrow columns and laid the hair carefully on the bright silver surface behind the support, letting the ends dangle off the table. The hair was very soft and it was yielding to my hands now and I could see this hair hanging perfectly against the back of her pale blue *ao dai* as she and Ly strolled away across the square near the Continental Palace Hotel.

I wish there had been some clear moment, a little scene; I would even have been prepared not to seem so solid and level-headed; I would have been prepared to weep and even to speak in a loud voice. But they were very disarming in the way they let me know how things were. We had lemonades on the veranda of the Continental Palace Hotel, and I thought it would be like all the other times, the three of us together in the city, strolling along the river or through the flower markets at Nguyen Hue or the bookstalls on Le Loi. We had been three friends together for nearly two years, ever since we'd met at the club. There had been no clear choosing, in my mind. Ly was a very traditional boy, a courteous boy, and he never forced the issue of romance, and so I still had some hopes.

Except that I had unconsciously noticed things, so when Thuy spoke to me and then, soon after, the two of them walked away from the hotel together on the eve of Ly's induction into the army, I realized something with a shock that I actually had come to understand all along. Like suddenly noticing that you are old. The little things gather for a long time but one morning you look in the mirror and you understand them in a flash. At the flower market on Nguyen Hue I would talk with great spirit of how to arrange the flowers, which ones to put together, how a home would be filled with this or that sort of flower on this or that occasion. But Thuy would be bending into the flowers, her hair falling through the petals, and she would breathe very deeply and rise up and she would be inflated with the smell of flowers and of course her breasts would seem to have grown even larger and more beautiful and Ly would look at them and then he would close his eyes softly in appreciation. And at the bookstalls—I would be the one who asked for the bookstalls—I would be lost in what I thought was the miracle of all these little worlds inviting me in, and I was unaware of the little world near my elbow, Thuy looking at the postcards and talking to Ly about trips to faraway places.

I suppose my two friends were as nice to me as possible at the Continental Palace Hotel, considering what they had to do. Thuy asked me to go to the rest room with her and we were laughing together at something Ly had said. We went to the big double mirror and our two faces were side by side, two girls eighteen years old, and yet beside her I looked much older. Already old. I could see that. And she said, "I am so happy."

We were certainly having fun on this day, but I couldn't quite understand her attitude. After all Ly was going off to fight our long war. But I replied, "I am too."

Then she leaned near me and put her hand on my shoulder and she said, "I have a wonderful secret for you. I couldn't wait to tell it to my dear friend."

She meant these words without sarcasm. I'm sure of it. And I still did not understand what was coming.

She said, "I am in love."

I almost asked who it was that she loved. But this was only the briefest final pulse of naïveté. I knew who she loved. And after laying her head on the point of my shoulder and smiling at me in the mirror with such tenderness for her dear friend, she said, "And Ly loves me, too."

How had this subject not come up before? The answer is that the two of us had always spoken together of what a wonderful boy Ly was. But my own declarations were as vivid and enthusiastic as Thuy's—more vivid, in fact. So if I was to assume that she loved Ly from all that she'd said, then my own declaration of love should have been just as clear. But obviously it wasn't, and that was just as I should have expected it. Thuy never for a moment had considered me a rival for Ly. In fact, it was unthinkable to her that I should even love him in vain.

She lifted her head from my shoulder and smiled at me as if to expect me to be happy. When I kept silent, she prompted me. "Isn't it wonderful?"

I had never spoken of my love for Ly and I knew that this was the last chance I would have. But what was there to say? I could look back at all the little signs now and read them clearly. And Thuy was who she was and I was different from that and the feeling between Ly and her was already decided upon. So I said the only reasonable thing that I could. "It is very wonderful."

This made Thuy even happier. She hugged me. And then she asked me to comb her hair. We had been outside for an hour before coming to the hotel and her long straight hair was slightly ruffled and she handed me the pearl-handled brush that her mother had given her and she turned her back to me. And I began to brush. The first stroke caught a tangle and Thuy cried out in a pretty, piping voice. I paused briefly and almost threw the brush against the wall and walked out of that place. But then I brushed once again and again, and she was turned away from the mirror so she could not see the terrible pinch of my face when I suggested that she and Ly spend their last hours now alone together. She nearly wept in joy and appreciation at this gesture from her dear friend, and I kept on brushing until her hair was perfect.

And her hair was perfect now beneath my hands in the preparation room. And I had a strange thought. She was doing this once more to me. She was having me make her hair beautiful so she could go off to the spirit world and seduce the one man there who could love me. This would be Thuy's final triumph over me. My hands trembled at this thought and it persisted. I saw this clearly: Thuy arriving in heaven and her hair lying long and soft down her back and her breasts are clearly beautiful even in the white robe of the angels, and the spirit of some great warrior who fought at the side of the Trung sisters comes to her, and though he has waited nineteen centuries for me, he sees Thuy and decides to wait no more. It has been only the work of my hands that he has awaited and he lifts Thuy's hair and kisses it.

I drew back from Thuy and I stared at her face. I saw it in the mirror at the Continental Palace Hotel and it was very beautiful, but this face before me now was rubbery in death, the beauty was hidden, waiting for my hands. Thuy waited for me to make her beautiful. I had always made her more beautiful. Just by being near her. I was tempted once more to turn away. But that would only let her have her condescending smile at me. Someone else would do this job if I did not, and Thuy would fly off to heaven with her beautiful face and I would be alone in my own shame.

I turned to the sheet now, and the body I had never looked upon in its womanly nakedness was hiding there and this was what Ly had given his love for. The hair and the face had invited him, but it was this hidden body, her secret flesh, that he had longed for. I had seen him less than half an hour ago. He was in Mr. Hoa's office when I arrived. He got up and shook my hand with both of his, holding my hand for a long moment as he said how glad he was that I was here. His eyes were full of tears and I felt very sorry for Le van Ly. A warrior should never cry, even for the death of a beautiful woman. He handed me the bag with Thuy's brush and makeup, and he said, "You always know what to do."

What did he mean by that? Simply that I knew how to brush Thuy's hair and paint her face? Or was this something he had seen about me in all things, just as he had once seen that I was a very good tennis player? Did it mean he understood that he had never been with a woman like that, a woman who would always know what to do for him as a wife? When he stood before me in Mr. Hoa's office I felt like a foolish teenage girl again, with that rush of hope. But perhaps it wasn't foolish; Thuy's breasts were no longer there for his eyes to slide away to.

Her breasts. What were these things that had always defined my place in the world of women? They were beneath the sheet and my hand went out and grasped it at the edge, but I stopped.

I told myself it was of no matter now. She was dead. I let go of
the sheet and turned to her face of rubber and I took out her
eye shadow and her lipstick and her mascara and I bent near and
painted the life back into this dead thing.

And as I painted, I thought of where she would lie, in the
cemetery behind the Catholic church, in a stone tomb above the
ground. It was often necessary in New Orleans, the placing of
the dead above the ground, because the water table was so high.
If we laid Thuy in the earth, one day she would float to the surface and I could see that day clearly, her rising from the earth
and awaking and finding her way back to the main street of Versailles in the heat of the day and I would be talking with Ly, he
would be bending near me and listening as I said all the things of
my heart, and suddenly his eyes would slide away and there she
would be, her face made up and her hair brushed and her breasts
would be as beautiful as ever. But the thought of her lying above
the ground made me anxious as well. As if she wasn't quite gone.
And she never would be. Ly would sense her out there behind
the church, suspended in the air, and he would never forget her
and would take all the consolation he needed from his children
and grandchildren.

My hand trembled now as I touched her eyes with the brush,
and when I held the lipstick, I pressed it hard against her mouth
and I cast aside the shame at my anger and I watched this mouth
in my mind, the quick smile of it that never changed in all the
years, that never sensed any mood in me but loyal, subordinate
friendship. Then the paint was all in place and I pulled back and
I angled my face once more into the flow of cool air and I tried
to just listen to the grinding of the air conditioner and forget all
of these feelings, these terrible feelings about the dead woman
who was always my friend, who I had never once challenged in
life over any of these things. What a coward I am, I thought.

But instead of hearing this righteous charge against me, I
looked at Thuy and I took her hair in my hands and I smoothed
it all together and wound it into a bun and I pinned it at the nape

of her neck. She was a fifty-year-old woman, after all. She was as much a fifty-year-old woman as I was. Surely she was. And at this I looked to the sheet.

It lay lower across the chest than I thought it might. But her breasts were also fifty years old, and they were spread flat as she lay on her back. She had never let her dear friend see them, these two secrets that had enchanted the man I loved. I could bear to look at them now, vulnerable and weary as they were. I stepped down and I grasped the edge of the sheet at her throat, and with the whisper of the cloth I pulled it back.

And one of her breasts was gone. The right breast was lovely even now, even in death, the nipple large and the color of cinnamon, but the left breast was gone and a large crescent scar began there in its place and curved out of sight under her arm. I could not draw a breath at this, as if the scar was in my own chest where my lungs had been yanked out, and I could see that her scar was old, years old, and I thought of her three years in California and how she had never spoken at all about this, how her smile had hidden all that she must have suffered.

I could not move for a long moment, and then at last my hands acted as if on their own. They pulled the sheet up and gently spread it at her throat. I suppose this should have brought back my shame at the anger I'd had at my friend Thuy, but it did not. That seemed a childish feeling now, much too simple. It was not necessary to explain any of this. I simply leaned forward and kissed Thuy on her brow and I undid the bun at the back of her neck, happy to make her beautiful once more, happy to send her off to a whole body in heaven where she would catch the eye of the finest warrior. And I knew she would understand if I did all I could to make Le van Ly happy.

———

Robert Olen Butler has published seven books since 1981, six novels and a volume of short fiction (*A Good Scent from a Strange Mountain*), which won the Pulitzer Prize, the Richard and Hinda Rosenthal Foundation Award from the American Academy of Arts and Letters, and was a nominee for the 1993 PEN/Faulkner Award for Fiction. His stories have appeared in many literary magazines and have been anthologized in *The Best American Short Stories* and *New Stories from the South*. Butler served with the U.S. Army in Vietnam in 1971 as a Vietnamese linguist and is a charter recipient of the Tu Do Chinh Kien Award for outstanding contributions to American culture by a Vietnam veteran. He is an associate professor at McNeese State University, Lake Charles, Louisiana, where he teaches creative writing. His new novel, *They Whisper,* will be published early in 1994.

PHOTO CREDIT: GRAY LITTLE

Through *1989 and into the spring of 1990 I wrote one short story after another, fifteen in all. They were all first person stories, each in the voice of a different Vietnamese expatriate living in southern Louisiana, and they ultimately made up my book,* A Good Scent from a Strange Mountain. *"Preparation" came near the end of this very odd period that produced the first stories I'd written as a mature writer, after six published novels. The origin of "Preparation" was a simple phrase in the notes I'd made for this volume: woman doing the hair for a corpse. That notion was years old. When I was in college, an aunt of mine was asked to do the hair of her dead friend, and the image of that stuck with me. When I finally turned to it to see what was there, I heard the voice of this middle-aged Vietnamese woman and with very little forethought on my part I put down what she said. I experienced the revelation of this story at precisely the moment she did; it was every bit as surprising to me as it was to her.*

Lee Merrill Byrd

MAJOR SIX POCKETS

(from *Blue Mesa Review*)

Tennessee sprang out the car door the minute John turned the handle, barking across the low rainy meadow at the four steaming cows; they lumbered down toward the stream, their leader—the biggest one—turning suddenly, clumsily, pawing the ground.

Daddy! shrieked Andy. They're going to kill Tennessee. But no, said Daddy, it was not true. That cow who pawed the ground was a woman, Daddy said—can't you see her tits hanging down? —and women cows are hopeless in the face of a dog like Tennessee.

Now, if that was a bull, said Daddy, raising his eyebrows. Um um um . . .

Yes, said Andy, raising what little eyebrows remained to him, if that was a bull. Um um um . . .

John hung out the car door, marking the landscape like a tour guide, while Daddy bumped the Mazda down into place beside a pile of branches. Here, said John, is the firewood. And here is a bush. Yes, here is where we park. There is the water.

Daddy said, Here it is, the perfect camping spot. Just like I told you from the beginning. We got out of the car and stood looking up at the soft gray clouds that huddled at the mouth of the canyon. Susie got out and stood beside Daddy, and John and Andy came and fell in place. They looked things over, the indolent sky, the steep mountains, the flat meadow skirted with chokecherry bushes, the pile of branches, the white rocks already set for a campfire. Up above, a long distance off, a last lone car rumbled on through the San Juans.

Here it is, said Andy. The perfect camping spot.

Here is where it began, with Tennessee and the imitation bull and with the finding of this spot, the perfect camping spot, as Daddy called it. Here is where it began, the vacating, the vacation, here on the low secret meadow, hidden in a pocket of the ragged mountains.

But it had started for Daddy a long time before that, the talking about it, the working out of it. It had started for Daddy almost from the beginning, before they knew about Andy, which way he would go, before he lost the ear and his hair and then the fingers on his left hand; long before it became apparent about John and his face. It had started for Daddy almost from the beginning, when Andy lay on a high bed, in isolation, wrapped in white gauze and did not talk. Daddy would talk to him, would talk to him about it, about the trip we would take, about the vacation, about the mountains and the perfect camping spot. Daddy said they would catch fish, they would catch rainbow trout, they would catch browns and cutthroats, they would use flies and worms and salmon eggs, garlic-flavored marshmallows and grasshoppers, and they would take the fish and Mother would cook them over the campfire in a pan filled with butter. Daddy said they would ask Susie to fry potatoes, too, and there would be Cokes and Jewish pickles and later some dessert.

One day in March after a long night and a high fever, Andy in a thin and broken whisper said he wanted pie. Cherry pie. The nurse said they didn't have any. Daddy's voice began to shake. He told her it didn't matter, that Andy didn't want the cherry pie now, he wanted the cherry pie for later, for after the fish. Wasn't that right? Daddy asked Andy and Andy shut his eyes and nodded solemnly.

Daddy, when he went to visit John on the ward, told John all about the plans he and Andy had been making. Daddy said he'd talked to Andy about where Eskimos lived, and that Andy seemed to agree that that might be the perfect place for a camping trip. Did John know that there in that place where Eskimos lived everyone slept together naked under a mound of caribou furs and there were lots of girls and all the girls liked to dance?

John listened intently, chewing on the bandages that covered his hands. He did not think that he wanted to camp in a place like that. He would rather camp in a place that was just so-so where if there were any girls they didn't dance and if you slept under caribou furs you could wear your pajamas.

Daddy talked to Ronnie Tate in the bed next to John's and wondered what kind of son he had who did not like girls who danced. He asked Carnell Hughes on the other side of the room what he thought about sleeping naked and the three young boys giggled and waited for Daddy to come back. When he did he sat on a chair in the middle of the room and brought news of Andy and the latest plans.

On the first of April, they took Andy out of isolation and put him in the big room with John and with Ronnie Tate and with Carnell Hughes. Andy looked at John and said, His skin, and John said in his most matter-of-fact way, He's bald. Daddy laughed until he cried and began to sing, Christmas is a-coming, the geese are getting fat, and clapped his hands until John wailed, Oh Daddy, stop.

That same day after lunch Daddy went to Colonel Bubbie's Army-Navy Surplus and bought a pair of shorts, Italian six-pockets, and filled the pockets with stuff for the trip: a pocket knife, some fishhooks and salmon eggs, fishing line, and candy bars and they spent the afternoon eating Milky Ways and looking over Daddy's Italian six-pockets and talking about Alaska and the Ozarks and New Mexico, about the Rockies and the Blue Hills and other perfect camping spots.

But April was no better. Andy's blood was full of infection. The antibiotic they gave him to cure it made him throw up and he could not talk. The tub men came to get him in the mornings, to scrub the dead skin away from the burns and Andy screamed and Daddy walked the halls. He wasn't sure where we would go anymore and he agreed with John, that a so-so place would be just as good as a place where Eskimos lived.

The doctors said they needed to operate on Andy again and that John had a staph infection in the graft on his cheek and must have more IVs. Ronnie Tate said would Daddy tell them again about the Eskimos and the dancing girls but Daddy said he'd have to wait, he did not want to talk about the trip anymore for a little while.

In the evening two days after Andy's surgery, Daddy and the nurse lifted Andy onto a chair and the nurse said that Andy would have to sit there awhile for a change and Andy cried and cried and said he hurt and the nurse finally asked Daddy to step out in the hall. Later, Daddy and the nurse put Andy back in bed, one under his head, one holding his feet, there being no place in between that they could touch and they covered him with a sheet and tucked it in and Andy began to talk and did not stop. He said to John that he was sorry about John's corduroy coat, that he had worn John's corduroy coat that day and that it had gotten burned and that did Daddy know where the corduroy coat was or his blue pants, the ones he had worn while they played in the fort and had he lost his sneakers too, the new ones, and did John remember how Morgan had thrown dirt on him to make the fire go out and did John remember the ice cream man who called the fire engine and did Mom know how to cook fish and that after the fish they would have cherry pie. He shook all over, he talked so fast and he said that he liked the Italian six-pockets and he called Daddy Major Six Pockets and Daddy sat down and could not talk.

Then the plans began in earnest. And every day they discussed another place. There were the Cherokawas and the Sangre de Cristos, the Smokies in Tennessee where Daddy was born, the Mississippi and the Shenandoah. There was Missoula and

Butte and Chaco Canyon and Mesa Verde and Cheyenne and the Florida Keys and the Yucatán and the Black Hills.

But—much later, when the boys were home again—Susie said she just wanted to go to Colorado, because, after all, that was where she was born; and according to the things that she had heard about Colorado from Daddy, there was a cottage there in a big meadow, a little honeymoon cottage where she had once lived and surrounding that cottage were hills and mountains where elk and deer roamed, snakes and mountain lions and coyotes. And in the meadow bulls moaned and pranced and down around all of it came crashing the mighty Rio Grande. She was a true Colorado girl and needed to go back. As proof, she reminded the boys that when she was hardly a day old, she had played naked in ten or more feet of snow. Hadn't Daddy said so?

And so the vacation was to Colorado, to Susie's ancestral homeland because, Daddy said, Susie is the oldest and even though we won't get to go where the boys wanted to go, all the things that they had dreamed about and talked about while they were in the hospital were right there in Colorado: cherry pies and caribou furs and dancing girls and sleeping bags and perfect camping spots. And anyway, Daddy said, it would have to be Susie's trip because the fire had been the boys'.

Andy took Dr. Phineas, the green frog, and Smudge, the stuffed bear. Also, he needed a backpack. He filled its pockets and corners with erasers and magnets, some photos he had gotten from Grandma, pennies, crayons, and a ruler. Dr. Phineas nearly fell out, even with Smudge crammed in beside him, so it seemed necessary to bring a second brown bear to make the fit complete.

John had books, many more than one, because of Andy and all the things that Andy had in his backpack. And John brought tapes and what were tapes without the tape recorder?

Daddy helped Susie hide her violin between the cooler and the backseat beneath two sleeping bags. She put a shoe box containing her diaries and some pesos and soap and a small tea set and something she was crocheting under the front seat and stuffed her jacket in behind it.

Daddy brought books and a pad of paper to write on in case of a poem. There was mayonnaise and peanut butter and salami and crackers and instant coffee, plenty of bacon, sacks of oranges and apples, a pineapple from Mexico, and some sugarless chewing gum. There was a hatchet and a shovel and two delicate fishing rods jammed in between the seats and the doors. The trunk strapped to the roof held a change of clothes for every person for every eventuality, but for the most part, it was full of pressure garments for the boys and splints and ace wraps and gauze and adhesive tape.

Well, said Daddy. None of this takes up much room.

Susie sat in the front seat and talked. She said that Texas was all right. Though it was hot. Though of course El Paso was not as hot as the rest of Texas. El Paso was not really at all like any other part of Texas. In the first place there were no Texans in El Paso. In the second place there was Juarez and all of that. Daddy listened and dreamed and Susie talked intently. John snoozed, his left eye partly open even while he slept and Andy colored, Dr. Phineas looking on. Tennessee turned and sighed between the cooler and the violin and the five extra pairs of shoes.

Daddy drove on up through Hatch and Truth or Consequences, on past Albuquerque and Santa Fe and Española, all in one day, driving toward Colorado and the perfect camping spot. Why did you and Mom ever leave Colorado in the first place? asked Susie. I mean, if you worked for Texas millionaires and ate venison and had the honeymoon cottage all to yourselves and the Rio Grande in your backyard?

John and Andy leaned forward to listen. Your mother and I, said Daddy, had things to do.

Yeah? said Susie. Like what?

Your mother and I had work cut out for us in the big city. We couldn't work for Texas millionaires forever. It was too easy.

Anyway, he went on, we were warned in a dream that John would arrive any minute and that he intended to be born in Albuquerque, in a little rented house in Albuquerque where the landlord next door was always drunk, so we had to quick hustle and pack up and move down the Rio Grande.

Oh, Daddy . . .

Tres Piedras had a cafe and a grocery and two gas stations.

Well, said Daddy, there was a second dream. It said, Leave any minute for Las Cruces for Andy intends to come howling and screaming forth from his mother's belly at exactly five in the morning on the twenty-fifth day . . .

Andy sang to himself all across the high plain between Tres Piedras and Antonito, hanging his good arm out the window.

John peered into the tape recorder listening to the Lone Ranger talk things over with Tonto. The Cavendish gang had just killed the Lone Ranger's brother and all his friends. Those evil men knew the Lone Ranger by sight. If they know that one man escaped their ambush, worried the Lone Ranger, they'll look for him and kill him.

Them not know one man escape, said Tonto. Tonto bury five men, make six graves. Crook think you die with others.

Good, wheezed the Lone Ranger. Then my name shall be buried forever with my brother and my friends. From now on my face must be concealed. A disguise, perhaps, he considered. Or maybe a mask. That's it! A mask . . .

Daddy wore his Italian six-pockets: two pockets on the side, two pockets in the front, two pockets behind, with four buttons up the fly that he never managed to button all at once. John and Andy wore their masks, brown elastic hoods that held white life masks in place. Susie wore a straw hat and people stared. Daddy stopped in Albuquerque for gas and people stared. We stopped in Ojo Caliente for lunch and took the boys' masks off so they could eat and everyone in the restaurant grew quiet and tried to pretend they didn't notice. In Antonito we stopped to buy flies and hooks and everybody watched while Daddy discussed salmon eggs loudly and deliberately with his children, Andy breathing hard and fast from the pressure of the mask on his nose, John, solemn and intent, just his eyes, his lips.

From Antonito on, Daddy drove hard, pushing on into the mountains, looking for that conjunction of the perfect camping spot and the setting sun.

The road from Antonito toward Platoro was all dirt and rocks and Daddy drove it fast, the Mazda eclipsed by the rising dust. Tennessee stood up, his nose pressed against the window, swaying as Daddy took the curves. Susie said how late it was, and John said that Daddy drove too fast. After a few miles there was a sign, a tent pitched upon solid rock, and behind the sign among the trees a neat circle of cars and RVs just settling down for some outdoor adventure and Susie said, There it is, Daddy, there's the perfect camping spot, but Daddy only drove faster, on past more signs with pitched tents, drawing up toward the edge of the wrong side of the road from time to time to peer down through thick forest, over sheer cliffs. We're getting closer, he said, as eager as Tennessee.

The forest opened up into meadow that rolled away from the road toward the hills. Daddy slowed to look, sticking his head out the window, talking it over. There's a stream. Too close to the road. What do you think?

But nothing seemed quite right and Daddy drove on.

There is no perfect camping spot, said Susie. It will be dark and we'll be lost and it will be cold and it will rain.

Daddy turned off the road, to the left, down a rutted path that crossed a little bridge and went up on top of a hill. Let's look around, he said.

Andy and John and Daddy got out and stood looking through the trees at the flat green meadow below. They walked down some and the three of them peed while Susie sat in the front seat and watched until they disappeared and watched the same spot until they came back again. They got in the car.

Well, Sus, said Daddy, I think we've found it.

*   *   *

The road down from the hill to the perfect camping spot was pitted with animal holes and big hidden rocks and at one point was so slanted that the Mazda felt as if it would tip over. The last curve revealed the meadow, empty and waiting.

The sun began its long summer descent at one end of the slender canyon while the ragged clouds pushed for entrance at the other; down in between, in the long flat meadow, our camp took its shape: tent and Mazda, firewood, cooler, trunk, sleeping bags. Daddy built a fire for the supper and said he thought he might try to fish while he waited for the fire to make coals. The kids declared that they would go first, until Daddy said that for tonight since it was almost dark, he was the only one who could fish. But that they could watch. And if they were good maybe they could each hold the pole once. Maybe twice. And that though they would bring the second pole, they probably wouldn't use it since fly-fishing was an art that had to be taught and it was getting too dark to do any teaching.

They walked up the meadow, carrying the two poles, looking for a pool of water in the stream where trouts and browns and cutthroats would be congregating. Tennessee made wide circles around them. Daddy in his six-pockets and sneakers, Susie in her straw hat, the boys masked and splinted. Just as the sun hit the edge of the mountain, they were back, unmasked and unsplinted, shoes and shorts and six-pockets soaking. Daddy said here was proof that every camping trip required an extra set of shoes and they all changed and stood around the campfire while Daddy told them again about his backpacking trip through the Winamoochies with Uncle Steve and how Uncle Steve and he had been caught in a driving rain and had to quick set up their tent and how he had had to rub Uncle Steve's hands and feet because Uncle Steve was shaking so hard from the cold. But how that was the price a person had to pay when he went camping with skinny people.

After supper Daddy said, Let's get up early and go fishing first thing. The kids got into the tent and laughed and argued for a long time, about whose head should be where, and about who would have Tennessee sleeping next to him, and about how loud John snored with his mask on. Daddy roamed around the camp-fire, getting things ready for the morning, looking up at the sky from time to time. He had a cigarette and some tequila and sat on a log, staring into the fire, listening to the kids talk. Much later, when they had finally fallen asleep, he covered the coals with dirt and made a bed on the ground near the door of the tent, but the minute he got in his bag it started to rain, so he came up into the Mazda, where the backseat was pulled down.

Think you're smart, do you? he said, making room for himself. We slept the way you sleep the first night on camping trips, just so-so, sometimes resting so deep inside the sound of the rain, sometimes sore, turning and turning to find just the right posi-tion. Then just before dawn, he woke up suddenly and said, I think the kids are having fun, don't you? and went back to sleep as if that was that: the very last thing on his mind.

That first morning he taught them to fish. They went back to the deep pool up the meadow before breakfast. He showed them how to cast, how to let the attractive, glittering flies float along the water as if they were alive, how to turn the reel quickly and strike again to catch the attention of those trouts and browns and cutthroats who lay waiting fat and sleek to take the bait. The flies caught on every rock and bush and Andy when they came back described the way in which Major Six Pockets had waded in and out of the deep pool to recover the line and how they hadn't caught anything this time because Tennessee had been leaping up and down the stream and barking after cows and scaring the fish and how Susie and John had taken much more than their share of turns. When Susie wasn't listening, Daddy said she fly fished as if she'd been casting in the womb.

For breakfast there were eggs cooked in plenty of bacon grease, the sun coming up sly and warm along the mouth of the canyon. Afterward, Daddy boiled water over the fire and took it and Andy to the stream to bathe. From a distance Andy looked like he wore a coat of armor across his chest and back, the skin was so scarred there and still so furious and red and it drew down tight against the soft whiteness of his stomach. Daddy washed him all over with warm water and then made him lie down quick to rinse off. He said how Andy was the only boy he knew who had only seven fingers but ten belly buttons and together they traced the convolutions that erupted on the upper part of his body. Andy said that John and Susie had to take a bath too but Daddy said no, that Susie being not burned could bathe every three or four days the way you did on camping trips and that John having no more open spots on his body could wait until tomorrow. Andy fussed and cried and said it was not fair, that just because he was burned he had to bathe every day. Daddy carried him to the Mazda and lay him down so he could pick the dead skin away from the open spots. Andy studied the slow movement of the sterile tweezers in Daddy's hand while Daddy strained and squinted to avoid the raw skin and Andy's screams; and rubbed cream on him, ranging slowly and methodically over that small eroded chest with his fingertips, massaging the withered arm with his whole hand; and wrapped both with ace wraps and put the pressure garments and the splints and the mask back on. Tennessee licked the bacon grease out of the fry pan and Daddy said that he would like to try fishing on the other part of the stream. Susie and John grabbed the poles. Let your mother go first, said Daddy. Susie came next, pressing close, then John, then Daddy and Andy with Tennessee behind and in front and behind again, announcing himself to the trout and browns and cutthroats who waited fat and sleek in the deep pools at the top of the meadow.

The stream crossed the meadow east not a hundred yards from the perfect camping spot. There was a little trail there on the other side but Andy said he could not walk, that his shoes were so wet from walking across the stream with them on and that Daddy would have to carry him. He cried and fell down in a heap insisting that he could not keep going, that his squeaking shoes hurt his feet and Daddy stopped, not sure whether to go on or to go back. Susie said that Andrew was a baby and John said that it was nothing to walk in wet shoes and Andy wailed. We walked on ahead, Susie and John looking back every little bit to watch Daddy kneeling beside Andy, taking his shoes and socks off and squeezing the water out; they could see Daddy talking to Andy and trying to shut him up. Susie called back for them to hurry up and Daddy told her just to go on and mind her own business. Susie yelled to Andy that her shoes were already dry and Daddy said to shut up, just shut up, so we went on, up where the choke-cherries got thicker and the trees were taller and the sun not quite so bright to hurt the boys' skin.

After a while Daddy came up with·Andy behind him sulking. One of the fishing lines was all tangled up and Daddy sat cross-legged on the ground trying to straighten it while Susie demonstrated the art of casting to her brothers. She stood on a big rock and repeated all of Daddy's instructions on fly-fishing as if they were her own and John and Andy watched her, caught by the volume of what she knew, mesmerized by each toss into the glimmering pool. Daddy looked up and looking, was arrested by the sight of the children: Susie, high on the rock, in her eleventh year suddenly so tall and beautiful; John, his face turned up to listen to her, that face that no amount of studying could change, the one side ravaged by fire, the other side handsome, perfect; Andy, at the age of six, bald, without an ear, with only seven fingers. Daddy looked. They played, mindless of him, mindless of themselves, laughing. And the line lay tangled across his knees.

We fished there an hour, then walked on up the canyon, up a trail toward the steep mountains, climbing until Andy's complaints were unbearable and then found a place to sit while Daddy took out the map. He traced the road between Antonito and Platoro with his finger and located the perfect camping spot somewhere in between. Susie said if we drove farther up we would find Blowout Pass and Cornwalls Nose and John said, Look, here is Elephant Mountain and Handkerchief Mesa and Andy because he could not read screamed until he could squeeze in close to Daddy and touch the map himself. Daddy took Andy's finger and led it all over the local terrain until it fell with a thud into Lost Lake.

Then Daddy lit a cigarette and pointed to the mountains in front of him, mountains that erupted from the earth, pocked with sinuous ridges, and red the color of dirt, and said those were called the Pinnacles and John wanted to know why and how come they were the way they were. Daddy looked at John awhile and didn't answer, as if he hadn't heard, so John asked again and Daddy said abruptly they were called the Pinnacles because they went straight up and were like towers and that the Pinnacles and all the mountains around, the whole range of the San Juans, were formed by fire.

They fished all that afternoon, before and after supper, but it wasn't until the next day, until they began to act as if they'd been in that canyon all their lives, that anything was caught. It was just before supper and they had gone again to that deep pool where they had gone the first time; and John came back across the meadow alone, his hands behind him and grinning, with the fish and the story. It was Susie's fish, he said, and her line had been so tight and she screamed, Daddy, it's a fish, but Daddy had gotten mad and said he was tired of wading out into the pool to untangle their lines and that people were going to either have to learn to cast or learn to wade. Susie screamed and screamed and Andy and John screamed and screamed, trying to persuade Daddy that this was no false alarm, but Daddy said it was a rock and that this was the last time, that in nothing less than two days he had nearly ruined his sneakers.

John said, Daddy waded out and put his hand down to get the line and when he brought it up, there it was, the fish, and Daddy laughed and slapped the water and Susie said, See, Daddy. See,

Daddy, and Daddy sent John back to spread the news. Come on, Mom, he said and we walked back across the meadow to hear the story again, once from Daddy and once from Susie and once more from Andy. We stayed there by the pool until they could barely see, until two more fish were caught and then came back to the perfect camping spot and ate them, cooked over the campfire in a pan filled with butter, each bite causing Daddy to tell the story again, until Susie's first catch had settled forever in the memories of the children, until just the smell of fish or the sight of the moon or the feel of mountain air on their bodies would remind them again all through their lives of their daddy and the trip he took them on into the mountains that first year after the fire.

That night the kids went to bed early, right after they ate, because they wanted to get up first thing and catch another fish. Tennessee crawled in the tent beside them, exhausted. Daddy wanted to talk. He sat beside the fire. He said he wondered did every parent think that only his own kids were remarkable? He smoothed a pattern into the dirt with his shoe, going over and over it until it was a perfect little fan shape, edged on both sides. Don't you think the kids are remarkable? he said. He could not believe how the fire had changed them all, he could not believe how happy they always were. It was what he would have wanted them to be, but never just by telling them could have made them that way. Do you see what I mean? he asked. It was like the fire itself had given them what we never could have.

He leaned forward, his elbows on his knees, and took a piece of his hair and twisted it around and around his finger, staring off to where the mountains lay like paper silhouettes against the sky. After a while he said, Don't you think John's face is getting better? Don't you think that eye is not pulling down quite so much?

They fished all that week, most often in the deep pool just down below the perfect camping spot, but sometimes up the meadow; once Daddy even got everybody in the car and went on up the road as if he were going to Platoro. He stopped at Saddle Creek, a wide stream that wound like a snake through a damp high grassed plain. It was flat there and the wind blew.

There was a man at Saddle Creek. He came walking up the stream wearing high rubber boots with his pole in his hand and his fish basket across his shoulder, walking slow, his eyes on the water. He was the first person we had seen since the vacation began and Daddy when he saw him got excited and said so quickly, Say, how's the fishing? The man looked up and blinked at Daddy and then past Daddy and past Susie at John and Andy and no farther. Andy had his splint off and John wore his mask. The man stopped and blinked again; and Daddy remembering moved back some and directly in front of Andy. How's the fishing? Daddy said again.

The man had been drinking. It was noon and he smelled like cheap wine. He didn't move. What do you have there? he said to Daddy. Daddy's face got tight. Behind your back? said the man. Daddy said, It's my family. The man opened his mouth so slow and looked as if he was going to fall forward; he sneezed suddenly and took an old handkerchief out of his pocket to wipe his nose.

Yeah? he said. He stared at Daddy. They're my sons, said Daddy. He brought Andy forward, his hand on Andy's shoulder.

Hey, sonny, said the man real slow. He looked at Andy for a long time, squinting, going from the bald spot to the ear to his arm. What happened to your hand? he said finally.

Andy looked down at the water. He was in a fire, said Daddy.

Playing with matches? said the man. The sun by then held at the center of the canyon, directly overhead.

No, said Daddy. The color drained down from his temples.

The man looked over at John. It was another boy who had matches, said Daddy quickly, it was an accident, these boys don't play with matches.

Yeah? said the man. He dropped his pole, an expensive bamboo one, and his fancy fish basket into the stream and began to try to get something out of his back pocket. Daddy bent over to get the basket and the pole out of the water, but the man flapped his hand at him to let him know it didn't matter. Finding nothing in his pocket he rubbed himself all over the front of his shirt, but seemed to forget for a while what he was after. I'd have killed my kids if I found them playing with matches, he said, his hands poised over his belly. He began searching again.

He found what he was looking for in the pocket of his pants: a roll of money. He thumbed through the bills, lots of twenties and tens, deliberating, then tugged at one, releasing it, and leaned over, nearly falling, to stick it in Andy's hand. You better find some other friends, little buddy, he said. He stood up and looked at Daddy out of one eye. What did you do to that kid? he asked. Did you kill him?

Well, said Daddy. He searched along the meadow past the man's head, biting at his upper lip. That boy is our friend, said Daddy quietly. He's one of the boys' good friends. And then a frantic burst of enthusiasm: How long you been up here? Have you caught anything? Where are you from?

Yeah? said the man. He sneezed again, wiping his mouth off with the back of his hand and began to reconsider his money.

Have you caught anything? Daddy said again, a little louder, but the man seemed intent on the roll of bills. Listen, said Daddy, his eye on the money too, these kids don't need money. He took hold of Andy's arm, trying to push him on up out of the stream.

Sure they do, the man went right on counting. Kid can always use a little money. Can't you, buddy? he said looking over at John. Here, he said. He breathed out of his mouth, short and hard. Here's something to buy some candy with. It was a twenty-dollar bill. What's the matter, buddy? You can't use a little money? John looked over at Daddy and then at the money Andy had clutched in his hand. He came forward looking down at the stream. The man held the bill out but wouldn't let go of it.

Say, tell me something, pal, said the man, what's this thing you've got covering your face?

These kids don't need money, said Daddy. Come on, John let's go, we have to go on.

Whoa, now, pardner, said the man. Don't get yourself all worked up. I'm just asking, just curious. Just wanting to know what happened to these poor little fellers. You don't always act like this when people try to do something nice for your kids, do you?

Look, said Daddy, slowly and deliberately, my boy is wearing a mask. He has to wear a mask because he was burned on his face, and burned skin will scar unless you keep pressure on it to keep it flat.

Yeah? said the man. He studied the twenty-dollar bill he held in his hand. Well, you know what I always say, said the man, putting the bill back into the roll of money. I always say that nothing is so bad you got to hide it.

Look! exploded Daddy. He's not hiding anything. He has to keep it on. Daddy pushed on John's arm to make him go on, up out of the stream, and looked back at Susie to get her to come follow, but her eye, like John's, was caught by the roll of bills.

What about the girl? said the man, suddenly aware of her. Girl could use a little money, too, couldn't she? Couldn't you, honey? The thumbing through the money began again, that process now at the very center of the canyon, the man studying each shift of his finger, droning on about matches and fires and the way he raised his own kids to be decent while Daddy, grabbing and pushing, severed Susie and John from the sight and the sound of him, striding out ahead across the high plain toward the car, dragging Andy by the hand.

Daddy had said he would take the kids to Platoro after they fished, to the store in Platoro so they could get some candy, but he turned instead and drove back along the edge of the canyon toward the campsite. He stopped the car finally just short of the pile of firewood, but nobody moved. He stared out over the flat meadow, chewing on his lip, then looked back as if to talk but didn't say anything. Andy still held his treasure tight in his hand where the man had stuck it. Daddy studied it.

How much did he give you? said Daddy. Andy opened his hand but would not look up. Twenty dollars, said Daddy. I want you to share that with your brother and sister, hear? he said and turned back, straight in his seat.

It was hot and no one moved. Finally Daddy said, He was drunk. And said again, after a while, Your mother and I are real proud of you kids. You know that? He turned to look at the three of them. Don't be afraid when people stare, he said, when they ask questions. Just be polite, just do the best you can. He looked down at his hands, empty before him, and then back up at the kids. Okay? he said.

We didn't do much the rest of that day, a little fishing, a little gathering of firewood, some half-hearted naps. For supper there were ranch-style beans and bacon and tortillas. Nobody mentioned the cherry pie that Daddy had planned to buy in Platoro. Daddy and John and Andy stood around the campfire with their hands in their pockets while Susie drew jagged lines in the dirt with a twig.

Whoa, now, pardner, said Daddy suddenly, in a deep slow drawl. The three of them looked over at him. Whoa, now, pardner, Daddy drawled again, why ya'll don't always act like this, do you?

Why, no, pardner, said Susie, standing up, brushing herself off. Whenever we see that much money we always act just like this. She froze with her eyes popping out of her head and her mouth wide open. John blinked in amazement. Yeah, he said, just like this, imitating his big sister. Daddy let his jaw drop, too.

Did you see how much money he had, Daddy? shrieked Andy, running over to tug on Daddy and get his attention.

Did I see how much money he had? said Daddy. He flopped down suddenly on the ground and lay like a dead man, with his eyes and mouth gaping open, even the rigors of death unable to erase the astonishment he felt at the drunk man's wealth.

Daddy, Daddy, Daddy, John sputtered, did you see it? Tens and tens and tens and tens and twenties.

I saw a fifty-dollar bill, said Susie.

Daddy, said Andy, what if he had given me a fifty-dollar bill?

Daddy sat up. He leered at Andy and said, Here you go, little buddy—plunking a rock down in Andy's hand—but you better find yourself a new daddy.

Yeah, said Susie, and while you're at it, pal, get rid of your mother.

And your brother and sister, too, said John.

Move to a new city, pard, said Susie.

Daddy stood up and went outside the circle of the campfire where they couldn't see him and came back inside, stumbling along with his eyes down on the ground and aiming straight for Andy. He rammed right into him and fell back, startled, whining, Why . . . Why . . . what happened to your hand, buddy?

His hand! said Susie, and grabbed Andy and turned him around, pointing to his head: This kid is bald.

Yeah, said John, did you notice that this kid is bald?

Why . . . did something happen to your head, little pal? moaned Daddy.

It went on like that for a long time, Daddy playing the drunk man, weaving in and out of the circle, the innocent and guileless cowpoke lurching smack up against that disconcerting vision of Daddy—played by John—in his half-buttoned six-pockets and Susie in her straw hat, of the real John in his mask and Andy without his splint; the wad of money coming in and out of his pocket, dropping from time to time all over the ground, being doled out according to the more or less pitiful merits of the one upon whom he had stumbled, his generosity spun out by Daddy before their eyes so they could squander and spend.

It was nine or past before they could be got into the tent, still talking and laughing and John almost beside himself with the ramifications of the drunk man's eyeful. Susie, Susie, Susie, he kept saying to get her attention, bursting with some new aspect of the case and it was his voice that we listened to as we sat beside the fire, that stalwart, practical, ancient voice trying to drown out Susie and Andy, suddenly as talkative and confessional as he had been heard but once or twice in his short lifetime.

The moon made its way along the top of the canyon while the three of them talked; we listened, not moving for fear of losing the opportunity. They talked it all through that night, the whole thing, about the party, about Susie's tenth birthday party and how Susie in purple stood at the top of the front steps and waved the boys good-bye as they went to stay at Morgan's house; about how—did Susie remember?—John sat in the backseat with Morgan and had a plate of party cupcakes on his lap. The fort in Morgan's yard had been built the week before of palm branches and an old Christmas tree and John said there were voices in the alley, voices and girls laughing and then the smell of smoke and suddenly the whole thing went up in flames and Morgan ran out and then back and John was stuck on a branch and pulled away and then Andy could not get out, could not get out, and Morgan pulled him out covered with flames.

And threw dirt on him, Susie said. And began to tell it her way. Susie, Susie, Susie, said John, until she shut up.

Listen, he said, it started spreading around. I felt real scared. I felt like I was going to die, except that Morgan found a way for us to get out. So when Andy got out there was fire on his clothes and I felt real scared.

You were stuck inside, said Susie, matter-of-factly.

Listen, Susie, said John, I was already out and I'll tell you what it was like. The easiest part in the whole thing to go through was getting out. And he went on from there, his story: about the plane ride down to Galveston and his eyes and his mouth swollen shut, about Johnson and Jackson in the tub room and how they told jokes and how they always let him watch the TV when they scrubbed him, about the surgeries and the shots and the doctors in their white coats standing in crowds around his bed talking about his face and how they could fix it. And all this time thinking it was the girls laughing in the alley who had thrown a match, just like Morgan told his mother, until Morgan flew down to Galveston and told them how he had seen a book of matches—did they remember?—just before he had come into the fort for the last time and he had struck one and thrown it aside, thinking it was out and that he hadn't meant to do it and that he was sorry.

Well, Susie wanted to know, what did you tell him, what did you say?

And Johnny said, I said, Sure, okay. But did Susie remember about the time when she had been there when he was finally out of the hospital and they were just waiting for Andy to heal up so they could go home and they all went to the bookstore on the Strand and bought comic books?

Daddy stood up. Um, he sighed and chewed his lip and sat down again for lack of anything else to do while John went on, on, and on remembering only moments of pleasure: the comic books and the Strand and the funny old stores and how Daddy had stood in the middle of the room one night and read *Alice in Wonderland* to him and Andy and Ronnie Tate and Carnell Hughes. His voice pressed forward steadily, cheerfully from the tent; up above the moon crossed the Pinnacles and then suddenly there was a story we had never heard before, he had never talked about. The first week of school—did Susie remember the first week of school when they finally got back home?—when John had to wear his mask all during school?

Yeah, what about it? Susie wanted to know.

Well, said John, did she know the big boy with the black hair in his class, the one that he had invited to his sixth birthday party whose name he couldn't remember?

Oh yeah, said Susie, that one.

Well, said John, that boy, whatever his name is, made a bunch of the kids who could not speak English take stones and throw them at me.

Oh yeah, Susie said. Did it hurt?

But that was the last Daddy heard, the last thing he listened to. He stood up then and walked away, on up the meadow, as far from the sounds of their voices as he could get.

Daddy brought the Mazda up away from the perfect camping spot exactly one week after he had brought it down and went on a half day's bumpy ride to descend into the San Luis Valley, there at South Fork, where Susie was born; and spent the next hour sightseeing. Here he said, is the honeymoon cottage and there beside it the road up into the mountains where Mother carried Susie on her back each afternoon and there the bushes full of rosehips that Mother made into a syrup to feed Susie when she got sick. And there! the bulls that she stood at the window ledge and stared at, the moaning prancing bulls; and O Lord! two buffalo! but of course—every Texas millionaire had a buffalo or two amongst his longhorns. And see! the Rio Grande, crashing around in the backyard, just like I said, Daddy said.

But they hardly listened. Andy fell asleep while Daddy toured the countryside and Johnny read and even Susie after a while was not so interested, ancestral territory or not, and turned down Daddy's offer to drive her by the hospital where she was born. She began to talk about school, about getting ready for school, about notebook paper and pencils and a ring binder and whether or not she would get Mr. Lafarelle for homeroom again. Daddy drove down through Del Norte and on through Monte Vista while she and John made lists of school items and the absolute minimum of clothes that would get them through: 2 pr. jeans, 2 pr. socks, one sneakers, shorts for P.E. The Mazda entered Alamosa and from there passed south, back toward Antonito; the flat plains of Manassa, the quaint stores, even the deep silences of the Sangre de Cristos and the San Juans unnoticed. They were already home. There was school and Sarah and Greg and Jeannie and Junior and John Maxfield and the cat to get back to and it appeared that the trip was over though they still had miles to go.

Lee Merrill Byrd was born and raised in New Jersey, but has spent the last twenty years of her life in the southwestern United States, most particularly in Texas. With her husband, poet Bobby Byrd, she established Cinco Puntos Press, a regional publishing house focusing on the literature of the Southwest. They have three children and live in El Paso, a border city claimed neither by Texas, New Mexico, or Old Mexico. A collection of her short stories is due out from Southern Methodist University Press in the fall of 1993.

PHOTO CREDIT: JAMES DEAN

In 1981 our two sons, John and Andy, were burned in a playhouse fire. The fire and its effect on my family have been the subject of much of my writing. I have written technical articles about being burned, a nonfiction piece about the event itself, a story about my coming to terms with the boys' scars, and a testimony. But I also wanted to write another kind of story, a story that was about how I saw my family surviving and gaining strength from the fire, about all the good I saw that had come to us from it. The vehicle for all the emotion I was feeling was a camping trip that we took up in Colorado about a year after the fire.

APPENDIX

A list of the magazines consulted for *New Stories from the South: The Year's Best, 1993,* with current addresses, subscription rates, and editors.

Alabama Literary Review
253 Smith Hall
Troy State University
Troy, AL 36082
Semiannually, $9
Theron Montgomery, Editor-in-Chief; James G. Davis, Fiction Editor

American Short Fiction
Parlin 14
Department of English
University of Austin
Austin, TX 78712-1164
Quarterly, $24
Laura Furman, Editor

The American Voice
The Kentucky Foundation for Women, Inc.
332 West Broadway, Suite 1215
Louisville, KY 40202
Quarterly, $12
Frederick Smock, Sallie Bingham

Antaeus
The Ecco Press
100 West Broad Street
Hopewell, NJ 08525

Semiannually, $30 for 4 issues
Daniel Halpern

Antietam Review
82 West Washington Street
Hagerstown, MD 21740
Once or twice a year, $5.25 each
Ann Knox and Susanne Kass

The Antioch Review
P.O. Box 148
Yellow Springs, OH 45387
Quarterly, $25
Robert S. Fogarty

The Atlantic Monthly
745 Boylston Street
Boston, MA 02116
Monthly, $15.94
William Whitworth

Black Warrior Review
The University of Alabama
P.O. Box 2936
Tuscaloosa, AL 35486-2936
Semiannually, $11
Glenn Mort

Blue Mesa Review
Creative Writing Center

University of New Mexico
Albuquerque, NM 87131

Carolina Quarterly
Greenlaw Hall CB# 3520
University of North Carolina
Chapel Hill, NC 27599-3520
Three times a year, $12
Will Phillips, Editor

The Chariton Review
Northeast Missouri State University
Kirksville, MO 63501
Semiannually, $5
Jim Barnes

The Chattahoochee Review
DeKalb College
2101 Womack Road
Dunwoody, GA 30338-4497
Quarterly, $15
Lamar York, Editor; Anna
    Schachner, Fiction

Cimarron Review
205 Morrill Hall
Oklahoma State University
Stillwater, OK 74078-0135
Quarterly, $12
Gordon Weaver

Concho River Review
c/o English Department
Angelo State University
San Angelo, TX 76909
Semiannually, $12
Terence A. Dalrymple

Confrontation
Department of English
C. W. Post of L.I.U.
Brookville, NY 11548
Semiannually, $10
Martin Tucker, Editor-in-Chief;
    Julian Mates, Fiction Editor

Crazyhorse
Department of English
University of Arkansas at Little Rock
2801 South University
Little Rock, AR 72204
Semiannually, $10
Judy Troy

The Crescent Review
1445 Old Town Road
Winston-Salem, NC 27106-3143
Semiannually, $10
Guy Nancekeville

Crosscurrents
2200 Glastonbury Road
Westlake Village, CA 91361
Quarterly, $18
Linda Brown Michelson

CutBank
Department of English
University of Montana
Missoula, MT 59812
Semiannually, $12
Peter Fong and Dennis Held,
    Co-editors; Claire Davis,
    Fiction

Epoch
251 Goldwin Smith Hall
Cornell University
Ithaca, NY 14853-3201
Three times a year, $11
Michael Koch

Esquire
1790 Broadway
New York, NY 10019
Monthly, $15.97
Rust Hills, Fiction Editor;
    Will Blythe, Literary Editor

Fiction
c/o English Department
The City College of New York
New York, NY 10031

Three times a year, $20
Mark J. Mirsky

The Florida Review
Department of English
University of Central Florida
Orlando, FL 32816
Semiannually, $7
Russ Kesler

The Georgia Review
The University of Georgia
Athens, GA 30602
Quarterly, $18
Stanley W. Lindberg

The Gettysburg Review
Gettysburg College
Gettysburg, PA 17325-1491
Quarterly, $15
Peter Stitt

Glimmer Train
812 SW Washington Street, Suite 1205
Portland, OR 97205-3216
Quarterly, $29
Susan Burmeister and Linda Davies,
    Editors

Granta
2-3 Hanover Yard
Noel Road
Islington
London
NI 8BE
ENGLAND
Quarterly, $29.95
Bill Buford

The Greensboro Review
Department of English
University of North Carolina
Greensboro, NC 27412
Semiannually, $8
Jim Clark

Habersham Review
Piedmont College
Demorest, GA 30535
Semiannually, $8
The Editors

Harper's Magazine
666 Broadway
New York, NY 10012
Monthly, $18
Lewis H. Lapham

High Plains Literary Review
180 Adams Street, Suite 250
Denver, CO 80206
Three times a year, $20
Robert O. Greer

Indiana Review
316 North Jordan Avenue
Bloomington, IN 47405
Semiannually, $12
Allison Joseph

The Iowa Review
308 EPB
The University of Iowa
Iowa City, IA 52242
Three times a year, $15
David Hamilton

The Journal
The Ohio State University
Department of English
164 West 17th Avenue
Columbus, OH 43210
Biannually, $8
Michelle Herman, Fiction Editor

Karamu
English Department
East Illinois University
Charleston, IL 61920
Subscription info not listed
Peggy Brayfield, Editor

The Kenyon Review
Kenyon College
Gambier, OH 43022
Quarterly, $22
Marilyn Hacker

The Literary Review
285 Madison Avenue
Madison, NJ 07940
Quarterly, $18
Walter Cummins

The Long Story
11 Kingston Street
North Andover, MA 01845
Annually, $5
R. P. Burnham

Louisiana Literature
P.O. Box 792
Southeast Louisiana University
Hammond, LA 70402
David Hanson, Editor

Mid-American Review
106 Hanna Hall
Department of English
Bowling Green State University
Bowling Green, OH 43403
Semiannually, $8
Robert Early, Senior Editor; Ellen
    Behrens, Fiction

Mississippi Quarterly
Box 5272
Mississippi State, MS 39762
Quarterly, $12
Robert L. Phillips, Jr., Editor

Mississippi Review
Center for Writers
The University of Southern
    Mississippi
Box 5144
Hattiesburg, MS 39406-5144
Semiannually, $15
Frederick Barthelme

The Missouri Review
1507 Hillcrest Hall
University of Missouri
Columbia, MO 65211
Three times a year, $15
Speer Morgan

Negative Capability
62 Ridgelawn Drive East
Mobile, AL 36608
Three times a year, $12
Sue Walker

New Delta Review
English Department
Louisiana State University
Baton Rouge, LA 70803
Semiannually, $7
Catherine Williamson, Editor

New England Review
Middlebury College
Middlebury, VT 05753
Quarterly, $18
T. R. Hummer

The New Yorker
20 West 43rd Street
New York, NY 10036
Weekly, $32
Tina Brown

Nimrod
Arts and Humanities Council of
    Tulsa
2210 South Main Street
Tulsa, OK 74114
Semiannually, $10
Francine Ringold, Editor; Geraldine
    McLoud, Fiction Editor

The North American Review
University of Northern Iowa
Cedar Falls, IA 50614
Six times a year, $18
Robley Wilson

Ohioana Quarterly
Ohioana Library Association
1105 Ohio Departments Building
65 South Front Street
Columbus, OH 43215
Quarterly, $20
Barbara Maslekoff

The Ohio Review
290-C Ellis Hall
Ohio University
Athens, OH 45701-2979
Three times a year, $12
Wayne Dodd

Old Hickory Review
P.O. Box 1178
Jackson, TN 38302
Semiannually, $12
Dorothy Stanfill and Bill Nance

Ontario Review
9 Honey Brook Drive
Princeton, NJ 08540
Semiannually, $10
Raymond J. Smith and Joyce Carol
   Oates

Other Voices
Department of English
UNIL Box 4348
Chicago, IL 60680
Semiannually, $16
Lois Hauselman and Sharon Fiffer

The Paris Review
Box S
541 East 72nd Street
New York, NY 10021
Quarterly, $24
George Plimpton

Paris Transcontinental
Institut du Monde Anglophone
Sorbonne Nouvelle
5, rue de l'Ecole de Médecine
75006 Paris
FRANCE

Semiannually, 130 F
Claire Larriere

Parting Gifts
March Street Press
3006 Stonecutter Terrace
Greensboro, NC 27405
Subscription info not listed
Robert Bixby, Editor

Pembroke Magazine
Box 60
Pembroke State University
Pembroke, NC 28372
Annually, $5
Shelby Stephenson, Editor;
   Stephen E. Smith, Fiction Editor

Ploughshares
Emerson College
100 Beacon Street
Boston, MA 02116
Three times a year, $19
DeWitt Henry, Editor; Don Lee and
   Debra Spark, Fiction Editors

Prairie Schooner
201 Andrews Hall
University of Nebraska
Lincoln, NE 68588-0334
Quarterly, $17
Hilda Raz, Editor-in-Chief

Puerto del Sol
Box 3E
New Mexico State University
Las Cruces, NM 88003
Semiannually, $10
Kevin McIlvoy, Editor-in-Chief;
   Christopher C. Burnham, Fiction

Quarterly West
317 Olpin Union
University of Utah
Salt Lake City, UT 84112
Semiannually, $9
Bernard Wood and Tom Hazuka

Redbook
The Hearst Corporation
959 Eighth Avenue
New York, NY 10019
Monthly, $14.97
Ellen Levine, Editor-in-Chief; Dawn
    Raffel, Fiction and Books

River Styx
14 South Euclid
St. Louis, MO 63108
Three times a year, $20
Lee Fournier

Sewanee Review
University of the South
Sewanee, TN 37375-4009
Quarterly, $15.00
George Core

Shenandoah
Washington and Lee University
Box 722
Lexington, VA 24450
Quarterly, $11
Dabney Stuart

Snake Nation Review
110 #2 West Force Street
Valdosta, GA 31601
Semiannually, $15
Roberta George, Pat Miller, and
    Janice Daugharty

The South Carolina Review
Department of English
Clemson University
Clemson, SC 29634-1503
Semiannually, $7
Richard J. Calhoun

Southern Exposure
P.O. Box 531
Durham, NC 27702
Quarterly, $24
Eric Bates, Editor; Susan Ketchin,
    Fiction

Southern Humanities Review
9088 Haley Center
Auburn University
Auburn, AL 36849
Quarterly, $15
Dan R. Latimer and R. T. Smith

The Southern Review
43 Allen Hall
Louisiana State University
Baton Rouge, LA 70803-5605
Quarterly, $15
James Olney and Dave Smith

Sou'wester
Southern Illinois University at
    Edwardsville
Edwardsville, IL 62026-1438
Three times a year, $10
Fred W. Robbins

Southwest Review
6410 Airline Road
Southern Methodist University
Dallas, TX 75275
Quarterly, $20
Willard Spiegelman

Stories
Box Number 1467
East Arlington, MA 02174-0022
Quarterly, $18
Amy R. Kaufman

Story
1507 Dana Avenue
Cincinnati, OH 45207
Quarterly, $22
Lois Rosenthal

StoryQuarterly
P.O. Box 1416
Northbrook, IL 60065
Quarterly, $12
Anne Brashler, Diane Williams, and
    Margaret Barrett

Tampa Review
Box 135F
401 W. Kennedy Blvd.
Tampa, FL 33606-1490
Semiannually, $10
Richard Mathews, Editor; Andy
Solomon, Fiction

The Threepenny Review
P.O. Box 9131
Berkeley, CA 94709
Quarterly, $12
Wendy Lesser

TriQuarterly
Northwestern University
2020 Ridge Avenue
Evanston, IL 60208
Three times a year, $18
Reginald Gibbons

Turnstile
Suite 2348
175 Fifth Avenue
New York, NY 10010
Semiannually, $12
Mitchell Nauffts

The Virginia Quarterly Review
One West Range
Charlottesville, VA 22903
Quarterly, $15
Staige D. Blackford

Voice Literary Supplement
VV Publishing Corp.
36 Cooper Square
New York, NY 10003
Monthly, except the combined issues
of Dec./Jan. and July/Aug., $17
M. Mark

Weber Studies
Weber State College
Ogden, UT 84408-1214
Three times a year, $10
Neila C. Seshachari

West Branch
Bucknell Hall
Bucknell University
Lewisburg, PA 17837
Semiannually, $7
Karl Patten and Robert Taylor

Wind Magazine
RFD Route 1
Box 809K
Pikeville, KY 41501
Semiannually, $7
Quentin Howard

ZYZZYVA
41 Sutter Street
Suite 1400
San Francisco, CA 94104
Quarterly, $20
Howard Junker

PREVIOUS VOLUMES

Copies of previous volumes of *New Stories from the South* can be ordered through your local bookstore or by calling the Sales Department at Algonquin Books of Chapel Hill. Multiple copies for classroom adoptions are available at a special discount. For information, please call 919-967-0108.

NEW STORIES FROM THE SOUTH: THE YEAR'S BEST, 1986

Max Apple, BRIDGING

Madison Smartt Bell, TRIPTYCH 2

Mary Ward Brown, TONGUES OF FLAME

Suzanne Brown, COMMUNION

James Lee Burke, THE CONVICT

Ron Carlson, AIR

Doug Crowell, SAYS VELMA

Leon V. Driskell, MARTHA JEAN

Elizabeth Harris, THE WORLD RECORD HOLDER

Mary Hood, SOMETHING GOOD FOR GINNY

David Huddle, SUMMER OF THE MAGIC SHOW

Gloria Norris, HOLDING ON

Kurt Rheinheimer, UMPIRE

W. A. Smith, DELIVERY

Wallace Whatley, SOMETHING TO LOSE

Luke Whisnant, WALLWORK

Sylvia Wilkinson, CHICKEN SIMON

New Stories from the South: The Year's Best, 1987

New Stories from the South: The Year's Best, 1988

Barbara Kingsolver, ROSE-JOHNNY

Trudy Lewis, HALF-MEASURES

Jill McCorkle, FIRST UNION BLUES

Mark Richard, HAPPINESS OF THE GARDEN VARIETY

Sunny Rogers, THE CRUMB

Annette Sanford, LIMITED ACCESS

Eve Shelnutt, VOICE

NEW STORIES FROM THE SOUTH: THE YEAR'S BEST, 1989

Rick Bass, WILD HORSES

James Gordon Bennett, PACIFIC THEATER

Madison Smartt Bell, CUSTOMS OF THE COUNTRY

Larry Brown, SAMARITANS

Mary Ward Brown, IT WASN'T ALL DANCING

Kelly Cherry, WHERE SHE WAS

David Huddle, PLAYING

Sandy Huss, COUPON FOR BLOOD

Frank Manley, THE RAIN OF TERROR

Bobbie Ann Mason, WISH

Lewis Nordan, A HANK OF HAIR, A PIECE OF BONE

Kurt Rheinheimer, HOMES

Mark Richard, STRAYS

Annette Sanford, SIX WHITE HORSES

Paula Sharp, HOT SPRINGS

New Stories from the South: The Year's Best, 1992